Meadowsweet

GALLERIES OF STONE - BOOK ONE

C. J. MILBRANDT

OLEXI

Galleries of Stone, Book 1
Meadowsweet
illustrated edition

Illustrations: Hannah Lavender | studiolavender.com
Jacket design: Elza Kinde | bumblebess.com

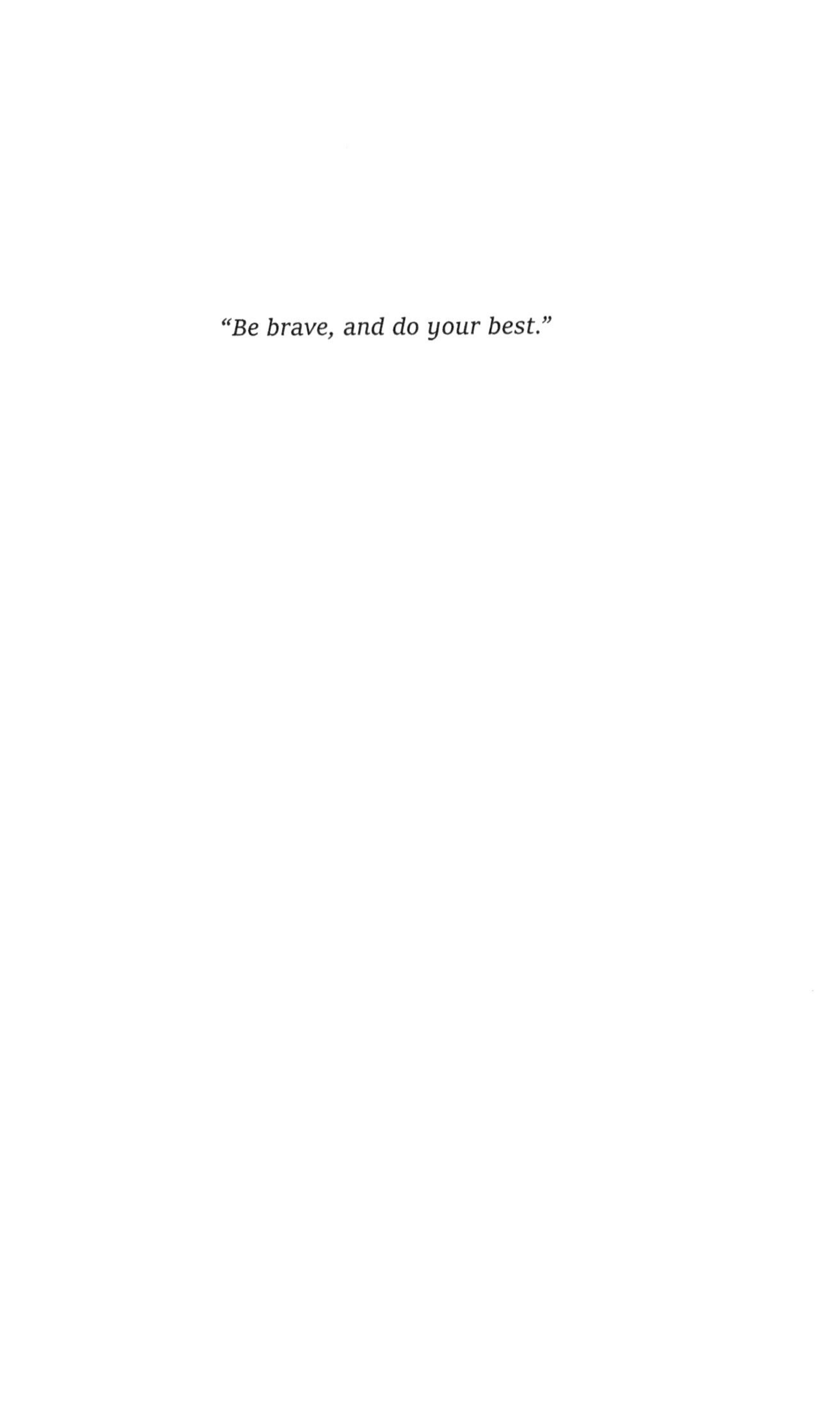

"Be brave, and do your best."

table of contents

Meadowsweet

PROLOGUE

No one could fault the Rakefangs. From the Far Continent to the Last, their line was recognized as one of the oldest, proudest, and most vicious. Conquest ran hot in their blood. Ambition sharpened their fangs. Fear lent them fame. But on a moonless night in summer, the head of their clan called a secret meeting.

"We are assembled, sir."

Lyall Rakefang glanced up from the mess of stone on his desk. A clubbed ear. A tiny paw. There were hardly any pieces large enough to identify the shattered figurine as feline. Wiping the dust from his dagger, he sheathed it with a snap. "My daughter?"

"She's quiet."

Lyall bared his teeth. "Death comes silently. Watch her."

"Aye."

Rising from his place, the clan leader asked, "And that man?"

Disdain crept into the other's tone. "A coward to the end."

Fury hardened Lyall's expression. Since when were his men so free with their opinions? If he delayed any longer, they might begin calling *his* courage into question.

Rebellion. Division. Bloodshed. The threat to the Rakefang clan was real. So tonight, he'd deal a fatal blow, lay bare their shame, and then purge it. Without fail. Without mercy. Without regret.

Lyall snarled, "Aye, let's end this."

Men and women arrived on silent feet, slipping through shadows with predatory grace. Shuttered lanterns. Furtive glances. Whispers at the door. And from the deepest shadows of the gardens, a young man watched with held breath and heart sick. Ulrica had smuggled him, though she'd done so under protest. If he was discovered, father would flay him alive. But Freydolf didn't lack courage. Only excuses.

For a while, his family made them on his behalf:

"He'll come into his fangs in his own time."

"Vanora's Keeper tapped him for studies. He's tied up with language tutors."

"Can he hunt? Aye, you'll not find a better tracker."

Evasion. Blinds. Half-truths. They were enough for a while. But at seventeen, he was well past the age of proving. Freydolf Rakefang's family could no longer cover for him, so they turned on him.

Uncles. Cousins. Aunts. They were terrifying, and he'd always been proud of their strength. Freydolf mouthed their names in silent greeting as each passed through the gates of the family estate. Nay. He was bidding them farewell. And it hurt.

He couldn't find it in his heart to blame his kin. Why should their reputations suffer because of him? But Frey's hands shook as he dragged them through unkempt hair. These who had taught him to walk, passed down their lore, laughed at his jokes—would they let Father shun him?

Doors shut. Guards set. And over the distant shush of waves, Freydolf could hear the deep growl of his father's voice call their clan to order. The tall, rangy Pred sounded angry, but Freydolf couldn't hear what he was saying. And he wanted to hear for himself the words that would cut him adrift. To see if anyone would challenge Lyall. To know if he was the only one who would shed tears.

Was it worth the risk to move closer?

Freydolf eased away from his hiding place only to freeze at the faint sound of a latch. One of the house's tall windows swiveled open. For a moment, the light from within set sparks in golden eyes that swept the gardens. Then the lean figure slipped out of the house, dropping to the ground and melting into the shadows without a sound.

So he wasn't the only one Ulrica had smuggled in.

Wary of discovery, Freydolf sank back into deeper shadows, listening intently. If the other intruder was lurking nearby, he didn't betray his position. But he'd done Freydolf a favor. Voices now carried from indoors, and they snared his full attention.

Lyall Rakefang cut straight to the bone of the matter. "I have no son!"

Murmurs followed, and Freydolf strained his ears, hoping against hope for a challenge.

Father wasn't done. His voice drowned out all others. "That man's branch is severed from our tree. His star is fallen from our sky. His name is cast into the sea. May the depths take him." Silence hung heavy in the house as the clan leader cursed his own son. "May his blood spill, may his bones break, may flames consume him. He is an enemy of this house. Should he trespass upon this clan's holdings, my own dagger will spill his entrails, my own hands will wring the breath from his lungs. That man will meet his end."

Waves of nausea swept over Freydolf, who couldn't afford to retch into the bushes. Not now that Father had pledged to kill him for trespassing. With Lyall Rakefang, there were no idle threats.

Freydolf cringed when his mother spoke next. "None will speak his name. None will acknowledge his former place. We spit upon him. We strike him from our history."

Into the next lull, Freydolf's younger sister spoke, her voice husky with anger. "I am a proud daughter of the house of Rakefang. I will bear sons, and they shall be heirs ... but do not ask me to forget my brother's name. I cannot banish Fr–"

A slap cut Ulrica off, and Freydolf started forward. But he'd only rolled to his knees when an arm slipped around him from behind, pressing a cold blade against his throat.

"*Don't.*"

"She might need ..."

" *...help?* From you?" His captor's murmur dripped with sarcasm. "Let her finish."

From inside, Ulrica's voice rang clear and defiant. "Behold, a mystery! My father has no son, yet I cherish a brother."

"Put away your blades, daughter." Mother's voice was deadly soft. "This is a peaceful assembly."

"If you want *any* peace, then let me grieve!" Ulrica snarled.

After a tense pause, their father said, "This once. Never again."

Freydolf shivered. Ulrica was treading dangerous boards, but she strode with enviable confidence. She began anew. "Do not ask me to forget my brother's name, nor to banish him from my heart. He can never be heir to this house, but do not brand Freydolf a coward. He has courage enough to defy Lyall Rakefang, which is more than can be said of any in this room."

"Excepting herself."

Turning his head, Freydolf caught a glint of admiration that matched the whisper of a smile in his captor's tone. He opened his mouth to warn off the would-be suitor, but the young man's hand clamped over his mouth. Golden eyes glinted warningly, and Freydolf caught the subtle shift in their surroundings.

Tension in the air. An uneasy silence. Others were on the prowl, and *they* were the prey. Poised for flight, Freydolf offered the barest of nods. They needed to bolt, and fast.

Into the unnatural lull, Ulrica's farewell rang loud and clear. "Chase the tracks left by your tears! Hunt the voice that haunts your dreams! Lay claim to a quarry worth keeping! And by my blades, keep your guard up!"

1

Rocks and Hard Places

As a rule, Freydolf kept to himself. His exile was partially due to location. Morven's cliffs loomed well above the tiny villages tucked amidst her foothills, and the narrow trail that zigzagged up the legendary Moonlit Mountain's precipitous face discouraged casual visitors.

Seated on the rim of the cistern at the edge of the outer courtyard, Freydolf tossed back a dipper of water before casting another onto the tumble of herbs crowded haphazardly against its sides. They looked as thirsty as he was. A bad sign. "That didn't take long. Has it even been a fortnight?"

None of the nearby statues responded. Their stony silence stretched, but not uncomfortably. By now, the man was used to one-sided conversations. "Poor lad. His knees never did stop knocking." Despite the towering inconvenience, Freydolf felt bad for his missing servant. After a thoughtful pause, he murmured, "I hope he made it home safely."

As Morven's Keeper, Freydolf received a certain amount of respect, but the locals didn't exactly welcome him. His heritage was too obvious. Tall and broad, his bushy brown hair was drawn back in a long tail that reached the belt of his dusty breeches. Heavy brows flared menacingly over wide-set dark eyes, and his swarthy complexion marked him further.

Freydolf was every inch a Pred, and therefore suspect.

His countrymen were a bloodthirsty lot—warmongers, mercenaries, conquerors. No matter what he said or did, Freydolf couldn't overcome the obstacle of his race's fearsome reputation. Even though he'd lived peacefully amidst the Flox for more than two decades, it made no difference. Friendly Pred simply didn't exist. So Freydolf had retreated into his galleries, leaving the Flox in peace. He'd been an outcast among his own people, as well, so all that had changed was the view.

"Now what?" he sighed, already knowing the answer. Without a servant to pester him to eat and sleep at regular intervals, he tended to do without. Judging by the pinch of hunger in his stomach, Freydolf had already been alone for two or three days. If he didn't want to work himself to death, he'd need to find a replacement, and that meant descending the mountain.

Hauling himself to his feet, he thrust out a hand to steady himself against a lichen-encrusted column. Claws scraped lightly against the weathered stone, and he gave the venerable support an apologetic pat before cutting across the inner courtyard and leaving by the gate.

"I'll be back before nightfall," he casually informed the stone hounds that flanked the Statuary's impressive entrance.

From the trailhead, Freydolf considered the clusters of houses dotting the rolling hills below. One village was as good—or as bad—as the next. "Hayward," he decided aloud. It had been a few years since he'd hired somebody from their midst, and he was on decent terms with one of their elders. Maybe *this* time, things would be different.

"Nay," he admitted, allowing reality to check his natural optimism. With a wry smile that showed off a bit of fang, Freydolf muttered, "That would be too much to ask."

Not wanting to alarm the villagers, Freydolf stuck to the middle of the road as he entered Hayward. Within moments, heads were turning, and whispers tickled at his ears. Eyes downcast, the sculptor kept his thumbs hooked into his belt, his gait steady, and his shoulders relaxed. For all the good it did. It was incredibly hard to appear non-threatening when you stood head and shoulders over the tallest person in the vicinity.

As usual, the Flox scattered.

Freydolf's expression saddened.

He'd once harbored hopes of fitting in with these gentle folk. They were a pretty race, petite and pale, with nimble feet and clever hands. By far, the Flox's most distinctive feature was their horns. Adult males bore sets that curved magnificently against curling hair that ranged through a variety of light hues: silver, buff, gray, and gold.

Their way of life was refreshingly simple. Though small, the homes he passed were neat, with thatched roofs, bright shutters, and blooming window boxes. He stole glances out of the corners of his eyes into walled gardens where food and flowers grew side-by-side. As an artist, Freydolf appreciated the obvious pride the Flox took in craftsmanship. Placards hung outside the buildings lining the town's square—carpenters, masons, weavers, potters, and a blacksmith.

His nose twitched as he caught the scent of baking bread, and his stomach rumbled. But he held himself in check, knowing from past experience that it would take time to gather prospects. "First things first."

Ducking his head, Freydolf stepped into the village's trading post and approached the shopkeeper, who eyed him warily.

"Good morning, Master Freydolf. How can I be of service?" the bearded man inquired with reedy politeness.

"I'm looking for help."

It took less than a minute to outline his expectations and name a price, and within five, the merchant's runners were sent flying to broadcast the news. "Wait a bit, Master Freydolf," the shopkeeper urged. "They'll gather in the square by midday."

While the sculptor might have enjoyed passing some time exploring the store's shelves, he had pity on the trading post's other customers, who were cowering in the corners. With a short bow, he excused himself.

Back in the square, he gazed toward the mountain that was both his refuge and his responsibility. Already, he could feel the restless pull to create and the wrongness of empty hands. He flexed his fingers, then balled them into fists, wishing for his workshop, his chisel, and the endless galleries of stone. Lonely as his lot in life might be, he preferred it to watching people duck and cringe.

Freydolf followed his nose into Pennyflax & Quince, badly startling the woman behind the counter. Remaining just inside the door, he held up a coin and asked, "May I buy some bread?" Long ago, he'd learned that there were only two ways of getting around the villagers' skittishness. The first was to leave the errands to a servant. The second was to pay *very* generously for what he needed.

His coin was enough to keep the apron-clad matron from vanishing. "How much?" she asked.

"Is this enough for four loaves?" he inquired, keeping his voice light.

She nodded and slipped fresh bread into paper sleeves, trussing them together with string. After a moment's hesitation, she placed the bundle near the edge of the counter and stepped back.

"Thank you," he said, moving forward to slide the coin across the counter and collect his purchase. With a hand over his heart, Freydolf inclined his head, then escaped.

Choosing a place under one of the trees on the edge of the square, he tore greedily into his high-priced meal. "Can't blame them."

The sun was high when villagers began herding youngsters into the square. Many had damp curls, evidence of a fresh washing, and several were undoubtedly dressed in their best. Freydolf had lived on the fringes of their society long enough to know that most boys were sent out to work as soon as their horns came in. They earned their own keep or brought home wages to help support younger siblings.

Flox throughout this area had served Keepers for centuries. Under Freydolf's predecessors, it had been considered a great honor to be chosen for work atop the Gray Mountain. That attitude had shifted drastically when Morven was bequeathed to a Pred, but enough still allowed their children to apply for work with him. Probably because he paid well ... and in advance. By and large, the villagers were poor, and their homes were crowded. A handful of coins could be very persuasive.

Freydolf waited until the shopkeeper arrived, for he'd paid him an extra fee to act as mediator. "They're all here," the bearded man announced briskly.

Slowly rising, Freydolf scanned the prospects. Working for him could spare one of them from a few years in the fields or quarry. And a generous wage would offset the perceived risk of working for a Pred. Judging by the villagers' nervous glances, they wouldn't thank him for the honor.

He sighed and wondered how to go about making up his mind. Choosing the cleverest boys never worked out. They were the first to run. Perhaps this time, he should aim lower—dull and dutiful. A servant only needed to be canny enough to mind the fires, push a broom, and boil the thin soups and slops that made up Freydolf's diet.

His last choice had been a strapping lad of sixteen, but bigger hadn't proved braver. "Maybe one of the younger ones?" he mused. He was hardly fit to tend a child, and the very idea of a Pred raising a Flox was laughable enough to inspire a low chuckle.

"Are you ready to begin, Master Freydolf?"

"Nearly," he stalled. "Before we start, can you recommend a dependable worker? You *know* those lads."

"I'm sure *any* of these boys would do Hayward proud," the shopkeeper replied vaguely.

His diplomatic response was understandable, for every family here wanted a fair chance at the fat purse of gold coins that hung from the sculptor's belt; however, Freydolf didn't miss the way his eyes drifted toward a youngster who stood by himself off to one side.

The boy looked barely old enough to blow his own nose, but the nubs of horns poked through his white-blond hair. More intriguing, the lad's gaze held his with a grim determination that was impossible to ignore.

Nodding thoughtfully, Freydolf said, "Aye. Let's begin."

Freydolf held out a collection of polished stones that were usually used when searching for children with affinity. He'd come to rely on these oddments for striking up conversations with nervous prospects and their parents. "Which one do you like?" he inquired of a blue-eyed boy who looked far too pale. "Can you point to one that pleases you?"

The applicant's mother prodded her young son forward, but with a wobble of his chin, the boy burst into tears, whirling to hide his face in his mother's apron. She quickly wrapped her arms around him, crooning comfort as she rubbed at the base of his horns.

Freydolf shook his head and kindly said, "Keep the lad close a while longer, marm."

Frightening children to tears might have distressed the sculptor more if it happened less. So far, Freydolf had spoken to ten boys ranging in age from eleven to fourteen. Only three had been brave enough to converse with him, so the pickings were dismally slim. With a weary glance at the bearded shopkeeper, the sculptor signaled his readiness to move on. "How many more?"

"A few," the man replied, nodding toward the knot of villagers awaiting their turn.

The boy he'd first noticed still stood apart from the rest, his slender frame practically vibrating with tension. Freydolf asked, "Doesn't that lad have parents?"

"Most children do."

"Granted," he replied with a crooked smile that quickly faded. What kind of parents sent their child alone to face a Pred? With a stirring of pity, Freydolf said, "I'll speak to him next."

"Certainly," the shopkeeper agreed, leading the way.

Freydolf followed more slowly, gathering first impressions. The boy was the smallest of the lot, which made him seem far too young to leave home, but perhaps he was just puny. Gray-green eyes stared up at him with solemn intensity. Crouching down to make himself smaller, the sculptor waited while the shopkeeper did his part.

"This is Master Freydolf, Morven's Keeper. Mind your manners."

"I will."

"Hello, lambkin," Freydolf offered softly. Fascinated by the boy's unwavering gaze, he asked, "Aren't you afraid of me?"

"I am."

The big Pred blinked in surprise and asked, "Then why are you still here?"

"Mother said to stay. And to look you in the eye."

Freydolf's bemusement grew. "So you're here because she told you to come, not because you want to work for me?"

It took a while for the child to untangle the sentence, but once he did, he nodded.

Lowering himself further, the sculptor sat on the ground. "You have nothing to fear from me, lambkin."

"That's not what people say," he replied bluntly, still not breaking eye contact.

Freydolf had to smother a smile. "Aye, people do say otherwise." He held out his collection of stones, asking, "Can you tell me which of these you like best?"

The lad glanced without much interest at the stones, which was mildly surprising. Most people showed *some* spark of interest, especially in the crystals.

Inspiration struck, and Freydolf made his invitation an order. "Point to the sphere."

A slim hand reached across the space between them to touch the marble.

"Now, point to the green stone," Freydolf commanded.

Without hesitation, the boy tapped a jade disk.

"The pyramid?"

The boy's fingertip brushed across the tip of a buff-colored stone.

"Obedient little thing." Freydolf asked, "Do you have a favorite?"

With a small shrug, the lad replied, "No."

"Not one for pretty baubles?" Freydolf had hired enough petty thieves in his day to be grateful for small mercies. Normally, he would have passed over a prospect this young, but it was so rare for a Flox to face him squarely. "What are you called?"

"Tupper."

"Tupper," he repeated, testing the odd name. "Would you like to come with me?"

The lad hesitated, then announced, "Mother said to go with you if you asked."

Freydolf glanced questioningly at the shopkeeper, whose expression was unreadable. Then, he asked the child, "Do you want to tell her goodbye?"

"No," Tupper replied in a soft voice.

He wasn't sure if the boy meant he didn't want to speak to her … or he didn't want to leave at all. Either way, compassion welled up in the Pred for the waif-like boy, whose eyes widened, then lowered for the first time. While Freydolf tucked away his assortment of stones, he glanced at the shopkeeper. "This one. I'll hire Tupper."

Nodding curtly, the man sent away the other villagers, then accepted the advance on the boy's wages, promising to pass it along to his mother. Placing his hand on Tupper's shoulder, the shopkeeper admonished, "Do your best for Master Freydolf."

"I will," he replied faintly.

The sculptor rose, eager to start home now that he'd made his choice. Beckoning to the boy, he called, "Follow me, Tupper." Not until he reached the village's limits did Freydolf glance over his shoulder. He smiled at finding the lad trailing obediently in his wake. It was a promising start.

2

Keepers and Keeping

Tupper had never seen a man as big as Freydolf. If he was a man at all. Many in the village called him a monster. News of his arrival in town had been followed by terrible rumors about wolf-like men from a faraway land, where the sea ran red with the blood of their prey. Rachel had begged Mother not to send him out, and Farley had warned Tupper not to get eaten. The fuss had seemed silly until he caught his first glimpse of Morven's Keeper.

His new master was a giant. Or he seemed like one to a boy who barely reached his hip. And he was dark all over—skin, hair, eyes. Only his teeth flashed white, making it easy to see how sharp they were. And then there were his claws. Surely, *they* were proof that the Keeper was a beast, and a bloodthirsty one, if the tales were true.

Except Freydolf didn't act very scary.

His voice was deep, but it didn't growl. He almost sounded happy, and he talked a *lot*. Tupper wasn't sure why the man rambled on about the things they passed, but he would glance over his shoulder from time to time to check if Tupper was listening. A nod seemed to satisfy Freydolf, so the boy's head bobbed every time he paused. He'd promised to do his best, after all.

"Do you know what that is?" inquired the big man, pointing

toward something in the foothills.

For several moments, Tupper simply stared at Freydolf's finger, wondering how sharp its claw was, but when the man repeated his question, the boy looked down. Far below, there were rows of what looked like drab stacks of hay. "No," he answered honestly.

"That's Hayward, your hometown." With a searching look, Master Freydolf added, "You won't be able to see it once we go around this bend, so make your last look a good one."

Was this really the last time he would see his home? Carden and Ewert had jobs, too, but they had home days. Tupper wouldn't. As the Keeper's servant, he would live on top of the mountain ... maybe forever. Addy had said he'd be lucky to earn the Keeper's gold, but Aggie had cried.

"Ready, lad?" Freydolf asked.

Tupper nodded, and they climbed higher.

To the boy's surprise, they didn't have much farther to go. He'd always assumed that Keepers came from the tippy-top of the mountain, but they were only about two-thirds of the way up Morven's northern face. Around the bend, the trail opened onto a very wide ledge, and before them stood an imposing gate.

"That's the Statuary. Or the way in, anywise," Freydolf announced. The sweeping arch framing the wide entrance was bordered by intricate carvings, row upon row, each different than the next. "This is called the Apprentice Gate."

Tupper nodded dutifully, but he didn't move to follow when the sculptor ambled on. Rooted to the spot, he peered at two enormous animals crouched on either side of the path. Their rusty red pelts stood out against the gray of the surrounding rock, and they were poised to pounce.

Too many things had happened too quickly on this day, and Tupper reached the limits of what bravery he possessed. Without really meaning to, he took a step backwards.

His master noticed, and retraced his steps. "Are you frightened?"

"Yes."

"Of me?" Freydolf asked, a small frown causing a crease between his dark brows.

Tupper avoided that question by pointing to the hounds

who threatened him with bared teeth and raised fur. His hand trembled.

"Ah," his master breathed, looking relieved. "The hounds are the guardians of this gate. They're statues, Tupper."

Looking closer, he realized that Freydolf was right. The ferocious dogs were carved from red stone, and they hadn't moved once since he'd spotted them.

"They're meant to look fierce, but you'll get used to them," the sculptor said in soothing tones. "I'll need to introduce you sometime, but we'll save that for another day."

Tupper offered another mute nod, his gaze still fixed on the terrible dogs. How could something made from stone look so real?

"Are you still afraid?"

"Yes."

Freydolf shifted his weight awkwardly from foot to foot. "It's safe here. Well, *mostly*." Extending his hand, he promised, "I'll be with you."

Among Flox, such a gesture was an offer of peace, but this offer looked more like a trap, lined as it was with deadly-looking claws. Tupper didn't like making decisions, but he faced one now. Very slowly, he reached up to touch the Pred's open palm.

When Freydolf's work-roughened hand closed over the boy's smaller one, it didn't hurt. Instead, its warmth stopped Tupper's trembling, and a small squeeze startled him into glancing up. The Pred's lips quirked. "Are you more afraid of them than you are of me?"

"Yes."

With a shake of his head, Freydolf said, "You're a small wonder, lambkin."

Unsure how else to respond, Tupper nodded.

The Apprentice Gate cut through a thick stone wall. Once Tupper was near enough, he could see its heavy doors flung wide. They were studded with weathered metallic disks that overlapped like green scales. Or maybe a suit of armor. Glancing back at the red hounds, Tupper wondered who would dare attack the home of such a fearsome man.

Freydolf had slowed his steps to accommodate his young companion, but he didn't stop. Leading Tupper by the hand, he strolled through the gate. The boy had no choice but to follow. There was an air of finality to crossing that wide threshold, but in the next moment, he traded his half-formed regrets for amazement.

They crossed a courtyard that was taller than it was wide, making the sky seem very far away. It was shadowy and cool in this sheltered space, where the native rock was mottled by moss and lichen. Masons had been at work, for stone towers hugged the mountainside. Narrow windows graced by elaborate stone lattices marched up their bowed walls, three tiers high and topped here and there with a scalloping of tiles. Having grown up in a snug hut with a thatched roof, Tupper was agog.

"Nearly there."

Although the man seemed to be talking to himself, Tupper nodded to show he was listening. Not that there was much to hear. Since Freydolf had talked so much during their climb, he'd expected more of the same, but his master's chatter lapsed into a silent intensity that made Tupper uneasy. The Pred's pace quickened, and a strange gleam lit his eyes.

They passed niches filled with statues of birds and beasts. Urns topped stout columns, and stately figures posed under cupolas. Squat buildings that looked like tiny houses were edged with stone filigree, and even some of the paving stones were engraved with pretty rosettes. Had Freydolf made it all? It hardly seemed possible.

After living with all his brothers and sisters in their tiny house in Hayward, the stillness was a little eerie. Not necessarily bad. Just very different. All Tupper could hear was the pit-pat of his own bare feet. He was trotting now, trying to keep up with the man's lengthening strides, but he stumbled to a stop when Freydolf arrived at a strange door. Doors? It was a door *within* a door, for a man-sized entrance had been cut through the center of another that looked as if it had been made for a giant.

Dropping his servant's hand, the sculptor opened the inset door and disappeared inside without a word. Tupper waited uncertainly, then tiptoed through, closing the door behind him.

The room in which he found himself was big and bright, lit by tall windows. Their glass was decorated by a tracery of stone latticework that caused the summer sunlight to dapple worn wooden planks that felt smooth underfoot.

Freydolf was acting strange. Maybe. Since he didn't know the Pred, it was hard for Tupper to be sure. Hovering nervously, the boy waited to see what he would do next. When the big man donned a heavy apron, Tupper wondered if Freydolf was planning to cook dinner. When the Pred next reached for a sharp-looking tool that might have been a weapon, the young Flox began to panic. Maybe Farley had been right after all.

Tupper tensed, ready to run, but Freydolf didn't attack. Instead, the sculptor murmured something to a misshapen column of bluish stone on a stand in the center of the room. The Pred smiled as if it had answered his greeting, then picked up a hammer and set to work.

The boy slowly relaxed, then looked for a place to sit down. Being forgotten might have distressed him more if it happened less. Choosing a bare patch of floor in the corner where he could keep an eye on his master, Tupper settled in to wait.

Freydolf remained completely absorbed until twilight's shadows dimmed his workshop. Why had no one lit the lamps? He often sculpted long into the night, so lanterns were suspended at regular intervals around the room. But their brass cages were dark. Annoyed to be forced to lay aside his tools so early, he cast about for the match tin. Some servants were better than others about putting things where they belonged.

Still half-lost in thought about the dragon slowly emerging from the blue stone supplied by his most recent commissioner, Freydolf methodically lit the lamps. Their familiar glow filled the room with flickering shadows, and he enjoyed the harmless tricks they played on his eyes. Blue scales seemed to ripple; stone eyes winked with warm reflections.

"Much more homey; though it's not fire you need, is it, beauty?" he crooned to the statue-in-the-making.

The Statuary was the first and only place where Freydolf felt he belonged. His holdings upon Morven were extensive—gallery upon gallery, vault within vault—but their Keeper mostly kept to three rooms. This workshop was his home, and he rarely left its confines. Out of necessity, he maintained a kitchen in an adjacent room. A bathroom was located on the level below, not far from the well.

With a grunt of discontent, Freydolf drifted toward the water pitcher on the stand in the corner and found it dry. An odd sense of déjà vu swept over him, for it had been empty this morning, too.

All at once, recollection came crashing down around him, and Freydolf whirled. He was accustomed to losing servants, but not like this! Had the boy abandoned him already? Worse, was he wandering unsupervised through the galleries? He hadn't even taken the time to warn Tupper not to ...!

Freydolf's inner diatribe screeched to a halt the moment he spotted the small figure huddled in the corner. "Safe," he breathed, shoulders sagging.

The sculptor crossed the room and dropped to one knee before the sleeping boy. He felt sorry for the poor lad, who looked so peaceful in repose. Freydolf gently grasped his slender shoulder. "Lambkin?"

Clearly, Tupper was a sound sleeper. With great care, he scooped him up, marveling over how little he weighed.

Freydolf had no idea which of his predecessors had added

a bed to the workshop, but they'd spared no effort on their creature comforts. A niche had been carved directly into the mountain. Sculpted ivy and flowering vines climbed the recess's interior, fanning out across its concave ceiling, transforming one of life's more commonplace necessities into a work of art fit for a king. A very *short* king.

Whoever had designed the bed certainly hadn't done so with a Pred's powerful frame in mind. The space was far too small for Freydolf, so the luxurious accommodation was relegated to his servants' use. The cot in the corner was sufficient to his needs. Although nothing fancy, the pallet was sturdy enough to collapse onto when he reached the edge of exhaustion.

Drawing back the niche's heavy tapestry curtain, Freydolf tucked in Tupper, then stood back to consider the lad's cherubic face. Despite rumors to the contrary, Freydolf didn't eat the children he carried off. Indeed, he couldn't remember the last time he'd eaten meat.

Creating was his food. Shaping stone satisfied him. He was perfectly happy to lose himself in his work, which was *exactly* why his sister had forced him to promise never to live alone.

Rumpling the boy's shining curls, Freydolf murmured, "Aye. Strange as it may sound, I need you, lambkin."

Tupper slept on, and Freydolf gave the top of his head one last pat; this time, his thumb brushed across one of the lad's nubs. Even after all these years, he'd never actually been this close before, and his curiosity got the better of him. Freydolf ran sensitive fingertips over the horn, which didn't feel anything like stone, and without thinking, he gently scratched its base.

Sleepy eyes blinked open. "Papa?"

Freydolf winced. "Nay, lambkin. Do you remember where you are?"

The boy's eyes widened, all drowsiness vanishing. Plucking at the blankets, he asked, "Are you going to eat me?"

"Nay."

Tupper accepted this with a small nod and peered at his extravagant new surroundings. Eventually, he asked, "Are you going to take care of me?"

"Nay. *You* are going to take care of *me*."

"Aren't you big enough to take care of yourself?"

"Nay," Freydolf glibly replied. "There are a few things I'm very good at, but there are a great many more things I cannot manage alone."

"Like what?" the boy asked dubiously.

"Cooking and cleaning, mostly."

The wheels of the boy's mind were turning, and he seemed a mite worried.

Hoping to put him at ease, Freydolf explained a servant's duties in the simplest possible terms. "You're here to fetch water, mind the fires, make sure I eat, and sweep up the messes I'm always making."

"You need a mother," Tupper decreed.

Freydolf had learned early that smiling was *not* the best way to set a Flox at ease. They mostly blanched, stared, or in one memorable case, fainted dead away. Thanks to his fangs, his friendliest expression had a way of inspiring dread. As a result, the Pred resorted to tight-lipped near-smiles, but Tupper's frankness was his undoing.

With a chuckle, he countered, "Mothers are too bossy."

"*Sisters* are bossy."

"Truer words were never spoken," agreed Freydolf, enjoying the novelty of actual dialogue. "However, you're the one I hired, so the duty is yours."

Tupper was obviously puzzled. "You want me to be your mother?"

The lad didn't seem very bright, but Freydolf didn't mind. "I suppose you could *try* to mother me, but I shall warn you now ... I'll be a difficult child!"

"Are you disobedient?" Tupper asked, his tone suggesting that this would be a terrible failing.

Folding his hands together on the bed's edge, Freydolf confessed, "I keep odd hours, and I'm forgetful. Like today." He bowed his head. "I'm not an easy man to live with."

Tupper's next question came out of the blue. "*Are* you a man?"

"What else would I be?"

In a softer voice, he asked, "Are you a monster?"

"What, because I have these?" Freydolf inquired, tapping one elongated canine tooth with the tip of his claw. Tupper nodded, and the Pred posed, "Before I found my way to Morven, I'd never seen a people with horns before. Are *you* a monster?"

"No."

"Aye, and neither am I." With solemn authority, Freydolf explained, "We're not the same sort of man, but we're both men. Well, you'll grow into one given enough time."

"Here?" Tupper asked.

The sculptor blinked. "Are you asking if you'll grow up here?"

Another nod.

Freydolf hardly knew how to respond. Past servants had only stayed long enough to line their purses with gold before hurriedly taking their leave ... or simply leaving. It almost sounded as if the lad anticipated living here for far longer, and the sculptor latched onto the prospect of Tupper's company with unexpected fierceness. It had always been too much to ask, but maybe this time, he could adjust the list of responsibilities to include cooking, cleaning ... and *conversation*.

Once the boy realized how many strange things lurked in Morven's galleries, he'd probably change his mind, but this chance was too rare not to seize. Leaning closer in his urgency, Freydolf asked, "Would you like that?"

Tupper shrugged.

The sculptor realized his mistake, for the only thing that seemed to register in the lad's wooly head was a direct order. Daring to give those glossy curls another pat, Freydolf urged, "Stay with me, Tupper."

Small hands tightened on the blankets, and wide eyes wandered over the lamp-lit workshop and all the wonders it contained. Then, Tupper met his master's gaze and answered, "I will."

3

Necessary Things

Tupper had never been in a bed so high or so soft. He only wished it was also clean. Mother *believed* in clean, so he was used to sheets that smelled of soap and sunshine. These blankets were nice and thick, but their faint mustiness made his nose twitch. But a much more pressing issue caused him to sit up.

Even though it was far past a normal person's bedtime, Freydolf was still awake. Surrounded by a ring of glowing lamps, the sculptor chipped and tapped away at his stone. Tupper had watched and dozed by turns, but now, he slid to the floor and padded over, hoping to catch his master's attention. Minutes passed, and the boy fidgeted; finally, desperation drove him close enough to tug at Freydolf's sleeve.

The big man blinked down at him, and Tupper quailed slightly, worried that the interruption might have angered him.

Heavy brows that looked as if they'd been made for scowling simply lifted, and dark eyes flashed with confusion. "What is it, lambkin?"

"I gotta go."

It took a few seconds for his meaning to reach the Pred, but when it did, he laid aside his tools and brushed his hands against his apron before removing it. "Aye, I'd best show you the way," he said briskly.

Taking the nearest lantern from its hook, Freydolf handed it to Tupper, then collected a second for himself. Almost as an afterthought, he grabbed a bucket from the floor next to the door.

The man led him along an open-air passage toward the end of the building. At home, there was an outhouse, so heading out-of-doors made sense. That's why Tupper was confused when his master entered another door, this one set directly into the mountain. Inside, the boy lifted his lamp higher and peered blankly around an empty room with six sides, one of which was dominated by a tall, shuttered window.

"We go down," Freydolf explained. "Mind the turns."

Against the wall in the corner, the floor fell away, and a wide set of stairs spiraled into the darkness below. Tupper followed the sculptor underground. Except a mountain was actually high above the ground, so it was probably more proper to say they went deeper into the stone. It was all around them, cool and quiet.

Freydolf's hand skimmed the wall as they descended, caressing the stone with his fingertips in an almost reverent manner. Stopping on one wedge-shaped stair, Tupper pressed his own hand to the rock, not sure what he was expecting to feel.

"Tupper?" Freydolf called, lantern-light illuminating the concern on his upturned face. "Do you need my hand?"

"No." He hopped down the remaining stairs without trouble.

"The necessary room is this way," his master said, nodding along a wide hall with arched ceilings supported by stout columns.

Right away, Tupper's ears picked up the soft *plash* of water, reminding him of his need to relieve himself.

"There's a fountain above the well," Freydolf explained. Pausing before a white door with a curved top, he said, "Everything you might need is inside, lambkin. I'll be waiting right over there."

Tupper nodded and pushed through the door. He quickly found the alcove where he could relieve himself. Afterward, he took his time exploring the lavatory's stone fixtures—innumerable bowls, basins, and even a deep bathtub. His whole family could have washed up in this room at the same time.

Making liberal use of a fat bar of soap that smelled of herbs, he scrubbed his hands and face, then collected his lantern and went to find Freydolf.

The sculptor's lamp rested on the rim of the fountain he'd mentioned, and Tupper followed its beacon to the wide passage's end. On a pedestal in the center of a dark pool, the statues of three women poured never-ending streams of water from stone pitchers. Beyond the fountain, Freydolf stood before a wide set of mullioned windows, looking out at the stars. He turned and asked, "Can you remember your way back the next time?"

Tupper nodded confidently.

With a satisfied smile, Freydolf held out the empty bucket and said, "Fetching water is one of your jobs, so you may as well learn the ropes." The boy looked uncertainly toward the fountain, but his master shook his head. "Fresh water comes from below. Let's see if you can manage the well-stone."

For the next few minutes the sculptor patiently talked him through the process of drawing water. Tupper sloshed the heavy bucket, blotching the floor in his efforts to lift it free from the shaft, but he succeeded without help.

"Good lad," Freydolf praised. "We'll cover the rest of your jobs tomorrow, but there's one thing I need to tell you before I forget."

His solemn tone made Tupper listen up, for he hoped to make his master smile again.

Crouching down, the Pred held his gaze and spoke very slowly. "The Statuary is filled with unusual things, and not all of them are completely tame. I don't want you to wander where they might be wandering." With a searching look, Freydolf asked, "Do you understand?"

Tupper honestly thought he did, so he nodded and said, "Yes."

The sky had already begun to lighten before Freydolf dropped onto his pallet, an arm flung over his eyes in an attempt to stave off the sun's rays. Sleep came hard and fast and probably would have lingered late, were it not for Tupper. It must have been mid-morning when the sculptor felt a touch, then a tug.

Thinking back, Freydolf was quite certain that this was a first. By his own accounts, the Flox were a tactile folk, hands-on learners and openly affectionate, but not with him. Even the bravest of his servants had never intruded upon his personal space, not that he expected it. Among his people, physical contact usually amounted to a bid for dominance. A Pred trusted few and permitted the touch of fewer, so Freydolf watched with mingled disbelief and amusement as Tupper attempted to tuck him in.

Keeping a servant was a practical necessity, but Freydolf had already begun to hope for more from the odd boy. Tupper was too young to offer much, but perhaps he would come into his own. If nothing else, the sculptor found his forthrightness amusing.

Freydolf pondered the concentration in Tupper's expression. The set of his chin was stubborn, but nervousness still lingered in his eyes. His slender arms were barely up to the task of dragging the heavy quilt up over the big man's shoulders, and Freydolf wondered anew what would come of his impulsive choice. "Are you mothering me?" he asked, his voice roughened by sleep.

Tupper froze guiltily. "Is that bad?"

"Nay," he replied, yawning hugely. "Is breakfast ready?"

The lad's eyes widened, and he slowly shook his head.

A noisy rumble alerted Freydolf to the boy's own hunger. Belatedly, Freydolf realized Tupper probably hadn't eaten since this time yesterday. On the heels of this thought came another, and he asked, "Can you cook?"

"No."

Wonderful. With a sigh, Freydolf admitted, "That makes two of us."

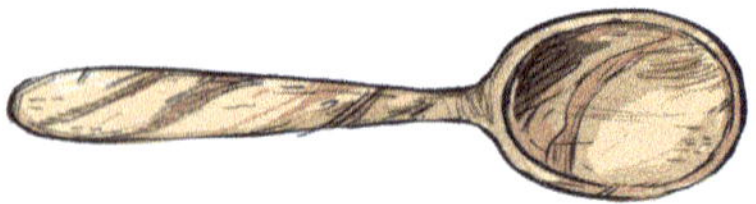

Tupper's mother would often ask him to stir the pot at home, but he'd never paid much attention to what went into it. Even so, Freydolf had left him to fend for himself in the kitchen, a cluttered room that smelled faintly of scorch and soot. Breakfast certainly sounded nice, but it wasn't looking like much. Still, Tupper labored over the copper kettle, hoping against hope that the porridge would see fit to thicken.

Freydolf strolled into the room and inquired, "How are the cook and his cookery coming along?"

Tupper's qualms increased. He knew the smell of good cooking, and this wasn't it. Bad as it was, it was the best he could do, so in that respect, he'd kept his promise.

Timidly ladling some of the mess into his master's bowl, he carried it to the table, and the sculptor took his seat, eating without complaint. A faint grimace over the aftertaste was the only reprimand Tupper received, but he felt it keenly.

Freydolf hated to lose more time in training his new servant, but he knew the value of a solid foundation. Though his hands were twitching to get back to the flowing mane of the dragon he was in the midst of carving, he turned his back on the statue and asked, "Can you grow things?"

Tupper nodded, offering, "Mother has a garden."

Most Flox did, which made things easier. Beckoning for the boy to follow, Freydolf led the way out and up a flight of stairs. As they climbed, he explained, "We're high and dry here, so anything that's planted requires watering. My trees will need you."

Again, the curly head bobbed.

They proceeded through a narrow, wrought-iron gate set into a natural gap in the stone; the passage opened onto the outer courtyard. Because it was nearer Morven's summit, this wide terrace enjoyed greater exposure to the sun. A garden of sorts was planted here, though there was no rhyme or reason to the jumble of plants that managed to survive in the shallow, rocky soil. Each Keeper had added to the collection depending on their tastes.

Freydolf's contribution was a set of oft-neglected fruit trees, which were espaliered against the cliff face along a narrow ledge overlooking the courtyard. His sister had badgered him into planting them during her first visit, complaining loudly and in great detail about his ineptitude at hunting and foraging. These trees were both a concession to her concern and a reminder of home, where orchards sprawled along the coastal plains.

Even though he only fussed with them when his sister took the time to check up on him, Freydolf's meager grove survived; indeed, it thrived. A dozen trees lined a rock face with a westerly angle, so they benefited from sun-drenched afternoons. Here, the air was thick with the scent of ripening peaches, and the usual stillness was broken by the hum of bees. It would be several weeks before any of the pears would be ready to pick.

"Mind the edge," he warned, glancing back at Tupper. The sure-footed lad didn't balk at the sheer drop they were skirting, which was a mercy. If there was one thing the Statuary had aplenty, it was heights.

In this region, summers were hot and dry, and winters were cold and wet. Between rainy seasons, this small orchard relied on him—or rather, his servant—to sustain it. "You'll need to tote water from the cistern," Freydolf explained, pointing to a small stack of upturned buckets.

Glancing at the lad to receive his usual nod, the sculptor was surprised to find that Tupper wasn't paying attention to his instructions. His nose twitched as he cast longing looks into the laden branches. Breakfast *had* been a paltry affair. Freydolf cleared his throat. "Help yourself, lambkin."

In a twinkling, Tupper was up the nearest tree, barely bending its thickly-gnarled branches with his scanty weight. Feet swinging, eyes roving, the lad reached for one of the blushing fruits hidden amidst green leaves. He pressed the softly-fuzzed peach to his lips, but before he took a bite, he plucked another. Freydolf thought the boy a trifle greedy ... until Tupper held it out to him.

"Aye, thank you," he said warmly. Freydolf knew he was better at picking rocks than picking servants, but for once, he knew he'd chosen well.

With nothing but a vague suggestion that he put the kitchen back to order, Tupper was at a loss. His master's words implied that the room had once *been* organized, but all he could see was a hopeless mess that would have scandalized his mother. The boy poked his nose into cupboards and peeped under the lids of unwashed pots with a growing sense of purpose. Tupper's cooking might have been a failure, but he knew how to scrub.

Standing on an upturned water bucket, he fiddled with the latch on the window until he figured it out, then threw the shutters wide. Fresh air and sunshine heartened him, and he rolled up his sleeves. Even though Mother might never see his new home, he would clean it well enough to make her proud.

Several hours later, Tupper refastened the shutters. Shadows were lengthening, and he sat wearily upon the bucket to survey his handiwork.

He'd emptied all the cupboards in order to scour them. Pitchers and plates were stacked upon the chairs. Pots and pans were heaped in the corner. Cups and cutlery took up much of the table. Oddities were fanned out in the middle of the room—mismatched goblets, delicate egg cups, a set of heavy irons, an hour glass, and an enormous mortar and pestle. He'd cleared all the ashes from the hearth, then boiled the rags, which he spread to dry before the wide hearth.

At first glance, all he'd done was make matters worse; the room was twice as cluttered as before.

The sculptor's larder was partially stocked with sacks of meal and dried legumes, and there were dusty bunches of brittle herbs strung up in one of the corners. They hardly looked useable, but the fat rope of onions looked newer. Tupper had sniffed and sneezed at the assorted tins that held salt and spices, but he had no idea what to do about dinner. His stomach growled a soft complaint, but he was at his limit.

"Lambkin?" Freydolf called, giving his shoulder a small shake. "Have you been cleaning this whole time?"

Tupper blinked up at the Pred and realized that he must have dozed off. "Yes."

Freydolf peered around the kitchen with an odd half-smile on his face. "You go on downstairs to wash up, and I'll make dinner."

The boy couldn't have been more relieved, and with a nod, he went to collect a lantern.

After some poking around in the necessary, Tupper found the big copper cauldron that was used to heat bathwater. He was too tired to bother now. Splashing cold water on his face, he wondered if every room in the Statuary would need a good scrubbing. The prospect was daunting, especially on an empty stomach.

Even before Tupper opened the little door set into the big door that led to Freydolf's workshop, he knew something was very wrong. He darted to the kitchen to find his master waving a damp rag over a smoking pot. Crossing to the window, Tupper struggled to open the shutters once more, then turned to the sheepish Pred.

Freydolf poked at their dinner and ventured, "I wonder if we can still eat it?"

Both of them were hungry enough to try, so the man divided the contents of the pan onto two plates. Freydolf asked, "Do you think this needs a fork or spoon?"

"Spoon?" Tupper guessed.

"Aye." Offering the utensil, he urged, "Eat up!"

There were flakes of char throughout the lumpy porridge, and Tupper pushed them aside before taking a bite. It was *horrible*. Still, he took another mouthful, gulping it down before the scorched flavor could hit his taste buds. His eyes watered as he reached for his mug of water.

Before he could pick up his spoon again, Freydolf grumbled, "This is awful!"

"Yes," the boy agreed.

Master Freydolf shoved aside his plate. "What do you say to a bit of fending before nightfall? There must be *something* in the garden more edible than this."

Tupper pushed back his own plate. "Yes, please."

On the way to the outer courtyard, Freydolf confessed, "I thought I'd have time to finish a bit more of the detail on the dragon's tail. By the time I remembered our dinner, it was already too late." His glance was apologetic. "This happens more often than I like to admit."

Nodding, Tupper scanned the wide terrace for plants he knew and wished for a gathering basket as possibilities multiplied.

"I'll pick more peaches. See what else you can find," suggested Freydolf.

"Yes." In the fading light, Tupper scurried back and forth, using the loose front of his tunic to hold all his finds. Lambsquarter grew like weeds, and he discovered a ramble of shell beans sprawled over an urn with pretty handles. A fat bulb of fennel pleased him greatly, as did the discovery of a shrub with tart berries. When Freydolf reappeared with an armful of fruit, Tupper proudly displayed his accumulation.

"Is this enough?"

"Aye, we'll eat like kings." In a more rueful tone, he amended,

"Or like rabbits. I could *do* with a rabbit, but this is better than nothing."

"It will do nicely," Tupper quoted, using one of his mother's favorite sayings.

Freydolf's expression shifted when something in the distance caught his eye. "Moon's on the rise. We'd be wise to get inside."

As the last bit of daylight faded in the west, Tupper jogged to keep up with his master's long strides.

To him, the reason for Freydolf's hurry seemed obvious. The sooner they reached his workshop, the sooner they could eat!

Eyes fixed upon the big man's back, Tupper never noticed the way silvery shapes and shapely shadows turned to watch them go.

4

Picking and Choosing

Tupper wasn't very good with open-ended instruction. Mother always gave clear directions and checked to see if he'd followed through, but Freydolf wasn't nearly as particular. His master's last offhanded suggestion had taken him three days to complete, and even though the kitchen was now clean and orderly, Tupper couldn't be sure it was *right*! Since Freydolf didn't seem to know himself, the boy supposed he'd never know. It was quite vexing.

Breakfast that morning had been a qualified success. His porridge had finally thickened—maybe a little *too* well. The viscid mass had solidified by the time he called Freydolf from his bed.

Unperturbed, the Pred suggested cutting the glop into pieces and toasting it over the fire. The crisped chunks had been tasty, and for once, Tupper's belly felt full.

As soon as Freydolf returned to his sculpting, Tupper dragged all their blankets to the outer courtyard and spread them in the sun, but after that, he was out of ideas. Taking a seat under the tall windows, he waited to see if his master would give him another job.

After several minutes had passed, it occurred to the boy that Freydolf had very big feet. Unlike Tupper, the sculptor owned a pair of boots, but the Pred didn't use them; he hadn't bothered with them since returning from Hayward.

Freydolf's feet were just like the rest of him—huge, hairy, and dangerous-looking. What really fascinated Tupper was that each toe was tipped by a sharp claw. Wriggling his own toes, the boy wondered how often his master's socks needed darning.

While Freydolf worked, he stepped with care, scuffing aside the sharp bits of stone that littered the floor before setting his foot. After watching this ingrained habit for several minutes, Tupper's eyes widened and he sat up straight, for inspiration had struck.

He spotted a stiff brush and a dustpan propped in the corner, and he padded over to collect them. Beginning behind the dragon statue, he worked his way around to where Freydolf stood. It took a matter of minutes to whisk away all the chips and chunks of bluish stone, and Tupper felt very pleased with himself ... until another piece clattered upon the wooden planks.

He chased it down.

And the next one.

And the next.

Finally, he realized that Freydolf had paused in his work and was staring. "You needn't catch each fleck as it falls, lambkin."

"You'll hurt your feet."

The sculptor smiled crookedly. "I'm tougher than I look. Besides, if you're underfoot, *you* could be hurt."

Tupper nodded and waited, unsure what to do next.

Freydolf seemed to understand his quandary. "Chase cobwebs in the balcony for a bit."

"Where?"

His master nodded upwards, repeating, "The balcony. Up there."

Following his gaze, the lad was surprised to see a stone railing spanning the entire back wall of the lofty room. It was high overhead, Tupper hadn't noticed it.

"Balcony," he echoed, testing the new word. "What's it for?"

"This and that," Freydolf replied vaguely. "You'll see for yourself if you can find the way up."

There were no stairs that Tupper could see, nor ropes or a

ladder. He wanted to ask Freydolf to show him the way, but the sculptor caught his eye and shook his head.

"Seek it out, lambkin. You don't have far to go."

A challenge. He'd never been good at them. His brothers and sisters were all quicker and cleverer than he. But none of them were here, so Tupper knew he would reach the balcony first. Brightening considerably at the prospect, he nodded his acceptance.

Freydolf busied himself with the graceful coils of the dragon statue, but his puttering was a pretext. It was far more interesting to watch Tupper. The lad stood gazing upward, his brow creased with concentration; then, he paced the length of the room a few times. Slow as it was in coming, Tupper finally realized that the entrance to the balcony couldn't be in the workshop and drifted off toward the next room.

Chuckling to himself, Freydolf shook his head. The boy had spent the last three days scouring the kitchen from top to bottom without once looking behind the door that stood in its corner.

In his admittedly limited experience, children were inquisitive creatures. Although Freydolf had reason to appreciate this incurious quirk in the lad's personality, he knew he needed to explain things soon. Ignorance could be even more dangerous than curiosity.

Leaving off his tapping, Freydolf listened for sounds of progress.

In the breathless silence, a soft *chink* and *clack* filtered down from above.

He grinned and muttered, "Good lad."

It was at least an hour later when it occurred to Freydolf that Tupper had been much noisier when cleaning the kitchen. Chasing cobwebs probably didn't require the same rattle and clatter as kettle-washing, but the prolonged hush piqued his interest. Setting aside the tools of his trade, he went to investigate.

The narrow door in the corner of the kitchen had been painted a dusky shade of orange by a previous tenant. Its warm hue had always struck Freydolf as appropriate, for the balcony was a welcoming place. Not every Keeper had been as alone as he was; some had brought wives to the Statuary, and their children and grandchildren had ranged through its galleries. The balcony had clearly been designed to keep busy youngsters close, yet out from underfoot.

Thick carpets, deep chairs, and a trio of matched fireplaces spread across the long, narrow space, and various nooks and crannies were stocked with the whimsical creations of doting sculptors. Freydolf mostly used the space in wintertime, when Morven's stone grew chilly.

Pausing at the top of the curving stairwell, he spotted his servant. "He's a child, after all," he mused in an undertone.

Tupper had discovered one of the games that had been gathering dust for untold decades. Small tiles with letters carved upon their smooth surfaces had been collected in a lidded basket, but the boy had them fanned out across the rug. The Pred didn't even have to try to be quiet as he stole up behind his servant; Tupper was engrossed in sorting the tiles by color. Freydolf knew without counting that there would be twelve sets.

He was pleased to see that the boy had been schooled. At least, he knew his own name. Green, gray, blue, and white tiles spelled, **TUPPER MEADOWSWEET.**

"So you *do* know how to play," he teased.

Tupper started and turned, then ducked his head guiltily. "Sorry. I wanted a basket, and ... this one was full."

There were cobwebs clinging to one of the abashed boy's horns, testament to the work he'd done before making such a beguiling discovery. Freydolf knelt and said, "You haven't done anything wrong, lambkin."

Tentatively, Tupper nodded.

"If you were to put to order the rest of the balcony, you might find even more interesting things," he said, giving oblique permission for future exploration.

The lad gave the plush rug an almost possessive pat. "I will."

Turning his attention to the scattered tiles, the Pred plucked up eight and laid them straight beneath Tupper's name, creating, **FREYDOLF**.

The lad regarded him expectantly.

Freydolf scratched awkwardly behind one ear, for he had nothing more to give.

"What is your second name?"

"I don't have one."

"Your family name," Tupper insisted.

"That name was stripped from me when I left home. My clan—*most* of my clan—no longer claims me, and I was forbidden to use their name."

Tupper's gaze grew solemn, then sad. Gathering the necessary letters, he added a new row. "I'll share."

Even though he was already on his knees, Freydolf found he needed to sit down. It was rare for cast-outs to be taken in by another clan, yet Tupper had innocently offered to undo his shame. Such a gentle surname was all wrong for a Pred, but he'd never been a very good one. **FREYDOLF MEADOWSWEET** had a nice ring to it.

Reminding himself that this was a child's game, nothing more, Freydolf swallowed hard and replied, "Aye, that's a fine idea, lambkin. Thank you."

Hefting the bucketful of bluish chippings that Tupper had swept up, Freydolf showed the boy where to put them. Upon entering the outer courtyard, the sculptor did a double-take, for the ground was strewn with blankets. *His* blankets. Freydolf hadn't even noticed their absence, yet here they lay, their corners weighted by stones lest a fitful wind carry them off. "When did you do this?"

Trotting over to the nearest quilt, Tupper lifted the edge to his nose and sniffed. With a nod of satisfaction, he replied, "Before."

Freydolf huffed in amusement. Did the boy ever say more than a word or three? He might have to start keeping count. "This way," he urged, striking out toward the terrace's far end.

Just beyond the outer courtyard lay great piles of stone, the leftovers of countless carvings. Most of it was the gray stone native to Morven. The rest was roughly divided into eleven other sections, and Freydolf stepped carefully over the sharp gravel to the blue heap. "Whenever you sweep up after me, the dustbin must be emptied here. Match stone for stone," he directed, upending the bucket with a rattle. "Freshstone from the blue mountain, here. Red, green, pink, white, flecked, and so on," he listed, pointing to each mound in turn.

"Yes," Tupper agreed, bending to pick up a stray pebble and setting it amidst other stones with an orange cast.

"This way," Freydolf repeated.

Beyond the chippings was a downhill slope, where larger pieces of every color were jumbled together. Choosing a seat on an outcropping overlooking the collection, he checked on his servant. Tupper seemed at home in the rocky terrain, leaping lightly from one stone to the next. He caught up and gave the sculptor his full attention.

There were many things that needed to be said, but Freydolf disliked lecturing. He'd endured too many dull and distempered tirades while training under his predecessor. Maybe it would serve them both better if he simply *showed* Tupper what being a Keeper meant. That was surely the first step to understanding the rest.

Pleased with his plan, Freydolf relaxed into a smile. "Do you see those stones?" he prompted, pointing to the tumble.

Tupper shifted his focus and considered the rocky slope. "Yes."

"Pick one."

The boy's solemn gaze swung back to his, silently begging for clearer direction. Freydolf laced his fingers together and explained, "These are the remnants of thousands of sculptures. They weren't needed for the statue they sheltered, but that doesn't mean they have no worth of their own. I want to see if you're a picker."

"What's a picker?"

"A picker is what we call someone who can see the potential in a thing. It's said they can find stones with aspirations." Freydolf chuckled at the boy's baffled expression and said, "Go on, lambkin; see if you can find a good stone."

"How will I know it's good?"

"Hard to say," Freydolf admitted. "It might be the color, the shape, the feel. All you need to do is find a stone that makes you want to pick it up. You'll know it's the *right* one if you don't want to set it back down again."

With a short nod, Tupper accepted this new challenge.

Tupper scanned the heap of stones in blank dismay. He wanted very much to obey his master, but he didn't know how. There were so many stones! How was he supposed to choose just one? If this was some kind of test, he was sure to fail.

Doing his best meant getting started, so Tupper hopped to a flat, green stone, then onto a pock-marked, golden one. Since all the rocks around Hayward were the same gray as their mountain, it was strange to see stones in so many colors—dark red, petal pink, and a creamy-hued stone with metal threads that sparkled in sunlight. They were pretty, but did that make them *good*? And good for what? Freydolf hadn't said.

Squatting down, Tupper tried to sift through thoughts as jumbled as the hillside, but he was unequal to that task as well. With a small sigh, he pushed aside the clamor inside his head. Not-thinking was much easier. Besides, what was the use in pondering when there was a job to be done?

Freydolf had given him a hint. All he needed to do was find a stone that wanted to be picked up.

Tapping each stone within reach, he silently asked each, *You? You? You?*

Tupper couldn't imagine why he was talking to them as if they were people … except that they did have a sort of personality. The brown stone was rough and rugged. That blue stone rippled smoothly. But was one better than the other? He couldn't tell.

He worked his way down the hill, pausing from time to time to poke, pat, and prod chunks of rock. He picked up a few, but he carefully put them back. Maybe they would have been good enough, but he'd been told to find something *good*. Although he couldn't have explained why, Tupper knew there was a difference.

Eventually, he came across a lump of white stone so smooth, it felt waxy under his fingertips. He turned it over and caressed its underside, which was marred by chisel marks, and asked, "Are you the one?"

Laying his cheek against it, he admired its silky surface; then he held it to his ear, listening intently. The rock did not say *no*, so perhaps the answer was *yes*. His logic may have been flawed, but Tupper cradled the pure white lump to his chest and trotted back uphill to his master. Shyly offering his pick to Freydolf, he asked, "Is it good?"

The sculptor took the chosen stone in one clawed hand and inspected it. His mouth quirked at one corner, and dark eyes searched Tupper's face. "This is from my homeland," Freydolf revealed. "My people come from the shores below the white mountain."

"Is it good?" Tupper needed to know.

"Aye, *very* good," the man assured.

He fidgeted. "For what?"

Freydolf's eyes took on a shine. "I'll show you."

5

Rasps, Rifflers, and Realizations

Freydolf allowed Tupper to carry the white rock, but already, his fingers were twitching. It had been years since he'd indulged in a small carving, and he was eager to begin. If the stone was cooperative, he could finish before the lad's bedtime.

On their way back, Freydolf took the time to collect their sun-drenched blankets. Shouldering the small mountain of bedding, he strode toward his workshop, mentally cataloging what would be needed.

He glanced over his shoulder and smiled at the picture Tupper made. The boy clasped the rock to his heart as if it were some great treasure ... or a *good* one, at the very least.

Slowing his steps, Freydolf tried to coax him into dialogue. "I'm Morven's Keeper. A master sculptor. Do you know what that means?"

"You make stone things."

"Well, yes," he allowed. "But there's more to it than that."

Tupper nodded, and Freydolf sighed. The boy really was a terrible conversationalist.

"There aren't many who can do what I do." Feeling rather foolish for boasting, he admitted, "Not many care." Fewer still would trade places with him if they knew the sacrifices that came with the inestimable honor of hearing a mountain's call.

Instead of responding, Tupper jogged ahead to open the door for him, and Freydolf felt a pang of disappointment. Was anything he'd said getting through to the lad? A little enthusiasm might be nice. Then, Tupper locked eyes with him, and the Pred's hopes soared. No mistaking it! The boy definitely understood that *something* was about to happen, and the glimmer of his interest added fuel to Freydolf's creative fires.

Anticipation left him giddy.

Whisking past the dragon on its pedestal, he tossed his burden of blankets into the corner and scoured the workbench for the tools he'd need. Once armed, he gave the blue statue's whiskered muzzle an apologetic pat. "Tomorrow," he promised, then held out his free hand to Tupper.

Without missing a beat, the lad placed the white stone on his outstretched palm.

Freydolf's predecessor used to complain that decent pickers were hard to come by. According to Master Platt, like called to like, and most men were fools. It had been Freydolf's uncommon aptitude for picking just the right stone that won him grudging approval ... and a place as the crotchety old Drom's apprentice.

Freydolf turned Tupper's choice this way and that, a gleam in his dark eyes, for the stone was exceptionally good. Inspiring, even.

Tucking it into the crook of his arm, he paused long enough to ruffle the boy's bright hair. He had no idea what was going on inside Tupper's head, but one thing was certain—the lad's heart was sound.

Though this sculpture would be small, Freydolf knew it would be perfect in every regard.

Freydolf hastened up the narrow stairs to the balcony and pushed aside clutter on the small workbench situated at its far corner. A sculptor of a Keeper's caliber rarely idled. At any hour of the day or night, they were wrapped up in the act of creation, so tools were always close to hand. Small sets for fine work were kept here for leisure-time fashioning; indeed, most of the toys and games tucked away on the surrounding shelves had been crafted on the spot.

After much rummaging, Freydolf found what he needed and belatedly tied on a work apron, slipping a variety of chisels, rasps, and rifflers into its pockets.

He was just fitting the white stone into the bench's clamp for some rough shaping when he realized that his audience was missing.

Scanning the length of the balcony, he confirmed that his servant hadn't followed him upstairs, so he strode to the railing and leaned over. Tupper had remained in the workshop, making up Freydolf's pallet with the freshened blankets.

He called, "Will you be much longer?"

Startled eyes swung upward. "Yes."

Suppressing a smile, Freydolf urged, "When you finish with that, come up."

"I will," Tupper replied, next turning to his own bed.

Draping his arms over the railing, Frey watched the boy wrestle heavy bedding into place, smoothing and tucking until both beds looked completely respectable. Tupper took much more care than anyone else ever had, himself included, and Freydolf wondered what inspired the lad's persnickety tendencies. Although he'd initially assumed the boy's family didn't want him, the care with which Tupper tackled his responsibilities hinted otherwise. "If this is how he mothers, then this is how he was mothered."

Tupper hurried up the balcony stairs as soon as his task was complete and found Freydolf immersed in his work. Padding across plush rugs that made him want to stop and wiggle his toes, the boy peered around the big man just in time to see him split the white stone with a sharp tap of a small mallet.

For a moment, Tupper was afraid that Freydolf was smashing his good rock to bits, but the sculptor slowly loosened the clamp, turned the rock, and prepared to make another break. This wasn't reckless damage. Tupper had watched Freydolf enough to know that this breaking was a part of making statues.

As he sidled closer on tiptoe to see if his rock looked like anything yet, the movement caught his master's eye. "There you are, lambkin."

"I'm here." Where else would he be? Hadn't Freydolf told him to come up?

"This part won't take much longer." He tightened the clamp and angled his chisel. "Then, we can make ourselves more comfortable."

Tupper nodded. He *liked* this balcony. It was so much higher than Ewert's tree house, and unlike his stingy brother, Freydolf was willing to share its treasures.

With a satisfied grunt, the sculptor loosened the clamp and smoothed his hand over the stone. "Aye, this will do."

Instead of a lump, the rock was now more of a block. Tupper couldn't tell what plans Freydolf had for it, but if the man could coax a dragon from a rock, then there could be just about anything hiding inside the smooth white stone.

Freydolf strode to a sitting area midway across the balcony and lowered himself to the floor. Leaning against the arm of a chair that was too small for his large frame, the Pred stretched out his long legs, crossing his ankles.

Tupper hovered uncertainly.

Freydolf's brow quirked. "My hands are busy, but yours are empty."

Holding them up, Tupper replied, "Yes."

Lifting his stone, the sculptor suggested, "I'll play with this, and you play with something from one of the shelves."

Thinking it very strange that a grown man was planning to *play*, Tupper nodded and turned to obey. Almost immediately, he realized that he was facing another choice. Looking back at his master, he ventured, "Anything?"

Freydolf nodded distractedly, for he was already chipping away at the rock. "Aye, and you needn't stop at one thing. We'll be here all afternoon."

Pleased beyond telling, Tupper hurried toward a set he'd first noticed when dusting that morning. A dozen stones had been shaped into perfect spheres, much larger than the marbles that the village boys used in their games. Touching the white one, the pink one, and the brown one by turn, he picked up the green one, marveling at how heavy it was. He would need to carry them one at a time!

While he ferried the matched spheres over to where Freydolf sat, the man began a sing-song rhyme. "Blue for sweet waters; white for the brine. Gray under moonlight; gold calls for wine."

Tupper stared perplexedly at the rich golden hue of the orb in his hands. Rocks couldn't be thirsty. Could they?

Freydolf chuckled and said, "Don't mind me, lambkin. Gather the rest."

He happily complied, and when he joined his master on the carpet, Tupper arrayed the spheres before him, fiddling with the order until he was satisfied. Smooth as glass, cool to the touch, and uncommonly pretty—he silently greeted each in turn by its color name.

The second to last one stumped him, and he looked at Freydolf. "This one?"

"Hmm?" he responded, glancing from boy to ball and back.

"What do I call her?"

"Her?" Freydolf echoed, the hint of a smile tugging at the corner of his mouth.

Nodding, Tupper backtracked, pointing to the earlier stones in his lineup. "Blue, gray, green, and ... this?" he prompted, again pointing to the sphere in question. It wasn't only one color, or even two; several shades of brown and a warm pink were daubed together, then sprinkled with black speckles.

"Aye, I understand," the sculptor replied seriously. "Dapple. We call her kind dapple."

Tupper nodded and turned his attention back to the last in the row. The red stone reminded him of the monsters guarding the gate, and he rested his palm atop the ruddy sphere, remembering. He had been so frightened then, but he wasn't anymore.

Peeping at his master from under his lashes, he admitted that while the man still *looked* fierce, it was hard to stay scared of someone like Freydolf. He was patient with his rocks, kind with his words, and generous with his treasures.

Farley had been all wrong about the Keeper, and Tupper was more than a little relieved. He'd tried so very hard not to break his promise to be brave, only to discover that bravery hadn't really been necessary.

"Which one is from my homeland?" quizzed Freydolf, interrupting the boy's train of thought.

He pointed to the pristine white stone that was a match for the one in the sculptor's hands.

"Aye, and which one is Morven's get?"

Tupper touched the gray stone, and on the game went.

The day passed quietly, but Tupper didn't mind. Freydolf's stones put interesting ideas into his head, and there was plenty of time to think them over. Was there a land where everyone's front step was red? His house's threshold was gray, but in a land where rocks were yellow, gray might seem strange. Also, how did rocks from all the places Freydolf talked about find their way here? Did Keepers trade stones like the village boys traded marbles?

After a short break to wash and a skimpy supper, Freydolf hurried back upstairs. Mindful of the lowering sun, Tupper brought lanterns with him.

"Good thinking," the sculptor praised, pulling over a small table to use as a lamp stand. Aided by its glow, Freydolf lost himself in his work.

Tupper climbed onto the chair against which his master was

leaning and hung partway over the arm, glad to have found such a good vantage point. More quickly than he could have imagined, the tiny sculpture took shape in Freydolf's hands, changing until Tupper could make some sense of what he was seeing—a broad back, sturdy legs, wee hooves, and a tail.

At first, Tupper wasn't sure what kind of animal it might be, but he liked watching as Freydolf added reticulated lines until the tiny animal looked shaggy and real. Then, he switched his attention to the creature's head, teasing away unneeded flakes of stone until a muzzle poked out, sloping to a broad brow adorned by a pair of curving horns.

As Freydolf used a shiv to give them texture, Tupper glanced warily at the sculptor's face. His people were sometimes picked on for their passing resemblance to herd beasts. To his relief, the Pred's expression was one of serene concentration. His half-smile bore no hint of malice or mockery, so the boy relaxed.

Finally, Freydolf asked, "What do you think, lambkin?"

"A ram?"

"Aye," he said, offering him the finished sculpture. Its head tilted at a proud angle, and there were curls on its chest and fetlocks. "He's a noble little thing."

Tupper inspected every masterful detail. "He's perfect."

"Nearly." Freydolf carefully watched the boy's face. "The rest will have to wait for nightfall."

The rest? Cocking his head to one side, Tupper tried to figure out what was missing. Finally, he was forced to ask, "Why?"

With a mischievous smile, Freydolf replied, "Because white stone needs starlight."

Tupper leaned against the wide ledge in front of the workshop's tall windows, waiting for day's end. The sunset sky cooled into blues, and one by one, stars twinkled into view. Freydolf rattled around at his workbench, putting away the small-scale tools and locating a set that was finer still. He was nearly as excited as the boy, for he knew what was coming. The finishing touch had always been his favorite part.

Once the sun slipped below the far horizon, he had Tupper place the tiny ram upon the sill where starlight could reach, then lined up the tools necessary to add his maker's mark. With a rueful smile, Freydolf added a dish of ash from the kitchen hearth to the collection.

"We can be grateful for a clear night," he remarked, glancing toward the spangled sky. "Come, lambkin, let's douse the lamps."

With a nod, Tupper hastened to those he could reach.

One after the other, they snuffed the lantern flames, plunging Freydolf's workshop into darkness. The Pred's eyes adjusted quickly, and he waited for his servant's gaze to find his. "Can you see, lambkin?"

"A little."

"We can wait."

"For what?"

"Until the stars are bright enough to see by." There was no way he'd proceed before Tupper could watch. Freydolf searched for a preamble that wouldn't spoil the surprise. Kneeling down, he explained, "Morven is a miraculous place. Some would even call it magical."

The boy considered his words, then asked, "Truly?"

"Aye, and as Keeper, I have a fair amount of say-so over what happens here."

Tupper nodded.

Freydolf tapped the white ram's head. "He may be small, but this fellow is a proper guardian stone; rather, he *will* be once I'm done with him."

Although it came more slowly, Tupper nodded again.

"Have you heard of guardian stones?" the sculptor quizzed.

"No."

"Ah." Unsurprising, considering what little contact the Flox had with recent Keepers. Centuries may have passed since the people who lived in Morven's shadow had seen any of its wonders. "They're plentiful enough in the Statuary, but that's beside the point. Put simply, a guardian stone stands guard over something ... or someone. This one is meant for you."

Tupper looked between the ram and its creator, puzzlement plain upon his face.

Freydolf shook his head and conceded, "It will make more sense if I show you. Watch carefully."

"I will," the lad promised.

Taking up the small guardian-to-be, Freydolf smoothed a small, circular patch on the ram's back leg, then incised a signature of sorts. His mark was intricate enough to defy imitation and had to be applied in just the right way, so a breathless silence surrounded the pair for the space of a few minutes.

Eventually, the sculpture laid aside his tools and turned the mark toward the window to inspect his workmanship. "Aye. This will take," he confidently declared. "Which brings us to a name. Can you choose one?"

"For him?" Tupper pointed uncertainly at the statue.

"Aye, for him."

After some fidgeting, the boy said, "No."

"How about Olexi?"

"Is that a good name?"

Freydolf admitted, "It's a common choice for first guardians because it means *defender*. Where I come from, they're a traditional gift, so most children have one."

"Olexi," Tupper echoed, giving the name a try. "Olexi is good."

"That's settled. Now, the uncomfortable bit."

Tupper made a small noise of dismay when his master sprinkled some of the collected ash into his own eye. As Freydolf grimaced and blinked, the boy whispered a sympathetic, "Ouch!"

"Aye," agreed the sculptor with a short laugh. It was irritating, but it was also the simplest expedient. "With white stone, sea water is best, but tears do in a pinch."

Catching one glistening drop upon his thumb, Freydolf swiped it over the ram's nose, along its back, then pressed it against the mark branding its hindquarter. "Olexi," he called gently. "Wake up!"

The ram's ears twitched toward the sculptor, and eyes blinked; with a silent sneeze, the tiny creature performed a full body shake, as if trying to fluff out its shaggy coat. Freydolf chuckled at the rapt expression on Tupper's face. Clearly, this was an unexpected turn of events for the lad. "We want him to look to you, so tell him his name."

Tupper edged closer to the animated statue, nearly cross-eyed as he stared. "Olexi," he obediently repeated.

Freydolf watched indulgently as Olexi minced forward on stone hooves and bowed his head, accepting the child as his own. Then, the little guardian's stone eyes swept the room. Finding no sign of a threat, he capered along the ledge, taking note of the workshop's contents with far more curiosity than Tupper had ever shown.

The Pred stole another glance at his servant and felt richly rewarded for all his efforts. A cautious smile had stolen onto Tupper's lips as he watched the ram's antics.

"You made him."

"I *found* him. A sculptor finds what's hidden within stone, and a master sculptor unlocks its fullest potential."

"Is it magic?"

"I wonder." Some things defied explanation; they simply *were*. Recalling the boy's complete ignorance when it came to guardian stones, Freydolf said, "White stones are nightly defenders. Olexi will wake when starlight reaches him, and he'll stand guard over you until the last star fades from the sky at dawn."

"Always?"

"Aye. Keep him safe, and he will return the favor."

Tupper crooked his fingers, and Olexi pranced over. To Freydolf's amusement, the lad tried to pet the little guardian, and the ram tilted his head, leaning into each tentative stroke. Then, the softest of giggles rippled through the otherwise silent workshop.

Tupper looked up at him with happiness shining like stars in his eyes. "He's mine?"

"All yours, lambkin."

Folding his hands over his heart, Tupper extended them toward his master in his people's most earnest expression of gratitude. "Thank you," he whispered, breathless in his excitement.

With an upraised palm resting just below his heart, Freydolf dipped his head in the manner of his race. "My pleasure, Tupper Meadowsweet."

6

Delivery

Tupper woke to a *creak* and clatter of unfamiliar sounds and reached for Olexi.

"Easy now! *Easy!*" demanded an imperious voice. "This is priceless cargo, and I don't want a single chip gone before its time!"

"You *could* lend a hand," growled Freydolf.

"*Surely* you jest!" came the haughty reply.

There was a grumble and a grunt, and then a *thud* that seemed to shake the whole room.

Clutching his stilled statue to the front of his nightshirt, Tupper peeped around the edge of the tapestry that partially hid his bed from the rest of the workshop. For the third day in a row, Freydolf had stayed up until all hours, fussing over the finishing touches on his dragon statue. The sculptor had told him to draw his curtain and get some rest, but Tupper had played with Olexi long into the night, so he was a little short on sleep himself.

Rubbing his eyes, the boy tried to make sense of the early morning ruckus.

Freydolf had guests.

Four men stood around a rough column of stone, and the one who immediately caught Tupper's attention was an unfamiliar

Pred. Easing back behind his curtain, the boy eyed the outlandish newcomer warily. He wore a snug coat with fancy trim over a ruffled shirt, and jewels glittered at both his collar and cuffs. There were even gems dangling from his earlobes.

"This is a good stone," Freydolf announced, his hand resting upon its buff-gold surface.

"A magnificent specimen!" the stranger boasted, leaning casually against the thick column and tilting his head at a saucy angle. "Thank me properly, Frey!"

"For doing your job?" he scoffed.

"Stingy!" accused the other Pred, giving lustrous auburn hair a toss. It fell in loose waves well past his shoulders, making Freydolf's slightly frizzy ponytail look unkempt in comparison.

"Greedy!" countered the sculptor with a knowing smile.

The man was nearly as tall as Freydolf, but leaner and lighter on his feet. As he circled the new stone, rambling on about the triumph of his negotiations with a Keeper whose hideaway was half-lost in the middle of some far-off desert, he oozed confidence. Twin daggers were strapped to his thighs, and although he used careless gestures, they didn't quite match the prowl in his steps.

"Dangerous," Tupper whispered to Olexi. This person was the embodiment of all the stories he'd ever heard about this race of foreign conquerors—skin like bronze, draped in jewels, and armed to the teeth.

Dragging his gaze away from the Pred, the boy glanced at the other two men, whose lighter hair and curling horns marked them as locals. With a start, Tupper realized that he knew them both. Old Gruff was an elder in Hayward, the overseer in charge of everyone who worked the quarry; he was big for a Flox and fearless. The tense young man next to him had gray-green eyes that darted here and there around the workshop as if searching for something.

"Carden," Tupper breathed, for this was his oldest brother. He crawled a little closer to the edge of his bed, but he wasn't sure what to do. As much as he wanted to go to his sibling, he didn't want the strange Pred to notice him.

Just then, Gruff elbowed his companion and nodded significantly in Tupper's direction. Carden turned, and relief washed over his face. Eyebrows lifted in silent inquiry, as if to ask, *'Are you okay?'*

Beaming, Tupper held up Olexi in both hands, wanting to show off his new treasure.

His brother blinked, and Old Gruff snorted and cuffed Carden's shoulder, clearly to say, *'I told you so.'*

Carden made a few gestures, relaying messages that made Tupper happy and homesick all at once. Mother must have asked Carden to check on him, and Gruff had found a way.

Freydolf was oblivious to the exchange, but it wasn't lost on the other Pred. He did a double-take upon catching sight of Tupper, his predatory golden eyes widening slightly before narrowing with frightening intensity. The boy ducked back behind the bed curtains and listened in frank dismay as the stranger sent Gruff and Carden to see to the rest of the unloading.

As soon as they were gone, the Pred glided over and thrust aside the tapestry. "Well, now!" he exclaimed, leaning down for a closer look. "What have we here?"

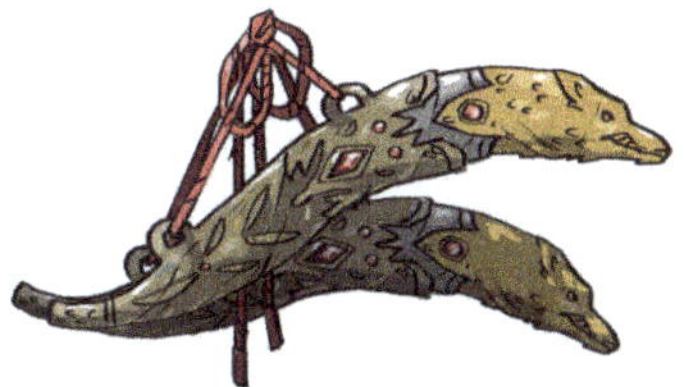

"Kind of small, isn't he, Frey?" the stranger demanded, his uncommonly-colored eyes alight with interest.

"Don't scare the lad," chided the sculptor distractedly, but he was busy with the new stone, smoothing his hands across its flat surfaces and rubbing his fingertips over the rough patches. "Who might you be, hmm?"

"Don't get ahead of yourselves over there," warned the new Pred with a dramatic roll of his eyes. "The customer wants something feline, so make sure it purrs!"

"Aye," Freydolf acknowledged, taking a stroll around the fat column, hands trailing. "I can see it."

Old Gruff trundled back into the room, wheeling a large trunk, and Tupper craned his neck to see if Carden would follow. His brother *did*, but the young man only stayed long enough to place a wooden crate inside the door and go back out for more. Tupper's sigh of disappointment turned into a squeak of alarm when he turned back and found himself nose-to-nose with the stranger.

"Planning your escape, sprat?" he asked silkily.

Clutching Olexi very tightly, Tupper shook his head.

With a hum that suggested disbelief, the elegantly-dressed stranger raised his voice once more. "What possessed you to choose this one, Frey? He's barely out of diapers!"

"The lad's just small for his age."

"He can't be much help!"

Freydolf's dark eyes flashed warningly, and his voice took on an edge Tupper had never heard before. "If you have a problem with my servant, you'll take it up with me. Now, stop frightening him."

"As you wish, Master Freydolf," the man acquiesced in gently mocking tones. Turning back to Tupper, he politely announced, "I'm Aurelius. The scruffy sculptor who hired you is my brother-in-law, so you'll be seeing plenty of me. Assuming you last that long."

Unsure how else to respond, Tupper fell back on the usual nod.

"Is it worth my learning your name? Or will you be running off, too?"

"You know, Aurelius," interjected Freydolf. "More than half of them ran once they got a look at *you*."

His brother-in-law's fanged grin was completely unrepentant. "Just weeding out the unsuitables!"

The boy's gaze drifted pleadingly toward Freydolf, and this time, the sculptor was watching intently.

Somewhat reassured and determined to prove he was a good pick, he lifted his chin and declared, "I'm Tupper."

"How cute." Aurelius offered his hand and commanded, "Shake."

"He's not a pet," groaned Freydolf.

"But he looks the part!"

Tupper didn't particularly want to be anywhere near Aurelius's manicured claws, but he couldn't ignore Freydolf's curt nod. For the second time in less than a week, he placed his small hand into a Pred's grasp.

Freydolf watched with a measure of chagrin as another trunk and several crates were added to the rapidly growing stack against the back wall. Aurelius certainly hadn't packed light. The larger of the two doors leading into his workshop had been swung wide to allow for the new stone's delivery, and the sculptor leaned against its sturdy frame, taking in the broadened view. His brother-in-law sidled up behind him, and he fought down the urge to tense. Aurelius was someone he could trust. Mostly.

Glancing in the direction of the finished dragon statue, Freydolf asked, "Will you be taking the blue?"

"Eventually."

"How long are you staying?"

"As long as it takes," Aurelius replied in longsuffering tones.

Somewhat startled, the sculptor took note of the angle of the sun and the chill in the air. "The season's turning already?"

"Do you have *any* concept of time?"

They both knew the answer to that; it was why Freydolf needed minding. Aurelius checked on him every year at summer's end, and his annual bout of meddling ensured the sculptor's survival through winter.

Aurelius prodded him. "Do you know that Flox?"

Freydolf eyed Carden, who was hefting another crate onto his shoulder, and answered, "Nay, I've not seen him up top. He probably works the quarry."

The Keeper had little or no contact with the Flox who labored on Morven's southern slope, harvesting blocks of stone. More than half the families in the area relied upon his coin for their sustenance, but management was left to Old Gruff, who served as a buffer between him and his skittish labor force.

"I think he's after your pet," Aurelius warned. "They were signaling to one another earlier."

"Really?" The sculptor took a longer look, then conceded, "There's a resemblance."

"How can you tell? These bleaters all look the same to me."

"Then you're not paying attention," Freydolf retorted, teeth on edge. There were times when Aurelius's elitist attitudes and petty posturing drove him to distraction, but he wasn't fool enough to let go the one tie that remained to his past. Keeping his voice even, he said, "Those two have the same eyes, chin, and hairline; I'll wager, they have the same father, as well."

"All the more reason to be suspicious!"

"Only if you're thinking like a Pred." Which Aurelius did with aplomb.

"Need I remind you that you *are* Pred?"

"No self-respecting citizen would claim me," Freydolf pointed out.

"I *dare* you to say that to Ulrica's face."

Freydolf grimaced, and Aurelius smirked. Not long after the Rakefangs cut ties and cast him out, Ulrica had followed him into exile, dragging along her peevish fiancé. Freydolf had been stunned to learn that his sister had made *him* part of a private prenuptial agreement. On their wedding day, Aurelius was contractually bound to Freydolf as his agent, ready and willing to inveigle and intimidate on the behalf of Morven's future Keeper.

The sculptor still wasn't quite sure if Aurelius had been very much in love ... or very shrewd. Either way, their business dealings were mutually beneficial. A generous percentage of Freydolf's earnings went straight into his brother-in-law's coffers, which meant Ulrica could live comfortably.

"You can't afford to lose a servant this close to winter," prodded Aurelius.

"Aye," he acknowledged, wheeling toward the kitchen. "Let's put your mind at ease."

"Mine?" he scoffed. "You're the one who'll freeze, starve, sicken ...."

Freydolf tuned him out and rapped a knuckle against the half-open kitchen door. When Tupper glanced up from his porridge-making, he asked, "Do you know my delivery men?"

"Yes."

"Is the younger one family to you?"

"Carden," the lad replied, his gaze drifting briefly toward Aurelius, who hovered just behind Freydolf. "My brother."

"And there you have it," the sculptor said, satisfied with the explanation

Aurelius regarded him pityingly. "You're a trusting fool."

Sighing, he turned back to Tupper. "Is Carden here to take you home?"

"No."

More to the point, Aurelius demanded, "Do you *want* him to take you home?"

Tupper didn't bat an eye. "No."

The Pred traded elbows, then Freydolf posed, "Would you like to go and greet your brother before his work takes him away?"

Eyes widening, the lad ventured, "Yes?"

"Aye, go on, lambkin," he urged. "I'll mind breakfast until you get back."

Tupper clung to the large, wooden spoon and said, "It might burn."

"Nay, I'll be more careful this time."

Tupper nodded and relinquished his place, plucking up Olexi before sidling past Aurelius and dashing out to find his sibling.

The moment he was gone, Aurelius hissed, "Frey!"

"Now what?"

Aurelius wore an expression of dismay and distaste as he crossed to the fire and peered inside the pot. "Meals have always been meager here, but do you mean to tell me this is *food*?"

"This *is* the kitchen."

With an equally straight face, Aurelius rebutted, "In your home, that means nothing! What is this ghastly mess?"

"Breakfast."

"Your cook can't cook!"

"It's hot. And filling."

Poking at the glop with the wooden spoon, Aurelius exclaimed, "It's a disgrace!"

"You're too fussy."

"That may be, but my high standards do not make up for your abysmal lack! You *need* proper nourishment!"

Frey wrested the spoon from Aurelius and gave the pot a stir. "The lad is doing his best," he defended grumpily.

Golden eyes fixed on him with cool calculation. For all his foppishness, Aurelius had impressive discernment; he understood people in much the same way that Freydolf understood stones. "Fine," he said snootily. "If you won't take heed on your own account, then consider this. Your slimsy *lambkin* needs proper nourishment even more than you do. Are you willing to put your pet into an early grave?"

Thunderstruck, Freydolf gaped at Aurelius for so long, he let the porridge burn.

When Tupper returned, the smell of burnt porridge hung thick in the air ... as did the silence. The scary new Pred looked as if he'd won a fight, for Freydolf's eyes never left the hands folded before him on the table.

Aurelius waved Tupper forward, rings flashing on his clawed hand. "First things first," he said in businesslike tones. "What's your role here?"

The boy wasn't sure he understood the question, so he simply fidgeted.

"Your *job*, sprat. What did Master Freydolf, world-renowned Keeper of the ancient galleries of Morven, the great Gray Mountain, hire you to *do*?"

"Mothering."

Aurelius blinked. "Pardon?"

Freydolf shot Tupper a look of such dismay that the boy thought he should add more to the list. "I water trees. I chase cobwebs. I pick lambsquarter. I light lamps." With a disappointed glance in his master's direction, he added, "I do not burn breakfast."

Steepling his fingers, Aurelius gazed at his brother-in-law, eyes glittering. "Your pet seems to be laboring under the misapprehension that he is your mother."

The sculptor's shoulders hunched miserably. "I was only using terms the lad would understand."

"Oh, I grasp the analogy. But do *you*?"

"What are you getting at?"

Freydolf's surly tones worried Tupper. Something was wrong, but what?

"If you cannot see it, all the better," said Aurelius. "Allow me to wrest the full potential from this situation!"

Freydolf shook his head. "You'll do as you please no matter what I say."

"Too true!" Sitting back in his chair, Aurelius crossed his legs decorously and fixed his gaze on Tupper. "Since your master can barely take care of himself, I shall take it upon myself to delineate your responsibilities."

Tupper's brow furrowed in confusion. Aurelius was going to take him? That didn't sound good, so he shook his head.

"He doesn't understand," Freydolf chided.

"Then, I shall simplify." Pointing to his brother-in-law, Aurelius adopted a patronizing tone. "This man has a job. Do you know what it is?"

"He makes stone things."

"Yes, Frey is a genius with stone," agreed Aurelius. "However, in every other respect, he is as helpless as a newborn babe."

"You exaggerate!" protested the sculptor.

"Only to make a point," soothed his agent before picking up where he left off. "When he's working, he forgets very important things—cooking, cleaning, eating, drinking, sleeping, and the basics of proper hygiene. Those things are *your* job."

Tupper was listening closely, but one part went over his head. "Hygiene?" he echoed uncertainly.

"Aye!" Aurelius exclaimed. "It's clear that he's been

neglecting his for *far* too long."

Freydolf muttered a few choice words under his breath, but his brother-in-law ignored him in favor of further elucidation. "Tell me, sprat, do you have a mother?"

"Yes."

"And does she make you wash?"

"Yes," he repeated.

"How often?"

Tupper glanced guiltily at Freydolf, for he already understood where he had been remiss. "Every other," he admitted quietly.

Freydolf scratched behind one ear and asked, "Every other … week?"

The boy shook his head. "Day."

"Excellent! I shall leave this vermin-infested, sorry excuse for a Pred to you, and you shall leave breakfast to me." Waggling his fingers in the general direction of the door, Aurelius wrinkled his nose and urged, "Go! Wash! Be clean!"

Tupper nodded and looked to Freydolf. "Bathtime."

"Aye, lambkin," he sighed, getting to his feet.

Aurelius wore a taunting smile, but deep down, he was mystified. Every other servant he'd ever questioned in this room had cowered behind the perfectly valid excuse that no matter what they did, Frey wouldn't listen. But this time, everything was different. "When his pet scolds, he lowers his head. Where his lambkin leads, he is sure to go." This new development would be very useful indeed.

7

Freshstone Menagerie

On the occasions when he bothered to avail himself of the necessary room's impressive bathing facilities, Freydolf counted himself fortunate that the predecessor who'd installed the tub had been more generous than the one who'd designed his bed. Long. Wide. Deep. The big Pred fit in the sunken pool with room to spare.

Slouching down in the hot water, he poked at bubbles with the tip of one claw. He hadn't realized he stocked such extravagances as bath foam. Aurelius had probably left it, and Tupper had insisted upon it.

The lad trotted back and forth, lugging a bucket between the well and the large, copper cauldron positioned at the foot of the tub. Once Freydolf was finished, there would be fresh water ready for Aurelius, who would undoubtedly wish to wash away every speck of travel grime.

A squat sort of fireplace with an ornamental chimney was part of a simple but ingenious system that allowed the heating of bathwater in any season. Draining was managed by removing a stone stopper at the tub's base, letting the water rush away to points unknown. Freydolf had never bothered to search for the outlet.

Tipping one last pailful into the big cauldron, Tupper gave the fire beneath it a poke before plopping down against the nearby wall. His cheeks were flushed from exercise, but Freydolf thought some of the color may have been embarrassment. Group bathing was common enough among Pred, but the lad's bashfulness suggested that Flox preferred their privacy.

"You may go back upstairs if you wish."

Tupper adamantly shook his head.

Freydolf didn't blame the boy for preferring his company over that of his brother-in-law. Aurelius had always been a terrible tease. Figuring the easiest way to get the boy to relax a little was to do the same, Frey let his eyes drift shut. If Tupper expected him to bathe every other day, there would be ample opportunity for him to get used to this sort of thing.

For his own part, Freydolf had fond memories of playing with his friends in shallow pools of steaming water in the public bathhouses.

A thought occurred to him, and Freydolf sat up quickly, sloshing water and startling his servant. Casting about, he spotted what he wanted on a nearby ledge.

"Do me a favor, lambkin?" He pointed to a row of small statues. "Bring those to me?"

Tupper leapt to his feet, clearly grateful for something to do, and carried over the first of the little animals. With great care, he set a small deer carved from freshstone on the tub's verge. "Like Olexi?" he asked, placing his ram beside it.

"Aye. Bring over the rest."

While Tupper fetched the next one, Freydolf shifted position so he could drape his arms over the rim. He studied the workmanship with fresh interest, for the animal wasn't from this part of the world. They'd probably been used to teach youngsters about a homeland that had been left behind.

It was an odd assortment—a deer with twisting antlers, a striped serpent, a large beetle, a turtle, and a sleek cat with some indication of spots roughed into its coat. Freydolf tried to recall which prior Keeper had come from the tropical forests over on First Continent. A quick check of the maker's mark confirmed his suspicions. "These are at least one hundred and fifty years old."

"Guardians?" Tupper asked, completing the set with a bird whose tail feathers draped behind like a train.

"Aye, they are. I suspect they were meant for bath toys, but these *are* proper water guardians. See? They bear a master sculptor's mark."

The boy knelt down to peer at each animal in turn. "Do they wake up?"

"Watch!" Cupping bathwater in his hands, Freydolf dribbled some over the turtle's shell. The stone creature's head lifted, and its eyes blinked placidly, first at him, then at Tupper, whose expression filled with wonder.

As the turtle began a slow shuffle along the floor, Freydolf offered, "You try?"

Scooting closer, Tupper scooped water and let it splash onto the small feline, leaving a soap bubble on its ear. The wee point flicked, and the cat sat back on its haunches to wash. "Oooh," Tupper breathed. He gave the beetle a similar dousing and gasped when it came to life and skittered away.

"They'll be able to move until they're dry again," Freydolf explained, sitting back to watch.

Tupper nodded and dipped the striped serpent into the tub. Lifting the wriggling reptile to eye level, he giggled when it coiled in the palm of his hand.

To Freydolf's relief, it only took a few minutes for these new playmates to drive away any hint of the lad's earlier shyness. Tupper sat in the puddles at the edge of the tub, his feet dangling in the sudsy water as he played contentedly with the menagerie. The bird ruffled its exotic feathers, the cat stalked passing soap bubbles, and the sculptor got down to the business of washing his unruly hair.

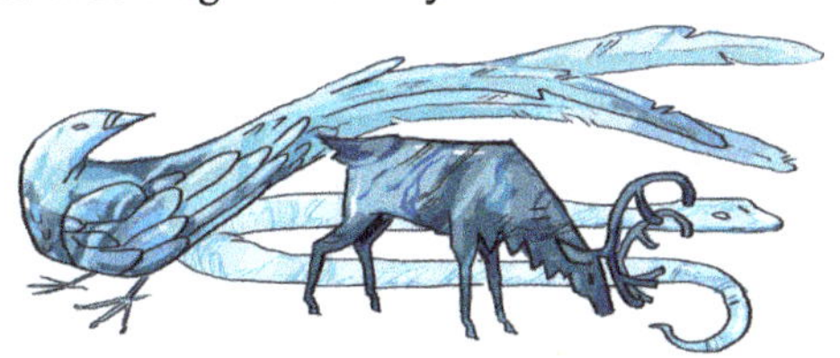

Tupper followed Freydolf upstairs, mimicking the way the big man trailed his hand along the stone wall of the curving staircase that led up from the lower gallery. Still wet, the Pred's thick brown hair was almost black, and when he strode out into the open-air passage, it glistened in the sunlight.

"Clean," Tupper murmured, pleased over a job well done. Aurelius couldn't scold them now that Freydolf had washed.

"Took you long enough!" groused the newcomer when they reentered the kitchen. He lounged in one of the chairs, his face alight with expectation. "Breakfast?"

It was a miracle! Tupper slowly approached the table and ogled the meal spread upon a scattering of richly-hued cloths. He recognized the mismatched dishes, for Aurelius had chosen the fanciest ones from the cupboard; however, none of this food had been in the pantry. Plates and bowls were heaped with delicacies—honeyed fruit, spiced nuts, tinned cookies.

The smirking Pred lifted a dark bottle and asked, "Isn't this better than mush?"

Frey grumbled, "If that's intended for the stone you just brought, don't you dare drink it!"

"Relax, I brought more than enough."

Tupper's astonishment spilled over. "You can cook?"

Freydolf snorted. "Aurelius can open crates."

The boy backtracked to check the large stack of boxes Old Gruff and Carden had left. Sure enough, several had been opened, their lids propped at odd angles. Straw, sawdust, and other packing materials littered the floor, but Tupper hardly minded the mess. Not when it presaged such a rare feast.

"I may not be a better cook," Aurelius said as he poured a rich, red liquid into Freydolf's goblet. "But I'm vastly more skilled at laying in provisions."

"Aye," his brother-in-law acknowledged.

Three places were set at the table, so Tupper slid into the remaining empty chair. Aurelius seemed quite prepared to play the genial host, or at the very least, to show off the extravagant fare he'd procured.

"Do you eat meat, sprat?" he inquired graciously.

"Yes, please," Tupper replied, accepting a strip of something dark and chewy. He tested it against the tip of his tongue, then sat back to gnaw on the savory treat while the Pred talked business.

At first, he listened intently, but his attention soon slipped, for they spoke of people and places only the two of them knew. He didn't feel left out, though. Both men kept putting new foods on his plate.

"This one's good, lambkin," Freydolf assured, proffering a wedge of yellow fruit on the end of his paring knife.

It *was* good, and Tupper happily accepted another piece.

Aurelius's choice tidbits were stranger, but sometimes interesting. The crumbly orange cheese had a sharp bite, and the salted fish smelled funny. Then, he pushed a bowl of glistening pickles toward him, saying, "Eat one of these. They're a favorite of Frey's."

Heat exploded in Tupper's mouth, and he quickly reached for his mug. He took several gulps, trying to wash away the lingering spiciness.

He gave Aurelius a watery-eyed look of reproach,

"You should have warned him." Freydolf popped one of the pickled vegetables into his own mouth. "Ulrica's peppers are definitely an acquired taste."

"I'm educating his palate."

Freydolf shook his head. "It's more likely you're testing his mettle. Or teasing."

Aurelius plucked a jewel-like preserved fruit and held it out. "Is this more to your liking, sprat?"

Tupper blinked at the pretty red berry, but he glanced at Freydolf first. "Is it good?"

"Taste and see," his master urged with a straight face.

This time, the new flavor was pleasantly tart, and he chewed contentedly.

"Braver than he looks," Aurelius remarked.

"Does as he's told," countered Freydolf.

"How fortunate for me!" Rubbing his hands together, Aurelius said, "I'll be putting your pet through his paces!"

Narrowing his eyes, the sculptor asked, "What are you planning?"

Aurelius's hand fluttered as if trying to shoo away his brother-in-law's suspicions. "My responsibilities are the same as ever, not that you'll even notice once you get cozy with that new rock of yours."

"I'm aware of how much you do."

"Good," Aurelius replied with a serene smile. "Then you won't begrudge me his assistance."

Tupper tensed as Freydolf's menacing brows drew together in a scowl that seemed to hold a warning. Was this the same thing they'd been discussing earlier? Did Aurelius want to take him away? He didn't like that idea, and it looked as though the sculptor didn't either.

"When?"

"Tomorrow is soon enough to start," said Aurelius.

Finally, Freydolf growled, "Aye."

With a discomfited wriggle, Tupper tried to figure out what their agreement meant for him.

That night, Tupper huddled in the far corner of his bed, listening closely for sounds from above. Aurelius was sleeping in the balcony on a fat mattress in front of one of the fireplaces, but the Pred was still too close for one little boy's comfort. Despite the man's many smiles and sugary tones, it was obvious he was planning something, and Tupper was afraid of what it might be.

Olexi butted his ankle, and he smiled at the brave guardian stone. No doubt the ram would try to protect him, but could he fend off a grown man like Aurelius? Shaking his head, Tupper whispered, "We're too little."

They needed a safe place to hide. Just in case. But where?

Tupper hunched his shoulders and tried to come up with a good plan. Honestly, there weren't many options—three rooms, the outer courtyard, the grove. The Statuary was vast, but these few places were all he knew.

That left just one option.

Crawling to the edge of the bed, he peeped around the curtain. Moonlight shone through the tall, latticed windows, casting pretty patterns on the otherwise dark workshop.

Freydolf's slow, deep breaths came from the pallet in the opposite corner, but the boy couldn't tell if Aurelius was sleeping. Maybe he was still awake. Maybe he was just waiting for Tupper to fall asleep. Maybe he was already on his way.

Scooping up Olexi, Tupper did the only thing he could think of. It wasn't a very clever plan, but it *was* a plan. Clinging to that faint hope, Tupper slid off the high bed. Nightshirt flapping around his knees, he made a wild dash toward safety.

Freydolf was in a blissful state—clean, warm, full, and between statues. The blue dragon was complete, so he no longer felt compelled to carve; the golden stone awaited his expertise, but it would take time to plan a piece that would suit his client's needs. Since there was no rush to begin, he was at ease with himself and his world.

A soft sound intruded upon the deepest slumber he'd had in months, but he clung to unconsciousness. He'd earned a rest! There was a dip, a rustle, and a tug before Freydolf roused enough to comprehend what was happening. Dark eyes blinked, then widened, for Tupper had joined him on the narrow cot and was sitting against the wall with his knees pulled up to his chest.

This was definitely a first. It took several moments for Freydolf to react, but he finally found his voice. "Are you lost, lambkin?"

"No," the lad whispered.

"You're in the wrong bed."

Tupper nodded, but he made no move to vacate the premises.

Freydolf could count on three fingers the number of times he'd dealt with his various nieces and nephews, but he did his level best to figure out what was amiss. "Did you have a bad dream?"

"No."

"Do you need the necessary?"

"No."

Olexi trotted across the hillocks formed by Freydolf's bedding and scaled the sculptor's blanket-covered hip, taking up a defensive stance between Tupper and … what? The man glanced around the quiet workshop, then back at the boy who seemed to be using him as a barricade. "What has you spooked?"

Solemn eyes flicked toward the balcony railing above.

Freydolf caught on. "Are you worried about Aurelius?"

"Yes."

And no wonder. Poor lad. "Does he seem dangerous?"

"Yes."

A thought occurred to Freydolf. "Don't *I* seem dangerous?"

Tupper pondered that for a moment, then answered, "In parts."

"Which parts?"

Tupper wiggled his fingers.

"Aye," Freydolf acknowledged, mirroring the boy's gesture. "Do you want a closer look?"

The boy offered a cautious shrug.

"Hold out your hands." As expected, Tupper immediately obeyed. Frey placed his hand into the lad's grasp, palm up, fingers relaxed. "I won't lie to you, lambkin. They're sharp enough to be deadly. Pred are predators, after all."

When gray-green eyes lifted to meet his, their expression seemed mournful.

"If it makes a difference to you, I can honestly say that *my* claws have never drawn blood. I didn't have the stomach for war, and I was too busy picking stones to complete a proper hunt." With a wry smile, he confessed, "My father was very disappointed in me."

Apparently, this *did* make a difference, for Tupper tugged

his hand closer, tucking it against his chest to get a better look. Childish fingers traced work-hardened ones, prodding at calluses, then carefully testing the tip of each claw. Finally, he pressed his palm to Freydolf's, comparing the sizes.

"Big," he murmured. "And sharp."

"Aye."

"And good," Tupper added with a pat. Glancing around, he located Olexi and placed the tiny ram on the sculptor's palm. "Making stone things is better."

Compliments came few and far between, and it was even rarer to find someone who didn't think him ill-suited to his calling. Freydolf was unaccountably pleased to earn Tupper's solemn approval for the one choice that had robbed him of everything, yet given him everything he now held dear. "Aye, I think so, too."

The ram jumped from his perch, returning to his former post and reminding Freydolf that there was a more pressing issue that needed addressing. "Do you have brothers, lambkin?"

"Yes. Three."

"Do any of them say or do things to pick on you?"

The boy's gaze slid sideways, and he quietly admitted, "Yes."

"Your big brother from earlier?"

"Not Carden." With a pout, Tupper said, "Mostly Farley."

"Is he older or younger?"

"Younger."

Freydolf hoped this frame of reference would be enough. "Aye, brothers can be both pest and pestilence, but if you were truly in need, would he abandon you?"

Tupper slowly shook his head.

"Aurelius is ...." Freydolf trailed off, searching for an appropriate description. None of the ones that came first to mind were appropriate for young ears. Starting over, he explained, "Aurelius is my bratty younger brother, by marriage. I'm not sure what my little sister sees in him, but those two are the only family I have left. He's a terror and a tease, but he's here to help us."

Two small hands tightened around his larger one, and

Tupper asked, "Will he take me away?"

"Is that what you thought? Nay, lambkin. He'll have you running errands, but this is where you belong." Reclaiming his hand, Freydolf pointed at the bed built into the opposite wall and amended, "Rather, *that* is where you belong."

Once again, those wide eyes pleaded with him.

Freydolf's brows slowly rose toward his hairline. Surely the boy didn't expect …!

However, the instant he folded back the corner of his blanket, Tupper scrambled under it, burrowing so close, one of his tiny horns jabbed the man in the ribs. Within minutes, the lad's breathing proved that he was fast asleep, leaving sculptor and sculpture to keep watch.

Olexi resumed his guard duties with an air of satisfaction, for his charge was finally calm. It took much longer for Freydolf to relax into this unaccustomed role. For years, he'd lived in an impenetrable fortress, crafting guardian stones for those seeking a sense of security, so he knew the lengths some people were willing to go to feel safe.

People came to him all the time, wanting his expertise. This was the first time he could recall someone coming to him because they wanted *him*.

Somehow, Freydolf had become Tupper's safe place.

8

Lost and Found

When Freydolf next woke, Aurelius was staring down at him with the oddest expression on his face. "Is this a new tactic, perhaps?" he inquired lightly.

"Tactic?" he grunted, unsure what he was talking about.

The perfectly-groomed man was adjusting the jeweled cufflinks on a deep blue silk shirt that had to have cost a fortune. Fleetingly, Freydolf wondered just who his brother-in-law was trying to impress. Moving to swipe unruly hair out of his face, the sculptor was hindered by the small body anchoring his shirtsleeve ... and belatedly recalled his young guest. Tupper was curled up snug against his side, still sound asleep.

"Oh. This?"

Judging by the glint in the other Pred's eyes, Freydolf would *never* live this down. "Since you consistently fail to *hire* decent servants, you opted to *raise* one?" hazarded Aurelius. "I'll give you credit; it seems to be working. How long have you been coddling him? Since he was weaned?"

"It's been a week."

That gave the other man pause, and his gaze shifted to the frizz of white-blond curls. "Truly? Is that all?"

"Aye."

Aurelius had met the majority of his servants over the

years, and he'd dealt with the villagers often enough to know that Flox and Pred did not mix. "How did you manage to circumvent the natural order of things?"

"I don't know," Frey admitted softly. "He's different than the rest."

"Clearly. Maybe the sprat has a stone heart?"

Aurelius reached for the boy, but the sculptor knocked his hand away, saying, "Leave him be."

"Why should I?" With a faint smirk, he pointed out, "Your servants have always been fair game!"

"Easy pickings, more like," Freydolf grumbled, "You frighten him."

"Of course I do! It's my birthright as a Pred!"

He had a point. Then, he made another.

"Every one of your hirelings came to you with fear and trembling, but this boy is the first to receive more than a share of coins back." Aurelius nodded toward Olexi and casually inquired, "Is that *your* mark branded on the sprat's guardian stone?"

"You know it is."

Aurelius gazed at the two of them for several moments, then pressed his hands together in a gesture of peace. "Relax, Frey. I won't scare off your pet. I'm not even sure I could."

He tugged the blanket closer around Tupper's shoulders. "I'll thank you not to try."

"Only a fool gets between a mother and her babe!"

Freydolf shot him a pained glance. "I'm not the lad's mother!"

"Aye," Aurelius conceded with a mocking smile. "But he thinks he's yours."

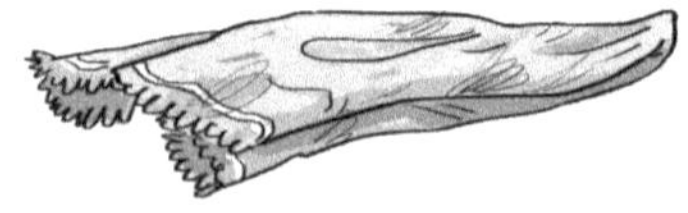

With a flurry of silk and sulk, Aurelius burst into the workshop and demanded, "Have you seen the sprat?"

Freydolf glanced over the top of the golden stone he was marking and inquired, "Recently?"

"Since breakfast," he clarified.

"I've been a little distracted."

"And I'm being driven to distraction! Do you know how much work is waiting?"

"Yes and no," Freydolf replied vaguely. "I usually leave such things to you."

Aurelius rolled his eyes. "Very trusting of you, but I thought we'd agreed that you'd be *entrusting* your pet to me for the duration."

"Aye."

"So you *haven't* seen him?" Aurelius prodded.

"Maybe he's hiding from you." Giving the other man a stern look, he added, "You *could* have been more polite at breakfast."

"I was!" he insisted. "For me."

Freydolf snorted. "If you don't bridle your tongue, you'll never win the lad over."

"I'll bridle my tongue when you collar your pet," Aurelius muttered. "He'd be easier to find if you kept him on a leash."

"Have you tried behind the rimbles in the upper loggia?"

The other Pred blinked. "The *what* in the *where*?"

"In the upper loggia." After offering a convoluted set of directions to the tucked-away spot, Freydolf said, "It's pleasant there, especially in summertime."

Aurelius stared dubiously at his brother-in-law. "Do you really expect me to believe that I'll find him way up there?"

"Not really," Freydolf admitted, turning his attention back to the stone and making a sweeping chalk line along its side.

With a growl, Aurelius exited the workshop.

Frey looked at the boy sitting on the floor between his feet and winked broadly.

Tupper's eyes shone with gratitude, admiration, and the rare delight of a shared secret. He was quite sure that *his* Pred was bigger and better than any other.

Tupper wasn't sure what Freydolf was doing. Well, he understood that the golden stone was going to become a statue, but that didn't really explain the swooping lines Freydolf was drawing across its surface. The markings didn't look like anything to him, but they clearly meant something to the sculptor.

Turning to face the new stone, the boy wondered who had picked it. It felt different than the white rock from which Olexi had been created, and he pressed his ear to the cool surface, trying to figure out how Freydolf knew there was a cat inside. Tupper liked cats, and a yellow one was a good idea. But the color also reminded him of Aurelius's eyes.

Glancing up at his master, he asked, "Will he be angry?"

"Only on the outside."

Resuming his spot, Tupper muddled over the difference between insides and outsides while poking at the floorboards. The wide planks were covered in scrapes and indentations, evidence of statues past. Aurelius was confusing because he was fancy on the outside, but scary underneath. Could there be something *else* deep down? Mother had always said that *saying* and *doing* were entirely different things.

Tupper scratched his head and sighed. All he could do was watch and see. "How long?" he ventured.

Chalk poised between dusty fingertips, Freydolf leaned past the near edge of the stone in order to meet his questing gaze. "What's that, lambkin?"

"How long will he stay?"

"Not sure," he admitted. "At least a fortnight, though."

Tupper nodded. Two weeks was a long time.

"You'll get used to him. Eventually," said Freydolf. "After a few years, you'll hardly notice his little affectations."

Tupper blinked. A few years was even longer.

Freydolf's bare feet made a shushing sound as he shuffled across the worn wood underfoot. Around and around, and with each passing turn, he grew more absorbed with the rock. A fierce light danced in the sculptor's dark eyes; he was seeing far off things, so he no longer paid attention to the things that were nearby.

That's why Tupper had no warning. At the same time one Pred lost sight of him, the other caught up with him. With a snitty *tsk*, Aurelius exclaimed, "*There* you are!"

They faced off in the kitchen, and Tupper did his best to be brave. His gaze never wavered as Aurelius glared down at him, arms folded over his chest.

"I suppose you think you're very clever," he groused.

"I'm not." After a brief pause, he stiffly added, "But Freydolf is."

"Aye." Aurelius's expression turning quizzical. "Are you attempting to defend him, sprat?"

He wasn't really sure, but he nodded for good measure.

"Because he's been naughty?"

No, that wasn't right. Tupper sternly said, "You are not his mother."

Quirking a brow, Aurelius inquired, "And therefore in no position to scold?"

"Yes."

"By any chance, did Frey tell you what *my* role is?"

"Yes."

"And?" the Pred prompted.

"Bratty younger brother."

Aurelius's expression blanked for a moment, and Tupper belatedly recalled his mother's frequent urgings to employ tact. A stealthy smile crept across the Pred's face, giving Tupper a good look at sharp fangs. This didn't bode well, and he braced himself for some kind of backlash.

Crouching down, Aurelius sweetly inquired, "Were those his very words?"

"Yes." The Pred seemed *pleased* to hear this, which confused Tupper. Once more forgetting the consequences of potential impertinence, he asked, "Why?"

The man propped his chin on his hand. "I never knew he

considered me a brother.”

“Is that good?”

“It’s a high honor, and one not lightly bestowed.” At Tupper’s uncertain blink, Aurelius gave a delicate snort and summarized, “Yes. It’s *good*, sprat.”

Relieved, Tupper resorted to another small nod.

“To business!” Aurelius decreed, rising once more to his full height. “Your illustrious master is much sought for his skills, but he cannot make beautiful statues if he sickens. Every year, it’s my solemn duty to procure suitable provender to see him through the winter.” Noting the boy’s confusion, he chose smaller words. “I need to make sure there’s enough food.”

Tupper liked the sound of that very much, for the cupboards were nearly bare. “You brought food,” he remembered aloud.

“Yes, and as honorary doyenne of home and hearth, unpacking it and storing it is your chore,” Aurelius explained. “Later, we’ll supplement these goods with local produce. And meat. I’m not sure how any Pred can survive so long without meat!”

It was strange how things were turning out. Even though Tupper had been dreading this confrontation, he was eager to help now. Opening all those crates and seeing what was inside sounded more like fun than work. Brightening, he said, “He could do with a rabbit.”

The man cocked his head to one side. “How do you know *that*, sprat?”

“He told me.”

Aurelius drummed his fingers against his thigh, then slapped it. “Aye, He’s right and so are you. I don’t suppose you can hunt?”

Ewert still did most of the hunting back home. When he’d taken work at the quarry the year before, Tupper had been passed over in favor of Farley for training in. He’d felt bad about it before; now, he felt worse. “No,” he admitted softly.

“Then it’s up to me!”

Tupper scanned the man’s elegant attire skeptically. “Can you hunt?”

"Do Pred have claws?" he returned tartly.

"Yes. And pointy teeth."

With a put-upon sigh, Aurelius said, "That was a *rhetorical* question. For your information, we're taught to hunt and fish from the time we're weaned."

The very idea was new and interesting, and Tupper asked, "Who?"

"Who *what*?" The Pred shook his head, bemoaning, "Your communication skills leave much to be desired!"

Rubbing sheepishly at the nub of one horn, he tried again. "Who teaches hunting?"

"Fathers," Aurelius replied. "Passing down these skills is a father's solemn duty."

He wilted a little, mumbling, "Oh."

Golden eyes that missed little narrowed slightly. "Don't you have a father?"

Tupper slowly shook his head. "Not anymore."

"Pity," Aurelius said lightly. Then he chose a new course. "With what's left of the day, you will unpack. I'll make arrangements with Gruff for the annual delivery of firewood, then hunt. I want embers suitable for roasting by sunset. Can you manage *that* much, sprat?"

"Yes."

"Progress. Finally!" Aurelius grumbled. "Once I'm sure the two of you will survive the winter, I'll be on my way. Am I correct in assuming you'll be glad to be rid of me?" he deadpanned.

"Yes," Tupper replied earnestly.

With a wry grimace, the Pred quipped, "Honest as blood, brutal as fangs."

The afternoon passed pleasantly for Tupper, although he had to do a lot of running back and forth. Most of the crates were too heavy for him to lift, so he was forced to ferry their contents from the stack by the door to the kitchen. He emptied the boxes of their precious cargo, stowing everything in his nice, clean cupboards.

All the while, he listened to the tap, crack, and rattle of Freydolf's first foray with the golden stone. By the sound of it, he'd need to sweep soon, but not until he tended to the fire. Aurelius seemed to think he couldn't manage good embers, which was silly. Fire-keeping was something mother had relied on him for!

As he raked the coals and lay the wood, Tupper wondered if he should have mentioned to the visiting Pred that he *did* know how to fish. To his way of thinking, hunting and fishing were two different things, but Aurelius had lumped them together. This gave the boy something to muddle over while he coaxed the flames to life. If hunting was for the land and fishing was for the brook, what did you call it when you wanted to catch birds?

Just as the sun touched the horizon, Aurelius stalked through the kitchen door with two gutted rabbits dangling from one hand. Tupper gawked at the sight, for the lean man was stripped to the waist, his glossy hair was caught up in a strict knot atop his head, and there was blood under his nails.

"I'll spit the meat while you heat bathwater," Aurelius ordered briskly. "You'll turn it while I wash."

With a quick nod, Tupper scampered away.

Once he reached the hexagonal room at the top of the curving stairway that led down to the fountain colonnade, he pressed a hand over his hammering heart. He didn't think he liked Aurelius without all his usual fanciness. The man had shed his frills and furbelow, leaving nothing but a predator, as dangerous as a blade pulled from it sheath.

"Scary," he whispered into the silence. However, Tupper was sort of relieved. Being sure of something was nicer than being unsure. Lurking monsters were more frightening than the ones you faced. Keeping that in mind, the boy trotted down the stairs to start the fire beneath the copper cauldron in the necessary room.

When Tupper returned to the kitchen, he peeped cautiously around the door frame. To his relief, Aurelius had at least washed his hands. Skewers of meat were arranged on a rack over the embers, and he was in the process of sharpening one of the blades he usually kept strapped to his thigh. The man glanced up from his honing and remarked, "You took too long."

The criticism seemed unjust, but Tupper bit his tongue.

Aurelius nodded toward the window, which showed a sky already sprinkled with stars. "I hope Frey warned you it's not safe to wander after dark."

"He did."

"Good," he muttered, sheathing his blade and moving toward the door.

Maybe Tupper should have let him go, but he blurted, "Why?"

Golden eyes fixed upon him, flashing with annoyance. "He didn't tell you *why*?"

The boy gave a small shake of his head.

"Then I know what the topic of tonight's dinner conversation will be," he announced with a reassuring dose of his usual haughtiness. "In the meantime, don't let the meat burn."

"I won't," he promised.

Aurelius left him to his thoughts, and Tupper stared into the fire, trying to sort out the new sense of uneasiness that the man's words had inspired. The warnings had been frustratingly vague, but their meaning was plain. Something unnamed and unnoticed lurked in the Statuary, and it was dangerous enough to make Pred wary.

Morven must be home to a monster!

9

Moonlight and Starlight

Afreshly primped Aurelius inspected the meat resting on the table, nose twitching. "It smells edible at least," he allowed. "Lure Frey over, and we can eat."

Tupper's belly was already rumbling in anticipation of a good meal, so he hurried into the workshop and stood inside the circle of lamplight, waiting for the sculptor to notice him.

Aurelius appeared behind him and tutted. "You'll never get his attention that way, sprat."

Partially propelled by the Pred's sudden proximity, the boy rushed to Freydolf's side and patted his arm.

His master blinked down at him. "What is it, lambkin?"

"Dinner."

"Aye, I'll be there in a moment," Freydolf replied distractedly.

From where he lounged against the nearby wall, Aurelius said, "He's lying."

Tupper shot him a shocked look.

He gracefully waved off his indignation. "Nay, I don't mean an intentional falsehood. I only mean that he's already forgotten you."

Startled, Tupper checked Freydolf's face. Sure enough, the faraway look was back in his eyes.

"Try again," prompted Aurelius. "Try harder."

His next two attempts were equally useless, and the frustrated boy appealed to the watching Pred. "Can you help?"

"I could, but I won't," the man replied with a smirk. "You'll shortly be on your own again, so *you're* the one who needs to make him mind."

Tupper's chin came up. "I will."

Only, he wasn't sure *how*. Getting between Freydolf and his statue might work, but the sculptor had told him to stay out from underfoot while he was sculpting. There had to be another way.

Just then, Freydolf's stomach growled audibly, and Aurelius chuckled. "His empty gullet knows what's needed even if he doesn't! If you're going to do him any good, do it quickly. Hunting works up an appetite, and I have half a mind to eat his portion."

There was no way Tupper was going to let that happen. Sweeping the rough-hewn golden stone with a practiced eye, he darted back into the kitchen. Returning with one of the skewers, he gripped it between his teeth to free his hands and nimbly scaled the rock. He plopped down on top, feet dangling over the edge, and waved the fragrant meat in front of Freydolf's face.

The man grunted in surprise, and Aurelius snickered as his brother-in-law's face registered confusion, disbelief, and then amazement when his servant leaned forward to push a tender strip of rabbit past his dropped jaw.

Using one of his mother's oft-repeated phrases, Tupper sternly declared, "Your work will keep, but dinner will not."

"Lambkin?" Freydolf mumbled around his mouthful. "How did you get up there?"

"I climbed."

"He's a regular little mountain goat," Aurelius dryly offered.

"Did you put him up to this?" asked Frey.

"Nay, it seems he's capable of a certain amount of ingenuity. The pet may yet train in his master. Now, come away. I'm hungry."

"So am I," Freydolf admitted, finally laying aside his tools.

To Tupper's chagrin, the sculptor picked him up and swung

him down as if he were still helpless and hornless. "I can climb!" he protested.

"That you can," his master warmly agreed. "Thank you, Tupper. You did well."

Tugging the man's sleeve, the boy echoed Aurelius's words. "Come away."

Freydolf reached across to pluck the skewer from Tupper's other hand and ripped off another piece of meat with his teeth. Humming contentedly, he answered, "Aye, and gladly."

Aurelius made good on his promise and steered the dinner conversation. "Tell me, Frey, how many servants have you lost because of the statues?"

"Not sure," the sculptor admitted. "Most disappear without a word."

"It's more likely their disappearances were accompanied by whimpers of fear and cries for their mothers. But did you warn them? Did you explain?"

Freydolf's face fell, and he muttered, "They're usually more afraid of *me* than anything. The poor things didn't trust me, let alone what I had to say."

Tupper's forehead creased. Servants had been lost? The statues were to blame? He nibbled at savory, skewered meat and tried to make sense of the adults' conversation. Could Morven's monster be made of stone?

"What about your precious *lambkin*?" demanded Aurelius.

"I warned him," Freydolf retorted defensively.

"Not properly. He has no idea what it means to live on one of the twelve mountains. Explain to him *why* he shouldn't wander."

By now, Tupper's eyes were wide, and he'd left off eating. This sounded bad, and Freydolf looked unhappy. With a *click* and *clop*, Olexi trotted across the table and took up a defensive stance between the boy and the two men, shaking his tiny horns threateningly.

Nodding to the small guardian, Aurelius pressed, "You gave your pet a pet, so he won't be put off by the notion that certain rocks can move about."

Suddenly understanding what they must mean, Tupper piped up. "Are there more?"

"Statues that bear a master's mark?" When the boy nodded, Freydolf did as well. "Aye, many more, but not all of them are this ... small."

"Or safe. Or sane," said Aurelius.

"That's not entirely fair. The truly dangerous ones have been confined to the vaults."

"And the accidentally dangerous ones?" challenged the other man. "What's more, it's not only the statues! I've seen enough of Morven's caprice to know the mischief runs far deeper!"

The sculptor pushed back his plate and sought Tupper's wide-eyed gaze. Smiling faintly, he said, "The Statuary is old. Even if I spent my whole life exploring its galleries, there wouldn't be enough time to discover all their secrets." He held out his fingertips for Olexi's inspection. "The Statuary is old, but the mountain is older still. I suppose the first thing you need to know is that Morven has a mind of her own."

Freydolf knew his place. Morven had called him. Morven had claimed him. Morven would keep him. He understood his duty to the legendary Moonlit Mountain, whose gray galleries were under his protection; however, that didn't make it easy to put into words the intangible tie he had to the stone beneath his feet.

"The dangers?" prompted Aurelius.

"You go too far!" Freydolf grimaced, for true threats were few and far between. He didn't want Tupper to fear *all* the statues because a rare stone ran amok.

Glancing toward the open window, Aurelius remarked, "The moon's high. Shall we take a little stroll along the colonnades and see if the sprat survives?"

He could brush off his brother-in-law's idle talk, but one look at Tupper's pale, pinched face cut Freydolf to the quick. "He only means you'd be frightened, lambkin. Many of my servants ran away because they feared the statues. They didn't understand why they could move."

"The Flox are so backward!" Aurelius said scornfully. "How can they live on the very slopes of one of the twelve mountains yet wallow in ignorance?"

"It's not their fault!" Freydolf insisted. "Nor is it the statues' fault. If you must blame anyone, blame me. As Keeper, the responsibility is ultimately mine."

"You've done nothing wrong!" argued the other Pred.

"I'm not searching for a place to lay blame," Freydolf countered in firm tones.

"Then lay out the facts! At the *very* least, warn him about that ridiculous pied beast that dour old Drom wrangled into existence!"

"Graven?"

"Wretched thing!"

Freydolf muttered, "Just because you hold a grudge ...."

"He's a menace!"

The sculptor lamely replied, "Graven's just lonely."

"There you go again, assigning them feelings!"

It was an old argument, one Freydolf had no interest in revisiting tonight. He understood his brother-in-law's perspective. They'd grown up in a culture where guardian stones were commonly given as children's toys, easy to come by and therefore taken for granted. Battered and broken. Cracked and chipped. Outgrown and unwanted. As a boy, Freydolf had taken in many a tiny cast-off. He supposed he was still doing it, but on a much larger scale.

"Aye, there I go again," Frey agreed amiably.

No matter how many times he witnessed the miracle, he felt that when a sculptor combined stone, shape, and seal, something was born. No, the rock wasn't alive in the traditional sense, but marked statues were unique individuals that took on a life of their own. They would always be real to him, no matter what others might say.

Tupper piped up. "Is there a monster?"

"Aye, more than one," Freydolf readily admitted. "Some of my predecessors had strange imaginations. Their workmanship bears little or no resemblance to the natural world."

"Are they bad?" the lad ventured, his gaze skidding Aurelius's way.

Freydolf said, "Nay, not really. They're simply trying to do what they were made to do. If you understand that, it's easier to understand their little quirks."

Aurelius thumped the table, rattling the cutlery. "That may be true of the rabble that roams freely through your courtyards, but there are *reasons* why so many of the Statuary's doors are fitted with heavy locks!"

"Aye. It's best to let some statues sleep. Their time is past. Or never came."

"And?" Aurelius prompted, gesturing insistently toward Tupper.

"And I shall make myself clear." Freydolf held his servant's gaze. "The places I've already shown you are safest. You're welcome to explore once your duties are done, provided you don't lose your way." After a stern look from his brother-in-law, the sculptor playfully added, "And don't go through any locked doors, since the very idea clearly worries Aurelius. Understood?"

"Yes," said Tupper.

A wriggle and a fidget led Freydolf to inquire, "Was there something else?"

"A stroll along the colonnades?"

Freydolf grinned triumphantly. "Aye, lambkin. We'll do just that ... and see if Aurelius survives!"

Tupper had already decided he liked his job, which was filled with so many strange and new things. By far, his favorite part was the way he was being included. Addy had warned him that servants were often pushed to one side, excused from family activities and made to feel invisible, but his master wasn't that way at all. Yes, Freydolf sometimes forgot about him, but not in the on-purpose way the village boys had done. Even though he was hired help, Tupper had been given a place at the table and a say during conversations. Coming from such a large family, he wasn't used to getting a word in edgewise, so having someone ask for his input was a novelty. "Nice," he murmured, happily swinging his feet under the table.

Aurelius pounced on the single word. "What's nice, sprat?"

There were too many nice things to list, but Tupper couldn't rightly say *everything* was nice because that would include Aurelius, and that might be stretching things. After some consideration, he settled on, "Here."

Freydolf stood and carelessly stacked the empty plates and platters, then carried them across the kitchen, setting the whole jumble in the washtub. "Ready to go?"

"Dishes?" Tupper asked worriedly.

"They'll keep," said Freydolf. "Besides, I'm as eager for this stroll as you are."

"Can Olexi come?"

"Aye, we'll all go."

Aurelius sidetracked into the workshop long enough to collect a lantern before joining them at the door. "The inner courtyard has smaller statues than the outer, and they're less cheeky."

Freydolf hummed. "The light slants through, as well. We should be able to catch several stones waking."

Breathless with excitement, Tupper trailed after the two Pred, glancing back and forth in the hopes of seeing something magical. The men ambled along, and their conversation rambled as well.

Aurelius noted, "You were right about the loggia. How long have you known about it?"

"Not long. One of the statues wandered down from a niche

not far from it, and I discovered its entrance when I followed him back. Such a lovely green. Rare, even here."

"What's a loggia?" Tupper asked.

Freydolf turned. "Do any of your houses have porches?"

"Yes."

"Then it probably makes the most sense to call a loggia a fancy porch. I'll show it to you another day."

Aurelius interjected, "That reminds me! What the deuce is a rimble?"

Frey chuckled and kept walking. "Did you find any in the loggia?"

"How would I know?" he retorted sourly.

Just then, something swished past behind Tupper. The boy whirled with an involuntary squeak, but there was nothing there. "What was it?" he asked, suddenly nervous.

"Nothing to worry about." Freydolf strolled up behind him. "Most of the statues around here are shy. You probably startled one."

"Shy," Tupper echoed, not sure he believed it.

The sculptor went down on one knee and asked, "Didn't you say you could climb?"

Accepting the subtle invitation, he clambered onto Freydolf's broad shoulders. When the man stood, Tupper fumbled for a handhold but didn't find what he was looking for, so he latched onto two thick hanks of hair, inadvertently giving them a good yank.

"Easy there, lambkin."

"You don't have horns," the boy explained.

"Aye, I am sorely lacking in that department." Big hands closed around Tupper's ankles, holding him in place. "I won't let you topple, so relax and enjoy the view."

As he resumed their stroll, Tupper obediently looked around. They were in the very first courtyard he'd seen on arriving. Several squat buildings were arrayed along its edges, and he remembered thinking that they looked like small houses. This time, he also noticed that none of them had windows, which was odd. They must be very dark inside.

While he watched, the moon crested the top of one of the tiled roofs far above, and light washed across the nearest building. Immediately, the stone crane at its peak spread wide its wings and snapped its beak.

"Oh," Tupper breathed. "Very good!"

"Aye, *grand*," Aurelius drawled sarcastically. He gave the bird a beady look, then muttered, "Until it hops down and tries to nip the buttons off your shirt."

"With your obvious love for glitter and gussy, he probably took you for a grave robber," Freydolf teased.

"Grave?" echoed Tupper.

Aurelius flashed him a menacing grin. "Aye, those are mausoleums! Once Morven gets hold of a man, she keeps him straight into the hereafter!"

This made sense to Tupper, who nodded and said, "Because they belong here."

Freydolf patted his leg. "Well said."

"One of these is yours, isn't it?" Aurelius mused aloud, holding his lantern high. "Well, not *yours* yours, but you decked it out."

"Every Keeper honors tradition by accomplishing three tasks," the sculptor replied, leading the way to the farthest of the low buildings. "On the day we are accepted as successors, we begin adding our border to the Apprentice Gate."

"Big job for a beginner."

"It can take an apprentice years to finish depending on how many other responsibilities their mentor heaps on them."

"I recall yours," the other Pred remarked. "It always makes me homesick."

"Aye." With a small sigh, Freydolf continued, "On the day we take on a Keeper's title, we begin ornamenting our predecessor's tomb." He gestured to the last in the row, saying, "This is Master Platt's."

Like the rest, the small building was constructed from tightly-fitted blocks of Morven's stone, but its trimmings were unique. Hundreds of rectangular stones formed a simple, yet colorful border, and even though it was hard to tell in the dim light, Tupper was pretty sure that every possible kind of rock had been used in the pattern. Aurelius strolled around the structure, stopping from time to time to scrutinize the workmanship. "How long did it take you?"

"Two years," Freydolf replied.

Tupper thought it was interesting that a sculptor took so much time to say goodbye to places and people, and he wondered if the last task would be as sad as the first two. "Third?" he prompted.

The sculptor's muscles bunched in a shrug. "A masterpiece," he replied in a flat voice. "Every Keeper leaves behind a masterpiece, his crowning achievement."

Aurelius returned to his brother-in-law's side, his expression carefully neutral. "Still no idea what yours will be?"

"Nay."

Three sad things after all. Tupper felt bad for Freydolf and gave his head a scratch right about where his horns should be.

The man glanced up at his small passenger. "What's that for?"

Falling back on his mother's pat answer for any show of affection, Tupper stoutly replied, "For keeps."

It was gradual at first, but the statues were definitely flocking to Freydolf. Lithe ladies, forest creatures, mythical beasts— from his perch atop the sculptor's shoulders, Tupper watched them come. Resting his forearms atop Freydolf's head, he leaned forward, eager to see all he could.

"Gray and white," he whispered, having realized what they all had in common.

"Moonlight and starlight," Freydolf said. "Orange stone wakes at sunset, but there isn't much of that here. Only .... "

A sudden rustle from behind sent Aurelius whirling into a defensive crouch, but just as quickly, he offered a truculent *tsk.* "A fortune in titian jade, wasted on an ignoble bit of mischief like you."

The dainty fox's plume of a tail waved saucily, and he seemed to yip in reply, but without making a sound. Tupper gasped at this additional discovery. Although the statues moved freely and gestured fluidly, the silence that hung over the courtyard was almost eerie. "No voices?" he asked.

Aurelius answered this time. "Aye, and they're light on their feet, which makes them deucedly sneaky."

Freydolf's shoulders shook in silent amusement. "Keeping an eye out for Graven?"

"*Both* eyes," grumbled his brother-in-law.

Tupper thought maybe he *should* be scared, but it was easy to borrow courage from his companions. Aurelius's blustering felt like a sham, and Freydolf's calm kept fears at bay.

Tapping the top of the sculptor's head, Tupper inquired, "Safe?"

The man turned his head enough to meet his gaze. "Aye."

Making up his mind, Tupper asked, "Down?"

To the boy's surprise, the Pred's crooked smile wasn't scary either, even with that little bit of fang peeping into view.

Minding his manners, Tupper added, "Please?"

"Good lad," Freydolf said approvingly.

Back on solid ground, Tupper dropped to his knees and wiggled his fingers at the orange fox. As it minced closer on neat paws, the boy set Olexi before him. For the first time in his life, he felt brave enough to take the initiative. Tupper suggested, "Friends?"

"I want a bench," Aurelius fretfully announced.

Freydolf waved at the inner courtyard's obvious abundance and replied with playful pomposity. "We have seating aplenty, my good man. Feel free to take your ease."

His brother-in-law hummed critically, then struck out toward one set into an alcove. "That one looks defensible."

"The statues aren't *attacking*."

Aurelius withdrew a silken handkerchief from within his vest and gave a token flick to a bench carved to look like a tumble of ivy. Setting his lantern upon the ground, he settled into place, calling, "I prefer to keep a wall at my back, thank you very much."

"Suit yourself." He turned back to check on Tupper, who was standing on tiptoe, trying to see into the cup held out to him by the statue of a pretty maiden. "She's offering you a drink, lambkin," Freydolf explained. "She was made to bring water."

Tupper's brow creased. "The cup's empty."

"Aye, because this courtyard's well ran dry." He nodded toward the pergola where both her pedestal and the old well were located. "She's still going through the motions, though. If you play along, it will put her at ease."

Nodding, the lad accepted the offering and pretended to drink. When Tupper returned the white maiden's cup, he said, "Thank you, lady. Good job."

She smiled softly, and Freydolf asked, "Shall we join Aurelius?"

Tupper glanced around and spotted the glow of the lantern across the way. Bending to pick up Olexi, he asked, "Is Graven scary?"

"That all depends on who you ask."

"*You're* not scared."

"Nay, and I doubt Aurelius is either." Thinking back, Freydolf said, "It's more of a grudge."

As they neared the ivy bench, Aurelius demanded, "Are my ears tingling?"

"You've made the lad curious about Graven," Freydolf relayed, dropping onto the opposite end of the bench. "I was about to explain your longstanding rivalry with a statue."

Aurelius crossed his legs and folded his arms over his chest. "He started it."

Freydolf patted the center of the bench and was gratified when Tupper accepted the invitation. To his amusement, the boy crowded close to him and placed Olexi on his other side, ostensibly to fend off Aurelius. The tactic wasn't lost on the man, who feigned disinterest. Freydolf explained, "The very first time Aurelius visited me here, Graven took him for a threat. It was a simple misunderstanding."

"That spiteful old Drom set him on me!"

"You represented a rare opportunity," Freydolf said. "I'm sure Master Platt was unable to pass up the chance to test his masterpiece."

"If that tired explanation was meant to mollify me, it fell dismally short!"

"Masterpiece?" interjected Tupper.

"Aye, lambkin. Graven was my mentor's crowning achievement, a guardian stone like no other."

Aurelius took a sour tone. "That piecemeal monstrosity looks more like a patchwork quilt than a proper statue!"

"Nonsense," countered Freydolf. "Even you have to admit he's a true masterwork."

"That concession awaits a full cessation of hostilities!"

"He's not hostile. Graven's only meant to corner intruders. Besides, it's not as if he's ever *caught* you."

"Is Aurelius fast?" Tupper asked, looking at the other man interestedly.

"And smart," Frey replied in conspiratorial tones. It was funny to see the instant improvement in his brother-in-law's mood. Aurelius had always enjoyed being the object of admiration, no matter the source.

The preening Pred admitted, "In all my travels, I've never seen Graven's like. Platt broke with tradition and created something truly unique." Aurelius flatly added, "Whether that's a *good* thing is another matter entirely. I still say the thing should be disassembled."

"You know I won't do that." Freydolf gazed around the courtyard and admitted, "I'm not even sure he's here. He's taken to wandering, just as Master Platt feared."

Tupper asked, "Where did he go?"

"He could be anywhere in the world, drawn by any of the other eleven mountains."

"Is that bad?"

"It's a nightmare!" exclaimed Aurelius. "That misbegotten guardian could turn up in any of the Keepers' holds and track me down!"

"He's *not* one of the Misbegotten." In sadder tones, Freydolf added, "And *you* are not the one he's looking for."

"Aye. I know it." Aurelius's gaze dropped. "Poor wretch."

By now, it was clear that Tupper was completely lost.

Giving the boy's hair a quick tousle, Freydolf started somewhere closer to the beginning. "The man who was Keeper before me was Master Platt, and he was very clever. It was his hope to create the ultimate guardian stone, a statue without inherent limitations."

The boy was using the palms of his hands to try to flatten the curls Freydolf had just ruffled. Pausing mid-pat, he asked, "Graven is the biggest?"

"Nay, I don't mean that he's *bigger* than other statues, although he's certainly not small." Aurelius muttered something about beastly behemoths under his breath, but Freydolf ignored him. "You already know that freshstone needs water, and white stone needs starlight."

"Yes."

Giving Olexi a friendly poke, the sculptor continued, "That means that this little fellow can only wake when starlight touches him. He can't move freely during the day. Or on a stormy night. Or if he's left in a place where the stars cannot reach him. Also, no matter when Olexi wakes, he always goes back to sleep when the sun rises. This is the way of white stone."

Tupper nodded.

"It's the same for *all* the stones. Each needs something different, and all of them remain active for a limited amount of time. Master Platt decided to make a statue cobbled together from all twelve stones. That way, no matter the time of day, no matter the change in weather, Graven would be on guard."

Again, Tupper's head bobbed.

"The only potential hitch to his plan was that displaced statues usually have ties to the mountain from which their stone was quarried. Usually, this is counteracted by a pedestal; every statue knows to return to its pedestal just before their resting state." Freydolf gazed into the square of starry sky high overhead. "Graven doesn't have a pedestal. Presumably, he didn't need one since he never sleeps. But I think Master Platt intended for his creation to be free."

Aurelius snorted softly. "Selfish old fool."

"Why?" Tupper asked. "Why are you sad for Graven?"

Freydolf sighed. "Instead of becoming attached to a pedestal like most statues, Graven bonded directly to his creator. On the day Master Platt died, his masterpiece lost its anchor. Now, Graven has taken to bouts of drifting, pulled in twelve different directions, searching for someone he'll never find."

"Poor wretch," repeated Aurelius in an undertone.

"Sad," agreed Tupper in a sleepy voice, leaning more fully into the sculptor's side.

"Aye," murmured Freydolf, placing a hand on the lad's slender shoulder, steadying him as he nodded off. Over the years, he'd done what he could for the restless statue, for he sympathized deeply with the creature's plight. "He's just lonely."

"We can go back inside by the fire," Freydolf offered, having noticed the slight change in his brother-in-law's posture. The stone bench was a thing of beauty, but not as comfortable as the deep, cushioned sofas in the balcony. He was also worried about Tupper catching a chill.

"You're too considerate of those around you. It's very un-Pred-like," Aurelius replied disdainfully.

With an unrepentant grin, Frey asked, "Is that consent?"

"Aye."

The sculptor laughed, and golden eyes scanned his face, then dropped to that of the boy tucked snugly against his side. "You're freer with him than the rest," Aurelius remarked thoughtfully. "Perhaps the sprat will help you unlearn some of your bad habits."

"Bad habits?"

"Abominable ones," Aurelius confirmed. "You're a shadow of the man my wife recalls."

Freydolf bristled at the assertion. "In what sense?"

"You don't even realize it, do you?" his companion sneered. "Ulrica goes on and on about her big brother. She remembers you for having the wittiest jokes, the widest smile, the longest laugh, and the surest path."

The sculptor gave himself time to collect his thoughts by gathering up his sleeping servant and standing. Aurelius had sharp eyes and a sharper tongue, but he rarely turned them on his brother-in-law except in jest. This time, the man was serious, and Freydolf wasn't sure how to react, especially since the criticism seemed to be wrapped in compliments.

Shaking his head, Frey prompted, "And in the intervening years, I've fallen into bad habits?"

"Unsightly, unseemly, inexcusably, indisputably bad!" Aurelius rose and dusted off his breeches.

"Can you be more specific?" Freydolf gruffly inquired, turning in the direction of the workshop.

Aurelius fell in step beside him. "Devastatingly so!"

"Go on, then," he invited, curious in spite of himself.

"The Flox are partially to blame, what with their propensity for panic whenever a Pred strolls into their midst. Those bleaters preyed upon your soft heart, leading to your downfall."

Freydolf snorted. "Still too vague."

"I can give specifics," Aurelius retorted. "For instance, you avoid direct eye contact."

"What does that have to do ...?"

"You never laugh aloud. You speak in an undertone. Your smile has changed."

With a blink, Freydolf asked, "It has?"

"Aye, for you fear to reveal your fangs." Warming to his subject, Aurelius continued, "You slouch your shoulders.

You hide your hands behind your back. You apologize with shocking regularity, even to those you have not wronged." With a scathing glance, he added, "It's as if you're apologizing for being Pred."

His words stung, mostly because they had merit. Freydolf hadn't realized Aurelius noticed how much he'd adapted in an attempt to put the Flox at ease. The little changes had never done any good, but at least he'd tried. "Aye," he replied softly. "Maybe I do."

"But not with him," Aurelius countered, stabbing a finger in Tupper's direction. Freydolf's hold on the boy tightened reflexively, and his brother-in-law smirked. "With him, you stand tall. You meet his gaze. You offer him your hand." As they strolled, his list lengthened. "Your smile is widening. Your voice is deepening. Your laughter is returning."

With an awkward shrug, Freydolf said, "It's only because he's not afraid of me."

"And because of that, *you're* not afraid of *him*."

They halted before the workshop door, and Freydolf shook his head incredulously. "Me?"

"Aye," Aurelius softly replied, reaching over to touch Tupper's head. "And that will change things. Indeed, it will change everything. And this time, for the good."

10

Three Little Words

The next morning, Aurelius loomed large, tapping his foot in dramatic impatience while he waited for Tupper to finish washing dishes after breakfast. "We have a schedule to keep!" the Pred griped.

Tupper didn't like to argue, especially when he didn't really understand. He'd finished the watering shortly after sunup, and the copper cauldron was filled to the brim, ready to heat for the evening bath. All the empty crates had been stowed, and the floor was freshly swept. Everything was *done*, so what was the hurry? He plodded along at his usual pace, for mother didn't approve of rushing through work. One of her many mottoes was *any job worth doing is worth doing well*, and pleasing her was more important to him than appeasing Aurelius.

When the last dish had been returned to its spot in the cupboard, the man muttered, "I can't decide if you're slow or stubborn."

He'd often been called slow, and not in the kindest of ways, so Tupper replied, "Stubborn, please."

Aurelius's brows shot up. "Is that so?"

Fidgeting, he answered, "Yes?"

The man snorted. "Duly noted. Now, come along. I'm taking you with me."

Taking? Tupper's knees locked, for he didn't want to be taken away from Freydolf. Surely his master wouldn't stand for it! The fancy-talking Pred should know better than to even suggest it!

Aurelius huffed lightly. "And what have I done to deserve *that* look?"

"I belong here."

The Pred folded his arms over his chest. "And you'd fight to stay?"

Tupper thought that over. He'd never liked butting heads with boys his own age, let alone a grown-up. Freydolf had called Aurelius fast and smart, and those daggers were still strapped to his thighs. No, fighting wouldn't work. Rubbing at one horn in hopes of inspiration, he finally ventured, "I could hide."

Keeping a very straight face, Aurelius inquired, "Because you want to stay with Frey?"

"Yes."

"Because you have a job to do?"

Honestly relieved that Aurelius understood, Tupper answered, "Yes."

"What if doing your job requires you to leave for a short time, then return?" Aurelius posed.

Was the man trying to trick him? The glint in those golden eyes had a sneaky feel to it, and Tupper reluctantly asked, "Go where?" A moment later, he thought to add, "How long?"

"Suspicious little thing, aren't you?"

Tupper nodded.

"I said it once before, so pay attention this time. I'm here to make sure your hopeless master survives the winter, and that means laying in stores." He flicked an imaginary fleck from the front of his extravagantly trimmed tunic and announced, "Gruff has my carriage waiting. We'll be going down into the villages to purchase foodstuffs. I'll return you to this very spot well before nightfall. Satisfied?"

Feeling a little silly, Tupper murmured, "Yes."

"Aye, then go tell your master we'll be off," he instructed. "Assuming he's not already too far gone on his next statue to notice you."

Escaping into the workshop, Tupper hurried to the sculptor's side. Freydolf was leaning against the wall between two of the tall windows, hip propped against the ledge that ran the length of the room as he took advantage of the light. Tupper was astonished to watch him add hatch marks to a large sheet of parchment stretched over a board, his fingers smudged with the charcoal from his fat pencil.

"You can draw!" the boy gasped.

Freydolf blinked, then smiled at his awed audience. "Aye, it's all part of what I do." He tilted the paper so it was easier for the boy to see a series of six rough sketches from different angles of a prowling feline with large paws and tufted ears. It looked as if it was climbing down from a high perch, eyes alert as it stalked its prey.

"The yellow cat?"

"It will be." The sculptor added a few more strokes with the charcoal, explaining, "I like to make up my mind before I begin, just in case the stone has other ideas."

"Doesn't the stone want to be a cat?"

With a chuckle, the sculptor said, "Mostly. I think it'll cooperate; however, some stones have different aspirations than the person paying me to craft them a guardian."

From the direction of the door, Aurelius interjected, "Like that time your client ordered a charging stallion, but I returned to find you putting the finishing touches on a stag."

Freydolf waved his hand in a vague way. "It all worked out."

"Thanks to my unparalleled powers of persuasion." Quirking a brow at Tupper, he said, "Speaking of which, weren't you going to relay a message, sprat?"

The boy nodded and turned to his master. "I'm going."

"With Aurelius?"

"Yes." Giving the sculptor's sleeve a tug, he promised, "I'll come back."

"With bread?" wheedled Freydolf.

Tupper's eyes widened, for he hadn't expected a request. Since he didn't have any money, he cast a pleading look at the other Pred.

"That can be arranged, provided the bakeries aren't sold out by the time we *finally* get down the mountain."

Though the Pred had answered in a roundabout way, Tupper knew what he meant. "Yes!" he quickly relayed to his master.

Freydolf smiled crookedly. "I'll look forward to that."

Nodding eagerly, Tupper dashed for the door, calling over his shoulder, "We'll hurry!"

Aurelius threw his hands into the air. "*Now* he hurries."

Freydolf watched Tupper bound away, and the light in his eyes flickered, then faded. "Which villages will you visit?"

Aurelius gazed steadily at him. "Why do you ask? You've never asked before."

"I was just thinking that for today ... perhaps it would be best ... that is ...." Taking a deep breath, Freydolf finished in a rush. "Maybe you should avoid Hayward."

"Oh?" Aurelius asked, his voice sweet and light. "If I remember correctly, they have the best bakery in the vicinity."

"Aye, but it's the lad's hometown."

Aurelius arranged himself on the opposite side of the tall window, mirroring his brother-in-law's comfortable pose. Turning his attention to the stone lattice that covered the glass, he inspected its intricacies with a critical eye. An openwork trefoil pattern was generously overlaid with carved vegetation—burled branches and twisting tendrils, luxurious foliage and exotic flowers, ripening fruit and camouflaged fauna. The decoration must have taken decades to complete and surely stood as a past Keeper's masterpiece.

Running a fingertip along the edge of a butterfly's wing, Aurelius casually asked, "Are you afraid the sprat will abandon you if he catches sight of whatever over-crowded hovel you extracted him from?"

Freydolf shrugged unhappily.

His brother-in-law's lips quirked slyly. "If you're afraid of losing him, increase his pay. *Or*, we could make his service contractually binding, quietly provide Tupper's family with a tidy sum as a bonus for signing him over to you. It's easily managed."

The sculptor's charcoal pencil snapped in two, and his incredulity changed into a fang-baring snarl. "I don't want to *buy* him!"

"You're easy prey, Frey!" Aurelius snickered. "I was jesting. Naturally!"

"Naturally," Freydolf muttered moodily. "Don't *ever* suggest such a thing again. And if I find out you've approached his parents ...."

"Parent," he corrected. "Your lambkin is fatherless."

Freydolf absently wiped his charcoal-smudged fingers against his breeches and softly admitted, "I didn't know."

"Aye."

"And I forbid you to interfere!"

"Aye, I won't go behind your back," Aurelius assured with an infuriating smile. "I have a good grasp on the situation, even if you don't."

The sculptor grunted and asked, "What is it you think you know?"

"You want him to stay, but you want him to *want* to stay."

That earned him another scowl.

Pushing off the wall, Aurelius said, "You worry too much about the wrong things, Frey! However, if it will put your mind at ease enough to continue with your work, I shall give you my word." The Pred gracefully lay his upraised palm below his heart and bowed. "Your surrogate mother will be here to tuck you in long before the hour when all good sculptors should be in bed."

"See that he is," Freydolf muttered, giving his brother-in-law a dismissive wave.

Aurelius simply laughed and left.

From the well-padded driver's seat atop his personal carriage, Aurelius kept a sharp eye out, more out of habit than necessity. Although he often traveled through territories where bandits posed a danger, the Flox were as decent as they were dull. He didn't begrudge them their boring lives, but the way they shunned Freydolf had always irked him.

Preposterous as it might sound to any other Pred, these peace-loving folk were his brother-in-law's greatest threat. In their fear, they neglected the softhearted dolt, and more than once, it had nearly been the death of him.

Aurelius planned to make sure that the scales finally tipped in Freydolf's favor.

Tupper sat as far from him as the wide seat permitted, his small hands locked in a white-knuckled grip on the armrest, and his eyes sparkling with excitement. Curious which part of their uneventful descent was putting the boy into such a tizzy, Aurelius asked, "Haven't you ever seen a horse before?"

"I have."

"*Surely* you're not afraid of heights?"

"No."

"Then what has you so antsy?"

The boy couldn't quite hide his exhilaration when he answered, "This is fast!"

Aurelius realized what all the fuss was about. "You've never ridden in a carriage?"

"No."

This child's life must have been truly sedate if a paltry buggy ride was enough to send him into paroxysms of joy. Smirking faintly, Aurelius said, "Apparently, we've reached a new epoch in your young life." At Tupper's blank expression, he resorted to patronizing monosyllables. "This is new, and you find you like it."

"Yes!" the boy agreed guilelessly.

Aurelius snorted and flicked the reins, giving the horses permission to pick up their pace along the straightaway.

Tupper's hastily-stifled squeak sounded suspiciously like happiness.

At least one of them was having a good time.

Morven's southern and eastern slopes bore almost no resemblance to the sheer face that overlooked the northern and eastern villages. A long road with frequent switchbacks wound through the forest above the quarry, a half-forgotten route that permitted the delivery of stone and stores to the Statuary. Aurelius suspected that his sporadic visits were the only time it saw any use.

He scanned the trees, picking out several splashes of yellow amidst the conifers. Autumn and its rains weren't far off, and once the temperatures dropped, even this reliable road would become impassible, for the cobblestones would be glazed with ice, then buried under snow. In winter, Morven became a prison, and in spring, there was usually a jailbreak. It was an incredibly vicious cycle for such a pastoral setting.

Eyeing Tupper, Aurelius asked, "How old do you claim to be?"

"Ten and a half."

The Pred chuckled. He remembered when his own sons were at an age when halves mattered. This scrap of boyhood wasn't *that* much younger than his youngest, but Aurelius was quite sure none of his get had ever been so puny. "And that's old enough to be useful?"

"Yes." The boy tapped one horn demonstrably. "Old enough."

As they slowed to round another bend, the man decided to tiptoe along the edges of Freydolf's warnings with regards to this servant. He wouldn't be meddling, *per se*. He'd simply reminisce aloud, and the lad would just happen to overhear.

Settling back in his seat, Aurelius began, "One of the first winters after Frey was made Keeper, there was an early thaw. Spring was coy and teased the world by warming it up, then turning a cold shoulder. The blizzard that slammed down shortly afterward was one of the worst this area has ever known." With a quick peek to make sure the boy was listening, he continued, "During that short thaw, Frey's servant bolted."

"Bolted," Tupper echoed uncertainly. "Does that mean sick?"

"Nay, he ran away." Aurelius *could* have mentioned that the bleater had also filled his pockets with a fortune in rare stones, but he didn't like putting ideas into impressionable minds. "He left Frey to fend for himself."

The lad's eyes widened. "Why?"

"Clearly, he didn't care what it would mean for his master." Aurelius shook his head and revealed, "When I arrived in the spring, I found Frey collapsed on his bed, cold as the ashes in his hearth. I had to resort to auscultation!"

Tupper seemed genuinely frightened, despite the fact that his master had clearly survived.

Amused, Aurelius strung him along. "Can you guess what I heard when I placed my ear to his chest?"

The lad shook his head, his gaze never leaving the tale-bringer's face.

"As it happened, I had stopped for supplies before making my way up this very road! Knowing that greedy fellow's penchant for the stuff, I was carrying several loaves of fresh baked bread." Waiting for the boy's eager nod, he revealed, "When I listened to see if his heart was still beating, I couldn't hear it ... because his stomach took to growling like a starved bear!"

Tupper's relieved sigh was gratifying.

The Pred nodded wisely. "I built up a fire and stuffed him full of food. Frey had no idea how long he'd been alone, but he was weak as a kitten. If I'd delayed another week, it may have been too late."

To Aurelius's surprise, Tupper sidled closer. Pressing a hand to his thin chest, the lad extended an upraised palm in Flox fashion, gravely saying, "Thank you."

A dozen years late in coming, and from someone who hadn't even been born at the time, the sentiment was a welcome surprise. Clearing his throat, Aurelius hastily explained, "That's why I make this trip at least twice a year—at summer's end, to make sure Frey has food, firewood, and a suitable servant before the snow flies, and as soon as the road is passable in springtime, to make sure he's survived."

After a considering silence, Tupper said, "That's good."

"Even though it means I'll be back?"

Tupper frowned. "He likes you."

"But *you* don't."

"No."

Aurelius laughed outright. "My wife would say you're a fine judge of character."

The jest apparently went over the boy's head, for all he said was, "I don't bolt."

Preening over the success of his cautionary tale, he feigned surprise. "Oh?"

"Master Freydolf won't be alone," Tupper explained.

"And why's that?" Aurelius prompted.

"He asked me to stay."

"Did he, now?"

"Yes."

"And so you'll stay?"

"Yes."

Aurelius wondered if this sort of answer would satisfy Frey. The boy did as he was told, but that wasn't the same as *wanting* to remain in the Statuary's confines. Borrowing from the boy's ridiculously limited stock phrases, he inquired, "Is that bad?"

Tupper straightened in his seat. "I'll do a good job."

He sighed. "I'm not doubting your abilities, sprat. I'm curious about your motives." The lad's blank stare inspired an even deeper sigh. "*Why* do you want to do a good job?"

"Why would you do a *bad* job?" he countered, sounding mystified.

Aurelius marveled at the boy's density and tried one last time. "Why do you *want* to stay with Frey?"

The question must have taxed Tupper's small brain nearly to its limits, for they rounded two more bends before he finally mumbled a bashful response. "He picked me."

11

Common as Curls

From what Tupper could see, Shepley was a lot like his own village, with rows of houses surrounding shops in the middle. Aurelius's fancy carriage turned every head as it rolled to a stop in the square, and the moment the Pred's boots hit the ground, people scattered.

Tupper climbed down from the high seat and peeped into the man's face to see if he was mad, but Aurelius didn't seem bothered by their rudeness. He scanned the vicinity, then strode toward the largest store, the boy close on his heels.

Pausing on the wide front porch, Aurelius turned slightly. "Wait here while I inspect their wares." As an afterthought, he added, "I wouldn't sit too close to the door, sprat. We'll have a stampede of fools within moments."

Sure enough, as soon as Aurelius ducked through the door, several women and a crying baby rushed out. Tupper obediently moved along to the far edge of the steps before sitting on the bottommost one. The wood planking had been stained bright green, and he thought it was pretty, though maybe not quite as nice as stone.

It was a comfortable feeling, being in a setting he understood. Even though he'd never been to Shepley before, the houses all had thatched roofs and walled gardens; the people passing by had fair hair, and men sported curving horns. Tupper sat and stared, wondering if anyone could tell he didn't belong in this sort of village anymore.

The shop door slapped shut, and Aurelius came up behind him. "Homesick?"

"No."

"This merchant barely stocks any basics!" He shook out his lengthy list and rattled off several varieties of tinned soups, canned vegetables, and fruit preserves. "To scrape together even a fraction of this, we'll need to travel to several different villages! It's the same every year."

Tupper thought Aurelius was being a little silly. Why would the stores stock those kinds of things when everyone grew their own?

"On top of that, Flox don't like doing business with Pred, so I'll have to pay triple the going rate. How am I supposed to negotiate with people who dive for cover?"

It was an interesting question, but Tupper didn't have an answer. Besides, he was too busy trying to figure out what the little old woman across the way was doing.

"Young'un!" she called in a stage whisper, beckoning with one wrinkled hand. "This way! Come over here, quick!"

Tupper pointed to himself. "Me?"

"Hurry, young'un! It's behind you!" she hissed urgently.

Aurelius blandly remarked, "I *believe* she's attempting to warn you that there's something dangerous poised to carry you off."

"You?"

The Pred rolled his eyes. "Set her straight before she raises a false alarm. I have a hard enough time doing business with your people. Accusations of kidnapping will only make matters worse."

Tupper jumped to his feet, for he knew just what to do. Grabbing an astonished Aurelius's hand, he tugged the man along with him as he crossed the street.

The old woman's pale blue eyes widened, but she stood her ground, the grip on her cane tightening. This was a very good sign, and Tupper was pleased. In every village, there was at least one busybody nosy enough to butt into everyone's business, even that of a boy from another town.

"Good morning, Auntie. I'm not kidnapped," he announced.

"Gracious, child!" she exclaimed, staring in frank amazement at the Pred who towered over them. "Is it safe?"

That was a question best left unanswered, so he fell back on courtesies. "I'm Tupper, and this is Mister ..." With a frown, he realized he didn't know his companion's full name.

"Aurelius Harrow," supplied the Pred, bowing with foreign flourish. "Agent to Master Freydolf, Keeper of Morven, the legendary Moonlit Mountain."

The old woman leaned closer to Tupper and whispered, "Where did you find such an peculiar ... man?"

"He's not Flox," Tupper solemnly explained. "No horns."

"How queer."

Tupper honestly agreed, but that wasn't the most important thing right now. Even a man without horns needed to eat. "Auntie," he asked. "Which lady in Shepley jars the best sauce?"

"Bea Watercress," the woman declared authoritatively. With a boastful air, she confided, "That's my daughter-in-law. Uses *my* recipe, she does!"

"Does she make soup?" Tupper quizzed.

"Do nettles sting?"

He grinned at the familiar saying, then asked the most important question of all. "Does she trade?"

"Who doesn't?" the old woman replied, eyes bright at the prospect of a good dicker.

With a solemn nod, Tupper said, "I want some, please."

"What do you have to trade?"

Recognizing his cue, Aurelius offered another bow, and with a slightly wicked smile, he spoke the magic word. "Gold."

Aurelius knew how to turn a situation to his advantage. A quick wit, a keen eye, a silver tongue, a sinister smile—these were the tools of his trade, and he made the most of them. Normally, he would have been irked by someone claiming they could do better in haggling a fair price for goods, but Tupper made no claims. The boy simply showed him up. Aurelius had no choice but to withdraw, leaving the fate of a fat purse of gold coins to a snip of a boy less than half his height.

Barter appeared to be common as curls with the Flox.

Borrowing a cushion from the carriage, Aurelius had retreated to the shade of a squat tree, for the sun had reached its zenith. Tupper stood at the center of a small knot of village women who showed off colorful jars of canned fruits and pickled vegetables. The boy offered assessments without pretense, and the old auntie by his side acted as agent, whispering advice on whose soups and sauces were worth their weight in gold. Reaching another agreement—his sixth of the morning—Tupper trotted over to Aurelius, who'd retained possession of the shopping list.

"Well, sprat?" Aurelius greeted.

The boy squatted next to him and reported, "Missus Bea's soup is nicest, and Granny Thistledown's red sauce is spiciest."

"Frey likes food with bite," Aurelius mused aloud.

"Yes," Tupper agreed. "Both ladies will trade twenty jars for two coins."

The Pred's brows shot up, for the price wasn't fair, it was a steal. "Only two?"

Tilting his head to one side, Tupper clarified, "If we return the empty jars next spring."

Aurelius could appreciate mutually beneficial business arrangements. Eat the food over winter, return the jars come spring, and likely place orders for the following autumn. "Aye, I'll make a note." Scanning the list, he remarked, "That covers the basics and then some. Shall we move along to the bakery?"

Tupper's expression shifted slightly, and Aurelius quirked a brow. With no further coaxing, the lad asked, "Can we go to the next village south?"

"To see the sights?"

With a shake of his head, Tupper explained, "Auntie Watercress's brother's son-in-law has a cider press!"

"And an orchard to go with it?" An extra stop might make them late, but the prospect of adding apples to Frey's stores was tempting. They certainly had coin to spare for a little extravagance.

Tupper hugged his knees and casually said, "A vineyard, too."

Aurelius was hooked, and they both knew it.

The boy was a natural.

Aurelius watered the team while he waited for Tupper to bid his farewells to Auntie Watercress and company. Despite his small stature, the Flox boy was definitely old enough to be useful. The Statuary's storeroom would be brimming with better fare than it had seen in two decades, and for half the gold usually squandered on less nourishing provisions.

Several bushels of root vegetables had even been spoken for, and they had yet to visit the neighboring village's vintner. Aurelius was growing rather fond of the lad. Purely for reasons of business, of course.

Tupper trotted over bearing a scrap of paper and a pot of fragrant herbs that must have been a parting gift. Handing off what proved to be a scrawled map to their next destination, the lad asked, "Is this good?"

"Aye, it'll do." Waving to the carriage, Aurelius said, "Stow your shrub, and I'll send you ahead to the bakery. We should buy bread while there's bread to buy."

With a nod, the lad quickly obeyed.

On impulse, Aurelius handed him one coin. "See how far you can stretch this. Make a good bargain, and you can keep the change."

"This is too much for bread."

Aurelius smirked and replied, "Don't underestimate Frey's appetite. Or mine. This will be our lunch, as well, sprat."

Nodding again, Tupper promised, "Lots of bread."

As the lad entered the bakery, Aurelius wondered if he realized that the more he spent, the less he could pocket. Given this morning's display of the youngster's business acumen, he probably did. Aurelius wouldn't blame the boy for skimping, but he needed to know what made Tupper tick. It was a test of sorts, for the merchant trusted few, especially when it came to Freydolf.

Springing lightly to the driver's seat, Aurelius guided his team to a standstill across from the bakery just in time to see Tupper stagger through the door. The lad was weighed down with more sacks and sleeves than he could properly carry, and Aurelius was forced to leap down and rescue several loaves before they toppled off his teetering stack.

"What possessed you to buy so much?" the Pred exclaimed, leading him back to the carriage.

"It smelled good."

"Aye, it does at that," Aurelius agreed, opening one of the side compartments in order to stow the unexpected abundance of baked goods. "But you didn't have to spend everything I gave you."

"I didn't."

The Pred looked sharp. "You managed to keep a few coppers?"

Once his arms were empty, Tupper held out his hand, readily showing his take. "Five silver and four copper."

Five and four meant he'd made a *very* good deal, and Aurelius demanded, "How did you manage that?"

"Last to buy always pays less."

His eyebrows arched. "You bought out the bakery?"

"Master Freydolf likes bread."

Shaking his head in disbelief, Aurelius thought to ask, "Do you have a pocket or purse for your riches?"

"No."

"Wait a moment," he ordered, gesturing for the boy to climb aboard. Aurelius disappeared inside the roomy carriage, which was lined with small cupboards and drawers. After shifting several jars of clear red jelly and a crock of pickled cabbage, he opened the drawer he needed, withdrew the item he sought, and snapped it shut with a satisfying *click*.

Returning topside, Aurelius gave the reins a snap to get the horses underway, then offered Tupper a pliable length of leather. The ends were joined with a small metal clasp, and there were two bright beads strung onto it, one carved from blue stone, the other from red.

"Do you know how this works?"

"No."

"It's a money cord. Undo the catch."

Tupper fiddled for a few seconds before discovering the trick for unclasping the ends. Poking at the blue bead, he asked, "Freshstone?"

"Aye, that bauble's from the blue mountain."

He rolled the other bead between thumb and forefinger. "What does red need?"

"Fire. Redstone calls for flames." Aurelius glanced down. The lad had migrated clear across the wide seat until he sat right at his side. Perhaps he'd purchased his trust?

"String the coins?" Tupper checked.

The Pred tapped the cord between the two beads. "Silver in the middle; copper to this side. If you had gold, it would go on the other side."

"Yes." Tupper patiently threaded the pierced coins into their proper places. Redoing the clasp, he held the cord up, then shook it so the collection jingled faintly. "Mine?" he asked, peeping at Aurelius out of the corner of his eye.

"Aye, sprat. You earned them."

As the boy looped the cord around his neck and tucked it safely away inside his tunic, Aurelius changed his mind. Frey had been right; Tupper wasn't a boy who could be bought. If he had a pittance of the lad's trust, it was because one way or another, he'd earned it.

Colors blazed across the clouds on the western horizon, and Aurelius glared at the setting sun. Between its inexorable drop and the longer-than-anticipated visit to the vintner's modestly impressive cellars, he feared they were going to be late. Clucking encouragement to his horses, he remarked, "I hope Frey's too busy to notice the hour. I promised to have you back before dark."

"Go faster?" Tupper suggested.

"I couldn't ask it of the horses," said Aurelius. "The carriage is full to bursting, and therefore heavy."

The orchard-keeper was a fussy little man who'd been quite willing to overlook his customer's race the moment Aurelius deemed his wines drinkable. After some tasting and tale-swapping, they'd nearly settled on a price, only to have Tupper sweep in with a brilliantly-timed inquiry if the man liked pears.

With visions of pear nectar dancing before his eyes, the farmer leapt at the chance to add to his orchard. Their excited discussion ended with a firm handclasp. Aurelius only had to part with a paltry amount gold, for Tupper had offered up both fruit and cuttings from Frey's grove. By the time they parted company, the beaming farmer had further weighed Aurelius's carriage down with three cases of wine, four bushels of apples, and two small kegs of sweet cider.

Tupper drew him from his thoughts by commenting, "Storm's coming."

"Aye."

"The blue stones will like that."

Aurelius only grunted. He preferred not to affix emotions to inanimate objects, even those imbued by the strange magic Freydolf wrought.

"And the white lady will be happy."

Mildly surprised by the boy's newfound talkative streak, Aurelius asked, "Pray tell, why would the lady be glad for a storm that will darken the sky and likely prevent her from stirring?"

"When she wakes up, her cup will be full."

The sun wasn't fully set when the horses clattered to a standstill near the sculptor's workshop, but its fading light was well-hidden behind the Gray Mountain's bulk. Shadows were already deep in the courtyards of the Statuary, but lamplight spilled across the stone pavement. Freydolf had left the inner door ajar. They were expected.

Tupper was fairly bouncing beside him on the seat, and Aurelius wondered if he needed the necessary. But the boy's gaze was fixed on the welcoming glow. "Glad to be home, sprat?"

"Yes."

"How about you let Frey know he has some unloading to do?" Aurelius suggested with a knowing smirk. Leaping down, he opened the compartment where they'd stowed the bread. Withdrawing a crusty loaf, he offered it to Tupper. "You can lure him out with this."

Eyes sparkling in the half-light, Tupper exclaimed, "Yes!"

The lad dashed inside, and Aurelius contemplated the rest of their purchases, making a mental tally of what should go where. As much as he hated menial labor, it was patently obvious that the lad would need help. All of it would need to be ferried across the threshold before the creeping clouds reached their mountain keep.

Recollecting that the horses and harnesses also needed attention, Aurelius bumped the heating of bathwater to the top of Tupper's to do list.

Since apples would likely get the second biggest reaction from his brother-in-law, Aurelius hefted a bushel of ripe fruit and strolled through the open door. He was surprised by the pervasive silence in the workshop, for the day had been rich with experiences that begged to be shared.

One look at master and servant was enough to explain the conversational lull.

Tupper perched atop the block of golden stone that Freydolf had begun shaping, judging by the rubble scattered around his bare feet. The sculptor's pose was relaxed—one elbow propped against his work-in-progress, one ankle crossed behind the other—and he'd traded his mallet for the loaf of bread. Well, *half* of a loaf. He'd torn it in two, and the pair chewed in companionable silence.

The sprat's swinging feet gave away how happy he was, and Freydolf lifted a hand in greeting.

Aurelius tossed him an apple, announcing, "Your servant's too scrawny, so you'll need to shift his harvest to the kitchen."

"*His* harvest?" Freydolf inspected the apple with interest before taking an enormous bite.

"And unlock the storeroom," Aurelius demanded haughtily. "*And* the stables, since it's too late to send the horses down to Gruff."

Grumbling around his mouthful, Frey surrendered his bread to Tupper and crossed to the workbench next to his cot. Lifting a large ring of keys from its hook, he said, "The stables I can understand, but the storeroom?"

"Aye, you'll need it this year. And you may wish to designate one of the lower rooms as your root cellar."

"What for?"

Tupper piped up. "Potatoes, onions, turnips, squash. And the cider."

"Cider?" echoed Freydolf, pausing in the act of handing Aurelius the keys.

His brother-in-law plucked them out of his hand. "And the wine, if we can locate a proper rack."

The sculptor's gaze swung back to him. He opened his mouth, then closed it again, opting to inspect the carriage's contents for himself.

Aurelius trailed after him, spinning the ring of keys on his finger. "You'll need a lantern."

Even with little light left to see by, Freydolf could make out enough of the abundance to be impressed. Muttering a soft oath, he asked, "So much?"

"And then some. I need to arrange for the delivery of the root crops."

The sculptor held up a jar of marmalade. "When did the shops start carrying home canning?"

"They don't."

"Then how ...?" Freydolf asked dubiously.

Aurelius coyly replied, "Your lambkin proved to be quite resourceful."

"Are you telling me that he found all this?"

"*I'm* not telling you anything. It's the sprat's tale to tell; coax it out of him."

Freydolf replaced the jar and glanced toward the door, where Tupper appeared with Olexi in hand, checking to see if the stars were bright enough to wake his tiny guardian. In an undertone, the sculptor said, "The lad's not what you'd call chatty."

"True, he's not the most loquacious of souls, but believe me, he's quite capable of stringing sentences together." With a sidelong glance at the youngster, he clarified, "*Short* sentences, using small words, but coherent nonetheless."

Tupper trotted over and pointed to the side compartment, helpfully announcing, "More bread!"

Aurelius snickered at the look Freydolf sent his way. He might be the sculptor's agent, but he wasn't about to play go-between here. "You're rather *chatty* in your own right, Frey. I'm sure you can pick up the slack until he pulls his own weight!"

"Speaking of weight," Frey grumbled. "Why don't you take another bushel inside?"

Giving the set of keys another rattle, Aurelius cheerfully replied, "Nay, I'll just take the team around to the stables. It will give you and the sprat time to talk!" To Tupper, he added, "I'll be wanting my bathwater sooner than later."

The lad nodded. "Baths before dinner."

As Aurelius strolled toward the horses, he listened as his brother-in-law tried to draw his servant into conversation.

"So what's all this, lambkin?"

"Soup."

Laughing quietly, Aurelius snagged one of the lanterns that hung from the carriage's front corner and located matches. He took his sweet time unhitching the team, eavesdropping all the while.

"Where did you find all these apples?" Freydolf tried.

"On trees."

Aurelius grinned wolfishly. He dawdled while the sculptor carried away box and basket, keg and crate. With any luck, he could prolong the care of the horses until the unpacking was done. Then, he could go straight to his bath. Gathering reins in one hand, he bent to collect his lantern and slowly led the team in the direction of the Statuary's roomy stables. Over the *clip* and *clop* of their hooves, he caught Frey's next question.

"Do you know how to cook these?"

"No."

Shaking his head, Aurelius ambled on. "The idiot will get it right eventually."

If there was one thing his brother-in-law had in abundance, it was patience. He was a sculptor, after all. Frey would keep asking questions, chipping away at Tupper's reticence until he figured out what lay beneath. Aurelius strongly suspected that what he found there would surprise them all.

12

Nice Manners

By mid-morning the following day, scudding clouds surrounded Morven's heights, blotting out the sun so that Freydolf had to stop work in order to light the lanterns. Aurelius had taken over one of the long tables against the wall. Its worn surface was now strewn with papers, and the Pred alternated between consulting a map and making notations in some kind of book. Tupper's duties were already done for the day, for they'd simply eaten apples and bread for breakfast, and there was no need to water the gardens or grove.

As the first raindrops pattered against the workshop windows, the boy hurried to peer through the glass. He'd never really liked rainy days because they meant his whole family would be crowded inside the house at the same time. Storms meant stuffy rooms, restless tussling, and grouchy sisters. This was nice, though. Peaceful. Quiet.

Not many minutes passed before Tupper realized that this wasn't a quiet rain. Winds whipped up, driving the downpour against the glass so that it looked almost as if the Statuary was underwater. Unsettled by the streak and swirl of droplets, Tupper backed away.

This was *nothing* like listening to rain on the roof of the snug house where he grew up. The storm felt closer, and it was trying to get inside. When lightning flashed, filling the workshop with its blinding glare, he gasped; when thunder *crack*ed and *boom*ed all around the mountaintop, he fled.

Tupper huddled in the corner of his bed, hiding from the storm's terrors. On the other side of the thick tapestry curtain, he could hear Freydolf and Aurelius talking in low tones, and he blushed in shame. Only babies skittered because of a little lightning. Another thunderclap made him duck, and he rubbed miserably at his horns, reminding himself that he was big now.

The low growl of voices came closer, and he could hear Aurelius snippily say, "For pity's sake, he's a valley dweller! What do you expect?"

"We're perfectly safe," Freydolf argued, though he sounded apologetic.

"Aye," agreed the merchant. "But that waif hasn't learned to trust Morven like you do. It's quieter *below*, if you catch my meaning."

Tupper thought he heard a soft sigh, and then the curtain was tugged aside. Freydolf's gaze held concern, but to the boy's relief, he didn't coddle.

"Aurelius has it in his head to look for a wine rack today, and I was thinking it's as good a time as any to show you some of the galleries." White light ripped through the room, and the air shattered in another echoing *boom*. Freydolf winced, then invited, "Shall we do some exploring?"

Slowly relinquishing his hold on the blankets, Tupper crawled across the bed toward his master. "Yes, please."

The man's big, warm hand rested lightly atop his head, gently rumpling his hair, then scratching at the base of a horn. "I'm sorry, lambkin. I forgot how noisy days like this can be." With a reassuring smile, he promised, "You'll get used to it."

Tupper nodded gratefully, then peeked past his shoulder to

see if Aurelius would make fun of him for acting so nubless.

The other Pred strode back and forth, gathering items and making a pile by the door. He didn't even spare them a look as he started handing down orders. "I'll check your stock of lantern oil while we're below. I can only *assume* the reason your lamps are burning low is because you neglected to tell your servant that they regularly require filling?"

"It slipped my mind," Freydolf admitted as he straightened.

"This could take a while; we should bring food and drink. Do you have a bag of some sort?"

"Aye, there should be something ... somewhere."

While Freydolf fished around in a set of nearby cabinets, Aurelius prowled over and fixed Tupper with a haughty look. "Bring your own lantern, for there are no windows where we're going."

Tupper slid off the bed. "The galleries are dark?"

"Dark and deep," Aurelius confirmed. Leaning closer, he dropped his voice conspiratorially. "There are only twelve of these mountains the whole world over, sprat. You've lived in the shadow of a legend your whole young life." Quirking a brow, he challenged, "Aren't you curious?"

The question was far too familiar. His younger brother often asked him the very same thing, always before diving into some new kind of trouble. Tupper didn't share Farley's knack for mischief, and he wondered if Aurelius meant to lead him astray. He warily shook his head.

With a small frown, the Pred asked, "Truly?"

How could he explain? Tupper rarely looked beyond whatever was right in front of him. Because of this, he had no worries, no regrets, and no plans. Being chosen by Freydolf and coming to live at the Statuary had changed everything about his life ... except him. Even in this strange and wonderful place, he was still plain old Tupper.

Being here was good, and for him, that was good enough. It had never occurred to him to look for something more. Holding Aurelius's gaze, he quietly asked, "Is that bad?"

The man drummed his fingers against the hilt of one dagger.

"Nay. Just unexpected."

A gust of wind sent a heavy sheet of rain against the windows, and Tupper flinched. To his relief, no burst of lightning accompanied its fury.

"Trade with me," Aurelius suddenly demanded.

Tupper blinked. Thanks to the two Pred, he was in the unique position of having something of value. While there was no way he would ever give up Olexi, he had a money cord now. Presented with the prospect of a barter, the boy's interest was piqued. "What?"

The Pred crouched so that they were eye to eye and asked, "Do you have any clothes other than the ones you're wearing?"

He glanced down at his homespun tunic and his pants, which were getting a trifle short. He'd left Hayward with nothing but the clothes on his back, but Freydolf had given him permission to use whatever his other servants had left behind. All the cast-offs in the small chest next to his bed were much too big, so he'd only adopted one item. "A nightshirt."

"What if I were to offer you a brand new shirt," Aurelius posed. "Something clean, bright, and new, perhaps with a pocket for your little friend?"

Tupper glanced toward the sill where Olexi stood. It *would* be nice to keep the tiny ram with him all the time. Curious what the man might ask in exchange, he asked, "For what?"

With a flourish, Aurelius held up three claw-tipped fingers. "Three things."

"Three bronze?" he asked dubiously. That might buy a loaf of bread, but not a tunic.

"Nay, three *questions*," the man clarified. "I want you to pay close attention to everything you see while we're in the galleries today. Watch for something that interests you. I don't care what or why."

Tupper could tell Aurelius wasn't done, but he nodded to show he understood so far. For once, the Pred wasn't using fancy words, and it helped.

"During our evening meal, you must ask your master three questions. If you can do that, I will fulfill my part of the bargain."

"What kind of questions?"

"That's up to you. My one requirement is that the questions be something only Frey can answer." He offered an upraised palm. "Do you accept my terms?"

If there was a trick in the man's trade, Tupper couldn't see it. He snuck another peek at Olexi, then one at Freydolf, who was leaning so far into a cupboard, he'd stuck out one foot for balance. Thinking up questions would probably be hard, but pockets were a luxury worth trading for.

Determined to do his best, Tupper placed his hand upon Aurelius's. "I accept."

It had been a few years since Freydolf last ranged deep enough into the galleries to warrant packing along food and water. Some of his predecessors had built *up*, but many had built *in*. Hundreds of lifetimes had been spent creating the mountain's maze of wonders, and it would take more than a lifetime to see them all. Freydolf had explored extensively during his apprenticeship, pushing beyond the passages recorded on Master Platt's maps.

A day's exploration appealed to the Keeper, and Aurelius was right; the storm couldn't reach them once they were safely below. Freydolf turned back to the room, both carrysack and canteen in hand, but his triumphant smile fell away at the sight of Tupper's small hand touching Aurelius's in silent agreement.

The pampered peacock had won him over.

Freydolf should have been relieved. After spending the past day with Aurelius, the lad seemed to have gotten over his fear of him. It was only natural. His brother-in-law was a father, after all. He'd raised boys and knew how to appeal to them. Still, Freydolf was surprised that his sharp-tongued, thick-skinned, fast-handed brother-in-law was even making an effort.

The sly wolf had found favor in innocent eyes.

Why did that bother him? The sculptor strolled toward the pair, unnoticed for the moment. Aurelius had been full of himself last night, preening over his superior knowledge of the boy and teasing Freydolf with hints about the heretofore unknown skills Tupper supposedly possessed. He'd been almost as proud as the time he'd bragged about the success of his youngest's first hunt.

Maybe this was a good thing. Maybe his brother-in-law was exactly what the lad needed.

Aurelius noticed him first and quirked a quizzical brow.

Tupper turned and peered up at him with those wide, watchful eyes, and Freydolf wrestled with the oddest mingling of annoyance and fear. Had he been supplanted so quickly? Then, the truth hit him like a chunk of rough-hewn brownstone—he was jealous!

His sudden epiphany was highlighted by a lash of lightning and a slap of thunder, and once its deep rumble faded, he looked down in amazement. Tupper was wrapped around his leg.

The poor boy's face was flushed with embarrassment, but Freydolf was elated. Tupper looked to him after all. Even if he wasn't as knowledgeable as his brother-in-law, Freydolf could clearly see what was needed.

Slinging the canteen strap over his shoulder, he tossed the carry-sack to Aurelius. "Tupper and I will get a head start."

"Surely not!"

"Aye." Frey tossed the lad over his shoulder. With a soft *oof*, Tupper scrambled to a more comfortable—and slightly more dignified—seat astride the man's shoulders. Freydolf strode to the door and handed up the cloak that always hung on the hook above his boots. To Tupper, he said, "This should keep the worst of the wet off. It's a short dash to the stairs."

The lad wrestled with the draping fabric so it covered them both. "Ready."

"Now, see here!" Aurelius peevishly exclaimed. "Do you expect me to carry all these supplies *myself*?"

Poised on the threshold, Freydolf only replied, "We'll meet you by the well!"

Freydolf sat on a step halfway down the curving staircase, catching his breath. His cloak hung beside the door in the six-sided chamber above, and its dripping could be heard, even over the rain outside. In the oldest sections of the Statuary, the walls were thick.

He'd covered the distance between outer doors in record time, grateful to have made it back inside before another bout of thunder could startle Tupper. The sculptor supposed it would have been wisest to bring at least *one* of the lanterns along, but he'd pulled open the creaking shutters on the entryway's window. Enough light filtered through to see by, now that their eyes were adjusting.

Tupper sat next to him, tucked safely between his greater bulk and the smooth stone of the wall. The lad rubbed at his nose, but showed no signs of worry or fear. He simply sat, eyes downcast, awaiting further instruction.

Freydolf inhaled deeply and exhaled on a sigh. "There are things I should tell you," he broached. "Maybe they will make things easier?"

Wide eyes sought his, and Tupper nodded.

Always nodding. Frey ruffled the boy's bright hair and spoke in a low, slow voice. "The Statuary is very high, but it's also very safe. The foundations are solid, and the walls are sound."

Tupper leaned close and whispered, "Lightning?"

"Aye, it's powerful stuff," acknowledged Freydolf. "But the first Keepers were good planners. There are lightning rods along the rooftops."

"No danger?" the boy pressed.

Freydolf hummed thoughtfully. "There are always reasons to be cautious. Up here, we must pay attention to where we set our feet." He extended a foot and wriggled his toes demonstratively, and Tupper followed suit. With a smile warming his tones, the sculptor explained, "When stone is wet, it's slick, so it's easy to slip and fall. On days like this, we're wise to stay inside."

"Like here?"

"Aye, you'll probably like this better than the workshop. The galleries are quiet."

"Quiet is good," Tupper replied earnestly.

Freydolf was used to quiet, or perhaps resigned to it. Most of his servants had only added to the Statuary's pervasive silence—afraid of bothering him, afraid of angering him, *afraid*. Their cringing, quaking silences were different than Tupper's stalwart presence. The lad didn't exactly spruce up the place with cheerful chatter, but his courage was something Freydolf wanted to protect.

Reaching over to press his hand to the stone wall, the sculptor said, "Morven has weathered many storms. You should trust her." To his amazement, Tupper touched his fingers to his lips, then pressed them to the wall. "What are you doing, lambkin?"

"Saying sorry."

"To whom?"

"To the mountain," he replied, blinking up at him.

"To Morven?" Freydolf asked, his lips quirking. This lad never did what he expected.

He nodded tentatively.

"You have nice manners. Is that how Flox apologize?"

"Yes."

"It's different where I come from," Freydolf offered, for as much as Tupper liked the quiet, the man liked conversation more. "We bow our heads to say we're sorry, but a kiss makes sense, too. I'm sure Morven is pleased by the gesture."

Tupper laid his cheek against the cool stone, listening. Just then, a flash of lightning blinked through the window above. In its light, Freydolf could see the boy tense for the thunder that was sure to follow, but the rumble was greatly muffled here. Tupper's sigh of relief was naught but a whisper, and then he patted the stone. "Thank you."

Freydolf caressed the wall with his callused hand, for he also had reason to thank Morven. She was his to keep, but she kept him, as well. Thanks to the legendary Moonlit Mountain, he would forever have a home. Glancing down at the boy who now shared it—at least for the time being—he murmured, "Aye. Thank you."

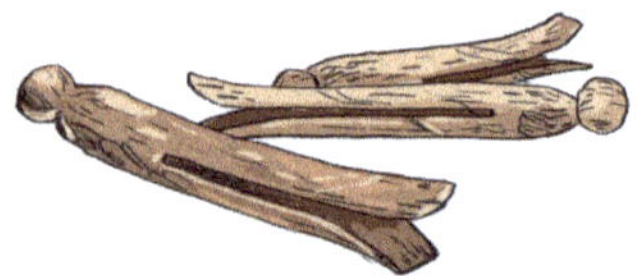

A very disgruntled Aurelius swooped along the wide passage, his boots squeaking wetly on the stone floor, his accumulation of gear clattering with every oncoming step. Tupper was already hurrying forward when the Pred sulkily called, "A hand, please? Two, if you can spare them."

Freydolf looked up from pouring fresh well water into a soft-sided canteen and chuckled. "Did you have to bring so much?"

"I would have had to bring considerably *less* if you had any shred of decency! Do you *realize* how difficult it is to open doors when one's hands are full?"

"Yet you managed it," Freydolf pointed out.

Aurelius's chin lifted haughtily. "At *great* personal sacrifice."

Frey capped the canteen and strolled over. "I take it you mean your hair?"

With a huff of annoyance, Aurelius relinquished the remainder of his burden to Freydolf, then pushed dripping hair out of his eyes. "For pity's sake, bring me a towel, sprat."

Tupper scampered into the necessary and fumbled in the dark for a minute before returning with two. The Pred were still trading jibes, but they didn't really sound angry. Their voices echoed a little in the stone passage—Freydolf's deep and fuzzy, Aurelius's smooth and sharp.

"You survived the ordeal without melting." Freydolf lit the first of three lanterns. "One would think you'd never endured a storm at sea."

"Quoth the perpetually landlocked," Aurelius returned

with a sniff. "Mercifully, I had the foresight to bring a change of clothes!"

"Is *that* what's in this great bundle?" Laughing outright, Freydolf said, "Your predicament is one of your own making!"

Tupper reached them as Aurelius let his soaked cloak fall with a *splat*. "You'll thank me once your belly recalls that it hasn't had lunch yet."

"Aye," the sculptor conceded, taking one of the towels from Tupper and tossing it over Aurelius's head. "Your praises will ring from the Cavern's walls, if that's what you truly want. However, I recommend a little more discretion, and I'd abandon those noisemakers on your feet. If Graven *is* here, he'll find you in a trice!"

With a withering look, Aurelius sat upon the rim of the fountain and proceeded to undo boot buckles. Peering into the shadows beyond the warm circle of light now cast by all three lanterns, he said, "Tread lightly lest the silence catch you unawares."

Despite his warnings, Freydolf didn't seem overly concerned. "Unless something's drastically amiss, he'd be the only one stirring."

Tupper edged closer and offered Aurelius the other towel. "Are you scared?"

"I'm *wet*," he replied shortly. The Pred's eyes almost glowed in the lamplight, and they flashed with annoyance. "What about you, sprat?"

"I'm not scared," he replied truthfully. "I like this quiet."

"Well, *I* like dry clothes. Any chance the fire's lit in the necessary?" Gesturing toward his sodden things, he said, "These would dry faster."

"I can do that," Tupper offered, glancing at Freydolf to make sure it was all right.

"Aye, lambkin," the sculptor agreed. "I'll check the lamp oil while we wait for Aurelius to make himself pretty."

Freydolf leaned to one side, neatly avoiding the boot flung at his head.

Tupper thought it best to get while the getting was good.

With a lantern to light his way, he pushed through the white door with its arched top.

By the time he had a decent blaze going, a much calmer Aurelius strolled in and dropped a heap of wet clothes in the closest basin. Tupper was a little surprised at how plain the man looked. Well, plain compared to his usual attire. His belted tunic's deep hem was covered in fussy embroidery, but otherwise, it wasn't much different than Tupper's own shirt, right down to the lacing at the collar. The Pred had removed nearly all his jewelry; only the deep green droplets dangling from his earlobes remained. His breeches were cuffed well above his bare feet, and the boy couldn't help staring, wondering what it was like to have claws.

"If you have questions, ask them," said Aurelius. "Though asking *me* won't count toward our bargain."

There *was* something he wanted to know. Tugging his own ear lobe, Tupper asked, "Does it hurt?"

Aurelius touched a gemstone earring. "Nay. Haven't you seen anything like this before?"

"No."

The Pred squatted down and waved him forward. "Take a gander, sprat. Pred are pierced once they complete their coming-of-age hunt. A brutal, bare-handed, and bloody rite of passage."

Tupper sidled up and gently poked one of the pretty gems, sending it swaying. It was the weirdest thing he'd ever seen. Instead of growing horns, they poked holes in their ears.

With a blink, he murmured, "He doesn't have them."

"Aye, and now you know *why*." Aurelius rose to his full height and slapped his thighs before briskly changing the subject. "In case you didn't realize, sprat, this room is set up for washing clothes. Naturally, the duty falls to you."

Immediately, the boy felt bad. Airing was good, but it wasn't the same as washing. Following the man over to a row of low basins, Tupper reached in to feel the ridges chiseled into its slanted side. Yes, this would work well.

"Use the cauldron and basins. Drying racks are in the far

cupboard." With a sidelong glance, he added, "It'll be a few years before you can hope to reach the clotheslines."

Tupper looked up, noticing for the first time that cords strung between the columns around the bathing area. Aurelius draped his wet clothes over the line closest to the fire, fixing them in place with stone clothespins from a nearby niche.

It *was* too high, but maybe if Tupper stood on a box, he could make it work. He was too busy with his plans to notice that Aurelius was done, so he jumped a little when a long, claw-tipped finger suddenly tapped his nose.

"Have you thought of three questions, yet?"

"No."

Aurelius didn't scold. He merely nodded and said, "It's a good bargain. Make the most of it."

"I will," he promised.

"I need to check the stock of soap, but you run along. Frey's in the room next door, which *may* be suitable for your root cellar if you clear it out."

Nodding, Tupper grabbed his lantern and did as he was told— both in going and in thinking. He paused outside the door, wondering if he needed a plan. Slowly, he shook his head. This was different than figuring out how to reach a clothesline. He couldn't stand on a box to reach Freydolf's secrets.

Sitting on the spot, the boy tried to think of the sorts of things only *he* knew. Holding up one finger at a time, he silently made his list—where he liked to hide when the house was too noisy, the best place to catch fish, which tree the honeybees had chosen, his fondest wish, the promises he'd made, the things he dreamed about at night, what made him want to cry. Seven fingers already!

Tupper had so many secrets tucked away in his heart mostly because no one asked him for them. Maybe it was the same for Freydolf, and *maybe* he wouldn't mind sharing three of them. So far, the man had been very generous, so Tupper figured it was possible. If he could come up with so many good questions for himself, *surely* he could think of some for his master.

Standing, Tupper gave his thighs an experimental slap and felt rather daring. He would show Aurelius. He would find the way into Freydolf's heart.

The door to the room next to the necessary was so wide, it was almost square. Tupper thought it was odd in a nice way, living in a place where the doors didn't match. He fanned his fingers for a quick tally, confirming that the house where he grew up had just five doors, and they were all the same size and shape. This one was thick and heavy, with a ring for a handle, and the entrance was broad enough for a wheelbarrow.

Peeping past the doorjamb, he spotted his master. Freydolf was down on one knee, counting fat candles in a long box. There were bulbous bottles of lamp oil lined up on the shelf behind him, and the room smelled faintly of the stuff, as if someone had spilled some without bothering to clean it up. Lifting his lantern a little higher, he scrutinized the floor. Sure enough, dark splotches mottled the stone. Tupper frowned, for someone had done a bad job.

Freydolf glanced up and asked, "What do you think about this room for all your squash and cider?"

"No."

The man seemed a little surprised. "It's convenient."

There was no way he was storing sweet apples in a room that reeked of oil, but he wasn't sure how to explain. Food and fuel didn't mix. Pointing to the floor, he explained, "It smells bad."

Freydolf looked, sniffed, then nodded. "Aye, you're right. No matter. You've more than enough rooms to choose from, so take your pick."

Tupper wasn't used to having his opinion matter, so the man's easy deference left him rather giddy. Unsure of a proper response, he quickly brushed his fingertips across his chest and extended them, whispering, "Thank you."

Aurelius appeared then, lantern in one hand, list in the other. "Well? How many candles are left?"

Freydolf looked down at the open box, then grinned at his brother-in-law. "Not sure. Lost count."

The merchant scanned the shelves and set down his light in order to make two notations on his list. "I'll place an order tomorrow, weather permitting. Come on."

Out in the columned passage again, a flicker of lightning caught Tupper's attention, for there were windows beyond the fountain at the far end. If thunder followed the flash, he couldn't hear it over the voices of his companions, who were discussing which section of the galleries to explore.

Freydolf said, "Let's start close."

"The first section of quarters on this level is completely picked over, but the second block is barely touched," said Aurelius. "Aye, they'll do. Any chance you have fire-bearers stashed close by?"

"Only if we go as far as the Cavern."

"Figures." Sparing a glance for Tupper, Aurelius said, "This way," and strode off in the opposite direction of the fountain.

"Acts like he owns the place," muttered Freydolf, favoring his servant with a wry grin. "He's right, though. The closest access to the galleries is through here. If you ever want to explore on your own, this is a good place to start because you can't get turned around."

The sculptor set an easy pace, not bothering to try to keep up with Aurelius. Tupper was glad for the chance to get his bearings. His sense of direction had always been good, and he reckoned they were under the workshop when the passage suddenly angled off to one side and narrowed considerably. To the left, there were doors, one after another. Each was a little different than its neighbors, especially in the decorative bands that were carved into the surrounding stone. These borders were fun to touch, and Tupper lagged behind to poke his fingers into the mouths of several fat frogs.

Freydolf didn't seem to mind waiting. He crossed to one of the niches across the way to greet the statue of a begging dog carved from red stone.

Tupper caught up and patted the little guy. He looked like a puppy version of the red hounds that stood guard at the Statuary's gate. To the boy's delight, there were *more* niches along the right side of the long hall, and he darted to each to see what they held. All the statues were of animals carved from various kinds of stone—blue, white, pink, green, and gold.

"I thought you might like these," Freydolf said. "From what I've gathered, these used to be like pets. Or maybe babysitters. They're especially fond of children."

Tupper hunkered down in front of a freshstone bear cub with an upraised paw and waved back. "They're good."

"This one has a clever design." The sculptor uncapped their canteen and dribbled water into a small, funnel-like opening on the top of the statue's head. Immediately, the cub blinked and wrinkled her nose, gazing expectantly between the man and boy. Freydolf said, "It takes a long time for the water to dry up, so she doesn't need constant splashing to stay awake."

The roly-poly cub found her feet and climbed out of her niche, looking up and down the long passage before trundling over to stand next to Tupper. She nudged his hand, and he wasted no time in petting her ears. They were cool like stone should be, but the fur was soft.

"What does she want?" he asked, looking to Freydolf for answers.

"She's a guardian made for minding children, so she'll want to tag along." He patted the cub's back. "I hope you don't mind the company?"

Tupper could hardly believe his luck. "She can come."

From further down the hall, Aurelius's voice taunted, "Couldn't you avoid adopting random statues for even *one* day?"

Freydolf whispered, "We're not *really* adopting her because she'll always return to this niche, but I think she'll enjoy a day's ramble. It's been years since she was invited along."

Tupper nodded, understanding the feeling.

The sculptor rose and strolled along after Aurelius, holding his lantern high as he inspected a section of the wall decorated with a complex series of interlocking circles. Glancing back, he said, "This way."

Tupper scrambled to his feet and collected his lantern, then smiled softly at the little bear, who rose up on her back paws. Pointing down the passage, the boy said, "This way." He took several steps, then peeked over his shoulder. To his delight, the cub dropped to all fours and followed.

Aurelius waited for them in front of a large, dry fountain. "Unless you have any objections, I'll start here."

"Be my guest."

Aurelius flung wide the door, his hand hovering near his dagger.

Tupper edged behind Freydolf's solid presence.

He glanced down, then back at Aurelius. With a soft chuckle, he promised, "There's nothing lurking, lambkin. He's just being overly dramatic."

The bear cub certainly showed no fear; she waddled in after Aurelius. Tupper felt a little better after that and followed her into a room that was as big as a small house. A wide fireplace marked the part that was a kitchen, and the frames of two beds were pushed against the opposite wall. A narrow ladder led to a tiny version of the workshop's balcony, which looked like it might be fun to explore.

Setting his lantern on a table, Aurelius strode to the corner and took hold of a heavy curtain, dragging it open to reveal a row of narrow windows. Rain spattered against the glass, and Tupper blinked in surprise. He'd forgotten the storm. It was closer here, but smaller, maybe because the windows were so much littler than the ones upstairs. Still, he eased back toward the door, bumping into Freydolf in the process.

The Keeper said, "These rooms were living quarters. In times past, the Statuary was a city unto itself."

Tupper tried to imagine a noisy village on top of Morven, but it wasn't easy. Freydolf's home was nice and quiet, like a secret hideout.

Just then, lightning flashed, and the sculptor tugged him out into the passage, distancing him from the *crack* of thunder that followed. He said, "I always thought it would be interesting if there was a stone that needed a flash of lightning to wake it."

"There isn't?" asked Tupper.

"Nay, it's just a fancy of mine."

"What else?"

"Hmm?"

"Starlight, moonlight, sunset, water," Tupper listed. "What else?"

"I see. Well, green stone is interesting stuff. Gives me the most trouble."

"Aye, because you're tone deaf," taunted Aurelius, who'd stalked out of the room, closed its door, and dusted off his hands. "Nothing there. Let's try the next!"

"But ...!" blurted Tupper.

"But what?" retorted Aurelius, his eyes widening at a sudden scrabbling noise.

Tupper dove for the handle and pulled the door wide enough to let the blue bear cub out. "She was still inside," he scolded.

Aurelius whisked away, muttering about chips and blocks.

While the merchant prowled into the next room, Tupper hung back and tugged at Freydolf's sleeve. "What wakes green stone?"

His master's dark eyes brightened. "It's quite unique. Of the twelve mountains, it's the only one that responds to sound. Green stone likes sweet music."

"Which is why Frey avoids it. His singing voice is brutish as a bear's." Quirking a brow at their tagalong, Aurelius added, "No offense."

"I can whistle," the sculptor protested.

"Tunelessly," scoffed Aurelius.

"It *works*."

With an air of superiority, the other Pred took up the lecture. "I've *been* to the green mountain, and I wouldn't mind returning. Lovely place, filled with bird cages and wind chimes." Slamming the door on the current room, he led the way down the passage. "Onward!"

Tupper thought Aurelius was acting like a finicky shopper, browsing for the best quality merchandise. He worked his way through the rooms, and it was interesting to see what they held. Each had a fireplace, windows, and a loft. Most were packed with stacks of unused furniture, but there were smaller things as well—crocks and cradles, pitchers and paintings, ink wells and washtubs.

All of it was good stuff, but Tupper noticed that Freydolf barely gave the clutter a second glance. He was more interested in the patterns carved on fireplace mantles or the mosaic of tiles on some of the floors.

"Oh, now this is promising!" exclaimed Aurelius, who'd spotted the outermost band of carvings on the next door he meant to try. With a sharp look at Freydolf, he demanded, "Did you *know* this was here?"

He shrugged. "I vaguely remember that pattern." Tapping the third border in, which was carved to look like birds in flight, he admitted, "This one is more to my tastes. It outshines the vines."

"Your poetry is pitiful," grumbled Aurelius.

Freydolf smirked. "Your persistence is plentiful."

While Aurelius forged ahead, Tupper checked to see what the fuss was about. "Grapes!"

"Aye, whoever lived here had a fondness for them," the sculptor confirmed. "It bodes well."

A crow of triumph echoed from within.

Freydolf amended, "And *that* bespeaks success. Let's hope the contraption's small enough to cart or carry."

"Is it okay to take?" Tupper ventured.

The sculptor chose a seat on the floor and stretched out his legs, smiling when the little she-bear bustled over and butted her broad forehead into his ribs. "These rooms and the things inside them aren't used anymore, so there's no harm in taking a few odds and ends."

Tupper gave him a hard look. "No stealing."

"We're *not* stealing. As Keeper, everything here is mine," With a crooked little smile he gazed down the long, empty passage. "There's no one else."

Tupper didn't like how sad that sounded, so he firmly corrected, "Except me."

Freydolf's smile straightened out. "Aye, lambkin. You and me."

13

The Cavern

They left Aurelius's wine rack standing against the wall, then delved deeper into the mountain. The passage took an inward turn that placed them in front of an imposing set of doors. Tupper thought they must be as tall as the Apprentice Gate and wondered if they were that big in order to be fancy ... or if they *needed* to be. Did something huge go in and out? He quickly checked, confirming that Aurelius's hands weren't anywhere near his daggers, and took that for a good sign.

Gesturing behind them, Freydolf explained, "This section was once filled with people, yet it stands empty; however, beyond this door is the first of the stone galleries, and it's filled to capacity."

"First of many," Aurelius said.

"Aye, but also first historically," Freydolf clarified. "The statues in the Cavern are Morven's oldest."

"Biggest, too."

Both men turned expectantly toward him, and Tupper realized they wanted him to do something. But what?

Lantern light added a shine to Freydolf's dark eyes as he said, "They're not locked."

Recognizing the implicit command, Tupper padded forward

and took hold of a door handle. He tugged, but nothing happened.

Aurelius snidely said, "*Push*, sprat."

He did, and the huge door swung easily inward, giving the boy his first glimpse of the largest room he'd ever seen.

Tupper had expected darkness upon darkness, but gray daylight filtered through from several sets of windows high overhead. He tiptoed forward, the blue bear cub right beside him, and picked out dozens of randomly spaced clerestories set into the irregular stone walls of an enormous cave. The most impressive windows were part of a twelve-sided cupola built over the Cavern's center. They illuminated a statue so huge, it took Tupper several moments to realize what he was seeing.

"What do you think?" asked Freydolf.

"*Big*," he breathed.

"Precocious as ever," commented Aurelius.

Tupper couldn't drag his eyes from the central figure, which towered above all the others. It *had* to be a masterpiece. Taking a few more steps forward, his awe suddenly shifted to speculation, and he was struck by an overwhelming desire. Although it might offend Morven and her Keeper, he simply *had* to ask.

Turning to Freydolf, he begged, "Can I climb it?"

Freydolf was flummoxed. Certainly, he'd expected Tupper to react more favorably than the rest, but even journeyman sculptors shied away from Thrall. On moonlit nights, nobody willingly entered the Cavern for fear of what she might do.

The Keeper's gaze swung to the enormous statue that dwarfed all others. The winged serpent's many coils looped in an impossible tangle atop a low pedestal, and her slitted gaze was fixed upon them. Needle-like fangs were on full display, and wicked talons adorned the elongated digits on all four of her sinewy forelegs.

Maybe he'd misunderstood. Meeting Tupper's pleading gaze, Freydolf checked, "Do you mean Thrall? The dragon in the middle?"

"Yes."

There was no mistake, and Freydolf's bafflement doubled. "You want to get *closer*?"

Tupper nodded hopefully.

"How would someone your size even manage the feat?" he muttered, half to himself.

Unperturbed, Tupper pointed to the Statuary's very first masterpiece. "Tail, back foot, scales," he explained before making a swirling motion. "Then up!"

The lad was right. The ridged end of the dragon's tail trailed onto the floor, and one of her hind legs cocked at an angle that might allow a determined soul into her coils. After that, there were toeholds aplenty amidst her scales. "Aye, it could be done."

Tupper waited patiently for an answer, but Aurelius lost his. Rolling his eyes, he demanded, "Haven't you ever climbed a statue, Frey?"

"For instructional purposes."

Indicating the looming dragon, Aurelius suggested, "Time for a refresher course?"

Freydolf rubbed the back of his neck and thought hard. There was no harm in letting the boy touch and see for himself. Thrall was generally given a wide berth, but she wasn't dangerous by daylight. Neither was she sacred. Like every other statue wrested from Morven's rock, she stood as a testament to her creator.

"Aye," he finally allowed. "Go ahead, lambkin."

There was a crisp *clack* as Tupper set down his lantern, and then he was off, weaving between the statues that lay between them and the mountain's matriarch.

Freydolf stood uncertain, but Aurelius jostled him from his thoughts with a sharp elbow. "I don't know about you, but I *refuse* to be outdone by that wisp of a boy."

"What are you on about?"

Aurelius's eyes glinted. "Ever been to the top?"

Two more lanterns connected noisily with the floor as both Pred bolted after Tupper. The race was on.

In the end, there was no contest. Aurelius's swift ascent of Thrall's bulk was a tribute to his single-minded intensity, but Freydolf was too easily distracted by little things like chisel-work ... and Tupper. Halfway up the statue's ridged neck, Frey paused to study the point where the dragon's two left arms joined her broad chest, then was further waylaid when he realized that his young servant wasn't climbing *up* so much as *in*.

From his triumphant lounge upon the crown of Thrall's head, Aurelius sulkily accused, "You have robbed me of any satisfaction! Did you even try?"

"Sorry. I was just ... looking."

His brother-in-law rolled his eyes, then asked, "Could *you* do this?"

"Do what?"

"A statue this big." He touched one of Thrall's many curving horns.

"In theory," Freydolf acknowledged. "But not in practice. If I wanted to complete something on this scale, I should have started two decades ago. And secured the assistance of a few journeymen."

Aurelius gazed out over the other statues that populated the Cavern. "So the longer you wait to begin, the smaller your masterpiece will be?"

Freydolf winced. "Aye."

"No matter. *Clearly*, bigger is not always better."

Chuckling at the leaner Pred's blatant self-aggrandizement, Frey changed course, retreating down Thrall's back in order to follow Tupper, who was working his way into the nest of the dragon's coils. "Looking for something?" he asked.

"Yes," Tupper answered, pointing into the shadows below. "Something's there."

"Sharp eyes," the sculptor praised. "Thrall does have a secret."

The boy's eyes took on a shine of anticipation, which slowly dimmed. "Will she be mad?"

"Nay," Freydolf assured. "She shares her secret with any who are brave enough to seek it."

"You know?"

"Aye, I found it years ago." He urged, "Go on, lambkin."

Nodding, Tupper continued his descent, now with his master following.

Thrall's pedestal was a smooth disk, half-buried under her overlapping coils, which draped over its edges in places. Whenever moonlight poured through the Cavern's high windows, she would stir, twisting and turning upon her small stage, flexing her talons, and baring her teeth at those who dared enter her realm.

It was a matter of some debate whether she stayed upon her pedestal because she couldn't leave or because she didn't *want* to leave.

Freydolf leaned toward the latter.

"She has an egg!" Tupper gasped, slipping to the very bottom

"Aye, she does." Scales encircled a circular space roughly the size of a small room, and a single egg lay hidden in its haven.

Tupper wrapped his arms as far as they could go around the curved surface, but the egg stood taller than he. Laying his ear against the stone, he furrowed his brows in concentration, as if listening for signs of what lay inside. "Will it hatch?"

"Nay. Though it would be wonderful if such a thing were possible."

"Yes," he agreed. "It's a good egg, though."

Freydolf offered a more proper introduction. "Thrall is the Statuary's first guardian, carved from a rock formation that the first Keeper found in this cavern. Everything else was built out from here, so this spot is where men and the Moonlit Mountain had their beginning." Caressing the smooth gray eggshell, he added, "Thrall's egg is nicknamed Morven's Heart."

Tupper wasn't satisfied until he'd scrambled over every possible plane of the dragon statue. He'd always loved rock-climbing, so he wasn't fazed by either the challenge or the heights. Even the occasional flicker of lightning through the clerestories didn't daunt him, for the storm was far from his thoughts. He was having too much fun.

Eventually, the boy noticed that Freydolf had moved two of the lanterns close to the place where Thrall's tail touched the ground. The sculptor was sitting on a blanket spread with food, playing with the blue bear cub, and Tupper felt bad for making him wait.

Leaping nimbly from ridge to scale, he hurried to join his master. Meals were supposed to be his job, but maybe picnics didn't count? He hoped Freydolf wasn't disappointed in him. Sliding to the ground near the big man, Tupper mumbled, "Sorry."

"For?"

Tupper wasn't sure anymore. He shrugged uncertainly, glad when the cub trundled over, giving him an excuse to lower his eyes.

Freydolf patted the blanket. "Sit and eat. Aurelius certainly wasn't stingy when he did his choosing, and the more we eat, the less there'll be to carry back."

Having worked up a considerable appetite, the boy was glad to obey. While he ate, Tupper glanced about for some sign of the third lantern and the other Pred.

"He went to choose another fire-bearer."

Those had been mentioned more than once already, but Tupper didn't know what they were. "Fire-bearer?"

"They're a practical necessity around here." Gesturing broadly, Freydolf explained, "Most of the galleries are carved straight into the mountain, and there are few windows. We rely on lanterns, candles, torches, and the like to light our way. Fire-bearers were designed to free our hands. They bring light into the darkness."

"Statues?"

"Aye, redstone statues." Nodding to a point behind the boy, Freydolf said, "I already brought one over, but I let him cool off so you could wake him again yourself."

Tupper turned to stare at a figure with an outstretched hand standing a short distance away. Setting aside his food, he went for a closer look.

"Bring your lantern. You'll need it."

He liked the way his master's eyes were sparkling. Something good was going to happen. Quick to do as he was told, Tupper studied the statue of a man dressed in strange armor; there was a sword at his side and a helm upon his head. The soldier wasn't like any person he'd ever met, for he had a large, hooked nose, and there were feathers where his hair should be.

"He's my favorite," Freydolf said from his seat. "According to the notation on his heel, his name's Brand."

"Redstone needs fire." Tupper looked to his master for further instruction.

"Aye, so turn up your lantern flame."

Tupper did so, and the circle of its glow widened to include the red statue.

"Hang it from Brand's hand so he can carry it for you." Once Tupper had accomplished this step, Freydolf said, "Now, pull the pin at the top."

Tupper located the slender rod, which was attached to the lantern's handle by a fine chain. It came away smoothly, and the top part of the lantern opened like the petals of a flower. The exposed flame licked at the fire-bearer's hand, and his long fingers immediately folded around the lantern's handle as he lifted it higher.

The statue looked to Freydolf before peering down his impressive nose at Tupper. Then, Brand smiled and lifted his brows in silent inquiry, as if awaiting instructions. The expression was so real, Tupper reached out, wanting to see if he was truly made of stone.

When he hesitated, the statue reached back, offering his free hand.

To the boy's surprise, Brand had curving talons on each finger, but the predatory feature worried him less and less.

Placing his hand upon the cool red stone of the man's palm, he said, "I'm Tupper."

With a slight inclination of his head, Brand acknowledged the introduction.

The boy thought the fire-bearer was nice and offered his mother's highest praise. "Good manners."

It startled him when Freydolf's voice came from right behind him. "He's never done that before!"

Although the statue seemed very tall to Tupper, the Pred was even bigger. He bent to peer into Brand's face, then prowled around the silent fire-bearer. Tupper trailed after him. Brand turned his head slightly to follow their movements with a quizzical expression.

Humming thoughtfully, Freydolf finally said, "Brand also serves as a guide. I suppose he could have been called upon to hold the hands of youngsters. That might explain it."

Tupper wasn't paying much attention. He was more interested in the statue's strange costume. Brand seemed to be wearing a feathered cape, but a sudden, crazy idea had him thinking hard. Pred were very different than Flox. Was it even possible?

Peeping around Brand's elbow to meet Freydolf's gaze, he blurted, "Are there men with wings?"

"That's a good question," his master replied, rubbing his chin. "Rumors are bandied about, but you can't believe half of them."

That wasn't a *yes* or a *no*, and Tupper frowned in confusion.

Freydolf explained, "The Keeper who carved most of the Statuary's fire-bearers was a Grif. Their people hail from the farthest continent, so it's difficult to confirm some of the more fantastical stories brought by merchants."

Tupper had never heard of the Grif, but he looked into

Brand's sharp-featured face with increasing interest. He wouldn't mind meeting a person with feathers, especially if they also had such a friendly smile.

Freydolf was still talking, but the boy only caught the end of his remark. "... like giving credence to widespread accounts of Pred having tails."

His eyes widened. Pred had tails?

Tupper had done his best to allow Freydolf privacy during bathtimes, but now he kind of wished he *had* peeked. Maybe the first of his three questions could be about tails? But then he realized that if *all* Pred had them, Aurelius could just as easily answer. It was no good.

A large hand landed atop his head. "What's on your mind, lambkin?"

Tupper cut to the chase. "You have a tail?"

The sculptor's bushy brows slowly climbed, and then Freydolf chuckled. "Nay, lambkin. What I meant to say was that hearsay is often false. Pred *don't* have tails, so I doubt Grif have wings."

Tupper nodded meekly. It was too bad, though.

"Aurelius probably knows, since he's been to the red mountain," Freydolf offered consolingly. "You should ask him ... perhaps at dinnertime? He's bound to spin the answer into a good story. Mind you, I'm not sure how much of it will be *true*."

The boy nodded, but he was only half-listening again. Questions for Aurelius came easily, but Tupper still didn't have any saved up for Freydolf. On top of that, he was feeling cheated. With a sad shake of his head, he sighed, "No tail."

"Lazy," Freydolf accused.

"Enterprising," Aurelius countered.

The sculptor's voice was serious, but his eyes twinkled in the lantern light. "You're also showing a *shocking* lack of chivalry."

"The lady hasn't complained once."

"Only because she *can't*."

Aurelius had returned a short time ago with his own fire-bearer, the statue of a graceful, feathered lady who balanced a wide basket atop her head with one taloned hand. The slender woman now carried all their baggage.

Tupper trailed after the two Pred, his fingertips resting lightly on Brand's. It wasn't that the boy *needed* his hand held, but playing along seemed to make the stone man happy. The tireless fire-bearer lofted the boy's lantern, illuminating the many statues they passed. Some were life-sized, but the majority took advantage of the spacious surroundings; they were larger than life.

Freydolf grunted and returned to a lecture that wasn't nearly as interesting as the friendly bickering. "There are twelve galleries that fan out from this central cavern. They're designated by the keystone set into each arch, but that's the extent of their organization."

"The Keepers made a mess," Aurelius complained. "This mountain is a maze, with intersecting passages winding back and forth, up and down."

"They're mapped," Freydolf countered.

"Not the *secret* passages!"

"Aye, there are those." Freydolf paused before a row of red statues and looked them over. "There aren't many on this level, and most of the ones we've found are locked."

"How many levels are there?" demanded Aurelius.

"It's hard to say," said Freydolf. "Several past masters were secretive, and most apprentices found ways to leave their own mark on Morven. There are hidden doors, half-levels, and off-shoots everywhere."

Aurelius eyed him curiously. "Did *you* have a pet project

back when you were apprenticed?"

Freydolf turned to Tupper and asked, "Which one shall I use, lambkin? You may choose."

Six fire-bearers stood along the wall, each unique. Brand helpfully raised his lantern so that Tupper could see, and the boy quickly sidled up to the smallest of the lot. There were no feathers, but it made Tupper happy to see another person with horns. He'd never seen someone with hooves for feet, though, and he crouched to examine the statue's goat-like lower half.

"This one?" he asked.

"Aye," Freydolf warmly agreed, passing along his lantern. "Wake the faun, then."

While Tupper gladly obeyed, Aurelius folded his arms over his chest. "You changed the subject. Did you think I wouldn't notice?"

Freydolf placed his hands on his hips and gazed around, completely ignoring his brother-in-law. "What color, lambkin?"

Tupper blinked. "Color?"

"Pick a stone, and pick the passage," his master urged. "Any of the twelve will do."

Aurelius sang out, "I won't let this go, Frey."

"Your hands are empty."

"So evasive!"

"I'm not hiding anything," said Freydolf.

"Morven hides it for you!" Aurelius accused.

Tupper traded smiles with the newly wakened fire-bearer. In their own way, the Pred seemed to be having fun. While their swift repartee added some liveliness to the otherwise silent chamber, the boy turned his thoughts to the stones. He'd learned them all, but choosing just one was hard. So instead of picking one, he asked for what he hoped Freydolf would like best. "White?"

His companions stopped mid-rebuttal, and Aurelius asked, "What was that, sprat?"

It seemed to Tupper that his master looked pleased, so he repeated himself with more confidence. "I want white."

Questions were *hard.*

Well, no. That wasn't quite right. Tupper's brows knit as he searched for the right words.

Good questions took cleverness.

Aurelius certainly made it look easy. He blithely led by example, plying Freydolf with all kinds of questions. Better ones than Tupper could have thought up. The boy found himself watching the merchant, hoping to learn the trick.

It was a little like bartering, but not for goods. Good questions netted the most interesting answers. Information, opinions, stories—Aurelius knew how to wheedle them out, and Freydolf shared generously from his store.

Aurelius paused in front of one of the numerous grottoes they'd been passing and tapped something carved into the wall beside it. "This one is his, as well?" he asked skeptically. "But the pattern varies widely from the last two!"

"Aye, he went through a geometric phase, but returned to his usual ferns after a few years. It's well documented." Freydolf smoothed his hand over the patterns that fanned out from the entrance. Each concentric band was roughly the same width, but unique from its neighbors.

Glancing at Tupper to include him in the conversation, Freydolf said, "These are signatures. They usually indicate workmanship or ownership. Often on larger pieces, these borders were added to the pedestal to show which journeymen and apprentices contributed their skills to the final sculpture."

"How can it be a *signature* if the pattern varies wildly depending on the mood of its maker?" scoffed Aurelius.

Freydolf shrugged. "There's usually something to distinguish it. For instance, *this* Keeper always includes at least one frog in his borders."

Aurelius grunted and moved on, but Tupper stayed long

enough to locate a pop-eyed tree frog half-hidden by the petals of a flower. He nodded, impressed. Aurelius was good at this!

"Coming, lambkin?" Freydolf called, poised at the bottom of a short set of stairs.

"Yes." Tupper padded after the men, pausing to make sure the bear cub could manage the steps. Aurelius was clever, and that's why the boy intended to follow his advice. The Pred had told him to pay close attention to Freydolf. That meant it was time to shift his focus.

Lagging behind as the path meandered deeper into the mountain, Tupper kept his gaze fixed on Freydolf with single-minded intensity. He would do his best to watch the man, though he wished he knew what he was looking for.

Freydolf was being his usual not-sculpting self—prone to rambling, quick to laugh, and happy to trade barbs with his younger brother. The man *liked* to talk, so he wasn't stingy with his answers. He probably wouldn't mind if Tupper's question wasn't clever.

They passed through a vaulted colonnade, followed a zigzagging set of stairs, then entered a hushed alcove graced by both a well and a necessary. Once everyone had availed themselves of the facilities, Freydolf shifted the well stone and peered downward. The little faun trotted over with his light, and the sculptor smiled at the red statue before announcing, "This one's full and smells fresh. Let's fill the canteen."

Aurelius plucked it from the basket atop his fire-bearer's head and tossed it over. Tupper hurried to help, and Freydolf offered him the rope to raise the bucket. While he pulled hand-over-hand, the boy noticed how different this well was from their usual one. Instead of being carved from Morven's gray stone, it was blue, and the well's sides were decorated with many borders, row upon row. Without too much trouble, Tupper spotted a tiny peep-frog, and he paused to give it a friendly poke.

"You're a fast learner," Freydolf remarked with a smile.

Tupper quickly shook his head, for he was *far* from clever. "I just like frogs."

"Aye," the sculptor replied, reaching into the well and hauling the bucket up the rest of the way. Wetting his fingertips, he christened the frog, who promptly reset delicate, webbed fingers tipped by sticky pads. "It's no hardship to learn more about something you already like."

When the wee frog cocked its head to one side, Tupper unconsciously did the same. Could it be as simple as that? With a soft gasp, the boy realized that there *was* something he wanted to know about Freydolf. He had his first question!

"So you like frogs?" Freydolf inquired.

Tupper's eyes widened, for he hadn't expected to be asked anything so personal. Did that mean his master was interested in him, too? A little giddy at the thought, he did his best to give a generous answer. Nodding three times for emphasis, he confessed, "Eensy green peepers are my favorite."

"And why's that?"

His face scrunched in thought. "They're small and cute."

Freydolf smiled. "Aye, I can see the appeal."

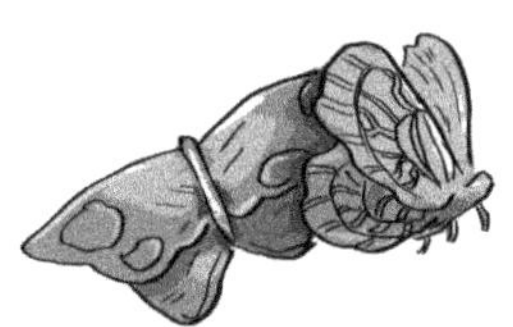

Tupper had sort of expected all the statues in the white passage to be white, but most were gray. He noticed that there were torch brackets and lantern hooks at regular intervals and wondered what the galleries would look like when lit. Wandering through the windowless darkness didn't bother him, but he felt a little sad for all the statues. They were tucked away where the moon couldn't reach them. Maybe their makers never woke them, so they didn't mind.

The boy had just spotted another stone frog on the border surrounding a niche when Aurelius demanded, "Are we lost?"

"We're exploring," Freydolf countered.

"But do you know where we *are*?"

"In a general sense."

"So we *are* lost!" Aurelius accused.

The sculptor waved his hand dismissively. "I wouldn't put it that way."

"You're the Keeper! You should be *ashamed* to be lost!"

"We're *not* lost," Freydolf calmly repeated. "Look there! See?"

They'd come to a place where the way split, and the master sculptor reached up to touch a white stone set into the wall. All three fire-bearers helpfully lifted their lanterns, so Tupper could see that there were shapes carved into its smooth surface.

Freydolf pointed to the left. "This will take us straight to where the white gallery ends on the far side ..."

"*Straight*," scoffed Aurelius.

Ignoring the snide remark, Freydolf indicated the right-hand path. "And this leads into the dapple gallery, should you be anxious to turn back."

Aurelius's golden eyes skimmed across the markings on the white stone, then conceded, "Aye, so it does."

Tupper stared in confusion at the series of crisscrossing lines on the plaque. They didn't look like a map, yet the Pred seemed able to read them.

Freydolf turned to Tupper and asked, "What do you think? Forward or back?"

The boy shrugged, willing to trust the decision to his master. All that really mattered to him was that he had a second question safely tucked away for dinnertime.

When they reached the end of the gallery, a long, circular tunnel spilled out into an open chamber easily three stories high. Windows took up a large portion of the far wall, and Freydolf strolled over to peer through water-streaked panes. Gray curtains of rain isolated them from the rest of the world, hiding what would have been an impressive view.

"The worst is over," remarked Frey.

Aurelius was gazing intently at the room's imposing occupants. Two towering warriors stood guard at opposite ends of the room—great, gray men armed with broad-bladed spears. Golden lions reclined at their feet. "Day and night guard?"

"Aye, if it weren't for the rain, the lions would be prowling by now," said Freydolf.

Tupper pointed to man and beast. "Moonlight, sunlight."

"Which way do these windows face?" Aurelius asked curiously.

"South south-west," he replied, letting his fingertips rest against the window. "The White Mountain is that way."

"Can you see it?" Tupper asked, going up on tiptoe to peer past the window ledge.

"Nay, it's many days' journey," Freydolf replied. "We're far from the sea here."

"Let's take a break," Aurelius proposed, beckoning his fire-bearer forward. "I'm feeling peckish."

"I could eat." Freydolf turned to find Tupper still hovering at his elbow. Crouching down, he asked, "Do you see any doors besides the one we came through?"

His servant glanced around and answered, "No."

"There are actually *three*," Freydolf confided. "See if you can find where they're hidden."

When the lad darted off, Aurelius waved for Frey to join him on the newly-spread picnic blanket and handed him a goblet. While they watched Tupper make a slow circuit of the large room, Aurelius asked, "How long has it been since you were this far from your den?"

Freydolf snorted. "Den?"

"It's an apt description since you hole up there for months on end." Aurelius pressed, "So?"

"Quite a while," Freydolf admitted. He smiled when Tupper resorted to trailing his hand along the wall as he walked, still searching for the exits.

"How long?"

Thinking back, Freydolf replied, "Four years."

"You shouldn't immure yourself completely in your work."

"It's all I have."

Huffing softly, Aurelius countered, "*Had.* You may want to consider changing these quadrennial tours to quarterly ones. Spend time with that boy. Teach him his way around." With unsubtle nonchalance, he added, "It wouldn't hurt for him to feel *at home* here."

"I wouldn't mind."

Restlessness between projects sometimes drove Freydolf into the galleries, where his brooding couldn't frighten whatever servant was currently in residence. But those solitary forays rarely satisfied him. The change of scenery was nice, but he vastly preferred days like today, when he could share the journey with others.

"I know you're enamored of rocks, but it's pitiful that your most longstanding relationships are with Brand and Graven."

Reaching for some bread, Frey let his gaze drift toward the fire-bearers who waited next to the tunnel entrance. "And you."

"Which shows a *scant* modicum of sense on your part," Aurelius haughtily rejoined.

Pleased at the prospect of introducing Tupper to the many wonders that Morven held, Freydolf took a long drink from his goblet, then amiably jibed, "Nay. *That* would have to be desperation."

Doors could be tricky! Tupper's search had a poor beginning because he started out looking for the kinds of doors he was used to. There were no rectangular entrances with hinges, lintels, knobs, or thresholds *anywhere* in the vast room. When his first reconnoiter came up empty, he made a slower, closer inspection, trailing his fingers along the walls as he looked for a seam.

A quick peek in his master's direction showed that Freydolf

wasn't in a hurry. He and Aurelius lounged under one of the tall windows, talking animatedly. Once again, he was glad for the chance to unravel the puzzle at his own pace. Farley was quick, Rachel was clever, and Aggie was lucky. *They* probably would have been done already.

It took many minutes, and the only reason Tupper found the first door was because a frog sat upon its handle. When he gave the old croaker on his lily pad a friendly poke, a squat panel swung silently on an invisible pivot point.

"Over here, Freydolf! I found one!" he called, totally forgetting to properly address his master.

"Very good! Do you want to come and eat before you hunt down the next?"

Tupper shook his head, determined to finish his quest. "Two more doors," he whispered to himself, renewing his search.

He discovered the next one near one of the stately warriors. A repeating pattern of arches decorated the entire wall behind his post, and a faint crack rimmed one of the tall, narrow sections. After some pushing and pulling, Tupper discovered the trick to making it slide to one side, revealing a wide tunnel.

As he peered into the darkness beyond, Brand came over, lantern at the ready.

"Did you know this was here?" Tupper asked.

The red statue's smile seemed wise.

Tupper shook a finger at him and warned, "No hints."

Brand inclined his head.

Circling the room twice more yielded nothing useful, so the boy struck out across the floor, thinking hard. A door in a window didn't seem likely. Could there be one in a statue? But where would it lead? Frowning in concentration, Tupper drifted over to one of the great, golden felines, gasped, then trotted triumphantly over to Freydolf. "Three!"

"You found them?" His master hauled himself to his feet and invited, "Let's have a look."

Delighted by the chance to show off his newfound knowledge, Tupper first led the way to the tall, narrow door, then to the squat one with its lily pad handle.

When he darted toward the third, Freydolf called, "Where are you going, lambkin? The last door is this way."

He was pointing to the opposite corner from where the boy was headed.

Tupper's heart sank. He was wrong? Slowly shaking his head, he said, "I found one, but I can't open it."

"Show me."

Nodding, Tupper led the man to the lion, then crouched before the beast and pointed to a spot beneath its near paw. Freydolf looked surprised. Maybe a door in the floor didn't count?

"I had no idea this was here!" He knelt to drag the tip of one of his claws along the visible cracks. "It's well-guarded."

Since Freydolf sounded pleased, Tupper relaxed. "Is it good?"

"Aye," the sculptor assured. "We'll have to come back on a sunny day in order to see where it leads."

"Save it for a *winter* wander," Aurelius interjected. The other Pred had slipped up behind them and stood with arms decorously folded across his chest. Freydolf shot him a stern look, but the agent only yawned and drawled, "It was *merely* a suggestion."

Tupper wasn't sure why Aurelius had earned a scolding, but his imagination was already spinning ahead to wintertime, when icy winds and heavy snows made life hard. Rainy days in a small house were bad enough; the long weeks of winter were far worse. He'd always disliked being cooped up, but that was impossible here. With a wondering gaze that took in the spacious room, Tupper murmured, "Long walks with no snow!"

Freydolf said, "Aye, lambkin... unless you find a door in the ceiling as well."

Back in the Cavern, they reclaimed their lanterns and a much-lightened load from the three fire-bearers. In the hallway beyond, Freydolf gently upturned the bear cub so her water reserve poured out. Setting her in her niche, the sculptor waited with Tupper until she lifted her paw as if to bid them farewell, then stilled.

"Won't she be lonely?" the boy asked wistfully.

"Not while she's sleeping," he assured.

The stroll back into increasingly familiar territory was monopolized by Aurelius, who could wax eloquent on any subject. To Freydolf's chagrin, the man's current topic was ... *him.*

"You listen to me, sprat. The twelve mountains are miraculous places, and their Keepers are venerable souls at the pinnacle of their craft. The acclaim of every master sculptor reaches to the farthest corner of the four continents!"

Tupper's brow creased, and he turned an uncertain gaze upon Freydolf. "Are you important?"

While Aurelius held his sides, Freydolf tried to formulate an answer that would make sense to the boy. He certainly didn't consider himself a person of any importance, yet there was no denying his unique position. Diminishing his role was tantamount to insulting the mountain he'd sworn to protect.

With a sigh, Freydolf grudgingly answered, "Important? Aye, perhaps to Morven."

"Oh, he's *famous.* Frey's the first Pred in history to heed a mountain's call ... and prolific to boot! He is both oddity and commodity!"

"Call?" Tupper echoed, looking mystified.

"Aye, it's a *noble* call, a *miraculous* gift, a *prestigious* honor!" the merchant said grandly. "This man is one of the rare few willing to pledge their lives to a heap of rock. The lords of every land know his name, praise his skill, and covet his handiwork!"

Freydolf was annoyed by his brother-in-law's ridiculous cant. He might spin such yarns for customers, but what was the point in heaping this nonsense on Tupper? Even if his name counted for something in the court of some far-off nobility, the sculptor would still eat mush every morning and chip away at stone long into the night.

"Are you trying to sell the lad something?" he asked waspishly. Freydolf didn't want his prestige to influence Tupper's opinion of him any more than he'd wanted his heritage to intimidate the boy.

Aurelius smirked. "He needs to know."

"To what end?" He'd always been uncomfortable with boasting. Wasn't it enough that his statues pleased those who looked upon them?

"Idiot," Aurelius chided. Peering haughtily at Tupper, he announced, "These mountains don't take a fancy to just anyone. Morven wanted Frey for her own, and he accepted her call. In *most* cases, the sacrifice involved is balanced by rewards in abundance."

Tupper peeked up at his master, then nodded tentatively.

Aurelius went on to archly decree, "At least *one* person in these parts should know Frey's worth and give him his due. For lack of other prospects, this duty falls to you, sprat."

Freydolf was mortified. "See here! I neither *want* nor *need* ...!"

Cutting him off without so much as a glance, his brother-in-law fixed Tupper with an assessing look and tersely inquired, "How much of that did you grasp?"

"Not much," the boy admitted.

"Which parts made sense?" Aurelius patiently prompted.

With a slight uptilt of his small chin, Tupper gravely replied, "Master Freydolf wants you to be quiet."

14

His Due

The fountain with its trio of ladies came into view, and Aurelius dropped lantern and baggage outside the door to the necessary. Rounding on Freydolf, he demanded, "What about my wine rack?"

"You need it *now*?"

"I'd *have* it now if you'd brought it along when I asked," Aurelius retorted peevishly.

"It was heavy!"

"You're sturdy," the man rejoined, waving vaguely at the sculptor's broad shoulders. "You lug rocks around for a living. What's one inconsequential little shelf?"

"If you think back, you might recall that it took *both* of us to shift that 'little shelf' into the passage. Carrying it was out of the question."

"Surely a sanctuary dedicated to stone contains the means to transport it!"

With a weary shake of his head, Freydolf said, "Aye, there's a cart in one of the storerooms. I'll go back for your precious wine rack if you'll start dinner."

Aurelius considered the offer, then countered, "I want my bath first."

Demanding as ever.

"I don't mind," he sighed, glancing toward Tupper.

The boy straightened. "I'll check the fire."

When he darted into the necessary, Freydolf muttered, "At least offer to help the lad tote well water."

Aurelius said, "Your little liege is young; he'll be fine. Youthful vigor, and all that."

Freydolf grimaced but let it go. It *was* the boy's job, and Tupper took his work seriously. He probably wouldn't thank either Pred for interfering. "Aye, I'll be off then."

Picking up the lantern, he strode purposefully along the columned passage. Lost in thought, it took several moments for Freydolf to register the patter of bare feet coming up behind him.

He stopped and turned just in time for a small body to collide with his leg. Lifting his lantern, Freydolf stared in surprise at Tupper, whose eyes were tight-shut as he hugged his master's leg. "Lambkin? What's wrong? Did something frighten you?"

"No."

Mystified, Freydolf asked, "Then, what's this about?"

"It's thank you."

The lad had been in such a hurry, he hadn't even brought his lantern. Freydolf could see it in the distance, still sitting on the floor in front of the necessary. Scratching awkwardly at the back of his neck, Frey asked, "For what?"

"Not *for*," Tupper answered. "*From*."

Puzzled, Freydolf fished for more information. "From you?"

"From Morven." The sculptor's brows shot up, but the lad wasn't done. "She must be happy."

Freydolf's throat tightened. "Aye, but ... why?"

"She has you."

With a final, fierce squeeze, Tupper whirled and dashed back the way he'd come. Thoroughly blindsided and beyond speechless, Freydolf stared after him, but it was hard to follow the retreating figure in the darkness. Not with the prickle of unshed tears blurring his vision.

Tupper had done it again, giving him just what he needed, probably without even knowing how much it meant.

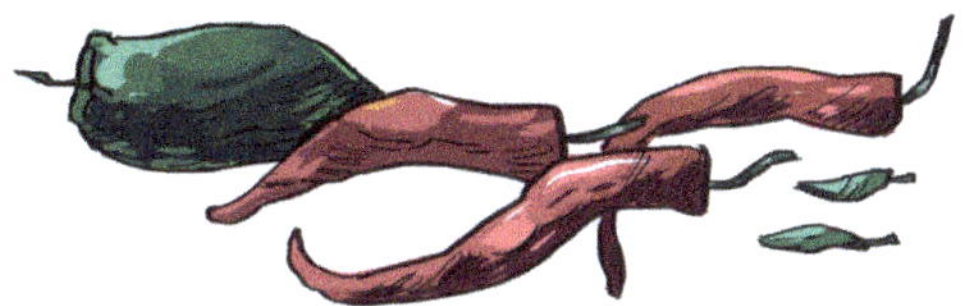

When Freydolf returned, dropping his damp cloak onto its hook, he found dinner already arrayed on the table and Tupper in his seat. Setting aside his lantern, the sculptor asked, "Where's Aurelius?"

The boy looked at the orange door in the corner, and the other Pred waltzed through as if on cue. A scant few hours remained before bedtime, yet the man had taken great care with his attire. Every ruffle and tuck was arranged, which accounted for the upswing in Aurelius's mood.

"Welcome home!" he exclaimed magnanimously. "What kept you? We've been anxiously awaiting your presence!"

"I was checking the horses," Freydolf admitted.

Aurelius quirked a brow. "I already took care of them."

"Aye, I noticed," he murmured. His brother-in-law might not look very reliable, but he wasn't neglectful. He tended to his own. "Something smells good."

"Toast," Tupper said, pulling back the corner of a cloth-covered platter. An entire loaf had been sliced and browned to perfection.

"And *I* made the soup."

Freydolf knew all Aurelius had done was open a jar and warm its contents, but he wasn't going to quibble. He was too grateful for a hot meal. Dropping onto his chair, he held out his bowl. "To the brim, please, and toss in a few of those peppers."

The first few minutes of the meal passed in relative silence, but Freydolf noted some nonverbal communication taking place between Aurelius and Tupper. His brother-in-law seemed to be signaling the boy, who was in turn concentrating on his soup bowl. Not until he'd swallowed the last drop did Tupper sit back and fix Freydolf with a solemn gaze.

Without preamble, the lad asked, "Was your front step white?"

Both Pred stilled, exchanged a glance, then focused on the boy again. Aurelius reached for his napkin and blotted a sly smile, leaving Freydolf to clear his throat and point out, "The threshold here is *gray*, lambkin."

Tupper squirmed and tried again. "My front step is gray because Morven is gray, but your mountain was white. Is it different there?"

The sheer length of the lad's statement was staggering, and it took a moment for Freydolf to pick up his jaw. "I see," he managed awkwardly.

Freydolf fiddled with his spoon as he thought back to a time when the afternoon sun bounced off white cobbles and merchants called to passersby from under the brightly patterned canopies that stretched over walkways leading through bazaars. Ulrica had fit in so well, with her vivid silks, jeweled combs, and coins jingling at her wrists and ankles. She'd swirled through the busy streets, and he'd trailed after, feeling dull by comparison. The family failure. The shameful son.

Home wasn't a place he'd lingered, but Freydolf remembered its threshold well enough. He'd loved it for its uncommon color, its soft voice, and its subtle promise that somewhere far away, other mountains beckoned.

"Aye, it was different there," Freydolf said. "There was white stone everywhere in the city where I was raised, but front steps were different. Ours was a spoil of war."

"Everyone who's anyone has a foreign threshold," confirmed Aurelius. "Raze their walls; seize their stones! Take their breath; leave their bones!"

Tupper shook his head. "I don't understand."

"War, lambkin," Freydolf gently explained. "My great-great-grandfather raided Far Continent many years ago, and as proof of his conquest, he carried home a threshold, probably from some fine house or public building."

"Why?"

"So the ones he defeated would always be under his heel." With a sigh, Freydolf muttered, "And that was just the *front* door. Every generation went to war, some more than once."

"Is it true that your house contained trophies from all twelve mountains?" Aurelius pried.

"None of the old families would discredit such a rumor." Freydolf eyebrows lifted. "I'm shocked you didn't poke your nose into every corner once Ulrica brought you home."

"Your father's a scary, scary man. He warned me not to snoop."

"How many varieties *did* you locate?"

"Five."

"Not bad," Freydolf conceded. "All told, the house boasts spoils from seven mountains. And as much as I hated the stories behind their acquisition, they were my favorite part of home."

"Counting our starstone, you already had a strong affinity for eight of the mountains," Aurelius mused aloud.

"Aye." Turning back to Tupper, Freydolf finally answered, "Pink. I grew up with a front step that loved the dawn."

Tupper hadn't expected his littlest question to receive such a big answer. Pred had strange traditions, but he was glad Freydolf had grown up surrounded by stones of many colors. That part sounded nice, but the rest made the man sad. Maybe it would be best to ask a new question so that he could move on.

Aurelius caught his eye and raised a finger, then nodded, and Tupper was delighted. His first question had been accepted!

Buoyed by this initial success, he leaned forward and patted the table. Freydolf noticed, and once eye contact was established, Tupper asked, "Were the scratches on the wall letters?"

Just like the last time, his master's eyes widened, but he answered more quickly, mumbling around a bite of toast. "In another language, yes." He took the time to chew and swallow before explaining. "I get along fairly well in two, and I know bits and pieces of the others. Aurelius is the linguist, though. He's paid to be fluent."

Tupper had guessed that the strange markings in the galleries were some kind of cipher, but this was even more than he could have imagined.

Aurelius looked amused. "You lost him at *language*, Frey. The concept of foreign tongues probably never even occurred to him."

"Demonstrate?" the sculptor suggested.

Propping his chin on his hand, Aurelius let loose with a string of gibberish. The crisp patter was utter nonsense, but Tupper leaned forward, not wanting to miss any of the foreign words.

When Aurelius finished his monologue with a little flourish, Freydolf snorted. "Only *you* could be long-winded in Terse."

Aurelius preened. "It's a gift."

Tupper gaped. It had been a stretch to imagine lands where all the stones were red, blue, or green. Now, he was trying to wrap his head around the idea that in different places, people used different words.

Freydolf said, "Those notations in the passage were in Terse, the language of Far Continent. On this continent, we read and write in what's called Verit. Bring my sketchbook, and I'll show you."

Tupper hurried to comply.

Pushing aside his bowl and shoving the last of a piece of toast into his mouth, Freydolf opened to a fresh page and slipped a charcoal pencil from its small sleeve. Using block letters, he scrawled **TUPPER MEADOWSWEET** across the top of the page. Underneath, he carefully etched a series of sharp, overlapping lines. "That's *Tupper* in Terse."

Crowding close, the boy watched him add a different set of characters under his last name. "Meadowsweet?" he guessed.

"Aye."

"Now yours," Tupper prompted.

Chuckling softly, the sculptor wrote **FREYDOLF** on the page, adding the Terse equivalent beneath.

The lad reached out and tapped the page. "You forgot *Meadowsweet*," he prompted, wanting to see him make the letters again. When Freydolf didn't move, he glanced up and sheepishly added, "Please?"

Freydolf's eyes were downcast, and he looked extremely uncomfortable.

Tupper was nervous that he'd inadvertently done something wrong and looked to Aurelius.

The other Pred was staring hard at his brother-in-law. "Frey?" he inquired sweetly. "Did the sprat give you his name?"

"He did."

"Does he have any idea what that means?"

"Nay."

Asking questions was much more dangerous than Tupper could have imagined. Things *happened* when their answers came to light. Wanting to defend his master, he tried to explain. "His was gone, so I shared mine. Is that bad?"

Aurelius held up a finger, demanding silence, his shrewd gaze still fixed on Freydolf. "His offer appeals to you?"

The man's eyes slid shut, and he muttered, "What do you think?"

"I doubt you could do worse." Aurelius plucking the pencil from Freydolf's limp hand and extended it to Tupper. "Not *bad*, sprat. Ludicrous, preposterous, and in arguably poor taste by Pred standards ... but not *bad*. Several generations of Rakefangs may howl in their graves, but their loss is your gain."

Tupper accepted the pencil with a tentative nod.

Aurelius pointed to the page. "You must be the one to add your name to his. Can you write?"

"Yes." With the greatest care, he added his last name. Then, he slowly copied out the strange pattern of lines that spelled Meadowsweet in Terse. Stepping back, he asked, "Is that good?"

"This will do nicely." Aurelius whisked away the book and removed the page, then imperiously held out his hand. Tupper returned the pencil and circled the table to watch the agent add several lines to the bottom of the page.

Witnessed on this, the fortieth day of the third season ...

Loopy letters detailed the year by Pred reckoning, which was followed by an extravagant signature.

Aurelius hummed in satisfaction, then looked to Freydolf. "Blood to bind?"

"I'd rather not," the man said with a pained expression.

Casting about, Aurelius snapped his fingers and reached for the open jar of his wife's peppers. "These are near as strong and close as kin. Share one of these, and I'll consider the matter settled."

Tupper couldn't stay quiet any longer. "Is this a bargain?"

"Aye. Are you concerned about the terms?"

"Maybe." He glanced at Freydolf, who was being unusually quiet. "Say it so I can understand."

Without a word of complaint, Aurelius explained. "It's very sad for a Pred to have no name. Frey must have been very glad when you said you would share. This paper will prove that someone wants him." Placing his hand lightly on the document, he added, "Where we come from, it's rare to offer such a gift."

"Master Freydolf?" Tupper waited patiently for the man to lift his gaze. Then he asked, "Do you like this bargain?"

"Aye, lambkin."

Nodding once, the boy said, "I accept."

"Then to finalize the matter, take a bite off of one of Ulrica's finest. Frey will finish the rest, and what's done is done."

Tupper accepted the pepper, took a deep breath, and crunched down on the spicy vegetable. His eyes were already watering when he held out the rest to Freydolf, but he could hear Aurelius just fine.

"Let it be known that Freydolf is no longer an outcast. His strength has been added to the clan Meadowsweet of the village of Hayward in the shadow of Morven, where Flox do reside. He is vouchsafed by one Tupper Meadowsweet, his newly-sworn... ah."

"Must you?" Freydolf asked in aggrieved tones.

"Oh, I *must*!" Aurelius laughed and said, "I was just wondering if I should say *mother*."

"Spare us a little dignity," the sculptor grumbled.

"Aye." Once Tupper downed the contents of his mug, Aurelius leaned close to confide, "According to our traditions, this makes Frey your brother."

Freydolf accepted a brimming goblet from Aurelius and watched with interest as his brother-in-law presented Tupper with a squat mug of sweet cider. The lad had already cleared away the remnants of their meal, but Aurelius had urged them all to sit tight, then returned with libations. With sugared nuts and sliced pears, they were settled in for a celebratory dessert course.

The sculptor was mildly surprised that his brother-in-law hadn't insisted on moving to the balcony, where the chairs were more comfortable, but if Aurelius wanted to prolong the dinner hour, he was content to linger. His gaze drifted back to Tupper, who'd carried over Olexi even though there wasn't any starlight to wake him. It was as if the lad wanted to keep everything he liked best close by.

Glancing through the kitchen door to the cluttered workshop beyond, Freydolf figured he understood the feeling. When you didn't have much, what little you had was precious.

Out of the corner of his eye, Frey caught a flicker of movement and turned to find Aurelius holding up two fingers.

Tupper seemed to find significance in the gesture, and Freydolf's curiosity was piqued. "Two what?"

Aurelius smiled serenely. "I just realized that this contract is in Verit *and* Terse, so it's binding on two continents!"

He knew the man wasn't telling the whole truth, but he didn't have time to press the issue. Tupper patted the table again, calling for attention. The sculptor was a little surprised by the seemingly sudden shift in the boy's manner, but maybe the young Flox was simply becoming comfortable enough to express himself.

Freydolf was rather charmed. "What now?" he invited with an amiable smile.

"I want to know," Tupper began, knotting his fingers together as he fumbled for words. With a small frown, he started over. "One liked frogs. Another had ferns. And another made feathered people. What do *you* do?"

The sculptor once more reached for the sketchbook. "I'll show you!"

Tupper hopped from his chair and hurried to his master's side, flatteringly interested in a simple sketch.

Freydolf took the time to add a bit of shading, then tilted the book for the boy to see. "My borders always incorporate at least one of these."

Tupper cocked his head to one side. "What is it?"

Freydolf blinked, for even if it was quickly made, his drawing was better than fair. "It's a *shell*, lambkin."

"Oh, a shell," the boy replied vaguely. Twirling his finger to imitate its tapering whorls, he said, "It's pretty."

"Collecting these was the closest I ever came to being a hunter. When I was a boy, I spent a lot of time on the shore."

Again, Tupper's brow creased. "Of a stream? We don't have those in our streams."

Suddenly, Freydolf realized they'd run up against a rather large cultural gap. With a measure of chagrin, he asked, "Haven't you heard of the ocean?"

The lad's eyes narrowed in thought. "Old Gruff sometimes talks about a place with water as wide as the plains. Ewert figures he made it up. But Farley likes the idea, so he says it's true."

"The ocean's real," Freydolf assured, wishing he could show the lad.

Aurelius drummed his fingers on the table, then rearranged a few of the dishes. "I come from a long line of voyagers, and I've traveled more than most," he announced with great authority. Touching the open tin of nuts, he said, "Let's say this is our continent, home to the Pred, Drom, and Flox. Three of the twelve mountains are located here—white, gold, and gray."

Tupper nodded, and muttered, "Verit."

"Aye, we all speak Verit," Aurelius agreed, then tapped the plate of pears. "*This* is known as the First Continent. It's the biggest land mass and quite tropical. The blue, green, and crystal mountains are found there."

The boy nodded, then looked expectantly at the Pred. "Far?"

"So you *were* paying attention!" praised Aurelius. He flicked the rim of his goblet, which was somewhat removed from the dishes at the center of the table. "Far Continent boasts the red, pink, and orange mountains."

"Terse."

"Correct again," he acknowledged, then pointed to the small dish set a little higher than the others. "And to the north is the smallest continent, usually referred to as Last Continent. It's cold there most of the year, but worth the trip if you're fond of precious metals. The brown, dapple, and dazzle mountains are there." He pointed to each representation once more, listing, "Home, First, Far, Last ... and everything *between* these four is water. This is the ocean Frey remembers so fondly."

"Ocean," Tupper murmured, trailing his fingers between the dishes. Turning to Freydolf again, he asked, "You lived next to lots of water?"

"Aye. I grew up in a port city, a place visited by many of the ships that traveled across the ocean."

"Like carriages?"

For lack of a better means of explanation, Freydolf began sketching. As he and Aurelius took turns explaining, he illustrated their conversation—ships and shores, decks and docks, porpoises and pelicans. With deft strokes of charcoal, he recreated a world where the air smelled of salt and seaweed, and where the inconstant sea was a constant presence.

"... and the waves rush and roar, carrying hidden treasures up onto the land."

"Like shells?" asked Tupper.

"Aye." Freydolf recreated several from memory. "They come in all manner of shapes, colors, and sizes. Some tiny as pebbles, but perfect in every detail; others large enough to use as bowls for fruit."

"I prefer the ones with pearls nestled inside," said Aurelius. "Treasures within treasures."

Tupper leaned into Freydolf's side, and begged, "What else?"

The Pred obligingly drew more things from the life he'd left behind—wise-eyed turtles, long-legged sea birds, horned whales, and whiskered seals. Aurelius suggested other oddments, like jellyfish, sea stars, and crabs.

With a sorrowful shake of his head, Tupper said, "There's nothing like that here."

"Nay." Aurelius watched Freydolf. "This mountain is about as far from the sea as a body can get."

"Too bad," the lad sighed.

"Because you want to see it for yourself?" his master guessed.

Tupper glanced between the many scattered pages covering the table and Freydolf and shook his head. Pressing his hand over the Pred's aching heart, the boy answered, "Because you miss it so much."

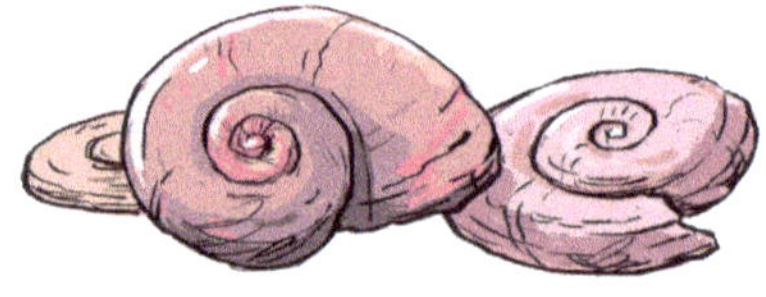

Aurelius called an end to the evening when Tupper nodded off at the table, one flushed cheek pressed against the drawing of the merchant vessel in which he sailed across the seas, bound for distant mountains on Freydolf's behalf. "Shall I put him to bed?" he offered.

"I'll manage," Frey replied, scooping up the boy and striding into the next room.

"Not much to him," Aurelius remarked as he followed.

"Aye," Freydolf agreed, for the limp child was naught but a featherweight. "Do you think he eats enough?"

"Probably." With a smirk, the Pred said, "I worry more about *you* than him, though less so this year. I can't *wait* to tell Ulrica about your little mother."

Freydolf tucked in his servant, then brushed at the smudge of charcoal on his cheek. "She'll laugh."

"Long and loud." Clapping the sculptor's shoulder Aurelius

said, "Goodnight, *Meadowsweet*."

With a grunt of acknowledgment, Freydolf drew shut the bed curtain and turned to face the familiar room. After all the day's events, he was too keyed up to sleep; however, the golden stone wasn't really tugging at him. His fingers twitched as new inspiration took hold, and he knew exactly which stone he wanted.

"Where did I put you?"

Lighting the lantern that hung over the largest of his workbenches, he rummaged around on its cluttered surface. Ages ago, he'd tucked the fragment away for a rainy day ... or a rainy night, in this case.

Freydolf worried that the stone might have been lifted by one of Tupper's predecessors, but he finally found it safe and sound in one of the many drawers that were better for losing things than organizing them.

"Aye, I can see it," he murmured, turning over a small chunk of dawnstone. "You'll be beautiful!"

He dragged a stool from under the bench and sat. With a dreamy smile on his face, he plucked tools from among those close to hand and set to work. Within minutes, his whole world narrowed until there was only the circle of lamplight, the persistent patter of rain against dark windows, and the stone in his hands. Tiny taps. Strategic nicks. Patient polishing. Caught up in his creation, Freydolf persevered until his eyes burned and his back complained.

Sunrise wasn't far off when he stood and stretched cramped muscles. Holding a tiny replica between thumb and forefinger, he inspected its graceful lines and smiled. "Aye ... beautiful," he whispered.

Compared to what Tupper had given, this small token was nothing, but he suspected the lad would appreciate his gift's significance.

Tupper reached for Olexi before he was completely awake, and when his questing hand came up empty, he pushed to his knees and patted around. The little ram *always* stayed with him! Had he fallen off the bed during the night?

Then, he remembered that rain had prevented Olexi from waking. He was probably still on the kitchen table.

Releasing his breath in a gusty whoosh, Tupper poked his head past the tapestry curtain to check on the weather outside and found something unexpected. Someone had placed his little guardian in his usual spot on the window ledge nearest his bed, and there was something else next to him.

The boy jumped down and went up on tiptoe to inspect the new item. Although he was no expert, he was certain that the delicate pink carving was perfect in every detail.

Picking it up with great care, he held it to his heart. Collecting Olexi as well, he trotted across the room.

Freydolf sprawled across his pallet, blankets askew, still dressed in his clothes, an arm flung over his eyes to block out the dim morning light. Without hesitation, Tupper climbed up next to him and shook his shoulder.

One of the man's eyelids cracked open.

The boy showed him what he'd found. "You made this?"

"Aye," Freydolf replied, his deep voice husky.

"Last night?"

His master hummed an indistinct affirmative.

Tupper leaned closer and whispered, "It's a *shell*!"

With a crooked smile, Freydolf repeated, "Aye."

"Is it mine?"

"If you want it."

Tupper nodded eagerly, then threw caution to the wind. With a clumsy flop, he draped himself over the big man's broad chest and squeezed. Freydolf was much larger than Papa had ever been, so it was like hugging a boulder ... or a haystack ... or one of the oldtrees ... except not as hard, prickly, or rough. Just big.

With a grunt, Freydolf complained, "See here, lad ...!"

Thinking he'd probably done something a servant shouldn't, Tupper quickly pulled back, mumbling, "Sorry."

Just as quickly, the Pred hooked one of his nubs and tugged him back down. "I don't mind *this*, lambkin. It's the *gouging* that's hard to take, so mind those horns of yours!"

"I'll be more careful," he promised.

Freydolf patted his head.

Tupper pushed up and sat on his heels. Turning the daintily spiraled shell this way and that, he said, "Thank you."

"Nay, thank *you*."

Tupper understood, then. Freydolf was giving him the shell because he had given his name. With a bashful smile, he confided, "I like sharing a shell better than sharing a pepper."

"Aye." The man draped his arm back over his face and yawned before mildly announcing, "But this cot is too small for sharing. Back to your own bed."

"But it's time to make breakfast."

"Have mercy, little mother," Freydolf begged. "I want more sleep!"

Tupper hesitated, looking between his master and the shell. Willing to compromise, he countered, "I will let you sleep if you will let me stay."

The man's eye opened again. "Are you *haggling*?"

"Yes."

With a low chuckle, Freydolf said, "Do as you please, lambkin. Just do it quietly."

Tupper tiptoed off, but he returned within minutes, reclaiming his spot on Freydolf's bed. For the rest of the morning, the boy played in a blanket-bound fortress, leaning against the sleeping man's warm bulk and playing with an assortment of stone figurines borrowed from the balcony, a stoically still Olexi, and one perfect, pink shell.

15

Stringers and Garlands

The following day dawned clear and bright. Right after breakfast, Freydolf started in on the golden stone, and Aurelius collared Tupper. "Stay with me, sprat. I have a plan."

With an obedient nod, the boy followed the Pred outside. He had to jog to keep up with the tall man's brisk pace, which carried them to one of the buildings alongside the stable. Aurelius opened a narrow door and withdrew a long pole tipped by a wicked-looking blade. Propping it over his shoulder, he struck a pose ... and held it.

Tupper belatedly realized this was his cue. "Are you going hunting?"

"*We*," Aurelius corrected. "And fish shall be our prey."

Fish sounded good, but Tupper wasn't sure how you could catch them with such a strange weapon. He held his tongue, though; he wanted to see the Pred use it. Rather excited about Aurelius's plan, the boy followed him along the road that led toward the quarry.

At the end of the first zig, right before it zagged, Aurelius stepped off the cobblestones and onto a narrow track leading downhill. He'd obviously been here many times before, for he slipped confidently through the bracken, silent as a shadow.

Tupper did his best to emulate his stealthy manner, but it

was hard to walk softly when the steep slope required him to hop from one mossy surface to the next. Even if the green stones offered a springy landing, he couldn't quite help the soft *oof* that accompanied his landings. Maybe that's why Farley was the family huntsman. Tupper's brother was better at being sneaky.

With his thoughts on his siblings back home, Tupper didn't look before his next leap, and he yelped in surprise when he stepped into thin air.

Aurelius, who'd been watching for him below, let his spear drop and neatly caught him. "Awake now?" he inquired in mocking tones.

Heart thudding and eyes wide, the boy gasped, "Yes."

"I suggest you keep what wits you have a little closer to the forefront of your mind." Aurelius set him on his feet and retrieved his weapon. "Don't you know this mountain at all?"

"Not this side."

"Morven is Frey's home and yours. If I were you, I'd learn her inside and out ... starting with the *out*," said Aurelius. "The contents of the Statuary may be splendid, but you need what's *here* more. For instance, there are three different streams at an easy distance, and all of them have fish. They're Frey's best chance for meat. Assuming you're teachable."

"I *can* fish."

Aurelius's eyebrows lifted. "Can you?"

"Yes," he stoutly affirmed.

The Pred lifted a hand for silence, then tapped his ear. Tupper tipped his head to one side, listening.

Not far ahead, he could hear the sound of rushing water.

With a smirk, Aurelius gestured for him to lead the way and challenged, "Show me."

Aurelius doffed his finery and knotted his hair. The Pred radiated self-assurance as he poised upon a flat stone midstream, clad in nothing but breeches and bronzed skin. Tupper had never seen someone with so many weapons—matched daggers, gleaming spear, and all those claws. Squatting on the broad, pebbled bank, the boy watched with undisguised awe.

This stream was perfect for fishing, with deep, shadowy spots near the bends and wide, sun-sparked shallows on the straightaways. According to Aurelius, there were several smaller branches and even a few waterfalls. Tupper promised himself a hike along the brooks to find the best fishing holes before winter halted any outdoor explorations.

Sleek, speckled shadows wove back and forth, swimming against the current. Aurelius remained completely still, eyes intent; Tupper thought he looked like a coiled snake gathered to strike.

Suddenly, the spear flashed, impaling a fat fish and lifting it from the water. As his prey struggled weakly on the end of the spear, Aurelius asked, "Care to try?"

"Yes," Tupper stood and rolled up his pant legs.

"Ever used one of these?" Aurelius indicated the spear.

"No." He waded out into the clear, cold water. "But I don't need it."

"If you say so, sprat." The Pred dropped into a crouch. "Do Flox herd their fishes?"

Knowing it would be easier to show than tell, Tupper chose a spot where the water wasn't too deep. The rocks were smooth under his feet, and the current tugged gently at his legs; this was familiar territory.

He wasn't as good at this kind of fishing as Rachel, but even his siblings had to admit he was next best. Mother counted on him for three things—fire-tending, foraging, and fishing. Still, Tupper was nervous. He'd never had an audience before.

Doing his best to ignore Aurelius, the boy bent forward and watched for his chance. He didn't have to wait long. With a quick dab, he tossed a gleaming fish onto the bank where it flipped and flopped in the sun.

Aurelius's eyes were wide, and he pointed imperiously to the stream. "Do that again!"

Nodding, Tupper waited patiently for the scattered fish to return. He smiled as a little one nibbled at his toes, but when a bigger one came within striking distance, he swooped again, swatting it into the air.

When it hit the bank, Aurelius tossed his spear aside. "I want to try!"

"That's good. It'll be faster with two." At the Pred's urging, he demonstrated his technique again.

On his first try, Aurelius only splashed ineffectually.

After Tupper cast his fourth fish onto the shore, the man managed to fling one into the air, but it fell short of the bank and escaped. The failures didn't discourage Aurelius, who murmured, "Catching it's only half the game; keeping it's just as important."

"Like this," the boy coached, showing him the little twist that made it easier to cut through the water.

With a curt nod, Aurelius tried again, exclaiming triumphantly when his prey thudded onto the bank. After that, it was a race.

Accompanied by splashes and whoops, one fish after another arced through the air. "Six for me!" the man exulted.

"I have seven."

Not to be outdone, Aurelius soon announced, "We're tied, sprat!"

As with everything, Tupper did his best, and he held his own against the proven hunter. Aurelius reacted with a wide range of good-natured taunts, foreign curses, and subtle compliments.

When the boy inadvertently hit the man upside the head with a particularly fine specimen, Aurelius lunged for it, lost his balance, and landed on his backside in the chilly water.

"S-sorry!" the boy stammered, hurrying over to help.

Aurelius took Tupper's slim hand and smirked. "I appreciate the offer, sprat, but you're on the scanty side to pull me up."

It was true. Even seated, the Pred was nearly as tall as the boy. "But I hit you with a fish," he mumbled.

"Aye. Which means *I'm* still ahead!"

Tupper rubbed his nose to hide a relieved smile. Aurelius wasn't mad.

Releasing his hand, the man asked, "How many fish can you eat in one sitting?"

"Lots."

Aurelius proposed, "Four more apiece?"

Tupper nodded his agreement, glad that their game wasn't quite over. He was having fun. When Aurelius sloshed to his feet and grinned fiercely at him, the boy realized something that made him even happier. They were *both* having fun.

Tupper was totally impressed. He'd never seen someone gut a fish with his bare hands before, but Pred claws were sharp enough to lay bare flesh and bone. The boy looked at his own fingernails, which were no match for Aurelius's. Even so, he was glad he wasn't similarly endowed. He might accidentally hurt himself. Or worse, someone else.

"We'll need a makeshift stringer, sprat," Aurelius said offhandedly. "Find something?"

At the base of an enormous oldtree whose leaves were beginning to turn copper, Tupper found a tumble of wild grapes. Climbing up amongst its hummocky roots, he rustled aside wide leaves, checking for signs of fruit and finding none. Even so, the plant could be useful; he wished he could take back the plentiful woody vines, but he wasn't sure Aurelius would be willing to help. The man complained a lot when there were things to carry.

Suddenly, there was a dull *thwack*, and Tupper looked up to see a dagger quivering in the bark of the tree just above his head. "Use that," Aurelius called.

The boy gawked. "You threw it?"

"Obviously."

"At me?" he squeaked.

Aurelius snorted lightly. "My aim is *excellent*, sprat. It's a loan, not a threat. Use it to cut what we need."

Although he was still a little rattled by what felt like a near miss, Tupper nodded and tentatively touched the dagger's jeweled hilt. It looked too pretty to use.

"What's the matter?" Aurelius asked impatiently. "Haven't you ever used a knife before?"

"I have," he replied defensively. "But not like this."

"Aye, it's too big for you, but that won't stop it from cutting. Don't you have a blade of your own?"

"No."

"Flox or no, a boy your age should have one," he said. "Now, make yourself useful!"

Tupper didn't waste time trying to pull the dagger from the tree. He simply drew a section of vine over it and tugged downward, slicing off a suitable length. He stripped its leaves and presented it to Aurelius, who tied a large loop at one end before threading fish onto the other.

It was a whole bunch—at least two dozen—but catching them had taken much longer than it needed to. Tupper flipped over a stone on the ground with his foot, then poked his toe into the soft dirt underneath.

"Well?" demanded Aurelius.

The boy blinked at the Pred, who was watching him keenly.

"I know that look full well, sprat. You *want* something. Out with it!"

With a sheepish nod, Tupper pointed toward the grapevines and asked, "Can I have more?"

"You want your own stringer?"

"No. I want to make a trap."

This time, Aurelius blinked. "For what?"

"Fish." With a small shrug, he explained, "One at a time is too slow when you need lots."

The man's gaze sharpened. "How many brothers and sisters do you have?"

Tupper checked on his fingers, then answered, "Seven."

"You make eight?"

"Yes."

"No wonder you're so good at this."

The boy nodded. He got a lot of practice.

"You usually use fish traps?" mused the Pred, eyeing the stream speculatively. "Why hasn't anyone mentioned the possibility before?"

Tupper shrugged. He didn't know of anyone else in Hayward who used them since the best stream for trapping was a long ways into the foothills. It was sort of a family secret. He wondered if Rachel had taken over his traps. Probably.

Aurelius carried the stringer of fish over to the oldtree and circled the bushy clump. "You can make a trap just using vines?"

"Yes."

"This I want to see. How much do you need?"

"Lots."

"So definitive," Aurelius muttered longsufferingly. Hooking their dinner over a nearby branch to keep it out of the dirt, he retrieved his dagger from the tree trunk. "Let me know when there's enough."

They worked in tandem, with the man untangling and cutting the woody stems, then handing them to Tupper, who deftly removed the leaves and coiled the sections so they'd be easier to carry. The whole process felt so familiar, for he'd done this many times with Carden, who'd taken Papa's place in teaching him how to fish and forage. Tupper's patient and practical oldest brother was his very favorite sibling, so he missed Carden most of all.

Hands busy, mind drifting, the boy never noticed how far Aurelius had gotten until the man exasperatedly inquired, "Are you planning to trap stream skimmers or a pod of whales?"

With a start, Tupper saw that the entire clump of vines had been reduced to a stump, and he probably had enough vines to make his trap plus a foraging basket. "Sorry."

"Nay," the man replied, waving aside the apology. "If you

can keep Frey supplied with fish, I shan't complain."

And he didn't. Not once. Even when he insisted on carrying both the stringer of fish and his spear stacked with garlands of grapevine all the way back up the steep slope.

Once again, Tupper was totally impressed.

Upon their return, Aurelius insisted on a bath before anything; afterward, he set up a grate over the kitchen fire and lectured Tupper on the finer points of rendering a catch edible.

"You said you couldn't cook, but this is the second time," the boy observed.

"According to my wife, holding chunks of meat over open flames doesn't count as true cookery." Aurelius offered an elegant shrug. "This is not so much cuisine as a part of hunting lore."

Tupper nodded, pleased by the idea of learning Pred lore. But in the end, it wasn't much different than toasting chunks of cooled porridge or slices of bread. As long as you didn't burn the food, it was good enough.

Trusting the manly searing duties to Aurelius, the boy ran from garden to cellar, collecting fresh greens, newly ripened pears, and another bottle from the Pred's wine rack. Once the table was set, Tupper hurried to check on Freydolf, who didn't appear to have noticed they were back. Tapping and chipping held all his attention.

The golden stone no longer looked like a block. Freydolf had changed its whole profile by knocking off unneeded corners and adding a sort of slope. Tupper figured it would be a long time before the sculptor found the feline drawn in his sketchbook. Maybe even all winter.

Noticing the mess on the floor, the boy retrieved his broom, but sweeping was difficult. There were too many big chunks in the way. As quickly as he could, he darted back and forth, toting them to the bucket in the corner. He knew what his first job would be in the morning, for it would take several trips to bring it all out to the rock pile in the outer courtyard.

Golden stone was nice, and in a different way from white stone. Instead of starstone's silky surface, the warm-hued rock had a subtle roughness that made it fun to touch.

Tupper hefted one of the bigger pieces and cradled it against his chest. Heavy, but not too heavy, he gave the stone a friendly pat. It was too bad this piece hadn't been needed for the statue because it felt good. He carried it over to his pail, but he hesitated over dropping his burden.

Remembering Freydolf's words about picking up a stone that you didn't want to put down again, he hugged it more tightly. Should he show it to his master?

Just then, Aurelius's voice came from the kitchen. "The fish is cooked, sprat. See if you can pull Frey away!"

Tupper was in a quandary. He looked between the kitchen, the sculptor, and the stone, then acted on impulse. Trotting across the room to his bed, he levered the rock up onto the high mattress, then pushed it under his pillow.

With a whispered promise and a final pat, he hastened to Freydolf's side and latched onto his arm.

When the man raised his mallet, he lifted the boy right off the floor and looked down in surprise.

Hanging there, Tupper cheerfully kicked his legs and announced, "We brought fish! Come eat!"

16

Trips and Traps

Shortly after dawn the next morning, Tupper clung to a steep section of Morven's uppermost slopes, calmly searching for his next handhold. He'd only meant to do his watering and collect some fresh fruit before breakfast, but out of the blue, it had struck him that he was *really* close to the top of a mountain, and he wanted to reach it.

"Where are you off to?" Aurelius called from somewhere below.

"Up."

"Better up than away, I suppose," remarked the man. "I'll meet you there."

The Pred disappeared, and Tupper persevered, scrabbling his way to the summit. He wasn't surprised to find Aurelius waiting for him, lounging against a tumble of boulders.

Dusting his hands on his shirtfront, Tupper said, "Good morning."

Aurelius bowed his head in acknowledgment. "This is the first time you ran off instead of coming straight back."

Tupper slowly nodded, for it was true. Was he going to be scolded for neglecting his duties?

"This is *also* the first time a runaway has gone up instead of down."

Had the Pred been watching him every morning? Aurelius was even more careful than he'd thought. Stepping up to face the man squarely, Tupper firmly declared, "I'm not running away."

"Aye, sprat, I'd long since figured that out."

Glad there was no misunderstanding, the boy glanced around. "How did you get here?"

"Oh, there's more than one way up," Aurelius replied breezily. "Though your route is arguably the most satisfying. A direct approach, as it were."

It *had* felt good to climb, so Tupper nodded.

Gesturing to the rock pile at his back, the man said, "If you mean to reach the top, you can't get any higher than this. Proceed!"

Tupper didn't need to be told twice. Within moments, his small feet found purchase on Morven's highest height. Feeling a little giddy, he turned around, trying to take in the enormity of the view.

Aurelius folded his arms over his chest and inquired, "What do you think?"

"Big!"

"Do try a little harder," urged the Pred in exasperation. "The scenery here is worth more than one syllable! Remit such praise as is due your homeland!"

Tupper spread his arms wide, saying, "The hills are green, and so is the forest!"

Aurelius sighed. "You're no poet, sprat, but it's a fair summary. Your people lay claim to the most verdant land on our continent."

"Verdant?" he asked uncertainly.

"Green," the man supplied.

Tupper blinked. "But that's what I said!"

Aurelius stuck his nose in the air. "But I said it better!"

"If it means the same, it should be worth the same!"

The Pred quirked a brow at him. "Are you arguing with me?"

"Yes." To his chagrin, Aurelius leapt lightly up the boulders, closing the distance between them. Finding himself nose to nose with the man, Tupper swallowed hard but held his ground.

"Really?"

Chin up, he repeated, "Yes."

Aurelius's lips twitched. "Most men would be wetting themselves about now."

Tupper could understand why and nodded sympathetically. "You're scary."

The Pred sat down next to him. "It's nice of you to *notice*, but it would be more gratifying if you *reacted*."

Wrinkling his nose, the boy pointed out, "I only have one pair of pants."

Aurelius laughed. "But you shall soon have two tunics." Pointing to the east, he announced, "There's a passable tailor in that village over there, and I mean to pay him a visit later today. What color would you like?"

"I don't know," he admitted. Every shirt he'd ever worn had been a hand-me-down, so he wasn't sure what to ask for. "What do you think?"

"How about something ... *verdant*?"

"Green," Tupper agreed.

Freydolf was jerked from a rather pleasant creative haze when Aurelius grabbed the thick hank of his bound hair and dragged him bodily away from his work. At his grunt of surprise, his agent addressed him in sweetly astringent tones. "Now that I have your attention, put down your weapons. We have guests. Or rather, the sprat does."

Curiosity piqued, the sculptor followed Aurelius to the workshop's open door in time to see Tupper fling himself at the same young man who'd accompanied the quarry overseer the other day. "His brother's back?"

"Aye, with the shipment of root vegetables."

A low wagon heaped with produce stood near the entrance to the lower level, and it made sense that Old Gruff would need help carrying it all below. "What a coincidence," Freydolf murmured lamely.

"Reconnaissance, more like," Aurelius said. "I don't approve."

"Is it so bad that his family cares about him?" Freydolf asked dubiously.

Tupper's older brother had gone down on one knee and opened his arms in greeting. There was no mistaking the concern in the young man's expression as he talked to the boy, stroking his hair and scratching behind his horns. However, Tupper must have put him at ease, for Carden was soon smiling.

Freydolf wished he could hear what they were saying; it appeared that the young man was sharing something of import. Tupper hugged his big brother, who folded his arms around the boy ... then looked over the top of his head at the two Pred watching from the doorway.

Carden's embrace tightened protectively, but his expression remained thoughtful rather than wary.

Lowering his gaze, Freydolf remarked, "They seem close despite the age difference."

Old Gruff stumped over and handed a list to Aurelius, remarking, "When their father died, Carden did his best to fill the gap. Fine man."

"Eldest son, then?" Aurelius pried.

"Yup," the old man replied, idly tugging at his beard. "I've my eye on him to take my place once I'm put to pasture."

Freydolf smiled faintly at the thought, for it would put him in close contact with yet another Meadowsweet. If that were the case, perhaps he should beg an introduction.

Aurelius hummed as he eyed the young Flox speculatively. "Does he have a good head for business?"

"All of Merona's do," the old man reported. "Sensible. Hard-working. Brave."

"Aye, good stock," Aurelius said. Old Gruff puffed up, and the Pred noticed. Golden eyes narrowing slightly, he leaned closer. "By any chance, are the Meadowsweets kin to you?"

The old man proudly replied, "Yup. Their mother Merona is daughter to my baby sister. I've always kept an eye on 'em for her sake."

Freydolf's gaze strayed back to the siblings. Carden had produced a bulky, paper-wrapped bundle, and Tupper untied its strings. He shook out a thick winter cloak and swung it around his shoulders. It was a little too long, for its frayed hem brushed against the paving stones.

Sharp-eyed Aurelius observed, "That's been mended more than once."

"Plenty of use left in it," Old Gruff remarked practically. "If Tupper minds it, Farley can wear it out in a couple years."

With a rueful smile, Aurelius said, "That brings back memories, and none of them good. My older brothers had *abominable* taste in clothes!"

The old Flox peered up at the taller Pred and asked, "You come from the tail end of a big brood?"

"He's the runt of the litter," teased Freydolf, chuckling over the way his brother-in-law bristled.

With a sympathetic *tut*, Old Gruff noted, "Those that have to fend early often fend best. I'll wager you made better than your biggers?"

Aurelius's smile had a vicious quality. "Well spoken, old man."

Freydolf was grateful that Tupper's family was making sure the boy was ready for winter atop Morven instead of trying to whisk him away. He hadn't given much thought to warm clothing.

Frowning to himself, he turned to Aurelius to ask about finding Tupper some boots only to receive an elbow in the ribs.

"Stop scowling," hissed the other Pred. "You're about to meet the family."

Tupper had his big brother by the hand and was leading him over. "This way," the boy urged. "You'll see."

The sculptor found himself the object of scrutiny by another pair of gray-green eyes and smiled in honest relief. Carden's steady gaze held interest and curiosity, not fear. This boded well.

Suddenly, Tupper broke away from his brother, saying, "Right back!" He wriggled right between the two Pred stationed in the workshop door, disappearing inside.

Freydolf watched the lad go, but Aurelius stepped forward, offering his hand. "Carden, is it?" he inquired genially.

"Yes, sir. Carden Meadowsweet."

"Aurelius Harrow, Master Freydolf's agent," the Pred smoothly returned. "So how long have you been working the quarry?"

As the men talked, Freydolf wondered if he should check on Tupper, but the lad reappeared from the direction of the kitchen with his trusty bucket, the one he used to reach things. Dropping it next to the door, he clambered onto his makeshift step stool and reached way up to hang his hand-me-down cloak on the hook next to Freydolf's. Judging by the shine in his eyes, the lad was very pleased with the secondhand garment.

"A cloak," Freydolf remarked in congratulatory tones.

Tupper beamed at him. "Mine's blue, too!"

"Now, we don't need to share," he joked.

First patting Freydolf's fine, deep indigo cloak, Tupper next thumped his dusty blue counterpart. "Now, yours won't be lonely!"

What a way to put it. Freydolf couldn't have agreed more, so he straightened the folds of both cloaks, then ruffled the boy's hair. "Aye, they look well together."

Suddenly, the sculptor realized how quiet it was. Conversation had fallen off, and all three men were staring at them. Aurelius was smirking, and Old Gruff was stroking his beard in a manner that suggested amusement. Carden was the only one who seemed stunned.

Freydolf *really* wished it didn't come as such an enormous surprise that he wasn't a monster.

With a resigned smile, he stepped forward to confirm the man's suspicions. Offering his hand, palm peaceably upraised, he said, "Welcome to the Statuary, Mister Meadowsweet."

Tupper was in a sudsy bath, playing contentedly with his stone friends when the door to the necessary swung wide, admitting Aurelius. With a startled squeak, the boy jumped away from the edge, inadvertently toppling the little freshstone feline and bird into the tub. Dunking under to rescue them, he came up and blinked away the bubbles dribbling down through his hair.

"Having fun?" the Pred inquired with a smirk.

He nodded, then mumbled, "You're back."

Aurelius had been gone for three whole days, on business in a large city to the east. "Aye, thanks to the Drom, there's now lamp oil aplenty." Removing the lid from one of the boxes he'd carried in, he showed off a fat, cream-colored bar saying, "And soap. This is for laundry, assuming you can lay your hands on Frey's clothes. Despite my best efforts to make him presentable, he's deucedly fond of that old tunic."

Tupper hunkered down at the far end of the tub and nodded. Freydolf always did wear the same red shirt.

"I'm surprised you haven't taken it from him while he's in the bath," Aurelius continued, busying himself with lining the shelf over the laundry tubs with neat rows of soap. Glancing Tupper's way, the man asked, "Haven't you tried?"

He shook his head, eyes downcast.

With a *tsk*, Aurelius said, "It's your best chance, and it comes every other day! What's kept you?"

Tupper wasn't sure how to explain. Every other evening, once the bathwater was hot, he pulled Freydolf away from his work and sent him downstairs. When the sculptor returned, always dressed in his same clothes, the boy had dinner ready. After their meal, Tupper washed dishes, then snuck downstairs to take his own bath ... in privacy.

The Pred strode across the room and picked up a bundle sitting atop the boxes that remained just outside the door. Carrying it over, he began, "*Speaking* of tunics...!"

Huddling against the far edge of the tub, Tupper's cheeks flamed red.

Aurelius finally noticed and dropped to a crouch. "What's wrong, sprat?"

He shook his head miserably.

An awkward silence lengthened, and the man finally asked, "Are you shy about bathing?"

Tupper ducked his head, hoping it passed for an affirmative.

"Ah," Aurelius said softly. Clearing his throat, he explained, "Pred aren't. For our people, meals are under truce, and baths are for bonding. These times are shared with those we most trust—friends and family."

The boy had expected teasing, and he glanced at Aurelius in surprise. The man had taken a seat on the floor, but he faced the wall so that Tupper could only see his profile. He studiously kept his eyes averted.

"In our culture, all the males in a household bathe together in rooms much like this one. The same goes for the females," the Pred shared matter-of-factly. "When I was small, this was my favorite part of the day—joking, gossiping, laughing. Knowing Frey, it was his, too. I've always thought one of the reasons he avoids bathing is because he has to face an empty room."

"Everyone at once?"

"Aye, a whole crowd," confirmed the man.

Tupper could hardly believe it. "And no one minds?"

"For us, it seems natural, but that's our upbringing," Aurelius explained. "Since I travel so much, I'm well aware of cultural differences. I apologize for causing you discomfort."

Unsure how else to respond, Tupper murmured, "Thank you."

Aurelius asked, "Would you like to see your new tunic?"

"Yes."

Crooking his fingers, the man said, "Come closer. You'll want a good look."

Tupper stayed low in the water, but he worked his way to the other end of the tub, turning loose the little cat and bird he'd been gripping. He folded his arms over the edge and quietly asked, "Is it green?"

"The most verdant shade I could find," Aurelius assured, undoing the bundle and shaking out the garment. "Also, I had some odd bits of trim stashed in the carriage … a little something I picked up from a dowager on Last Continent two summers ago."

With a soft gasp, Tupper reached out to touch the tunic's hem. A wide border had been added to the lush green fabric, and it gleamed softly in the lantern light—golden braids and twisting loops, as fancy as anything Aurelius wore. "For me?"

"Aye," the man confirmed with a smirk. "I even threw in an extra pocket for good measure."

He was right! There were *two* pockets! Shaking his head in wonder, Tupper said, "It's too much."

"Nonsense!" Aurelius retorted. "This is *exactly* what I had in mind when we made our bargain. Besides, if you show a little polish, perhaps Frey will make more of an effort."

The boy doubted it, but it didn't seem polite to argue at this point. He merely nodded.

"Tupper."

That startled him. He couldn't remember the man ever calling him by name. "Yes, sir?"

Aurelius eyes flickered briefly his way, then returned to the far wall. "If one of us treads on your tender sensibilities in the future, speak up more quickly." Lifting a hand to study his claws, he coolly added, "And if anyone *else* attempts something that makes you uncomfortable, give a shout. Frey or I will gut the offender."

Tupper gawked at the man, who rose gracefully and pinned the green tunic to the clothesline.

Eyes still lowered, Aurelius offered an apologetic bow. "I'll leave you to your ablutions, sprat."

Nodding mutely, Tupper sank to his chin in the bath, blowing bubbles as he thought about everything the Pred had said. Aurelius's gift was wonderful ... his promise was a little scary ... and his hint was impossible to ignore.

Tupper scrubbed his hair three times and washed between his toes, wanting to be extra specially clean. All the while, he gazed at the new tunic hanging from the clothesline. "Verdant," he announced to the tiny blue stag with its twisting antlers. "It means green."

The little deer shook its horns, then charged the beetle, who was teasing the prettily-plumed bird. Their antics made bathtime lots of fun, and Tupper wondered if the statues counted as company. After a while, he shook his head, for they couldn't gossip or joke around like people did. Statues weren't what Freydolf needed for the same reason they didn't make Tupper shy.

He dawdled until the water cooled, but finally, he opened

the drain and climbed out. Sitting upon one towel, the boy used another to dry his hair. He smiled when the little blue feline stalked his foot and wiggled his toes when an itty-bitty stone paw reached out to tap him.

"Pred are different than Flox," he informed it. "They take baths all at once."

The only person who'd ever helped him wash was Mother, back when he was little and nubless. Tupper's hands stilled as a thought occurred to him. Freydolf *was* nubless, and *he* was supposed to act as the man's mother. Did that mean it was his job to help? Surely not! At least, he hoped not.

All Tupper's worries vanished when he donned his pants and hopped onto a box to reach his new tunic. The green cloth was thick and soft, which would be nice in winter, and the tunic's full sleeves were edged with more of the fancy embellishments that decorated its hem. Tupper pulled the shirt over his head and smoothed his hands down the front, then noticed there was a heavy lump in one of the pockets.

Curious, he slipped his fingers inside and withdrew a knife.

Small enough to fit in the palm of Tupper's hand, its pointed sheath was decorated with a pattern of scales. Turning it over, he found a fin and eye worked into the leather—a fish! With something akin to reverence, he unsnapped the guard and withdrew the gleaming blade. Although he was no expert, the boy could tell this was a good knife, and he tested its edge by carefully trimming his fingernails as Carden had taught him. Making short work of ragged edges, Tupper resheathed it, his mind reeling. Cutting reeds, pruning trees, gutting fish—this would be so useful!

Dropping the blade back into his pocket, Tupper quickly collected the blue menagerie, setting them back on their shelf, and gave the rest of the bath area a lick and a promise. He picked up his lantern and ran upstairs, along the passage to the workshop, only to find it empty.

Voices drifted down from above, so Tupper shot up the balcony stairs, eager to thank the one Pred and show off for the other; however, he paused on the top step.

Freydolf and Aurelius sat on the largest of the couches, heads together as the agent pointed to some papers, then gesticulated broadly. It would probably be bad to interrupt, so Tupper hung back.

Golden eyes that missed little soon caught sight of the boy hovering at the entrance, and Aurelius drawled, "Are you waiting for an engraved invitation, sprat? Come here!"

Suddenly self-conscious, Tupper dragged his feet on the plush rugs as he made his way over.

Freydolf exclaimed, "Someone has replaced my servant with a princeling!"

"The lad cleans up well enough," Aurelius said smugly. "How's the fit, sprat?"

"Good," Tupper answered breathlessly. "*So* good."

Freydolf shifted over and patted the spot between him and his brother-in-law. "We saved a place, lambkin."

Noticing that his mug stood between their goblets on the end table, Tupper felt assured of his welcome. With a bashful smile, he mumbled, "Thank you," and joined the men.

Freydolf ruffled his damp hair, and Aurelius passed him his cider. Tupper tucked up his feet and basked in a delicious sense of belonging.

Giving his brother-in-law's shoulder a poke over the back of the sofa, the sculptor asked, "What are you up to, giving the lad such grand gifts? Have you taken a shine to him?"

Aurelius coyly returned, "Afraid I'll steal away your pet?"

"I'm more suspicious of your motives," countered Freydolf. "Are you trying to bribe him?"

"Would I do something so iniquitous?"

"If it suited your purposes, *definitely*."

"For your information, he and I had a gentleman's agreement. He *earned* his new finery."

Freydolf bowed his head, conceding graciously before tapping the Tupper's shoulder. "Are you pleased?"

"I have pockets," he confided.

With a grave nod, the sculptor replied, "Aye, you can never have too many of those."

Tupper was glad Freydolf understood.

Banter gave way to tales of Aurelius's visit to the Drom city, where he'd caught some interesting news and made several excellent trades. Tupper tried to make his cider last as long as possible, lest he be sent to bed and miss something interesting. The hour grew late, and his eyes grew heavy. Finally, Freydolf rescued his nearly-empty mug from tipping, and the boy blinked sleepily up at him.

"M'wake," he mumbled, glancing around in confusion. Aurelius was adding logs to the fire, which had burned down to embers, so it had to be very late indeed.

Even though Tupper was *almost* lying, Freydolf nodded and said, "You can stay."

Relieved that his master really did seem to understand what was important to a boy, he nodded and nestled closer ... to make room for Aurelius, of course.

He was fast asleep before the Pred could thank him for his consideration.

At breakfast the next morning, Tupper dared to speak up. Patting the table for attention, he looked to Aurelius and requested, "Will you show me the other streams?"

The Pred set aside his cutlery. "In the mood for some fishing?"

Freydolf said, "I certainly wouldn't complain. Those skimmers make good eating!"

"Aye," agreed Aurelius.

Tupper explained, "My trap is ready."

Freydolf's heavy brows drew together in confusion, but Aurelius's lifted. "Show me," he demanded.

Since he'd set it outside the door much earlier that morning, Tupper obediently trotted out, returning with the project he'd been working on during Aurelius's absence. This fish trap wasn't as big as the ones Carden had helped him make for their family, but there were only two people to feed—or *would* be, once Aurelius went away.

Surrendering his handiwork to the golden-eyed Pred, Tupper said, "I have enough vine left to make another."

"This is well made," Aurelius pronounced, gazing at the youngster over the top of the trap. "You've done this before."

Tupper nodded.

"I daresay this is evidence of a Flox cottage industry! What's your family's trade, sprat?"

"Mother is a basket-weaver."

"Aye, that makes sense," Aurelius murmured, sounding pleased with himself.

Freydolf accepted the trap and shook his head in wonder. "You made this, lambkin?"

"Yes."

"By yourself?"

Tupper nodded, but felt duty-bound to mention, "Mister Harrow cut the vines."

The Pred in question scoffed. "He called me *Mister Harrow*!"

"That *is* your name."

"Nay! It's my grandfather's name, my father's name, and even my eldest brother's name, but the rank and file of *lesser* siblings are not given such courtesies." Aurelius's smile was bitter. "We fend for the family with our given names alone."

"Since you call him *sprat*, he could call you *brat*," Freydolf proposed.

Aurelius steepled his fingers. "He refers to *you* as *Master Freydolf* ... though I suppose it could just as easily be *Mister Meadowsweet* now that he's taken you in."

"And?" gruffly demanded the sculptor.

"*And* under the circumstances, they're *all* entirely too formal!" Holding out his hand to Tupper, the Pred said, "You shall call me Aurelius."

Reaching across the table, Tupper brushed his fingertips across the man's palm, gravely echoing, "Aurelius."

The man looked pointedly at Freydolf. "You *know* you want to!"

"Aye." Frey set aside the fish trap and beckoned to Tupper,

turning to fully face the boy. He rubbed his hand on his pants leg before offering it. "Like Aurelius said, we're past formalities at this point. Please, call me Freydolf ... or even Frey, if you like."

Tupper was pretty sure servants weren't supposed to be so familiar with their masters, but at the same time, he and the sculptor were both Meadowsweets now. Placing both hands into the man's larger one, he shyly said, "Freydolf."

"How *cozy*," Aurelius observed sarcastically. Then he patted the table in Tupper-fashion to bring everyone's attention back where it belonged. "So, sprat! You are proposing a trip? To the streams?"

"Yes."

"Very well. I have no other pressing business today."

"Thank you."

Folding his arms over his chest, Aurelius added, "On *one* condition."

Tupper straightened, and Freydolf gave the man a hard look.

With a serene smile, Aurelius commanded, "We'll all go!"

"All?" Frey asked, clearly startled that anyone would suggest such a thing.

"*All*," Tupper breathed, obviously taken with the idea. He smiled hopefully.

Freydolf buckled immediately.

Having orchestrated the discussion perfectly, Aurelius summarily decreed, "All."

17

Quarry

Freydolf hadn't been in the woods since … *huh*. The man honestly couldn't remember the last time he'd strayed off the beaten path. Even then, it had probably only been a few steps to get a closer look at a rock.

The Keeper knew the lay of his land, for he'd explored extensively after arriving on Morven; however, once Master Platt had taken him on as an apprentice, he'd spent more and more time locked away in the galleries.

Autumn had graced the forest with a golden crown, and Tupper bounced along ahead of Freydolf, crunching through fallen leaves in Aurelius's wake. The lad's carefree manner was pleasant to watch, and his carelessness was amusing. It was just as well they were after fish today; all the noise he was making had undoubtedly sent any other prey scattering.

When they reached the water, Aurelius guided them upstream, saying, "There's a deep pool at the base of a waterfall this way. Will that do, sprat?"

"Maybe," Tupper replied. He hugged the neatly woven fish trap to his chest, eyes on the reeds that lined the bank. "I want to see."

Aurelius's lips twitched, and he said, "Suit yourself. Far be it from me to interfere with another hunter's methods."

Freydolf wasn't surprised by his brother-in-law's patience with the lad. For all his affectations, Aurelius was a good father. It was just strange to see him treating a Flox youngster with what amounted to respect. Frey asked, "Will there be a demonstration of this new fishing technique of which you're so enamored?"

"Certainly! Although with you here, we *could* bring down bigger prey."

An invitation to hunt together wasn't something a Pred offered lightly, and Freydolf was touched. Rubbing the back of his neck, he gave their surroundings an assessing look. The waterfall would cover any noise they made, so if they were patient, they might yet catch something unawares. "Perhaps in an hour or two," he suggested.

"Aye," agreed the other man. Quirking a brow, he asked, "How long has it been?"

"Not so long that I've forgotten what I know," Freydolf replied defensively. "I can track."

With a smirk, Aurelius said, "I'll give you the chance to prove it."

"Aye, these are good hunting grounds. I've no weapon, though."

"You have two hands. However, I'm willing to trade favors. If you can track down prey for me, I'll kill it for you."

"What if I were to corner a bear?"

Aurelius haughtily replied, "Then your belly would be full to bursting this evening."

Laughing over the man's cockiness, Freydolf glanced Tupper's way. The boy's eyes were round as saucers, and he couldn't resist offering, "Do you want to come, lambkin?"

"Can I?" he gasped, glancing between the men.

Arms folded, Aurelius drawled, "Are you sure about that, Frey? He has *no* idea how to walk."

Tupper looked down at his bare feet, then up at Freydolf. "I can walk."

"Like prey."

"I'll carry him," Freydolf offered, not wanting to leave out the lad.

Aurelius slowly nodded. "Beginners learn best by watching their betters. Aye, I'll accept that."

Freydolf checked the angle of the sun, then pointed to Tupper's burden. "Set your trap first. That way, if Aurelius fails to bring down any dinner, we'll still have something nice to eat."

Nodding, Tupper said, "I'll pick a good spot."

Aurelius strolled close and quietly said, "I *trust* the only reason you made such a *preposterous* insinuation was to make the sprat feel needed."

Smiling faintly, Freydolf countered, "As if your invitation wasn't meant to make *me* feel needed."

His brother-in-law sniffed. "As long as we're clear on who needs whom, I have no complaints."

The sculptor thought that over, then candidly admitted, "I need both of you."

Aurelius snorted. "Don't be so quick to leave yourself out of the equation, Frey. As much as it pains me to admit it, we need you as well."

Freydolf felt a little flustered, for his brother-in-law wasn't prone to heartfelt admissions.

He was almost relieved when Aurelius breezily concluded, "It's not as if we could hunt or fish these lands without the owner's consent!"

Tupper waded in the shallows along the stream's sloping banks, collecting the reeds that grew in abundance. With quick flicks of his new knife, he took the best ones and added them to a growing sheaf, for he was planning ahead for winter. From the time he'd been old enough to braid, he'd been taught that winter and weaving went together. This would give him something to do on snowy days while Freydolf worked on his statue.

At a sharp *slap* and *splash*, Tupper checked to see how his master was doing.

"Missed," sighed Freydolf, who was having a hard time getting the hang of fishing by hand. He wasn't nearly as quick as Aurelius, but he was twice as patient. Even though all he'd earned for his efforts were wet patches on his breeches, Freydolf kept trying.

"Like this," said Aurelius, who flipped another speckled fish onto the bank.

Both men had abandoned their shirts, and they'd rolled up their pant legs past their knees. After the first few times Freydolf's thick hair dragged in the water, he'd allowed Aurelius to knot it up out of the way. Tupper thought the odd hairdo made the men look dangerous, just like in stories about Pred conquerors. He could *almost* imagine that Freydolf was a powerful warrior who might attack his home and steal their front step.

Freydolf resumed his stance, eyes fixed on the shadows darting through the clear water. Suddenly, he tensed and reached very slowly into the stream, bringing up a smooth stone. Smiling softly, he crooned, "Well, hello there!"

Aurelius tossed his hands into the air, and Tupper giggled.

Freydolf grinned abashedly, then sloshed over, offering his find to the boy. "Put this in your pocket for me?" he begged. "I'm not sure how a bit of songstone found its way down here, but I think we should bring it home. It has promise."

Tupper took the egg-shaped rock and inspected it closely. There was a slightly transparent quality to the stone, which was a soft shade of green. "Will you sing to it?"

"Maybe one day," the man replied, planting his hands on his hips and stretching his back. Eyes on the sun, he announced, "It's no use, lambkin. You'll have to catch my share of fish for me."

"Fish will come to the trap," Tupper pointed out as he tucked the stone safely away. "We'll have lots."

"Sounds good." Freydolf joined him on the bank and sprawled on a sun-drenched patch of pebbles. Loosening the knot that held his hair captive, he folded his hands behind his neck and closed his eyes. "I'll leave it to you."

Even though his master couldn't see, Tupper nodded.

"I'll find enough wood for a small fire," said Aurelius. "Frey's stomach was growling loud enough to scare off the fish, and now he's collapsed from hunger."

"I haven't collapsed," argued the sculptor in a sleepy voice. "These pebbles simply wanted company."

Aurelius snorted and made his way onto the bank. Drying his feet with a lacy handkerchief, he donned his socks and boots, saying, "Better check him for fever, sprat. He's clearly delusional."

Tupper figured the man was teasing, but better safe than sorry. Putting away his knife, he set aside his reeds and knelt beside Freydolf. Holding one hand to his own forehead, he placed his other on the sculptor's.

When the man opened one eye, Tupper solemnly inquired, "Are you sick?"

"Nay," he assured. "So what will you do with all those long grasses?"

"Make things." Tupper sat cross-legged beside him.

"Like?" prompted Freydolf, his eye drifting shut again.

"I want a foraging basket. And maybe a snow hat."

"Very useful."

Tupper blushed at the approval in his master's tone and selected three reeds from his pile. Slender fingers flashed as he plaited them together, adding more to lengthen the simple cord he'd use to secure the bundle in order to carry it home.

As usual, while his hands were busy, his mind meandered. It was really amazing. He was doing all the same things he'd always done at home. But pitching in with his siblings had been utterly ordinary.

Nothing about his new job felt commonplace.

New experiences came few and far between in the Flox village. Up until now, the boy would have considered a double-yolked egg exciting, but a few weeks at the Statuary had changed everything. He lived somewhere magical, but the very *best* part was the way Freydolf relied upon him.

With a pleased smile on his face, Tupper murmured, "Useful."

The sun dropped behind the surrounding hills, bringing a false twilight to the woods. Aurelius stood and slapped his thighs, then touched the hilts of his daggers; glancing at Freydolf, he inquired, "Ready?"

"Aye," Freydolf agreed, then looked to Tupper. "Ready?"

Tupper nodded, but Aurelius scoffed, "Clearly not!"

Master and servant stared blankly at the Pred.

Aurelius touched his chest. "Men hunt like *this*. Set aside your finery, sprat. Blood is deucedly hard to get out of cloth!"

Even though he would only be along for the ride, Tupper wanted to fit in with the two Pred, so he nodded again and hurried over to where Aurelius and Freydolf had left their tunics. Wriggling out of his, he double-checked his pockets to make sure the rock and his knife were safe. Hesitating uncertainly, he asked, "Should I bring my knife?"

"Nay." Aurelius drew his twin blades, giving them an expert twirl. "This kill shall be mine."

Freydolf beckoned to Tupper, then crouched. "On my back this time. I'll need to bend down from time to time while tracking."

Tupper knew that much, even if he wasn't very good at hunting. He crossed to the man, hunching his shoulders a little, feeling shy over being shirtless. The Pred were so *big*. By comparison, he felt small and nubless, so he touched one horn for reassurance.

"Are you warm enough?" Freydolf whispered.

In answer, Tupper placed his hand on the man's arm; his fingers only *looked* pale and cold compared to the Pred's darker skin.

Satisfied, Freydolf pulled aside his hair. "Climb on, lambkin."

"And be *quiet*," Aurelius added. "No questions, answers, commentary, or chit-chat! If I hear so much as a squeak from either of you, I shall be highly displeased!"

Tupper had a feeling that a displeased Aurelius would be very scary indeed, so he nodded several times.

Freydolf took the warning in stride. "What of compliments?"

"During the hunt, you must content yourselves with *looking* impressed. Words of praise can be bandied about over dinner."

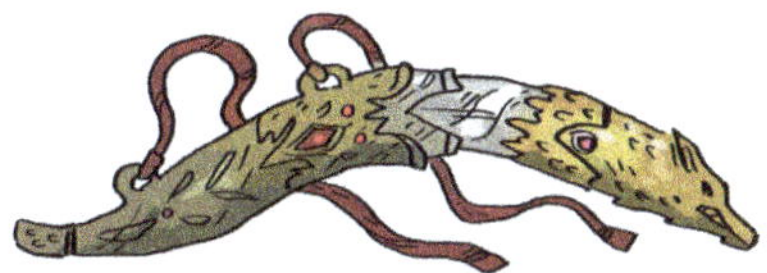

Freydolf's tracking skills could be considered superior, if and when he was focused. Conscious of the thin arms wrapped around his neck and the solemn eyes taking in everything he did, the man did his best.

Swift and silent, he led Aurelius further down the mountain, aiming for an ancient quarry, long-abandoned by masons. Blocks of stone had been removed, leaving a series of pretty little notched ravines where it might be possible for a single hunter to corner prey. Time had softened the angular edges left by past generations of Flox stone-cutters. Moss and fern, mist and lichen—Freydolf found them beautiful.

As expected, fresh tracks marked the deer paths. Pointing, he glanced to his brother-in-law, who signaled his wish to take the lead. Freydolf acquiesced, and Aurelius lithely slipped past, clearly up to the challenge.

They stole along the edge of a rise, alert for any sign of movement in the gray labyrinth below. Tupper's arms tightened a moment before Freydolf spotted the small deer, and he stilled, not wanting to spook the graceful animal. The young buck's ears turned this way and that, but he lowered his head to browse in the underbrush, unaware of his peril.

The rest was up to Aurelius.

As he watched the foraging deer, Freydolf recalled why he'd become so adept at tracking. He'd always loved stealing up on such noble creatures, but not with a weapon. Even now, his fingers twitched, wishing he'd brought a sketchbook. It had been more than a decade since he carved a deer, and his creativity stirred at the sight. The curve of its jaw, the slope of the neck, the dainty set of its feet—they would translate beautifully.

What he wouldn't give for a large section of brownstone. Or perhaps dapple. Aye, that would be perfect!

Then, Tupper scooted higher on his back and pointed, and Freydolf remembered why they were here.

Aurelius stole onto a rocky outcropping above the buck, blades drawn, muscles taut, poised to leap. It was impossible not to acknowledge the hunter's own unique nobility. Although Freydolf would never cater to the other man's ego by telling him so, he'd often thought that *this* Aurelius—the one stripped of all his ruffles and refinement—was worth sculpting.

Any second now, Aurelius would pounce, and Freydolf dreaded the strike. As much as he appreciated meat upon his dinner table, he hated this part. Foolish as it might sound to any of his race, he would rather do without than bloody his hands.

Horror welled up in his very soul, yet Frey couldn't tear his eyes away.

His dismay must have been obvious to his small passenger, for just as Aurelius leapt, Tupper's hands slipped up to cover his eyes. All he heard was a rustle, grunt, and *thud*.

Then, the lad's breath tickled his ear as he whispered, "It was fast. Aurelius is quick."

"Aye," he muttered, and when Tupper took away his blinders, he saw the other Pred kneeling beside his kill, stroking its fur. It almost looked as if Aurelius was apologizing to the buck, but he was probably just assessing the quality of its pelt.

Hanging his head, Freydolf said, "He is what I am supposed to be."

"No. Morven doesn't call hunters."

Freydolf knew it. Well he remembered the tug that had led him away from his home and into this haven. Up until then, it had been said that the mountains didn't call Pred. Many a journeyman had scorned Master Platt for fostering a barbarian, but the sour old man's ready answer was the closest thing Frey had ever received to a compliment—

"I don't give a flying fig who isn't called! Morven calls sculptors, and he's got rocks in his head just like the rest of us."

"Aye, lambkin. Morven calls sculptors."

"Yes. And one Aurelius is enough."

Nightfall found the trio replete, sitting idly before a fire on the balcony. The long walk, longer bath, and large meal left them all drowsy, yet they lingered in a comfortable jumble on the sofa, as if unwilling to end the day.

While he smothered a yawn, Tupper's freshly-clean hair was tousled and he glanced up at Freydolf only to find the man's hands folded in his lap. Startled, he checked Aurelius, but his hands were similarly folded.

At his baffled expression, Aurelius asked, "Imagining things?"

Tupper patted at his mussed curls, giving each man a longer look.

"Is Aurelius ruffling your feathers?" Frey inquired solicitously.

Snorting, Aurelius countered, "Are you going to believe a repeat offender?"

Freydolf's eyes shone with ill-concealed amusement, and Aurelius's glittered with a sharper, more vicious sense of humor. Tupper didn't know who to believe, but he knew where his loyalties lay. He scooted closer to Freydolf.

Tutting in disappointment, Aurelius said, "You've aligned yourself with the culprit. Don't say I didn't warn you!"

"I think he's wise to be wary of the likes of you," said Freydolf. "What are you up to?"

"Me? I have it on good authority that Frey's subtler than he seems, a real prankster."

"Once upon a time," the sculptor allowed.

Aurelius leaned close, his voice dropping. "He's taking pages from his own book, sprat! Watch out for him!"

Doubting that someone given to conniptions and conniving was any different, Tupper asked, "And you?"

"*Never* let down your guard!" Aurelius advised. "Assuming you *have* one."

"I have Olexi." Tupper pointed at the hearth, where his little white ram capered back and forth. The small guardian seemed to believe that his charge was safest when tucked up against Freydolf's side, so he wandered freely.

"Aye," Aurelius blandly acknowledged. "My ankles are in peril."

Another yawn took Tupper by surprise, and while he rubbed at tired eyes, fingers riffled through his hair. Both Pred answered his stern glances with pious looks, but Tupper didn't even consider abandoning his seat. After all, brothers teased. Maybe someday, he'd be big enough to tease back.

"Bed," Aurelius finally decreed, for Freydolf's yawns were becoming contagious.

Frey shifted slightly in his seat, reluctant to disturb Tupper, who'd dozed off more than an hour ago. "I'll have to carry him," he murmured.

On impulse, Aurelius said, "Let me."

Not giving the other man a chance to protest, he expertly gathered the boy up, cradling him in his arms. Freydolf quickly found his feet, looking anxious to take back his servant, but Aurelius rolled his eyes and muttered, "*Relax*, Frey! I'm not going to eat him."

"Aye." But he was practically wringing his hands as he hovered.

Aurelius adjusted his hold, marveling at how little the Flox boy weighed. It had been quite some time since his own boys were this small, and none of them had ever looked half so innocent. Pale skin and thin bones lent an air of fragility to all these bleaters, but Tupper had pluck.

The lad also showed promise in the appreciation of life's finer things. Aurelius watched closely as the boy turned his face against his chest and breathed deeply of the merchant's spicy perfume. With a small sigh of contentment, the sprat nuzzled trustingly against the soft velvet of Aurelius's tunic, then drifted into a deeper sleep.

"Little fool," Aurelius murmured. "I warned you not to let down your guard."

Freydolf asked, "Are you talking to him or yourself?"

Just then, something knocked against Aurelius's ankle, and he fixed Frey with a disbelieving look. "*Don't* tell me ...?"

With a low chuckle, the sculptor crouched to collect the tiny, white ram. "I doubt he still views you as a threat. Olexi simply didn't wish to be forgotten."

Humming skeptically, Aurelius strode lightly across the thick carpets, then down to the moonlit workshop where Tupper's regal bed awaited.

Freydolf helpfully lit a lamp, then drew aside the tapestry curtain and folded back the blankets.

In one smooth motion, Aurelius relinquished his small burden, brushing his fingers through Tupper's fair curls. Taking his sweet time, he fussed with the bedding, making sure the boy was neatly tucked in. Glancing at Frey, he asked, "Could you draw this?"

"What ... Tupper?"

"Aye. I want a picture to show Ulrica. Otherwise, she'll think I'm making him up."

Freydolf went for a sketchbook and pencil while Aurelius gazed at the odd child who had impressed him at every turn. Shrewd, stubborn, practical, loyal—Tupper wasn't the most adventurous of boys, but he might well be the bravest.

When Frey returned and propped his hip against the windowsill, Aurelius remarked, "Flox are plain folk, but far from simple. Every time I think I have him sorted, he does something incomprehensible."

The sculptor's dark eyes shone with amusement. "I seem to

remember you speaking similarly about my sister."

"I'm not talking about a woman's wiles." With a sniff, he muttered, "I'll wager he's just as great a mystery to you."

"I'd hardly call him a mystery," Freydolf countered distractedly. "He's just a boy."

Folding his arms over his chest, Aurelius retorted, "No? Then be so kind as to explain something to me, Frey."

"Hmm?"

"Why does your pet keep a rock under his pillow?"

18

Cultivating Curiosity

Over breakfast a few days later, Aurelius casually remarked, "I've procured all the ruck for both pantry and cellar and remunerated the riffraff on your payroll. All we're waiting on is the firewood; once that's delivered, I'll be off."

While the brothers-in-law compared notes, Tupper poked his spoon into his mush. Hadn't he been looking forward to Aurelius's departure? Thinking back over the last two weeks, the boy realized that he was sad the man was going away. Big changes could come quickly, and he wondered what else might happen to his heart while he wasn't paying attention.

No ideas presented themselves, so he supposed he would have to wait and see.

Propping his chin on woven fingers, the agent challenged, "Glad to be rid of me, sprat?"

Frowning a little, Tupper admitted, "No."

Aurelius's eyes widened and might have gone misty, but at that very moment, hooves clattered to a stop outside the workshop door.

Freydolf half-rose, asking, "Is that …?"

"How fortuitous!" his brother-in-law exclaimed, but his voice sounded a little flat. "I'll just let the two of you deal with the unloading. I have trunks to pack!"

When Aurelius disappeared through the orange door in the corner, Tupper looked to his master and whispered, "Will he leave?"

"Aye, soon," Freydolf replied. "He has a lot of ground to cover before winter gets its fangs into this part of the world."

"He could stay."

The sculptor chuckled. "It might please him to hear you suggest it, but he has a home and family; Aurelius belongs to them, not to us."

Tupper was still pondering that friendly-sounding *us* when they opened the door to find Old Gruff and Carden waiting out in the courtyard. With a soft gasp, the boy exclaimed, "You came back!"

"It's part of my job, Tupp," Carden replied, playfully tapping horns with his younger sibling. "Gruff promoted me, so I'll be back regularly."

"You're gonna help Freydolf?"

"*Master* Freydolf," the young man gently corrected. "And yes."

Tupper hung his head, for he didn't want Carden to think he'd forgotten his manners. "He *said* I should call him Freydolf—or even Frey—on account of being sworn," he defended.

"Sworn?"

"Yes. In Verit *and* Terse. Plus, we shared a pepper. It was spicy!"

His brother shook his head and smiled a little. "As long as he doesn't mind, I don't see any harm. Now, I have news of my own. Can you guess it?"

The boy's eyes grew wide. "Did it happen?"

"I told you last time that it would be soon."

"When?" Tupper squeaked. "And ... and *what*? And does Mother know?"

Carden chuckled, but it was easy to see that he was just as excited. "Two days ago, a little girl, and Mother is very pleased and proud."

"Me, too!" the boy promised, giving his brother's shoulder a pat. "Can I tell?"

"If you like," Carden agreed, his gaze wandering to where Freydolf and Old Gruff stood talking beside a wagon filled with good, seasoned firewood.

Even though he knew it was rude to interrupt, Tupper hollered, "Frey!"

The sculptor turned in surprise, then stooped to meet his servant's pell-mell rush. Swinging the boy onto his shoulders, he said, "You startled me, lambkin. Is something amiss?"

"Something is *good*."

Freydolf glanced between brothers. "I can see you're both happy. What's happened?"

Tupper leaned down to whisper his precious news. "You and me are *uncles*!"

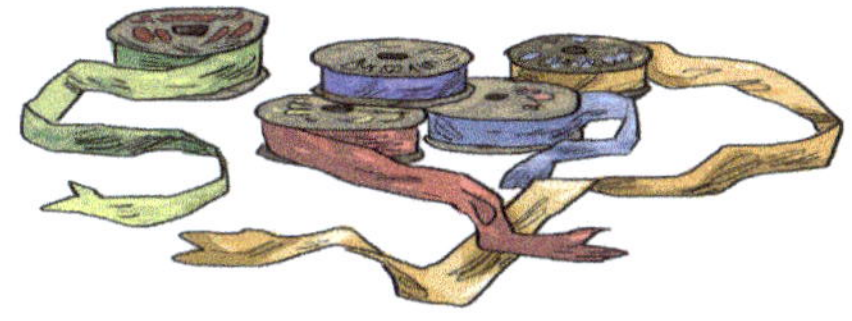

Although Tupper could tell the end was near, Aurelius didn't leave all at once. He'd had his carriage brought up from the shed behind the quarry's office so he could arrange everything for his homeward journey. The boy watched his preparations with interest, for Aurelius did everything with flamboyance—even packing.

His "last minute" details had already stretched to encompass two whole days. Without apology, he thoroughly distracted Freydolf from his work by flying back and forth between the balcony and courtyard, showing off foreign trinkets for trade and sharing tasty tidbits.

The sculptor was similarly distracted this morning, for Old Gruff had arrived early with a stack of new boards and his tool box. Together, he and Freydolf were making a new kind of mess on the workshop's floor. Instead of rocky rubble, they strew sawdust and wood shavings everywhere, and the smell of new wood set Tupper's nose to twitching.

He'd just finished the breakfast dishes when Aurelius breezed past, demanding, "Lend me a hand, sprat!"

With a nod, the boy followed him out through the workshop, where a crate for the dragon statue was taking shape. Bright boards and clean straw would keep the water guardian safe until it reached its new home across the sea. Tupper wondered how many men it would take to lift something so heavy. Maybe they would come up from the quarry when it was time to load the carriage.

"Are you *coming*? We have things to do!"

Trotting over, Tupper asked, "Things?"

"Aye! In you go!" the man directed, indicating the carriage's open door.

Tupper had never seen such a fancy rig, with its high wheels and decorative scrollwork. Aurelius's carriage was big, but then it *had* to be, since he used it to transport stone and statues. The first rung of the short ladder leading up was a bit of a stretch, but with a determined hop and scramble, he made it.

The interior made Tupper's nose wriggle anew, for there were lots of smells all mixed together—spices, beeswax, leather, and tea. Both the front and back walls of the carriage were made entirely of polished wood cabinets. Dozens of little doors and drawers were fitted with metal rings that probably jingled when the carriage was in motion.

Aurelius joined him, smoothly taking a seat upon a cushioned bench that looked long enough to double as the tall man's bed. Meeting his gaze, Tupper asked, "What do you want me to do?"

"Whatever do you mean?"

Tupper was thoroughly confused. Hadn't the man asked him for help?

The Pred simply sat there, gazing intently at him, and Tupper stared back, waiting. Aurelius was up to something.

Finally, the man inquired, "Is there anything you'd like to do?"

Right away, Tupper felt awkward. These were the kinds of questions he hated most, for he always seemed to come up with the wrong answer. Thinking hard, he reviewed his plans for the day and came up empty. His usual duties were done, and Old Gruff had already bid him leave the crate-making to carpenters.

Making up his mind, Tupper asked, "May I sit down?"

Aurelius's brows arched. "That's *all*?"

Tupper ducked his head, but answered honestly. "Yes."

With a put-upon sigh, the Pred snidely said, "Do as you please, O, adventurous one."

"Thank you," the boy murmured, sitting where he was, legs crossed and hands folded in his lap.

This was a very interesting place, and he was glad Aurelius was willing to let him stay for a while. Smiling a little to himself, he tried to decide if the citrusy smell he was picking up from amidst the potpourri of fragrances was made by real lemons. They were hard to come by, and mother loved them.

"This carriage has been on every continent." Aurelius languidly waved at the surrounding cabinetry. "It has contained untold treasures from faraway lands. Indeed, there are many extraordinary things still hidden in its nooks and crannies."

Tupper nodded, for he believed it. Merchants certainly lived interesting lives. Aurelius was still looking expectantly at him, and the boy fidgeted. Unsure what else to say, he offered, "That's good."

Aurelius crossed his legs and tapped his fingers on his knee. In an exasperated tone, he asked, "Aren't you the least bit curious what's in these drawers?"

Thinking it over, Tupper admitted, "No."

"How can a child *not* be curious?" demanded Aurelius. "Isn't there *anything* you want to know?"

"Yes."

Spreading his hands wide, the man urged, "Ask!"

"How can a carriage cross an ocean?"

With a sigh, Aurelius explained, "It cannot on its own. I drive it up onto my ship and lash it down so it cannot roll with the seas." Using his hands to illustrate, the man went on, "There is a special place to keep it below decks, not unlike a carriage house and stable."

Tupper tried to imagine such a place. "Do your horses like to sail?"

"They have little choice. However, after so many years, they're used to it. A few of them were even born aboard ship."

Horses that were born travelers because their master was a traveler. That wasn't much different than him, really. He lived on top of a mountain because that's what his master did. It made sense to Tupper, and he nodded.

"I'll set sail for Far Continent once I return home," Aurelius offered. "The blue dragon will grace a fountain in a land where stones are red."

"Won't your family miss you?"

"Nay. They're coming with me."

Tupper was impressed by Aurelius's plan. He would go on a great voyage without being lonely, for he wouldn't leave anyone behind. Except Freydolf and Tupper. The missing would be up to them. Already, he felt a little sad, which was silly, because the man was right in front of him.

Aurelius hummed in dissatisfaction. "I wonder if an incurious nature can be cured? Shall we find out?"

"How?" Tupper asked, even though he wasn't sure what the Pred meant.

Pointing to the many drawers lining the wall behind Tupper, Aurelius ordered, "Open one."

He hesitated. "Which one?"

"I don't really care, sprat. One's as good as the next, meaning they're *all* excellent."

Taking the man at his word, Tupper crawled over and tugged open a drawer by its ring. Inside were several spools of delicate lace and skeins of colorful ribbon, the sort of things his sisters would have exclaimed over. "Girl stuff." Belatedly recollecting how often ribbon and lace figured into Aurelius's attire, Tupper lamely added, "They're nice."

"Drom-made wares. Very fine." Wiggling his fingers imperiously, the merchant urged, "Now, another one."

Tupper counted over three, up two, and pulled. In this drawer, he discovered a single pair of earrings on a swatch of dark velvet. The blue stones seemed to wink at him. "They twinkle!"

"Aye," Aurelius said smugly. "Those come from the vicinity of the crystal mountain, where a well-treated stone can shine like the stars themselves! Choose two more drawers."

Salt and silks, bangles and beads, resins and oils—with each new discovery, Aurelius spun a tale, amazing his wide-eyed audience with tiny glimpses of a world he'd never dreamed existed. Tupper wasn't lending a hand. He was lending an ear.

Eventually, the boy didn't need to be prompted to reach for the next drawer, and Aurelius was quick to praise him for delving deeper and wondering aloud.

"That's the way, sprat. The more you look, the more you'll find; the more you ask, the more answers you'll receive. If you don't stretch your boundaries, your world will remain quite small."

"Is that bad?"

"Not necessarily. I've seen many small worlds, and they have their appeal. You're living in one now, since Frey's life is limited to this mountain."

"Morven is big!" Tupper pointed out.

"Do me a favor and remind Frey of that the next time the stone seems to be closing in around him."

The boy tipped his head to one side, then to the other, doing his best to see Morven the way a traveler might. "It's small?"

"At times."

"But it's *not*," Tupper argued.

"Exactly," Aurelius agreed with a cryptic smile. "You've pushed Frey's boundaries already, horning your way in as you have. Keep it up, sprat."

How could he when he wasn't sure what he had done? Rubbing a nub uncertainly, he asked, "What am I doing?"

With an expansive gesture, Aurelius replied, "Widening his world!"

Tupper could have spent several days investigating the contents of Aurelius's carriage, but he had responsibilities. "I need to make dinner."

"Aye, but first ...!" Aurelius exclaimed, leaning down and poking his finger into a recess at his feet. Hooking it, he lifted an entire section of floor, revealing a sizable hidey-hole. Tupper scooted to the edge and peered down as the merchant explained, "Every spring and fall, I bring one large stone, usually a guardian stone commission for some wealthy client. Most of the time, it takes Frey several months or even a year to finish these pieces; however, there have been times when he finishes early, and I hate to leave him with nothing but time on his hands."

"Stones!" Tupper breathed. "Are they gifts?"

"I'd call them a *tradition*, or perhaps a treat," said Aurelius. "Thanks to these treasures, your master is always glad to be rid of me. He knows I wait until it's time to leave to bring them out."

"To keep him company?"

"Aye, that's the sum of it."

"Good idea." Tupper reached down to touch the cool surface of a large, polished cube of dapple.

One by one, Aurelius showed off the smaller pieces he'd chosen, extolling their qualities and his cleverness in procuring them. Tupper was allowed to handle everything that was small enough for him to lift. He greeted each with a reverent touch—a fat column of red, a pale rod of pink, and irregular lumps of brown and orange.

"What will they be?" asked Tupper.

"That's up to Frey. These rocks aren't sent by a customer. They're his to do with as he pleases."

"Can we show him?"

"Aye. Normally, I leave them around the workshop for him to find, but this time I believe I shall leave them to you."

Tupper accepted this with a nod, but he couldn't help but wheedle. "Can we show him *tonight*?"

"We could give one an early unveiling. We'll slip it onto the kitchen table and witness his amazement together." He waved at their choices. "Which one, sprat?"

Without hesitation, Tupper touched the block of dapple,

with its mottling of browns and pinks. The merchant pouted in disappointment, and the boy cautiously asked, "Is it wrong?"

"Nay," Aurelius sighed. "Merely *heavy*."

Long after Aurelius retreated to the balcony for his beauty sleep, Freydolf remained at the kitchen table with a half-empty goblet, his sketchbook, and the sublime block of dapple. Too comfortable to go fetch a lantern from the workshop, the sculptor made do with the light of two fat candles while he indulged in planning a personal piece.

At first, he was so sure that the stone would be perfect for a buck like the one he'd admired in the old quarry a few days ago, but the stone had other ideas. Gradually, his sketches of noble stags gave way to those of a gentle doe. Nodding to himself, Freydolf tried positioning her several ways, but something was missing.

"What is it you need, hmm?" he mused aloud, his gaze resting upon the polished stone.

"Umm," came a soft response from the direction of the workshop.

Freydolf turned in his chair, surprised to find Tupper out of bed. The boy peeped around the door's frame, looking especially pale in his over-large nightshirt and hugging a sizable rock to his chest.

Aurelius had already snooped and reported that the lad was harboring a stray piece of sunstone under his pillow, but Freydolf had refused to question his servant on the matter. It would be hypocritical to scold the lad over a castoff, especially since Frey had done the very same sort of thing all throughout his own childhood.

He could guess at the reasons; still, he was curious if

Tupper's were the same as his. Was it possible the young Flox had an affinity for stone?

Beckoning him closer, Frey asked, "Trouble sleeping, lambkin?"

The lad shook his head. "I was playing with Olexi."

"And what do you have there?"

Tupper padded across the kitchen floor and hefted the stone up onto the corner of the table. "I picked it up," he explained. "I didn't want to put it back down. I think it's a good rock."

Freydolf gave the sunstone his full attention, turning it over in his hands and rubbing at its rough edges with his fingertips. A slow smile spread across his face, "Aye, you found something I missed."

With an expectant expression, Tupper edged closer. "Will it be a statue?"

"Not just a statue," Freydolf said. "A guardian."

"Like Olexi?"

"Aye and nay." Setting the golden rock beside the block of dapple, he picked up his pencil and began to sketch. "Starstone yields a nighttime companion, but sunstone is for the day. Your new friend will stalk your steps whenever the sun is shining."

"Mine?" Tupper whispered, crowding close to the sculptor's side to watch him draw.

After a few minutes, Freydolf turned the sketchbook so Tupper could see better. "If you can wait until after Aurelius leaves, I'll carve this little one for you."

"I can wait," the boy breathlessly assured.

"She's a little more complicated than Olexi, so I'll need to take my time," Freydolf warned.

"Can I watch?" Tupper begged.

"Aye," he promised. "Until then, you can keep her someplace safe. Perhaps under your pillow?"

The lad gaped at him, then pledged, "I'll keep her safe."

Freydolf messed up the boy's hair, then sent him and his rock back to bed. As Tupper trundled off with the sunstone in his arms, the sculptor smiled over the subtle symmetry they'd established. Tupper had protected her, and she would protect him.

"He's a wonder, that one," he remarked to the dapple. "A guardian of guardians and keeper of Keepers."

Pulling his sketchbook closer, Freydolf flipped back to the drawing in which his doe lay amidst grasses and fern, with spring flowers in evidence. With sure strokes, he added what had been missing and smiled in satisfaction at the spotted fawn nestled against her flank.

"How about that," he whispered in awed tones. "There were two of you all along!"

19

Waking a Dragon

"It's time, Frey." Aurelius pushed back his empty bowl. "Gruff and his Meadowsweet minion will be here soon to lend a hand."

The sculptor moodily poked at the remainder of his porridge. "Aye, I know it."

"Time for what?" Tupper asked.

"To wake the dragon," the merchant replied, rubbing his hands together.

Freydolf grunted his agreement, but he looked far less pleased about it.

Aurelius ignored the sculptor's lack of enthusiasm by breezily inquiring, "Do you have everything you need?"

"You know I do."

"Are those elements in readiness?" Aurelius prodded.

"You know they're not," Freydolf sighed.

Aurelius clapped his hands. "You and the sprat had better get busy! It's early, so you'll have all day to say goodbye. I won't leave until tomorrow."

Tupper thought he saw a flash of gratitude in his master's eyes.

Showing a little more optimism, Freydolf pushed back his bowl. "Stoke the fires, lambkin. We need heat!"

"Which fires?"

"All of them—kitchen, balcony, necessary," Freydolf said. "Then join me in the outer courtyard. We've rocks to gather."

Hopping from his chair to clear the table, Tupper asked, "Does freshstone need more stones to wake it up?"

"Not exactly." A bit of mischief showing in Frey's smile. "Watch and see."

When Old Gruff's wagon rattled into the courtyard, Tupper waved to his older brother from atop the pile of stones in his master's wheelbarrow. Freydolf hardly seemed to mind the extra weight of his young passenger as he trundled along from the direction of the outer courtyard.

The quarry manager eyed the load of gray rocks and remarked, "Been a while since you finished a blue."

"Aye."

"Need help with the drapings?" asked Gruff.

Tupper was startled that the old man seemed to know so much about the statues. Gruff certainly never spoke of such things in the village, but maybe that was good. People were already afraid of Freydolf. What would happen if they learned there were living statues on top of Morven?

Frey's smile included Tupper's older brother. "Thank you, both. That would be most welcome."

Cuffing Carden's shoulder, Old Gruff said, "What happens today comes with the job. May as well jump right in and see if you have the horns for it!"

By his brother's confused expression, Tupper guessed that he didn't know anything about Freydolf's magic, and he wondered if he should try to warn him. As Gruff steered Carden toward the workshop doors, the boy rubbed worriedly at one nub. "No one told him?"

"I doubt it," Freydolf admitted. "Is your brother brave?"

Tupper nodded, for how could Carden be otherwise?

His master's smile was rueful as he remarked, "A dragon for his first time ... not the easiest way to begin."

Tupper had at least a dozen questions whirling through his head, but the men didn't give him any chances to ask them. They strode back and forth, intent on their various responsibilities, chivvied on by Aurelius's curt commands and frequent grumbles. The boy finally crept back against the wall and sat down, tucking his knees up to his chin in an effort to stay out from underfoot.

Carden scaled the ladder Gruff brought in and knotted the corners of several lengths of heavy cloth to the lantern hooks, creating a makeshift tent around the blue statue. Freydolf manhandled six hefty stone basins from under one of the workbenches, rolling the squat cylinders across the floor, then standing them up in a wide ring around the dragon's pedestal.

"Is there enough water?" Aurelius demanded.

"Nay," Freydolf replied, his dark eyes seeking out Tupper and softening when he spotted him huddled in the corner. "Bring more from the well, lambkin. We'll be wanting it."

Glad to be of use, he promised, "I'll bring lots."

Three trips were needed before Frey was satisfied by the number of brimming basins, buckets, and pitchers in the room. In the meantime, Gruff and Carden carefully transferred hot stones from the various fireplaces into the squat basins, and Freydolf pulled the tarps around.

"Aye, that should do it," he said. "I'll only need a few minutes."

"For what?" Carden spoke up, clearly mystified by the proceedings.

"I'll be adding my mark to this guardian," Freydolf replied, lighting a lantern and plucking a few tools from the bench. He stepped inside the tent, but hesitated before pulling the draped cloth shut behind him. "Tupper? Do you want to hold the light for me?"

"Yes!" he blurted, dashing to his master's side.

The man's grin let Tupper know he was glad to share this moment.

Then Freydolf addressed the others. "In a minute or two, begin adding the water. Slow and steady, please."

"I remember the way," Old Gruff assured.

As soon as they were inside the tent, Freydolf handed Tupper the lantern and asked, "You remember how it was for Olexi? Starstone needed salt water to wake because the White Mountain is beside the sea."

Tupper nodded and held up the light while the sculptor circled his statue, looking for the best place to leave his mark.

"The Blue Mountain is in a tropical place," Frey continued in a low voice. "So while a guardian like him will only need fresh water from now on, the mark must be matched by ...."

Just then, the cloth was lifted at one corner, and a noisy *hiss* made Tupper jump.

"Aye, that's the way!" Freydolf called as more water hit the heated stones.

"Steam?" guessed the boy as water vapor billowed up around them.

"The very thing," the sculptor acknowledged, taking a seat on the floor.

Freydolf worked slowly, making careful incisions into one of the dragon's many scales. From time to time, he looked up at the vapor, which condensed against the cool stone and trickled down its surface. "More water, Gruff!" he bellowed. "I need it thick in here!"

"Yessir!" came Carden's voice, followed by another *hiss*.

Tupper's hair curled damply against his forehead, and his cheeks were pink, but he was glad to be next to his master during such an exciting time.

Freydolf wiped his brow with the back of his hand, then used the sleeve of his tunic to blot away some of the water that had seeped into his etchings. "Nearly done," he murmured, glancing at his companion. "You all right, lambkin?"

He nodded eagerly.

A few taps and scratches later, the sculptor sat back, eyeing the mark critically.

It was larger than the one he'd made on Olexi, and Tupper could see more detail.

Freydolf met his gaze and whispered, "Ready?"

Tupper's eyes were wide as he nodded once.

The Keeper waved his hand through the air, as if trying to capture the vapor, then cupped it over his mark. "Wake up, Dart."

A back paw flexed, scales rippled, and Tupper looked up in time to see the freshstone dragon blink its eyes, uncoil from its perch, and slither around until they were nose-to-nose.

Giggling at the way the stone guardian's trailing whiskers tickled, he happily greeted, "Hello, Dart. I'm Tupper."

When Freydolf pulled aside the curtain, releasing a billow of steam, Carden's eyes widened as the dragon statue glided sinuously out of the tent he'd helped rig. The young man backed up one step, but any further retreat was halted by Old Gruff and Aurelius, who hooked their arms through his.

"Not so fast, Meadowsweet," purred Aurelius.

With a rusty chuckle, Gruff remarked, "Figured you'd pass the test."

"This was a test?" Carden asked weakly.

"Aye," the Pred replied with a positively wicked leer. "Working with Frey's not for the faint of heart."

"And I passed?"

"You're still conscious." The old man thumped his assistant's back. "That settles it. Right, Mister Harrow, sir?"

"He *does* show promise."

"Statues that move," Carden murmured dazedly.

"Catches on quick," said Gruff. "This place is full of strange carvings like that'un. Guardian stones, they call them."

"A-are they safe?"

"That's an interesting question," Aurelius replied. "Would you say that Master Freydolf was *safe*?"

Carden slowly nodded. "I would. At least, Tupper is safe with him."

Golden eyes flashed to where the boy stood, blithely patting Dart's head. "Aye. Fortunately for you, well-made guardian stones retain their maker's intent. Frey's statues are famed the world over for being beautiful, loyal, protective, and deucedly affectionate."

The young man sighed in relief. "So the statues *are* safe."

Aurelius lips turned down. "That's *not* what I said."

Carden thought it over. "Oh, of course! Master Freydolf's statues are safe, but you can't vouch for those of other sculptors."

"Glad to see you have a few wits about you," said Aurelius.

With a chuckle, Carden said, "Well, this should make loading the carriage much easier. The statue can simply climb in by himself."

"Precisely!" Aurelius exclaimed in pleased tones. Easing his grasp, he instead draped his arm over Carden's shoulders, leaning as he drummed his claws upon the slender Flox's opposite shoulder.

Gruff was stroking his beard, a sure sign that they weren't finished teasing him, so Carden withstood the Pred's overbearing proximity; however, his nose began to twitch. With a sidelong glance at the man, he asked, "What spice is that? Perhaps ... cloves?"

Aurelius's brows arched. "Do you like it?"

"Very pleasant," Carden gravely replied.

Positively beaming, the Pred magnanimously announced, "You can keep this one, Gruff. Young Mister Meadowsweet is approved."

Tupper worried that the newly wakened dragon would have trouble with the stairs leading down to the lower colonnade, but Dart descended the curving obstacle with rippling grace.

"This way," coaxed Freydolf, who strode purposefully toward the sound of trickling water. "You'll like fountains. You were *made* for fountains!"

Without hesitation, Dart plunged into the icy water, plashing about in the shallow pool in a manner that was far from menacing.

Tupper dipped his fingers into the pool, then said, "A bath is better."

"For what, lambkin?"

"For playing. I'll refill the cauldron."

"But I had a bath just last night!" Freydolf protested.

Tupper shook his head and began drawing water from the well. "You'll catch cold if you play in the fountain. I'll make warm water."

Once the boy trotted off with his first pailful, the sculptor cupped his hand under the dragon's whiskered chin and gruffly said, "Now see what you've done? I'm being sent in for an extra bath, and you've been demoted to bath toy!"

Dart blinked happily over the attention, then squirted Freydolf in the face with a small jet of water.

Since the fires had already been stoked, it didn't take long for Tupper to fill the necessary with steam. Freydolf lured Dart through the door, then over to the sunken tub. "Not as wide, but *much* deeper! Wallow in here for a while!"

The living statue sloshed right into the bath, and Freydolf peeled out of his damp tunic, tossing it over one of the clotheslines. "You were right, lambkin," he said to the boy who quickly turned his back. "I was getting cold. This fellow likes to splash!"

"I'll add more wood to the fire," said Tupper.

Leaving his breeches on, Freydolf sat on the edge of the bath, dangling his feet in the steaming water. "Aye, do. The tropical atmosphere will horrify Aurelius. He always complains that the humidity on First Continent makes his hair unmanageable."

"Is he coming?"

"Once he's done lecturing your brother," said Freydolf. "I always make sure Aurelius is acquainted with the statues he escorts. Even if it's not important to him, I insist upon it."

Tupper added more wood to the fire, then brushed off his hands on his pants. "He says they're not alive."

"Aye, that's what he says." Changing the subject, the sculptor gestured to the roomy tub and invited, "Join us?"

He took the time to pull off and hang up his shirt. Kneeling at the edge of the sunken tub, he tried to see what Dart was doing. Suddenly, a blue snout poked out of the water, followed by a spurt of water. Tupper didn't hesitate to splash back, and a full-scale water war ensued.

"… and the bathing facilities are through here," Aurelius announced in pompous tones, pushing through the door to the necessary. "Ah," he muttered, lifting one elegant slipper from the puddle in which he'd stepped and giving it a small shake. "How droll."

Carden's eyes widened at the sight of his younger brother wrapped in the coils of the blue dragon, who was snapping his jaws at his creator. Tupper and Dart had apparently allied themselves against the bare-chested Keeper, who'd armed himself with a bucket. Freydolf dipped and pitched, and water sluiced through the air, accompanied by deep chuckles and shrieks of boyish laughter.

Smiling faintly, Carden asked, "Is this normal?"

Aurelius tutted as he removed his ruined footwear. "They seem to be headed that way, Mister Meadowsweet." Raising his voice, he demanded, "Is there room for two more in this ridiculous fracas?"

Frey straightened. "Is that a challenge?"

"It would be *uncivilized* to issue challenges whilst bathing!" scolded Aurelius.

The sculptor swung out of the bath and ambled across the slick floor. "Aye, that tradition is older than fangs, and I wouldn't *dream* of being so discourteous with a guest in our midst." Freydolf bowed graciously to Carden, then upended a bucketful of water over Aurelius's head. "However, it doesn't count as *bathing* if we leave the soap on the ledge!"

"That loophole is older than fangs," the other Pred noted sourly.

"Aurelius! Carden! Come meet Dart!" Tupper called, his arms wrapped possessively around the blue dragon's neck.

"Aye, sprat. And that's not *all* I'll do," Aurelius promised, pushing sodden tresses out of his face before meticulously removing his cufflinks.

Grinning unrepentantly, Freydolf turned to Carden. "I know Tupper would be pleased if you could stay a little longer. Please do?"

"Oh, he's staying," Aurelius interjected with a superior look. "It's all arranged."

Carden said, "It seems I'll be needed to harness the teams tomorrow morning, so Mister Harrow insisted I sleep here. I apologize for any inconvenience."

"Not at all," Freydolf automatically returned, looking rather shocked. "You're most welcome."

"Thank you, sir," Carden replied, slipping out of his vest and unbuttoning his shirt.

"Don't you have a young one at home?" the sculptor ventured.

"Yes. My wife and daughter are in Hayward."

Awkwardly rubbing the back of his neck, Frey asked, "Are we taking you away from them?"

"No." Carden patiently explained, "Most of us who work in

the quarry stay in the bunkhouse during our work allotment. Melina isn't expecting me home for two more nights." Freydolf's concern must have been apparent, for the young man added, "My mother and her parents live nearby; she and Dulcie aren't alone."

"Well, then," Freydolf said, beckoning to the bath where a waterlogged Aurelius was attempting to stare down Dart. "Make yourself at home. And choose sides with care. My brother-in-law plays to win, even when there's nothing at stake."

Carden chuckled. "Thank you for your hospitality."

Freydolf was so distracted by the novelty of having an honest-to-goodness guest in his home that he nearly missed Aurelius's counterattack.

A wet towel smacked the door and slid to the floor with a sticky *slap*. Carden and Frey traded a startled look, tentative smiles, and then dove into the melee together.

"We already loaded the pedestal into the carriage," Aurelius announced, wringing out his hair and twirling it into a knot atop his head.

Freydolf hummed noncommittally.

"It would be *best* to load this wretched prankster before dark so we can see to nail the crate shut."

"His name is Dart," the sculptor quietly corrected.

"Aye, and he's a menace," groused Aurelius. The dragon had singled him out during their water wars, nipping at the man's fingers whenever he came within range.

"Dart *likes* you," said Tupper.

"Wherever did you get such an absurd idea?" Aurelius demanded.

"He didn't *bite*. Only nibbled." Tupper sat on a folded towel with another draped over his head, and Dart lounged beside him, his muzzle pushed up against his leg. Dipping his fingers in a bucket of tepid water, Tupper smoothed his hand over stone scales, prolonging the guardian's fugitive consciousness.

Carden returned from the recessed stalls around the corner dressed in one of Freydolf's nightshirts. The garment made the slim man look far younger than his twenty years; however, his curving horns helped salvage his dignity, as did his uncanny poise. He said, "Thank you for the loan."

Waving off the remark, Freydolf assured, "It's nothing. Aurelius is always plying me with what he deems suitable attire, but most of it goes to waste." Eyeing the chartreuse sleepwear's impractically full sleeves with a shake of his head, he muttered, "Better you than me."

"You look like a butterfly," Tupper announced.

Stretching his arms wide, Carden asked, "Is that a compliment?"

The boy ducked his head to hide his smile, and his older brother ambled over to sit beside him.

Giving his younger sibling a poke, he whispered, "Thought not."

Dart raised his head to consider Carden, then wriggled a little closer, curling his tail around to include him in the circle of his protection.

Freydolf watched his creation's antics with a sad little half-smile, which the others pretended not to see. Saying goodbye to Dart was going to be hard on him.

Lightly clearing his throat, Carden asked, "He needs to stay wet?"

Tupper dribbled more water over the dragon's pointed ears and said, "Yes."

Adopting a sterner tone, his brother said, "But *you* need to be dry."

Looking down at his wet britches, the boy replied, "Yes. I'll change."

While Tupper snagged his hand-me-down nightshirt and disappeared around the corner, Aurelius slapped his own wet breeches and stood. Stalking over to where Freydolf's red tunic hung, he plucked it off the clothesline with thumb and forefinger, then plunged it into the water bucket. Flinging the sodden mass in the direction of the laundry basins, he decreed, "Consider that garment confiscated until such time as the sprat renders it clean."

"It wasn't *that* bad," grumbled Freydolf.

"Nay, it was *worse!*" Pointing imperiously at the garments he'd retrieved from upstairs a short time ago, he said, "There's something in there for you, as well. I even chose something blue, in honor of your scaled fiasco!"

"His name is Dart," Freydolf quietly repeated, but he hauled himself to his feet and lifted one corner of a vibrant blue tunic. "These things are too fancy, Aurelius!"

"Then by all means, admonish your servant to spend the rest of the day laundering your rags, for they are in no fit state to wear!"

Tupper reappeared, his eyes wide. "I will wash them!"

"Nay, lambkin," Freydolf sighed. "Leave the work. Today's too precious to squander on scrubbing."

Aurelius smugly picked up the red tunic and wrung it out over Dart's head, then returned it to the clothesline. "Very reasonable. I applaud your wisdom."

With a snort, Freydolf followed the Flox's suit by retreating into an alcove to change.

Crossing to his own pile of dry clothing, Aurelius looked to Tupper and said, "We should burn that travesty while we have the chance."

The sculptor's deep voice carried from around the corner. "I heard that!"

Carden and Tupper exchanged a glance while the agent gamely called, "'Twould be a kindness! There's your position to consider! You're the worst-dressed Keeper in the world!"

"No one cares! There's no one to see."

"Oh, that's just rude!" Aurelius drawled. "Have you forgotten your guest?"

The sculptor's voice was more subdued when he answered, "Nay, but that's beside the point."

"And you're missing mine!" Aurelius exclaimed, smirking at the Meadowsweet brothers as he waited for his brother-in-law's answer.

Freydolf stalked back into the room, brows drawn together in a heavy scowl, dark eyes flashing warnings. He looked positively regal in the fancy clothes Aurelius had supplied, but no one was brave enough to mention it. Making a grab for his favorite tunic, the sculptor flung it over his shoulder along with his breeches and stormed out of the room, muttering something about *safe keeping*.

Tupper gave Aurelius a stern look. "That wasn't nice."

"Aye, but it was needed."

The boy looked confused. "Why?"

Nodding significantly at Dart, Aurelius said, "If he's miffed, he's not being maudlin."

When Carden stepped back into the courtyard, he squinted at the sky, needing to reorient himself. The sun wasn't visible behind the bulk of the mountain, but judging by the angle of shadows, it was only mid-afternoon. Perhaps it was because they'd needed lanterns in the bathing room, or maybe it was because he and his brother were already clad in nightshirts, but he'd expected this surreal day to already be over.

Everything felt off-kilter, and there was little wonder as to why. Carden stepped aside to let Dart slip past, the dragon's lithe body rearing up as he peered around, searching for Freydolf. Spotting the man on a bench not far from Aurelius's carriage, the blue creature took off, moving with astonishing speed and silence across the cobblestones.

How could something carved from rock see, hear, and act like a living being? Carden never would have believed such a tall tale if he weren't witnessing the miracle firsthand.

Tupper tugged at his flowing sleeve and asked, "Isn't he good?"

Carden wasn't sure if he meant the dragon or the man, but in either case, he agreed. "Very good, Tupp."

"There's more," his little brother confided seriously. "Lots and lots more. I'll show you!"

The turnabout amused him, for he was used to being in the role of teacher. Tupper had only been four when their father died, and more than any of Carden's other siblings, the boy had clung to him.

Carden had never minded his silent tagalong, for he couldn't bear seeing the little guy isolated. He was too affectionate to be left alone. At the time, Mother's hands were full with Farley and Aggie, so Tupper had become *his*. Carden had quickly come to think of the boy as a boon, for they'd worked through their grief together.

With a small smile, the young man remarked, "You're happy here."

Tupper nodded eagerly. "Freydolf needs me."

"Oh? For what?"

Tugging his brother toward the man in question, Tupper listed, "Making fires, waking for breakfast, watering the trees, sweeping up ... stuff like that."

Carden nodded, for these were the sorts of jobs any Flox youngster expected to do the first time they were hired out. "I can give you a hand today," he offered.

Halting in his tracks, Tupper fixed him with a hopeful look. "Do you know how to cook?"

Quick about putting the pieces together, Carden ruefully admitted, "Probably no better than you can, Tupp. You know how Mother is about her kitchen, and Melina's much the same. I've never had to fend for myself."

"Too bad," sighed Tupper.

Aurelius strode past then, calling, "The carriage is open, Frey. Show Dart the way back to his pedestal before he dries off!"

Perhaps because the merchant actually used the dragon's name this time, Freydolf didn't argue. Slipping free of the statue's coiling embrace, he led Dart to the ramp Old Gruff had set up before heading back down the mountain. The old quarryman had declared the Pred merchant's carriage a carpenter's feat, for one entire side could be swung open to accommodate the loading of large stones and statues.

Freydolf asked, "Can you feel it, Dart? You know your pedestal is up here. Time to rest for your journey."

Without a fuss, the blue dragon ascended the ramp and stepped carefully into the straw-lined crate. Tupper clambered up after him and watched with interest as the dragon folded itself into a neat column of scaled loops. Reaching down to pat Dart's muzzle, the boy said, "You'll have a fountain all your own in a land where stones are red."

Freydolf climbed up to kneel beside the crate, checking statue and pedestal. "Aye, Aurelius will see you safely there. Don't give him *too* much trouble."

To Carden's surprise, Tupper leaned down to kiss the dragon's nose, saying, "It's not because he doesn't want you."

The sculptor's eyes widened, and he hoarsely muttered, "Never think that!"

Nodding in satisfaction, Tupper pronounced his final benediction, the same one Merona Meadowsweet always used when sending off her children. With a smile for courage, he urged, "Be brave, and do your best."

20

Send-Off

Not long after sunset, Aurelius announced that he was retiring early, claiming emotional fatigue due to the day's trauma. Freydolf suspected it was simply a ploy to get out of the work left over from waking the water guardian, but he didn't complain. His brother-in-law had briskly taken over when it was time to nail shut the crate, something the sculptor simply couldn't bring himself to do. Saying goodbye to one of his own was never easy, but Dart would have been particularly hard to seal away.

With Carden's help, the reminders were soon hidden from view. Tarps folded, rocks removed, stone basins stowed, and a few lanterns were lit to help stave off the deepening darkness. Tupper snuck into the balcony long enough to borrow a few favorite figurines, so he could show them off to his brother—a gangling knight on a pudgy pony, a princess with a crown of feathers, and a centaur with a quiver and bow.

Freydolf drifted over to the golden stone that was his next responsibility and caressed its roughened surfaces. The best cure for farewells had always been work, and his hands were restless after a day away. While he donned his apron and checked his tools, the sculptor stole glances at the Meadowsweet brothers as they settled in for the night.

"I've never seen a bed this grand," Carden remarked as he took the inside.

"Too big for me, too little for Freydolf."

"I see," the young man murmured, propping himself up against the wall. "Tupp, is there a *rock* under here?"

"Yes." The boy lifted his pillow to proudly display his chunk of sunstone. "She's mine. Frey said."

With a bemused glance at the sculptor, Carden repeated, "I see."

Freydolf rubbed the back of his neck, embarrassed over being caught eavesdropping.

Carden said, "From what Mister Harrow has told me, a gift of stone from a Keeper is pretty special."

"This is my third!" Tupper looked to the long ledge beneath the windows, then up at the sky. "Almost dark enough."

"For what?"

"Starlight. Olexi needs stars to wake him up."

While the brothers chatted, Freydolf idly chipped at the rock, making no progress but doing no harm. It felt good to do something, even if it was nothing. Lost in his own thoughts, it was a while before he realized that Tupper had fallen silent, and he turned to see if all was well.

Carden said, "He wore himself out."

"Aye." Frey couldn't help smiling at the picture the two made, with Tupper curled up against his brother's side, and Carden gently untangling the boy's curls. Glancing at the tools in his hands, Freydolf asked, "Am I keeping you from your rest?"

"No," the young man assured, his eyes following Olexi's slow march along the bed's perimeter. "I doubt I could sleep."

Freydolf wondered fleetingly if Carden was aware that they shared a name. It didn't seem likely that Tupper had brought it up. Little boys had their own set of priorities where news was concerned, and he'd apparently deemed pink shells and fish traps more vital than an oath of brotherhood. After all, the lad had plenty of brothers. What was one more?

With a sigh, the sculptor set aside his tools, for his heart was in no fit state for him to be touching a stone. The last thing he wanted was for this melancholy mood to seep into one of his sculptures. Carrying a chair closer to the bed, Freydolf dropped into it. "Did any of the lad's explanations raise more questions than they answered?"

"Dozens," Carden replied. "May I ask a few?"

"Aye," the sculptor agreed. "As many as you like."

"If you'll pardon my intrusion," the Flox began, "I *would* like to know ... what is my brother to you?"

Freydolf hadn't expected a personal question, and for several moments he sat with his eyes lowered, trying to find the words to express just how desperately he needed the boy. Unsure if Carden could grasp the full weight of his former isolation, he met the young man's gaze and earnestly answered, "Tupper is good company."

Tupper woke first. For a little while, he stayed in bed, putting off all the things that must happen next. But then he decided that it might be nicer if Aurelius found nothing to complain about on his last morning on Morven, and his bare feet hit the cool floorboards. It was time to light the fires.

He ran everywhere, for his morning tasks multiplied to include drawing an extra bath, locating a missing button, and polishing Aurelius's boots. Thankfully, breakfast didn't burn, and it only took two tries to get Freydolf out of bed. Carden helped where he could, but the young man had his own duties in the stable. Somehow, everything was accomplished before the sun had burned off the mists that lingered amidst the trees and in the valleys below the heights.

They would give Aurelius a good start for his long journey.

Four matched blood bays were harnessed to the fine carriage, looking strong and lively as they stomped their hooves and shook their dark manes. Carden stood aside as Aurelius checked his work and accepted the Pred's approving nod with a hand over his heart.

"You'll ride with me, Mister Meadowsweet, so tell your brother goodbye and climb up," the merchant directed.

"See you soon, Tupp," Carden said simply.

With a nod, the boy replied, "Hope so."

Aurelius took much longer in saying his farewells to Freydolf, for the man was the sort to give lots of last minute advice. Tupper didn't mind waiting since it meant Aurelius was still here. Tipping his head to one side, he closed his eyes and tried to memorize the way the men's voices sounded together—Freydolf's teasing rumbles and Aurelius's sharp grousing. He would miss their banter.

"Asleep on your feet, sprat?"

Opening his eyes, Tupper started, for Aurelius had stolen up in true Pred fashion. The man crouched before him so that they were nose-to-nose, and his eyes glittered mockingly.

Tupper opened his mouth to say his goodbye, but the word didn't want to come out. Ducking his head, he stared at his toes and blinked hard against the prickling of tears.

Aurelius gripped his shoulder and quietly said, "I'm counting on you, Tupper. Almost as much as Frey is."

He glanced up, surprised by the man's gentled tone.

With a little half-smirk, Aurelius said, "The big lout made me swear not to extract any promises from you, so how about some advice instead?"

Tupper slowly nodded.

Aurelius dropped a knee to the ground in order to lean close enough to whisper, "A mother is for bossing, but a brother is for back-up."

"I'm both."

"Aye. Can you handle it alone?"

He frowned a little and pointed out, "I won't be alone."

"Your logic never fails to astonish, sprat."

Tupper had a feeling that this goodbye was going poorly. "Is that bad?" he mumbled, his gaze pleading with the man to understand all the stuff he couldn't say.

For just an instant, Aurelius looked flustered, but then he launched into the same sort of diatribe Freydolf had just endured. "Make sure he bathes. Don't let him skip meals. Take him out for walks. And *do* try to diversify his wardrobe."

It was nice that Aurelius had reverted to his usual self—bossy and bratty. Tupper nodded at appropriate intervals as the agent's list of reminders grew longer, but finally he shook his head.

Aurelius cocked a brow. "No? You are opposed to clean hearths?"

Tupper didn't want to be a ninny, but he couldn't very well let the Pred go like this. Maybe it would make Aurelius complain, but he didn't know how else to say something without words. With a soft sniffle, he flung his arms around the man's neck and hugged him tight.

To his relief, Aurelius didn't get angry. Tupper found himself pulled into a steadying embrace.

The only scolding he received was when the Pred softly said, "Took you long enough."

21

Triads

Tupper wasn't needed every minute of every day, so he had to figure out what to do with all his leftover hours. Falling back on familiar things, he'd lugged blankets into the outer courtyard, weighting their corners against fitful breezes that smelled like change. Winter was coming soon, but he hoped it would wait a little longer. There were things he wanted to do first.

On his way back to the workshop, the boy noticed a narrow set of stairs leading up to the right and paused. Aurelius had said he should learn Morven inside and out. Was this a good place to start?

Tupper knew he had the time to spare, so he nodded to himself and checked to see where the steps led.

The passage climbed to a dead end, which was certainly strange, but when the boy turned to retrace his steps, he realized the builder had played a trick. "Found it!" he whispered as he fiddled with a clever catch that opened a half-hidden door.

Crossing into a neighboring stairway that led higher still, he soon discovered several niches with statues, a tiny bridge with stone railings, a chair so grand, it looked like a throne, and a swing that squeaked when it swayed.

His exploration ended when the meandering passages led him back down into the inner courtyard, which was currently bathed in sunlight. Choosing a smooth bench, he lay down and let the gray stone's collected heat warm him as he soaked in the quiet. The silence was complete, for there were no trees to rustle in the breezes that slipped in through the Apprentice Gate. All the plants and animals in this part of the Statuary were made of stone, so they wouldn't stir until moonrise.

Ever since Tupper could remember, he'd searched for peaceful places to hide away, but he'd never imagined the perfect spot was on top of a mountain. He supposed it made sense. You had to go where no one went if you wanted to be alone. Here, time passed slowly enough that he could keep up.

Just then, the sun slipped out of the patch of blue sky far overhead, leaving him in shadow. A flurry of whistling flaps startled him as four rock doves flew from the railing of one of the high balconies looming overhead, chasing after the day. Tupper lifted both hands, waving after them, for he didn't mind sharing the courtyard. After all, wasn't Freydolf sharing the Statuary with him?

At that thought, Tupper rolled to his feet and trotted off toward the outer courtyard to collect his master's bedding, certain that the quiet was helping him think more clearly. Otherwise, he might have forgotten something important.

Tupper liked quiet, but Freydolf was different. He seemed happiest when there was busyness and noise ... and someone to talk to. The boy had been away from the workshop long enough; it was time to go back and remind Freydolf that he wasn't alone.

Freydolf was alternately amazed and amused when Tupper resolutely joined him in the necessary during bathtime. "Do you suspect me of leaving parts unwashed?" he joked as he lowered himself into the hot water.

"Did you?" the lad returned, his eyes firmly fixed on his handiwork. Pink-cheeked and bashful, Tupper sat on the floor, a mess of vines at his side as he created the framework for a new basket.

With a noncommittal grunt, Freydolf dunked himself, then reached for shampoo. He glanced guiltily at his servant as he poured a generous amount into his hand. Was it possible the boy could tell he'd skipped washing his hair during his last two baths?

To the Pred's relief, the boy switched subjects. "Who made the fountain ladies?"

"Do you mean the statues at the end of this colonnade?"

"Yes."

Frey smiled, for the three sylph-like women had been charming apprentices for centuries. "They're said to be modeled after the three daughters of the third Keeper. We call them the Triads because there are actually two sets of them— those atop our fountain and another arrangement at the end of the westernmost passage leading off the Cavern. I should take you there in time for sunset one of these days. The titian jade is especially ...."

"There are three," Tupper interrupted.

"Three ladies, Freydolf agreed.

"Three sets," Tupper corrected, peeking out of the corner of his eye. "I found them in another place."

Freydolf stopped scrubbing at his scalp. "Where?"

"In a little room." Gesturing vaguely with one hand, Tupper replied, "Up, down, up, and up from the squeaky swing."

The directions made no sense to Freydolf, so he instead asked, "Are you sure it was them? There are a lot of statues of ladies around here."

The lad frowned thoughtfully, then nodded. "They don't have water jars, but their necklaces are the same."

Feeling rather foolish, Frey asked, "They have necklaces?"

Tupper went back to his basketry. "Yes. A lock, a key, and a moon."

Blinking away a dribble of soap bubbles, the man took the time to rinse his hair. A triad of Triads? He couldn't remember any mention of other sculptures of Master Tremont's daughters, but the oldest records were haphazard at best. "I've never noticed them roaming about. Are they in a place where the moon can reach?"

"They don't want the moon."

Frey's brows drew together. "*All* the oldest statues are carved from moonstone."

"These aren't. They're pink."

Nearly forgetting Tupper's preferences where modesty was concerned, Freydolf sloshed over to the end of the tub and propped his arms on the verge. "Dawnstone?" he asked excitedly. "Will you show me?"

With a sidelong look that was positively speculative, his servant haggled, "If I show you the sunrise statues, will you show me the sunset ones?"

"Aye! Tomorrow, if the sky's clear."

"You'll need to wake up early," the boy warned.

"Gladly," Freydolf assured, his eyes brightening further. "By any chance, does that mean these ladies of yours are master-marked?"

Tupper nodded. "They dance."

Freydolf readily admitted that there were untold mysteries in Morven's stone galleries—half-forgotten avenues, cleverly-concealed hideaways, and best-left-buried experiments. These were every Keeper's legacy and responsibility, and he'd always considered himself a careful caretaker. He'd been fairly certain he knew every nook and cranny in the buildings that loomed over the inner courtyard, for he'd climbed the stairs to every turret and investigated each terrace and tier. It was both humbling and humorous that in a matter of weeks, Freydolf's new servant had found a rare treasure hidden right under his nose.

"Higher still?" he inquired, lifting his lantern when Tupper paused at a juncture.

"Yes," Peering up at him in the predawn darkness, the lad warned, "It gets narrower."

Freydolf was already turned sideways in the snug little alley between buildings. "Lead on, lambkin. I'll manage somehow."

Given the route the boy took, it wasn't any wonder that Freydolf had never entered this section of the heights. The path was meant more for willowy boys than a man of his stature. At times, he was barely able to wedge his large frame through the tight archways dividing the maze Tupper navigated with ease.

Finally, the boy stopped before a squat door and patted its handle. "In here."

Bending low to enter, Freydolf found himself in a small, twelve-sided room. The three easternmost walls were completely taken up by windows that offered a magnificent view of the horizon, where the pearly sky was already touched with color.

In the center of the chamber, he could make out the forms of three slender young women and stepped closer to study their faces. "Dawnstone," he murmured in awe. Both the triad and the floor on which they stood were the distinctive rosy hue of the stone that waited for sunrise.

Quickly locating the maker's mark on the nearest statue, Freydolf excitedly relayed, "Aye, these are Master Tremont's daughters. Amazing!"

"They're nice," Tupper said, his eyes on the sky outside, where salmon pink was giving way to a warm yellow.

As soon as the bright rim of the sun broke into the sky, the trio lifted their arms in unison, bowed, then whirled into the steps of a lively folk dance.

The sculptor smiled at the pretty picture they made, and as the light gained, he was able to confirm the detail Tupper had mentioned. All three girls had necklaces. The one who wore a tiny key at her throat stepped out and offered her hands to Tupper. To Freydolf's astonishment, his servant set aside his lantern and executed a precise bow, then let her lead him to the middle of the room. Eyes sparkling, the lad wove between the ladies, clearly performing the male counterpart to their carefree dance.

"You know the steps?" Frey asked.

"Rachel taught me because Ewert wouldn't dance with her," Tupper explained without missing a beat. "This is the midsummer dance. It's easy."

Freydolf was aware of Flox celebrations, but he'd never attended one. "You're good at this, lambkin."

"I like it. Festival time is my favorite."

Smiling sweetly, the maiden whose necklace bore a small lock offered her hands to Freydolf, and he bowed, but in apology. "I'm afraid I don't know your dance, young lady. Thank you, but I'm content to watch."

As the statue rejoined her sisters and his servant, the Pred realized several things in a rush. All three girls were slender, and their hair was arranged in an abundance of curls. Tupper fit right in with them as they revolved through the traditional, local dance.

Frey blurted, "They're Flox!"

"Yes," agreed Tupper, who'd begun humming to himself.

"Master Tremont must have been Flox," Freydolf mused aloud. He wracked his brain, trying to remember what little was recorded about the ancient Keepers. If he remembered right, the third one had hailed from First Continent. "Or his wife was Flox, at the very least."

"He did good."

Indeed, he had. Admiring the graceful dance and the maidens' gentle expressions, Freydolf would even go so far as to call this Tremont's masterpiece. Setting aside his lantern, he watched Tupper play the part of a young gentleman, and slowly, another possibility occurred to him. As a stranger in this land, Master Tremont may have adopted the girls to liven up a lonely home. It was a pleasant thought.

When the young lady with a moon necklace next invited Freydolf into the circle, Tupper stopped dancing long enough to offer his hands as well. "It's fun," he coaxed.

Unable to refuse, Frey put his hands in theirs and joined the dance.

From the Cavern, Freydolf led the way to the gallery designated by a keystone of vividly orange titian jade, and Tupper couldn't have been happier. Just like the white gallery, it meandered deep into the mountain, with amazing things waiting to be discovered at every turn.

They had all day to reach the far chamber where the last of the Triads resided, so Freydolf set a leisurely pace. Tupper held Brand's hand much of the way—just to be friendly. It seemed to the boy that the red statue was glad for company, for the Grif warrior often smiled down on him and even patted his head once.

Losing track of time was easy in the galleries, so Tupper was relieved when a lofty colonnade opened into an elegant rotunda with windows high above. Sunlight spilled into the space at a sharp angle, letting them know that the day was near its end.

"We missed lunch," Tupper said with a chagrined glance at his master.

"Aye," the man agreed, though he seemed more interested in the mosaic on the floor than in his empty stomach.

The late afternoon light glowed warmly against chippings of red, orange, and yellow stone that had been fitted together to create a fiery bird. "We should eat here instead of waiting. The porch isn't enclosed, so it'll be too cold for picnicking."

Nodding, the boy trotted over to Brand. "Bag, please."

The statue slipped the strap of their single carry-sack from his shoulder and extended it, and Tupper made short work of laying out a simple meal. It was really too bad they were out of bread. Freydolf would have liked some bread.

"Ready."

Freydolf sat next to him, stretching out long legs as he gazed at the domed ceiling high above. "The ones who finished this section really took their time." Pointing toward the archway leading off to the left, he said, "There are small homes all along the next hall, so the builders probably lived and worked right here for years and years."

Tupper gazed around the six-sided hall with interest. On three of the walls, statues of wise-looking men with staffs reached toward the sky, and on the other three, there were archways. They'd entered through one, and Freydolf had indicated the second; however, the third was barred by a heavy door.

"What's that way?" he asked, for its heavy lock looked rather foreboding.

Pausing between bites, the Keeper replied, "There's a statue beyond there that's best left sleeping."

"Why?"

"Sometimes when a statue is woken, something goes wrong. It's hard to say if it's the fault of the man, the stone, or some quirk of magic. For instance, it's said that the quality of the wine used on sunstone can influence the statue's temperament, and there are tales that warn of waking moonstone while a cloud is passing over the moon." Freydolf gazed solemnly at the locked door. "Master Platt called them the Misbegotten."

"Are they bad?"

With a grimace, the sculptor admitted, "Aye, some are. Others simply make too much mischief to be left loose, so we close them away where they cannot wake. Drape and shutter, lock and key—most of the Misbegotten sleep in the lower galleries, but this one was too big to move."

They didn't linger over their food, for they were losing the light. Throwing everything back into their bag, Tupper beckoned to Brand, who accepted it with a wink.

Just as Freydolf had said, the final chamber wasn't far.

Columns decorated a wide veranda. They were thick with carved vines, and right away, Tupper noticed that they were studded by fat cones of orange stones like prickly gems. In the very center, protected by a copper-roofed gazebo, stood the same three ladies they'd danced with at sunrise. Only these statues were carved from moonstone. The girls remained still and silent as they watched the sunset with joined hands.

Freydolf had Brand help him light the torches, which wavered in the stiff gusts that swept the heights. "Where's your cloak, lambkin?"

Tupper rummaged in their baggage again, glad his master had insisted on bringing extra layers. Buttoning into his, he carried the indigo one to Freydolf, then checked the position of the sun. The entire western horizon was ablaze—orange, magenta, and violet blending into a deeper blue where the first stars shone faintly. The instant the bright rim of the sun touched the distant hills, Freydolf murmured, "That's it. Look!"

In the ruddy light of the setting sun, the points of vivid jade trembled, twirled, then unfurled their delicate petals.

With a soft gasp at the sudden display, Tupper stepped back to try to see everything at once, for the flowers seemed to glow in the last light of day. "Pretty!" he declared.

"Aye. A fair trade for your sunrise trek?"

Tupper's answering smile was secretive, for he knew he'd made the better bargain. Having Freydolf all to himself for the day had been even more fun than a midsummer festival, harvest festival, and birthday party all put together in one. With Flox formality, he offered his hand, saying, "The trade is good; may our next be better still."

Chuckling softly, Freydolf closed both his hands around Tupper's smaller one. In Pred fashion, he intoned, "Your satisfaction is mine. Let peace remain between us."

The deal was done.

Tupper woke because he was cold and muzzily reached for his blankets. Pulling them back to his shoulders, he peeked around the edge of his bed curtain to check the sky. In the pale light of dawn, he could see patterns of frost decorating the windows, but then he spotted something else. With a soft noise of dismay, he slipped from the bed, gasping when his feet hit the cold floor.

On tiptoe at the window, he watched between the lattices with wide eyes until another snowflake drifted across his line of sight. Winter had arrived?

He sighed in disappointment, for he'd planned to check the fish traps today and gather more vines. He wanted to weave little fences for the outer courtyard to fend off the rabbits who foraged there. It wouldn't do if they nibbled away any more of Freydolf's meager garden; actually, it was a wonder there was any garden left.

His trek down the southern slopes would have to wait until spring.

On his way to the kitchen to start a fire, Tupper noticed that Freydolf's scanty blanket was off-kilter and hurried over to tuck him in.

The man opened an eye and grunted a sleepy greeting. "Too early," he complained.

"You stayed up too late."

"Maybe."

"Winter came," he whispered, sharing the dreadful news.

"Too early for that, too."

"There's snow!"

Freydolf shrugged unconcernedly. "Won't stick yet ... but I think I'll hibernate until the sun's back. Good day to burrow."

Leaving his master to his rest, Tupper lit the kitchen fire, then one of the balcony fires for good measure. After that, a quick dash to the necessary left his feet painfully cold, so he searched the small chest next to his bed and located a lumpy pair of socks. They sagged around his thin ankles, and there were no less than three holes, but they were better than nothing.

Tupper padded to Freydolf's bed again and gave his shoulder a shake. "Do you want breakfast?"

The man yawned, showing off his fangs, then squinted at the boy. "Too early," he grumbled again. "Have mercy, lambkin! It's cold!"

Tupper knew that well enough. He was having a hard time keeping his teeth from chattering.

Frowning to himself, the man demanded, "Show me your hands." When the boy complied, Freydolf's large, warm hand closed around his, and his frown deepened. "You're freezing!"

Feeling like they were going in circles, the boy sighed and explained, "It's snowing."

Freydolf said, "I propose a trade."

"What kind?"

"You let me sleep as late as I like, and I'll let you loan me your blanket."

The boy sternly declared, "That's a poor trade."

Frey chuckled and amended, "We burrow until the sun's high, and I'll grant you a boon."

Tupper's mind whirled as he weighed his options, for there were so many things he wanted to finish before winter set in. He could only get so much done on his own, and it was hard to decide which parts were most important.

Suddenly, he knew what bargain would suit him best. Nodding once, he made his counter-offer. "If I loan you my blanket and burrow with you, you'll trade with me for today."

"Trade what?" Freydolf asked curiously.

"Places."

The Pred's heavy brows drew together. "How do you mean?"

"For the rest of the day, you'll be my servant."

22

Master of Hearth and Home

Sunshine assaulted Freydolf's senses, and he scowled in protest, burrowing deeper under his blankets, putting off the day for a while longer. His stirring disturbed his half-forgotten companion, but a short jab to the ribs refreshed his memory. With greater care, he eased to the edge of his narrow mattress, giving Tupper a little more room.

The Pred was still rather awed by this one young Flox's abiding trust.

Previous servants had carried warding charms and paled whenever he made eye contact, but this boy made a point of sticking close. Even now, Tupper was reaching for him. Freydolf watched the boy's hand pat across the gap between them, perhaps searching for missing warmth. Either that, or his little mother was worried about him.

Fingers bumped his chest, then latched onto his tunic, and with a wriggle, Tupper closed the distance between them. Freydolf tentatively patted the boy's back as he'd seen Carden do, and for just a moment, Tupper peered hazily at him from under pale lashes.

Frey froze, unsure how the lad might respond, but Tupper only smiled sleepily and nestled closer.

Incredible.

A crooked smile found its way onto Frey's face, and he wondered if this might not be the closest thing to parenthood he'd ever experience. Though their roles were muddled, Tupper definitely inspired familial feelings. He knew the lad wasn't properly *his*, but he desperately wanted to foster this sense of belonging that was growing stronger with every passing day.

Aurelius had been smitten with Tupper, and in his own devious way, his brother-in-law had set out to win *the sprat*'s admiration and affection. Freydolf was less sure of himself when it came to chasing after what he wanted. He was accustomed to taking things as they came and taking care of them as best he could. That's how he'd become Morven's, and she'd become his.

Maybe it would be the same with Tupper—gradual, mutual, and permanent.

"I hope so, lambkin," he quietly admitted, a little frightened by just how much he meant it.

"More?" asked Freydolf, glancing quizzically at his young taskmaster.

"More."

"How much more?"

Tupper glanced up from his own work. "Lots more."

Chuckling to himself, the Pred tugged down another vine to add to the boy's growing collection. They'd been busy since midday, and he was impressed by Tupper's management. At first, Freydolf had wondered if his servant would take advantage of the day's role reversal, but so far, he'd been given nothing but wholly reasonable commands.

Tupper only asked for help with things that would have been difficult for him to accomplish on his own. Indeed, they worked side by side—lugging in the last of the pears, mucking out the stables, and now gathering more vines.

Freydolf tossed another coil onto the pile and checked, "Are your feet warm enough?"

Hands busy with stripping leaves, Tupper said, "I'm fine."

He was sitting on a flat stone that was probably warm from the sun despite the air's chill, so perhaps he was.

"We should get you some boots before winter."

"That would be good."

"Aye," agreed Freydolf, knowing it would mean a trip down into one of the villages—and soon. Yanking a particularly stubborn bit of vegetation, he asked, "So what will you use all these for?"

"The garden. I want to make it better, but there are too many rabbits. These are for fences."

Freydolf was quietly thrilled. Most servants didn't last more than a season or two, but Tupper was making plans for the future. Smiling broadly, he said, "If the rabbits are getting out of hand, maybe Ember needs some day help."

"Who?"

"That little fox you liked so much," said Freydolf. "Ember is—or *was*—guardian of the Statuary's henhouse, way back when. Since he doesn't have a flock to tend, he entertains himself by making trouble for the rabbits that wander into the courtyards after sunset."

"Ember," Tupper softly echoed. "I didn't know that was his name."

"It's etched into that little mischief-maker's back paw. His creator had quite the sense of humor, putting a fox in the hen house."

"Do you like eggs?" Tupper suddenly asked.

"Aye."

The boy stared fixedly at him. "Eggs are easy to cook."

Freydolf caught on and asked, "Are you hoping to put Ember back to work?"

"Maybe." After a pause, Tupper amended, "Probably."

"We could talk to Aurelius about it in the spring," he offered. "Although he'll probably ask us why we don't just eat the rabbits."

"I didn't learn hunting," Tupper confessed. "Only fishing."

With a trace of chagrin, Freydolf admitted, "I was taught to hunt, but I didn't learn to like it."

"Do you want fish for supper?"

"Aye. Shall we check the traps?"

"Yes," he agreed. "But first more vines."

"How many more?"

With a small smile to hint that Tupper knew full well who was boss, the lad repeated, "Lots more."

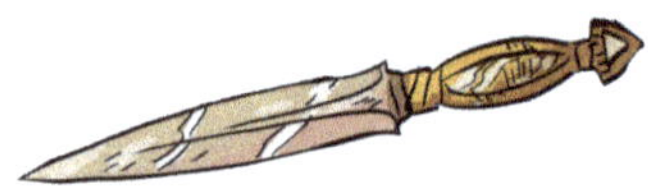

That evening, Tupper made it clear that he was still in charge of the cooking. Freydolf gratefully acquiesced, but insisted on doing the dishes afterward. The man was less happy when he was sent to warm water for their baths.

"We had one yesterday," he pointed out, an edge of petulance to his tone.

"Today, too," Tupper insisted.

"Aye, sir," the man sighed, shambling out.

While he was gone, the boy did several household chores that were easier done than delegated. He added wood to all three balcony fireplaces in hopes of doing a better job of keeping the workshop warm overnight. After similarly banking the kitchen fire, he added an extra blanket to Freydolf's bed.

"Better," he said, then reluctantly turned to the one task he'd been putting off.

A large trunk against the wall held all the clothes Aurelius had ever given Freydolf, and Tupper carefully lifted the lid. Rich fabric, fine tailoring, extravagant trimmings—it was almost like sifting through a treasure chest. Tupper sorted and sniffed, trying to find something Freydolf wouldn't mind wearing.

Choosing was hard. He'd hoped for something red, but maybe deep orange was close enough? Finally deciding that tucks were probably less offensive than ruffles, Tupper made his selections, grabbed his own nightshirt and cloak, and trotted along the passage toward the entrance to the lower level.

By the time he reached the necessary, Freydolf was already in the bath, and his gaze locked on the bundle of clothing in the boy's arms with frank dismay. "Surely not," he begged.

"I'm going to wash your clothes," Tupper firmly announced.

"You already did!"

"That was over a week ago, and I only washed your shirt. I need to clean your pants."

Freydolf grumbled to himself, then challenged, "What about yours?"

Tupper looked down at himself, then offered a small shrug. "I'll wash mine, too. That's fair."

While the boy disappeared around the corner to change, Freydolf called, "Will everything be dry by morning?"

"I hope so." Poking his head around the corner, Tupper said, "I don't have any other pants."

"We should do something about that."

"That would be good," he admitted. Especially since his current set was wearing a little thin in the seat. Padding over to the row of deep basins, Tupper reached for a cake of the creamy laundry soap and set to work while Freydolf dawdled in the tub.

An idea came into Tupper's head, and he asked, "Am I in charge of keeping the house?"

"You're in charge of *everything* at the moment, sir," Freydolf drawled.

Tupper absently pushed up his nightshirt sleeves. "But *usually* ...?"

"Aye," his master relented. "I thought you already knew that. The day-to-day running of my household has been entrusted to you."

"Can I move things?"

Freydolf chuckled and said, "I doubt it, lambkin. You're almost the smallest thing in the building, save Olexi."

"*May* I move things?"

"Aye. And if you need help with the moving, ask me. I don't mind lending a hand."

Taking Freydolf at his word, when the plug was pulled and

fresh clothes donned, Tupper asked him to haul a cumbersome drying rack out of storage and tote it upstairs.

"I didn't even know I had such a contraption," Frey admitted. "It's been collecting dust for decades. Are you sure it'll work?"

"Yes," Tupper said. "It's good. Big, too."

"Where do you want it?" Freydolf asked, grunting as he maneuvered it through the workshop door.

"Kitchen, please."

The Pred struggled to set up the folding rack in front of the hearth.

Tupper shoved his load of wet laundry into the man's hands, saying, "Let me."

In short order, he disentangled the rickety-looking frame, and Freydolf commented, "You're an expert!"

As the boy hung Freydolf's red tunic on one of the rungs, Tupper explained, "Mother uses hers in winter. It was my job to turn the clothes so they dried faster."

The sculptor hummed in an interested way, then draped his freshly-scrubbed breeches over one of the crosspieces. "Like this?"

Tupper straightened the garment, but nodded. "That's good. You can have them back in the morning." With a sidelong glance at the man he softly added, "But those clothes are nice, too."

Freydolf scowled at his finery. "These sleeves are too poofy, and the breeches are stiff."

"That's how new pants are," Tupper reasoned. "If you wore them more, they'd soften up."

The man's expression suddenly shifted. "It's a disgrace for me to complain about an embarrassment of riches to someone who has naught but these." Freydolf offered, "I'd share if I could."

Tupper shook his head. "Your shirts are taller than me."

Once their clothes were arranged, Freydolf ventured, "How about for my last duty of the day, I tuck in my young master?"

"I'm not a master."

"Nonsense," Freydolf countered, scooping up his servant and tossing him toward the ceiling. Tupper yipped in surprise, so the man did it again. Striding toward the boy's bed, the Pred jovially declared, "You are master of baths and basketry, streams and stables, hearth and home! And for today, you were master of *me*." Gently pitching Tupper onto his mattress, he placed his upraised palm under his heart and bowed deeply. "Thank you for treating me kindly."

Righting himself, the boy gawked at the man.

Freydolf awkwardly rubbed the back of his neck. "I'm sorry, lambkin! Maybe Pred play too rough. Did I frighten you?"

Feeling a little childish, but not caring in the least, Tupper shook his head, held out his arms, and firmly directed, "Again!"

The next morning, when Tupper roused him for breakfast, Freydolf wasted no time checking his old tunic and breeches, fingering the heavy cloth to see if it had dried. The boy made no comment when he snagged them off the rack, only smiling a little and nodding to himself.

To the Pred, it smacked of teasing, so he ruffled the Flox's hair and defended, "To each his own," before carrying his old favorites along to the necessary.

Glad to be shed of his elegant attire, Freydolf dug into his usual morning mush with good appetite. Once he'd worked the edge off his hunger, he noticed that his servant was quieter than usual ... which was saying something. Waving his spoon at the boy, he asked, "What's going on in that wooly head of yours, lambkin? It must be serious."

"Yes," Tupper replied simply. With an uncertain glance, he added, "I think so."

"Well?" he prompted.

"Would it be all right ...?" he began, trailing off with a soulful look.

Unsure what was behind the boy's sudden bout of fidgets, Freydolf asked, "What is it you want, lad?"

Taking a deep breath, Tupper announced, "I want to go home."

23

Luff

There were reasons aplenty for the boy to want to return to his people. He was young. He was probably homesick. It made sense that Tupper might want to see his mother, his siblings, and even the new niece Carden had spoken of with such fondness. Freydolf had no reason to object to a trip into Hayward ... except for a tiny sliver of fear.

What if Tupper returned home and decided he preferred to stay?

Sense said otherwise, but Frey couldn't help feeling uneasy as they entered the lad's hometown. Heads turned, and the Pred was forcibly reminded that most Flox still fled before him. His shoulders sagged, and keeping his eyes downcast, he trailed after his servant, who led the way to one of the village's thatched cottages.

For the most part, the Meadowsweets' place looked like all the rest. The garden may have been a little larger, and an addition on the back of the house suggested that their home had been expanded at some point to accommodate a growing family.

Pausing with his hand on the gate, Tupper gazed up at him and announced, "This is the one."

"Aye." Knowing that the presence of a Pred was sure to cause trouble, Frey gripped the boy's shoulder and said, "It may be best if I wait out here, lambkin."

Tupper looked between him and the house with a puzzled expression. Then, his confusion cleared, and he offered, "I'll hold your hand if you're afraid."

With a small smile, Frey reminded, "They'll be afraid of me."

"No. I'll explain," the boy assured, taking his hand and leading him into the yard.

The man was touched by Tupper's confidence, but he was older and wiser. Waltzing through any Flox's front door was likely to cause a panic.

Gently extracting his hand, Freydolf firmly said, "Your family won't be prepared for a guest such as myself. You go ahead." He indicated a small wooden bench standing inside the walled garden. "I'll wait over there."

With a reluctant nod, the boy left him alone.

Freydolf crossed to the bench and, after a longer look, changed his mind. The seat was a pretty little piece of carpentry, and the last thing he wanted to do was break it. Settling onto the ground instead, he was relieved to realize that the garden wall was high enough to hide him from passers-by. He preferred to remain as unobtrusive as possible, so long as no one spotted him and assumed he was lying in wait. Wincing over memories from a previous foray into another village, he muttered, "That was a *most* unfortunate misunderstanding."

Having nothing else to occupy his time, Freydolf plucked a twig from amidst a ramble of hardy herbs and dragged it through the smooth dirt of the path. Before long, he'd sketched several tiny dragons and a jumble of notes in both Verit and Terse, and he was wishing he'd had the presence of mind to bring along his sketchbook. "This may work!" he murmured excitedly.

Tupper reappeared then, followed by a woman who had to be his mother. Blonde curls were arranged in a knot at the nape of her neck, and her pale blue eyes were wide.

"Master Freydolf!" she exclaimed, looking both nervous and curious at having her son's employer show up on her doorstep. "You should not be loitering in my garden!"

Ducking his head in apology, Frey murmured, "I apologize, marm. I can take myself to the square."

The woman made a soft tutting sound. "I'm not running you off, sir. I'm inviting you in!"

"Are you certain? I don't want to cause any trouble."

She made that same tutting noise and turned to her son. "Go, fetch Melina from over by Carden's. Rachel's with her, and they'll be wanting to see you."

The lad obediently trotted out the gate.

Her gaze returned to Freydolf, and she said, "I'm Merona Meadowsweet, Tupper's mother. Please, come inside, sir. I'll make tea."

Freydolf stooped slightly to enter and found himself in a room that smelled of green things and good food. Reeds much like the ones Tupper had harvested were heaped on a clean cloth in the corner, along with several baskets in various stages of construction. A large kettle bubbled over the fire, and a tiny girl sat on the hearth, staring at him with enormous blue eyes. Her lip trembled, and he quickly lowered his gaze and aimed for the far corner, ignoring the room's few chairs. Taking a seat on the floor against the wall, he made himself as small as possible.

Suddenly, another child poked his head through a hole in the ceiling where a spindly ladder led to some kind of attic. He looked a good deal like Tupper; however, there were no horns showing amidst his fair curls, and this child's eyes were blue.

Without preamble, he exclaimed, "You're big!"

"Aye," Freydolf agreed, keeping his voice low lest he frighten the little girl any further.

"Do you want to buy a basket? Mine are first rate!"

"Farley, you know Master Freydolf isn't here as a customer," Missus Meadowsweet chided as she bustled between cupboard and table, preparing refreshments. "He's an important guest, and you'll treat him with all due respect!"

"Yes, Mother," the boy mumbled, though his bright eyes showed none of the contrition with which he infused his tone.

Freydolf knew a troublemaker when he saw one and smiled to himself. Farley was nothing like his older brother, except in one respect. "You're a brave lad," he remarked, trying to be friendly.

"You're not so scary," Farley said from the safety of the loft.

With a smug look, he reasoned, "If you didn't eat Tupper, you won't eat me."

"Aye. I wouldn't."

"Besides, I'm twice as fast and ten times smarter than him!" the lad boasted. With a speculative glint, he suggested, "Once my horns come in, you should take me instead!"

"Farley!" scolded Missus Meadowsweet.

With a sulky glance, the boy defended, "It'd be a good deal!"

Just then, Tupper burst through the door and looked around the room. Spying his master in the corner, he relaxed a little, and with a cautious glance in his younger brother's direction, he swiftly took a seat at Freydolf's side.

The lad pointedly positioned himself to fend off Farley's advances, and the Keeper couldn't have been more pleased. It wasn't so much that he needed protecting. Tupper was simply making good and sure he didn't lose something he wanted for himself.

The realization warmed the sculptor's heart. After all, he was here for the very same reason.

Freydolf worried some about his servant's pensiveness, but none of his family seemed surprised by Tupper's watchful silence. Merona had tea ready to serve when two more ladies arrived, hovering uncertainly just inside the door. They cast long looks at the Pred sitting on the floor in the corner, and Frey bowed his head in greeting but thought it best to wait for someone else to handle the introductions.

The younger of the two was obviously a Meadowsweet, for she had the same coloring as Tupper—a sister. That meant that the petite young woman with deep golden curls, bright green eyes, and a small bundle in her arms must be Carden's wife Melina.

"Rachel, come pour!" Merona ordered. "How's Dulcie, Melina?"

"Doing well, Mother Meadowsweet. She's a good baby."

Making another small tutting sound, the lady of the house expertly arranged biscuits on a plate, then took the first of the steaming cups over to her guest. With impressive confidence, she announced, "Master Freydolf, my daughter-in-law Melina and my daughter Rachel. Girls, this is Tupper's employer, Master Freydolf. Your brother brought him for a visit. Isn't that nice?"

At her pointed look, Rachel nodded, but Melina actually stepped forward. Dipping her head politely, she said, "My husband speaks highly of you, Master Freydolf. I'm pleased to meet you."

Freydolf placed his hand under his heart. "Thank you, Missus Meadowsweet. The pleasure is mine."

She dimpled prettily at his response, then looked to her young brother-in-law. "Would you like to hold Dulcie, Tupp?"

He lifted both arms. "Yes, please."

"Are you sure?" Rachel asked sharply.

"Tupper's good with babies," Merona declared in no-nonsense tones. "He used to tend Aggie for me all the time."

Rachel's unhappy glances suggested she was more concerned about her brother's proximity to a Pred than to the lad himself. Still, Tupper cast an injured look at his older sister, who tossed her curls. Shrugging off Rachel's pique, he once more held out his arms to Melina, who showed no qualms over surrendering Dulcie.

The lad fearlessly unbundled the newest little Meadowsweet. Humming softly to the squirming infant, he counted each toe on her tiny feet before earnestly declaring, "All there."

Dulcie's face scrunched, and she opened one eye, then the other. Freydolf looked on with rapt fascination, for he'd never been this close to a newborn before. Delicate fingers clutched at the edge of the blanket her uncle carefully pulled back into place, and the boy offered his own finger for her to hold.

Smiling down at her, Tupper murmured, "Good grip."

Freydolf glanced again at the fearful child huddled by the

hearth. This must be Aggie. Those big, blue eyes were fixed on Tupper with such wistfulness, it nearly broke Frey's heart. The poor little thing was too shy to approach her beloved brother because of the monster he'd brought home.

To his relief, Melina crossed to the girl and knelt down to whisper to her. A few moments later, she took the youngster's hand, slowly leading her over. "You've missed your Tupp, haven't you, Aggie?"

Blonde ringlets bobbed when she nodded.

Melina continued, "Tupp's a big boy, so he works for Master Freydolf now."

Merona interjected, "Don't be afraid of him, baby girl. Big doesn't necessarily mean bad."

"What about brown?" Farley checked. "He's mostly brown."

"So's molasses," quipped his mother.

To Freydolf's amusement, this appeared to be a point in his favor.

Gently urging Aggie nearer, Melina coaxed, "Can't you see how much your Tupp likes him?"

Tupper spoke up. "He's good. Promise." Then, he shocked everyone in the room by turning to Freydolf and lifting the baby. "Your turn."

"Nay, lad," the man demurred, glancing nervously at Melina. He didn't wish to anger or frighten her.

Tupper made a tutting sound much like his mother and said, "You're Dulcie's uncle, too."

Freydolf opened and closed his mouth, but he had no words.

Merona broke the awkward silence. "What's this, Tupper?"

Before the sculptor could stop him, Tupper said, "He's a Meadowsweet."

The woman's gaze swung to Freydolf, who cleared his throat. "When your son found out I left my family name behind, he graciously offered to share his. His gift was recently formalized."

"On two continents," Tupper helpfully added as he stroked Dulcie's cheek.

"You adopted a Pred?" Farley demanded.

"No. We're sworn."

His younger brother narrowed his eyes suspiciously. "What's *that* mean?"

Tupper's brow furrowed, and Freydolf stepped in again, saying, "According to the traditions of my homeland, we're brothers."

Farley's fair brows lifted. "Is that so?"

"Aye," the Keeper confirmed, glancing cautiously at Merona.

"Does that make you my brother, too?" the outspoken youngster persisted.

Freydolf slowly replied, "If you like."

Hurrying to his mother's side, Farley tugged at her sleeve. "*Is* it so?"

The woman was having a difficult time hiding her amazement, but she snapped to attention and shot her youngest son a warning look. "Tupper said as much, and Master Freydolf confirmed it. What more do you need?"

With a whisk of full skirts, Melina knelt at Freydolf's other side and urged, "You *should* hold Dulcie! Pass her along, Tupp."

Nodding, the boy pushed up onto his knees so it would be easier to transfer his precious cargo. To the little one, he whispered, "This is your Uncle Frey. Him and me live on the mountain."

Freydolf straightened and tried to avoid taking the baby. With a panicky look at Melina, he stammered, "N-nay, missus. I've never ...!"

Carden's wife giggled and asked, "Haven't you ever held a baby?"

"Nay," he repeated weakly.

"She won't hurt you," Tupper offered encouragingly.

"What about *him*?" interjected Farley. "His fingers are all pointy!"

"He's careful!" Tupper defended, leaning into his master's side.

Meanwhile, Freydolf stared down at the tiny person entrusted into his keeping. He probably could have supported the wee girl with just one hand, but he thought it best to follow Tupper's example, tucking Dulcie into the crook of his arm. The contrast they made was staggering. She was dwarfed by his bulk, and he instinctively cupped his hand around her, wanting her to feel secure. He was awed by her miniature ears and the downy fuzz of her white-blonde hair.

Unsure what else to say, Freydolf lamely offered, "Your father speaks highly of you."

Melina giggled again. "Carden hardly puts her down when he's home. Dulcie's sure to be her daddy's girl."

Curious about the grip Tupper had extolled, Frey slipped a finger under the baby's hand, which rested pale against his darker skin. Shaking his head in wonder, he whispered, "She's perfect."

Someone tugged at his sleeve, and Freydolf turned to find that Tupper had his lap full again, for Aggie had claimed her rightful place, her arms wrapped possessively around her big brother's neck.

The lad asked, "Can I borrow your hand? Aggie wants to see."

Frey met the girl's wary stare. "Aye."

With a solemn nod, Tupper tugged the man's free hand into both his own and gave it a pat, saying, "See, Aggie? Pred have claws, but no horns. And no tails."

"Hey! Lemme see!" exclaimed Farley, dashing across the room in order to drape himself over the Keeper's other shoulder. "Are they sharp? Do you file 'em? I bet they're good for pickin' your teeth! Or your nose!"

Freydolf hunched defensively, trying to protect Dulcie from the sudden onslaught, but the baby was more used to the noise than he. She simply gripped his finger with all her might and tried to focus on the man's face with solemn green eyes. He cast a bewildered look at Merona, whose reaction stunned him further. She was *laughing* at him!

Just then, Rachel nervously applied to her mother. "They say Pred can kill with their bare hands! He could be dangerous!"

The good woman tutted. "Have you lost the use of your senses, girl? *Look* at the man!" With a tilt of her head, Merona addressed Freydolf directly. "If you don't mind my saying so, sir, you're as mild as moonlight!"

Finding the comparison remarkably apt, Freydolf murmured, "Aye, marm. Thank you for noticing."

"Hey!" yelped Farley, grabbing a hank of the Pred's hair. "Didja see that? Lemme see your teeth again, mister Master! Are those *real*?"

Laughing again, Merona said, "Welcome to the family, Master Meadowsweet."

Much to Freydolf's astonishment, once tea had been served, Missus Meadowsweet deemed the social niceties accomplished and resumed her day. Farley was sent to the village well for water, Rachel settled amidst the reeds and took up her basket-weaving, Melina moved to peel vegetables for dinner, and Frey faded into the background as resident baby-tender. The man hadn't been part of any sort of family life for so long, he watched the bustle of normalcy with a greedy sort of gratitude.

One thing puzzled him, though. He still wasn't certain why Tupper had asked for this visit. He glanced at the boy, who seemed to take the look as his cue. With a small nod, he worked his way free from Aggie's clinging embrace, saying, "Wait here. Right back."

Tupper plucked at his mother's sleeve and said something to her. The woman frowned and murmured back, and when the boy replied, her gaze darted toward Freydolf with an expression of incredulity. She subjected her son to a rapid round of questions, to which he responded with quick nods or shakes of the head. Desperately wishing he could hear what they were talking about, Frey wracked his brain for possible topics of conversation.

Suddenly, Missus Meadowsweet straightened and asked, "Can you stay for a meal, Master Freydolf?"

"Nay," he admitted. "The climb back will take time. We cannot stay long."

"I understand." Tapping her finger against her chin, she and Tupper returned to their quiet conference. A few moments later, the woman crossed to a tall chest of drawers and rummaged inside, producing a few scraps of brown paper and the stub of a pencil.

Freydolf's curiosity was mounting, but just then, Aggie distracted him completely by climbing onto his lap. She worked her way into the crook of the arm that wasn't occupied by Dulcie, and he did his best to make sure she was comfortably settled. Then, her true aim became apparent, for she reached up to pet a stray lock of his hair, peeping up at him to see if he minded. Given the universality of Flox fairness, Frey supposed his darker coloring *was* unusual, so he turned his head temptingly. "Your Tupp makes sure I wash my hair every other day. Did I do a good job?"

Aggie pulled his thick ponytail forward and sifted her fingers through the coarse waves, even going so far as to sniff it. "All clean," she decreed.

Indulging his own curiosity, he asked, "How old are you, Miss Aggie?"

"'Most six."

With a half-smile, Freydolf confided, "I'm beginning to think that all the Meadowsweets are very brave."

"Are *you* brave?" she inquired seriously.

"Not especially," he admitted. When her little brows furrowed, he remembered to simplify. "Not as brave as you."

She nodded, setting her springy curls to bouncing, then asked, "Are *you* afraid of Pred?"

After a moment's thought, he quietly answered, "Aye."

Blue eyes blinked. "Are you afraid of yourself?"

His smile widened. "Nay. No one should be afraid of me."

"I'm not," she informed him. "My Tupp luffs you."

Rather flustered, Freydolf retorted, "Is that what you think?"

"My Carden wented to live with Melina because he luffs her," she reasoned. "They made a family."

"Aye, but that's different."

The girl shook her head. "Mother said you're family. You're Tupp's."

Freydolf chuckled, for he could see how it might seem the same in the eyes of one so small. Relenting, he said, "Aye, Tupper takes good care of me. Thank you for sharing him, Aggie."

"Welcome," she replied, nestling close and switching her attention to the babe in his other arm. "Melina's a Meadowsweet now. So Dulcie's ours, too."

"Carden is a lucky man." In truth, Freydolf was feeling rather lucky himself; at least, he *was* … until Farley returned.

Freydolf had long believed that no one could out-talk Aurelius, but he soon discovered that eight-year-old boys were relentless creatures.

"Do you have a sword?" the lad pried.

"Nay."

"Why's your hair so long?"

"It grows."

"Have you ever invaded anything?"

"Does my pantry count?"

"Do you have mountains of gold?"

"My mountain is gray."

"Are all Pred as big as you?"

"Aye, except for the ones who aren't."

On and on it went, an endless barrage of questions that ranged from the ridiculous to the intensely personal, but Freydolf rather enjoyed answering and evading by turns. The children were as much a novelty to him as he was to them, so time passed quickly. An hour must have slipped by when Tupper trotted over to kneel in front of them.

"I'm done. We should go before the shops close."

"Aye," the man agreed, giving Aggie a boost to her feet.

The little girl flung her arms around Tupper and begged, "Come back soon?"

"No," he replied, patting her head. "I'll be snow-stuck until spring. After that, maybe."

"That's a long time," she complained, her lip trembling.

"Yes," he agreed, making no excuses.

Meanwhile, Freydolf carefully stood, still cradling little Dulcie. It hadn't occurred to him that this was the first time some of them had seen his full height, so he inadvertently made a spectacle of himself.

Carden's wife gasped, "Gracious!"

Farley snickered and said, "Hope your ceilings are higher than ours!"

"They are," Tupper assured, manfully lugging Aggie onto his hip. He frowned at her and said, "You're bigger."

"I'm not the baby no more," his sister shyly boasted.

"Be Dulcie's guardian 'til I come back?" he bargained. They traded nods, and Tupper set her down.

Melina held out her arms for her baby and lightly said, "You are *very* tall, sir!"

"Aye," he acknowledged, carefully surrendering Dulcie. "It's useful for reaching things, but inconvenient for blending in." Turning to Mrs. Meadowsweet, he bowed deeply. "Thank you for your hospitality."

She folded her hands over her heart and extended them, replying, "Thank *you* for giving Tupper a place."

"And he, me," Frey mumbled, hoping the woman understood.

"Errands next," Tupper announced in businesslike tones. With a stern look at Farley, he added, "*No* tagalongs."

"He'll be sorting onions in the attic," Merona assured, giving her youngest son a pointed look. Farley stuck out his lower lip but didn't argue.

After one last round of farewells, Freydolf and Tupper were on their way. At first, they walked in silence, the man admiring his up-close view of the countryside that skirted Morven's eastern face. When a thought occurred, he curiously inquired, "Did you do everything you wanted to?"

"No," the lad admitted. Patting his pocket, which crinkled with the sound of folded papers, he added, "But this is better than anything else so far."

Freydolf hummed and might have inquired further, but they arrived in front of a clothiers. Pointing to the shopfront, he asked, "Do they sell boots and breeches here?"

"Yes." With a hesitant look, Tupper said, "They'll be costly."

Loosening the pouch at his belt, Freydolf said, "I've money to spare, lambkin. Take whatever you need."

The lad accepted the small bag, undid its fastenings, and explored its contents. "This is too much," he muttered.

Ignoring all the gold coins, he extracted several silver and a few bronze, then handed back the pouch.

"Is that enough?"

"We'll get a better deal with less," Tupper asserted. "Hide the rest."

Aurelius had urged Freydolf to leave all business transactions to the boy, so he nodded and asked, "Should I wait out here?"

"No. Come in." Without batting an eye, he added, "They'll bargain faster to get you to leave."

Freydolf winced. "I don't like to frighten people."

"Yes," Tupper replied. "But Gruff says that gold for trust is a bad trade ... and silver is enough for pants."

"And boots," the man reminded.

"And then bread?"

A slow smile spread across the Pred's face. "Aye, as much as we can carry!"

24

The Fox and the Henhouse

It only took two days to run through the cache of bread they'd purchased from Pennyflax & Quince. Freydolf woke on the morning of the third day and peered around the daylit workshop in confusion. Why had Tupper left him to sleep? The lad was regular as clockwork, which meant something must be amiss.

Noises drifted from the direction of the kitchen, but they were ordinary sounds, so Frey didn't hurry to investigate. Swinging his feet to the floor, he rubbed at his face and scratched his head, running his fingers through the tangled length of his hair before reaching for the tie.

Still rather drowsy, he shuffled over to the kitchen door to check on Tupper. The lad was surrounded by a mess of tins, bowls, and utensils. Flour dusted the old wooden table, where a small stack of brown papers had been anchored by Olexi's hooves.

Tupper scooted the wee ram aside and referred to the paper before measuring some white powder into a ceramic bowl decorated by orange stripes.

"What's all this, lambkin?" Freydolf asked curiously.

"I'm cooking ... I think. Mother told me what to do."

Freydolf crossed to the table and scanned the topmost paper, which amounted to a recipe. A combination of simple words and pictures depicted ingredients, quantities, and processes. "I see!" he murmured. "So *this* is what you were after!"

"Yes."

"Can I help?" the man offered.

"This is *my* job," Tupper firmly replied.

Accepting the lad's determination, Freydolf withdrew, feeling rather foolish for ever thinking the boy had intended to go home to stay. This whole time, Tupper had wanted to acquire the skills he lacked. And who better to give him lessons in mothering than his own mother?

Freydolf wouldn't complain if the lad's cooking repertoire expanded to include something more interesting than mush.

That morning, breakfast was very late, but there were lumpy biscuits on the plate in the center of the table. They were nothing like the fine, yeasty loaves sold in village bakeries, but they were the closest thing to bread ever served at Frey's table.

"May I?" he asked eagerly.

"Yes," Tupper replied, casting nervous glances at his master all through the meal.

Slathered in the tart jellies from their pantry, the biscuits were more than passable, and Freydolf ate one after another. When the last was gone, the man licked sticky fingers with a sigh of satisfaction. "Tupper!"

"Yes?" he mumbled.

"This was *good!*" Freydolf exclaimed. "*Very* good!"

With a deep sigh of relief, his servant promised, "I'll get better."

The sculptor only nodded. As far as he was concerned, Tupper was already the best.

Tupper thought hard while washing the breakfast dishes, and after giving the workshop a quick sweep, he donned boots and cloak, then slipped outside. Today, he intended to locate Ember's hen house. It probably would have been easier to simply ask Freydolf where it was, but Tupper wanted to find it on his own. He even knew the best place to start.

Filled with a sense of purpose, he took long strides, trying to emulate the Keeper. Tupper's new boots made him feel a little taller, a little older, and perhaps a little bolder. This was a good day for exploring, and if he was quick, he might still have time to empty the fish traps for their lunch.

"Ember needs to see the sunset," he reasoned aloud, following the cobblestone road toward the stables. Surely the people who built things would have kept the animals all together in one area.

Nothing inside the freshly cleared barn looked like it was meant for chickens, but Tupper poked his nose into every cupboard and corner just to be sure. Back outside, he got his bearings, pointing to the western horizon. "Facing that way," he murmured, turning to consider the buildings behind him. The stable wasn't the only structure on this vantage point, and he stared hard at the jumble of tiers and turrets that seemed to march the rest of the way to the summit.

Such a castle seemed too fine for chickens, but it was hard to tell with the Statuary. Maybe the kind of Keeper who would give their flock a titian jade guardian would also give their flock a fancy place to roost.

Tupper climbed several flights of stairs and discovered interesting niches, but all the rooms he found were definitely meant for people, not chickens.

Recalling that his new home was both tall *and* deep, the boy backtracked to see if there was a way down.

Sure enough, across the courtyard from the stable, not far from a row of fanciful hitching posts, he found a narrow stair that angled sharply down through solid stone. The manmade ravine led onto a wide ledge edged by stout columns and a low wall. A miniature colonnade supported a network of sheltering vines whose leaves littered the ground. Tupper double-checked the spacious balcony's vantage, which overlooked the rolling hills to the west. Perfect!

Given the height and the overhanging greenery, this secretive place felt like a giant tree house, and Tupper was completely delighted. He was already planning to come again when he turned and spotted Ember sitting in an alcove between two small, square holes in a bowed wall. "There you are!"

The orange statue didn't react, but Tupper didn't mind. He patted the bright fox's head and promised, "I'll bring my broom next time and sweep."

Even though he didn't know much about chickens, he could tell that the basics were in place—feed bins, watering troughs, and even a small cistern. Mother always bought her eggs from Auntie Rue, but Melina had a tiny coop in the corner of her garden with three hens to give her eggs. He'd always liked the speckled cluckers, who were as tame as pets.

Crossing to a wide door set into the far corner, he pushed it open on creaking hinges. Cobwebs and shadows blanketed the dusty, musty interior, so he patted his pockets and brought out a stubby candle and a matchbox.

The additional light was enough to show him the interior. A rusty shovel stood in one corner, and dozens of decrepit baskets hung from a series of stone pegs lining the wall. Roosts crisscrossed the space overhead, and moldering straw and dry leaves had blown into the corners.

"Needs cleaning," he decreed. "But still good."

He emerged and carefully shut the door again, then sat down in front of the fox statue in order to make a deal. Pulling out the money cord Aurelius had given him, he fingered his few coins that were strung with the beads. "Tomorrow I'll clean the hen house, and in the spring, I'll buy chicks." Even though he wasn't sure the guardian could hear him, he bartered, "Until then, help me keep rabbits out of the garden. It'll work out because by the time you have a flock, I'll have fences."

Giving Ember a final pat, he lit back up the stairs and headed toward the southern slopes, certain he'd made a good deal. Ember would like having chickens to mind, and Freydolf would like eating the eggs they'd lay. For the rest of the day, Tupper blissfully counted chickens that had yet to hatch.

Freydolf was laboring over delicate ear tufts when he saw a flash of white out of the corner of his eye and turned to see Tupper trotting to the door. He'd thought the lad was already asleep, but perhaps nature called.

But that wasn't it.

Now that the sculptor had stopped working, he realized that there was *another* source of tapping. Someone—or more likely, some*thing*—was at the door.

With considerable amusement, Frey looked on as his servant played doorman for Ember. Although Morven's plentiful statues occasionally sought out their Keeper, this was the fox's first time.

Ambling over, he gruffly inquired, "What are you after, bit of mischief?"

"He and I have business," Tupper explained seriously.

Frey was surprised, yet he wasn't. The lad had an uncanny way with marked and unmarked stone.

"Regarding rabbits?" he guessed.

"And chickens," the lad confirmed.

"Aye. Then, I suggest you move your conference to warmer climes."

"Like First Continent?"

Although the young Flox had never journeyed, the Statuary's mysteries were definitely fostering a fascination for distant lands. Mealtimes were often sprinkled with questions about far-off places and cultures. Tupper's interest was a little different from the sculptor's own, for while Freydolf contented himself with stone, his servant wondered aloud about the people who lived in, on, or near the other mountains.

"I was hoping for something closer to home."

Taking the hint, the boy hurried back to his bed, pausing to try to boost Ember up ahead of him. The fox was hardly the largest of statues, but he was still made of stone. "Heavy!" gasped the boy as he awkwardly wrapped his arms around the guardian's chest, leaving Ember's hind legs dangling.

The cheerful creature didn't seem to mind the indignity. His paws waggled, and his tail swayed.

"Let me," said Freydolf, hurrying over.

Tupper clambered into bed, and the sculptor easily lifted the fox after him. Poking the statue's nose, he said, "If you're going to make a habit of this, lambkin, have Ember sit by the hearth beforehand to take away the chill."

"Next time," Tupper agreed.

He'd been half-joking, but Freydolf strongly suspected that the die was now cast. The *only* way to get rid of their cheeky titian jade bed-warmer would be to give him a flock of chickens.

As Tupper snuggled down with Ember, the sculptor turned his attention back to the graceful feline who was emerging from the block of golden stone. Smiling as he tickled the big cat's ears, he slyly remarked, "Good thing that bed's as sturdy as Morven herself. The lad's well on his way to filling it with rocks."

A fortnight passed in ordinary ways, but winter didn't hold back any longer than that. Tupper woke to a world turned white. Excitedly, he pulled on his clothes and boots, snagged his cloak, and rushed out into the courtyard. Overnight, the heavens had emptied their stores upon the Statuary, blanketing his home in snow. Every peak and pinnacle now wore a pristine cap, and still more feathery flakes fell from the sky, sticking to everything. There was so much!

He waded through snow that nearly reached the tops of his

boots, creating a trail toward the door to the lower colonnade. Shoveling would have to be added to his list of daily duties, but work could wait just a little longer. Taking his sweet time, he continued his reconnoiter, switching directions to meander toward the stables. When he reached the top of the cobblestone road, he was startled to find footprints marring the endless stretch of white leading down to the quarry.

He didn't need Ewert's tracking skills to understand that they were big, deep, and fresh.

Walking over to the nearest, he stepped into the hole and wondered how big a person had to be to make such big prints. These belonged to a giant! Then, he noticed the shape and changed his mind. They belonged to a giant *animal*!

Suddenly, it seemed like a good idea to get back to Freydolf.

Tupper didn't see or hear anything moving all the way back to the workshop, and by the time he slipped safely inside, he'd convinced himself that the tracks must have belonged to one of Morven's statues.

Except ... there would have been no moon last night.

Shedding his damp cloak and boots, Tupper crossed to Freydolf's bed. The man must have heard him coming. Before the boy could give his master's shoulder a shake, the man grabbed hold of him, lifting him right off his feet as he dragged him onto the narrow cot, trapping him with one strong arm.

"You smell like fresh air," the Pred murmured conversationally.

"I was outside."

"Too early for such things," said the sculptor, who'd been up half the night adding fur to feline haunches.

"It snowed."

"You said that once before," reminded Frey. "Flurries aren't worth a fuss."

"We're snow-stuck."

"That so?" the man inquired skeptically.

Tupper reached up to pat the man's cheek with an icy hand, saying, "Almost knee deep and good for packing."

"I suppose you're at an age when playing in the snow still has appeal."

"You don't play?"

"I wonder," he answered vaguely, finally cracking an eye. "I *do* usually take a look around and give the hounds a run when the snow is thick enough to snuff any sparks they scatter."

"The gate guardians?"

"Aye. Would you like to be introduced?" Frowning a little, Freydolf said, "Might be wise to care for that sooner than later. They don't take kindly to strangers."

"Why not?"

"It's their job to be suspicious, I suppose," the Keeper casually replied. "If the Statuary ever comes under attack from the north-east, they're our first line of defense."

Tupper was mystified. "Who would attack?"

"No one these days, but during earlier eras, there was a scramble to occupy the twelve mountains," Freydolf explained. "Silly, really, considering Morven makes up her own mind about who she'll harbor. But there will always be those who have to learn the hard way."

Tupper wriggled free and stood next to the bed. "Do you want breakfast before or after we see the hounds?"

"Are those my only two choices?"

Tupper nodded.

Heaving a sigh, the man decided, "Before, provided there are more of those biscuits on the table when it's time to eat."

"I accept your terms."

Freydolf's deep indigo cloak flapped as he strode through snow that lay thickly in the inner courtyard. Tupper liked the way snowflakes looked when they stuck in the big man's dark hair. His master carried two special lanterns that were shaped like golden orbs, one in each hand.

"Are those to wake the statues?" he asked.

"Aye."

Tupper patted the box of matches in his pocket. "Are they fire-bearers?"

"Not quite," Freydolf replied. "This sort of guardian is referred to as a fire-eater."

"Why?"

Chuckling, his master said, "Hurry along, and I'll show you!"

Beyond the Apprentice Gate, the two red hounds crouched menacingly, hackles raised as they glared down the path, ready to defend their home. Tupper wasn't nearly as frightened by them now that he understood better about the Statuary. Still, the pair had left a lasting impression on him, and he was feeling just a little shy about meeting the snarling beasts.

Freydolf pushed aside some of the accumulated snow and climbed onto the pedestal of one of the great dogs, then waved Tupper over. "Matches, lambkin!"

Sheltering a tiny flame in the hollow of his hand, the Pred lit one of the odd lanterns. "I didn't add much fuel to these, so Itak and Ilam will only have a short run. If these lanterns were full, they could last for days!"

To Tupper's amazement, Freydolf reached right into the hound's mouth, and there was a soft *clunk* as the orb slid into place. The Keeper fiddled with something, and the flame bloomed brighter within the toothy maw.

Backing up, the boy watched closely, waiting for something to happen.

"All right, there, Itak?" Frey inquired in a deep, authoritative voice.

The hound executed a full-body shake, scattering an abundance of snow everywhere, including onto Freydolf.

With a grunt of surprise, the man gave his own hair a shake. "Thanks for that. Shall we wake your brother?"

Tupper lingered beside the copper-plated doors while the process was repeated for Ilam. Despite their imposing size, both hounds seemed light on their feet, and it was sort of funny to see them behaving like real dogs—snuffling around the wide ledge, their noses pushing paths through the thick layer of snow, and even lying down to roll in the white stuff.

They looked for all the world like two enormous puppies, and the way they vied for Freydolf's attention was so comical, Tupper laughed quietly to himself.

That may have been a mistake.

Immediately, the guard dogs' heads swiveled his way, and their hackles went back up. Tupper's eyes flew wide as the pair leapt for him; however, Freydolf was just as fast to react.

With a thunderous shout, he threw himself between the dogs and his servant, arms outspread. "What manners are these?" he scolded. "For shame!"

Tupper sidled up behind his defender, tucking himself under Freydolf's heavy cloak as he peeped up at the hounds. Their heads dipped, their ears drooped, and they exchanged a guilty glance before lowering themselves to grovel on the ground before their indignant master.

In lighter tones, the Keeper said, "I know you're eager for action, but I'll thank you to add this lad to your memories as one who needs guarding. Tupper Meadowsweet belongs to us, so take a good look."

Recognizing his cue, the boy edged out from behind Freydolf and offered a soft, "Hello."

Itak lay his great muzzle on the ground and gazed mournfully at him, and Ilam scooted forward on his belly, ears pricking hopefully.

Tupper rubbed abashedly at the nub of one horn and glanced up at Freydolf.

The sculptor addressed the hounds again. "Apology accepted, but next time, see that there's no need for one!"

Their gazes shifting between man and boy as their tails began to sway.

Frey rested his hand on Tupper's shoulder. "Sorry about that, lambkin. They're a couple of hot-heads ... if you'll pardon the pun."

"It's okay. You warned me." Tupper stepped forward to touch each hound's nose. Warm air drifted from their muzzles like hot breath in the cold air, and he crouched to see the lanterns set into the back of Ilam's mouth. An open flame tickled the roof of his mouth, keeping him alert. "Itak and Ilam," he greeted. "Their names are strange."

"The Keeper who carved them was a Fwan from the Far Continent, and they're words in his tongue. If I remember right, their names mean something like *belt* and *buckle* in Prose." Giving the red stone muzzles an affectionate slap, he explained, "The two of them together are considered Master Aln's masterpiece."

"I like that," Tupper murmured, filing away this new information for future consideration.

Once more speaking to the hounds, Freydolf said, "You have permission to check the boundaries, so make good use of what time you have! Off you go! Enjoy your run!"

Both dogs bounded up and frisked together, snapping at each other's ears and tails before amazing Tupper by scrabbling right up the rocky outcroppings beside the Apprentice Gate and disappearing around a bend in the mountain's bulk. Shaking his head in wonder, he considered the aftermath of Itak's and Ilam's romp. The new-fallen snow was churned up and trampled down, and there were huge footprints everywhere.

Remembering his earlier discovery, Tupper wondered if a statue really could have made the footprints up by the other entrance. With the storm, there had been no glimpse of sun, moon, or stars since yesterday. Puzzling it out, he finally asked, "Does snow wake stone?"

"Aye," Freydolf acknowledged. "Dazzle wants it. Why?"

So that was it! Nothing to worry about, then! With a small shrug, Tupper replied, "Just making sure."

25

Driven to Distraction

Freydolf's stomach growled, and he stopped work in surprise. When was the last time he'd been hungry? Ever since Tupper's arrival, the boy had been pulling him aside for regular meals. Patting his complaining belly, the sculptor muttered, "Is he late today?"

The golden feline was coming along beautifully, but she wasn't telling, so the man laid aside his tools and investigated. Kitchen and balcony stood empty.

Freydolf belatedly checked by the door. Both boots and cloak were missing. "He's out. But where would he go in this weather?"

Deciding a break was in order, Freydolf tugged into his boots, tossed his cloak over an arm, and snagged the nearest lantern. Perhaps the boy was in the lower colonnade, toting bath water or something. It wouldn't hurt to check.

Blowing snow made it hard to guess the hour of day, but Freydolf's gut insisted that Tupper was behind schedule. The lad was quirky, but his track record was sound; he'd shown himself to be wholly dependable when it came to his responsibilities. Holding his lantern high, the Keeper thundered down the stairs, letting his hand skim along the curving wall of the staircase leading to fountain level. He paused at the bottom to listen.

Adopting a more casual stride, he crossed to the necessary, opened its white door, and leaned inside.

"You here, lambkin?"

No answer came, and the man sighed. On a day like this, there was really only one place Tupper *could* have gone—into the galleries. Unable to guess where the lad may have wandered, Freydolf trudged upstairs and returned to the workshop.

He attempted to work, but focus was impossible. With an apologetic caress for the golden statue he expected to finish ahead of schedule, Frey asked, "Do you think he's all right?"

Companionship could be a distraction. Something Aurelius confirmed twice-annually, whenever he sashayed into his brother-in-law's life and made himself comfortable. The merchant's visits were grandiose interruptions to the sculptor's usual habits, but servants had always been a different matter. Their presence was supposed to make it possible for Frey to work uninterrupted.

The Pred took to pacing and watching the sky. What if the boy was lost? What if his lantern went out? What if he ran into something that frightened him? Freydolf wasn't used to worrying, but all he could think about was Tupper. How was he supposed to work like this?

Desperate for something to calm him down, Frey rummaged through the odd bits of stone on his workbench to no avail.

Inspiration flashed, and he strode to Tupper's bed, reaching under his pillow. Yes. This. Turning the chunk of golden rock over and over in his hands, he murmured, "You're exactly what he needs."

Wasting no time, Freydolf gathered his tools and took the stairs to the balcony two at a time. He added fuel to the fire and dropped onto the rug before it, basking in its heat and light.

This time, he was able to concentrate, for he poured all his pent-up concern into the precious piece of sunstone.

"You can watch over him when I cannot," he informed the rock he was shaping.

It was high time Tupper had a daytime guardian.

Nearly an hour later, Tupper returned, and it didn't take long for him to locate Freydolf in the balcony. The sculptor glanced up from his handiwork as the boy hastened across the rug-strewn floor, a hangdog expression on his face. Then, his gaze drifted to the golden stone, and all traces of apology vanished. "You started without me?"

"I haven't gotten far," Freydolf soothed, holding up the rough shape.

Nodding, Tupper recalled himself and quickly ducked his head. "Sorry."

"For?"

"We missed lunch."

"Aye," the man acknowledged, covertly looking the boy over to make sure he was both safe *and* sound. "Where were you?"

"In the dazzle gallery." A little more softly, he added, "It's hard to tell time with no windows."

"That's true. No harm done. Did you see anything you liked?"

While Tupper stoked the fire and added more wood, he offered a rambling explanation that centered around the discovery of several carvings of frogs and the search for a large dazzle-stone statue.

Shaking his head, Freydolf explained, "Most dazzle statues are small. The threads of metal make the stone more brittle than other types, so it's tricky to work with."

"No big ones?"

"Perhaps on Last Continent, but certainly not here."

Slowly adding one last log to the fire, Tupper gazed thoughtfully into the flames, then sighed and changed the subject. "Do you want to eat?"

"Aye," Freydolf replied, trying not to sound *too* eager. "Let's have our meal up here today. I'm of a mind to keep shaping this little one until she's done."

Eyes bright, Tupper exclaimed, "Right back!"

This time, the wait was much easier to endure, for the pleasant clatter of activity filtered up from the kitchen, dispelling all Frey's worries … and the loneliness that loomed nearer during the winter months.

The Pred could soon smell soup warming. His stomach growled in anticipation when Tupper appeared at the top of the stairs with a tray.

Setting it beside his master, he announced, "Nibbles. Until the rest is cooked."

Freydolf eyed the assortment and quickly discerned that they were all his favorites. "By any chance, is this meant for an apology?"

"Maybe," the boy mumbled. "Probably."

"The food is welcome, but the apology isn't necessary. Relax, lambkin." At Tupper's tentative smile, Freydolf went a step further. "After our meal, you could bring up extra lanterns and maybe your baskety things? We can keep one another company."

Tupper quickly replied, "Yes, but not after dinner."

"Oh?"

"After *bath*."

Freydolf drooped, then wheedled, "Couldn't you let me off this once?"

For just a moment, Tupper hesitated, but he answered with a firm, "No."

"Thought not." He plucked a pepper from amidst the delicacies on the food tray and popped it into his mouth, but paused mid-chew. Sniffing, he asked, "Were you also planning to ply me with biscuits?"

Tupper blushed, but gamely said, "They will be a thank you."

"For?"

"Not being mad."

With a twinkle in his eye, Freydolf said, "Then I hope you are generous in your thanks!"

Rubbing a nub, the young Flox admitted, "Two batches."

"Tupper," the man sighed, waiting for the boy to meet his gaze. "Two things."

"Yes?"

"Little stuff like this doesn't upset me. I don't need to be appeased." Tupper only stared blankly at him, so the man simplified. "Don't be afraid of how I'll react if you don't do your job perfectly."

"Oh." Holding up two fingers, he prompted, "And?"

"Bring up both kinds of jam?"

Tupper offered a shy half-smile and nodded, leaving Freydolf with a mingled sense of triumph and relief. Today's little upheaval meant something important: his conscientious young servant was comfortable enough to make mistakes.

Tupper had well and truly made himself at home.

It took two more days to finish the statue, for Freydolf took his time, wanting the little guardian to be perfect in every detail. With careful planning, he'd been able to make a near life-sized sculpture that stood roughly three times taller than Olexi, and he'd taken into account all the things a daytime guardian would need to keep up with an active young boy. Balance and agility were a must. Grace and speed would come naturally. Freydolf did his best to infuse the very stone with an attachment to Tupper that echoed his own.

"Done," he finally announced, passing the carving along to his servant.

The lad turned her this way and that, then murmured, "Good job!"

"We're in luck," Freydolf announced with a glance at the windows. "The sky's clear, and the sun's still strong enough to stir stone. Why don't we take a trip to the upper loggia. It'll be a bit brisk, but it's high enough to catch the light she needs."

"We can wake her *now*?"

"Aye. Sunshine and fine wine are all we require."

Jumping up, Tupper asked, "Which bottle?"

"Slow down, lambkin. I'll choose one myself and pour what

we need. You can bring some cider along as well, to toast your little one's waking."

The notion clearly pleased the lad, and he hurried into the kitchen, his golden treasure tucked under his arm.

Amused, Freydolf rubbed the big feline statue's head and remarked, "Already inseparable."

Tupper returned with two goblets.

Freydolf selected a local wine with a sweet, tart finish, then tapped into their cider reserve for Tupper. Carrying both goblets in one hand, he led the way up a convoluted route through halls and up stairs. Before turning down the passage that would take them to the loggia's entrance, he paused to ask, "While we're close by, would you like to see that songstone statue I was telling Aurelius about? It's just along here."

Tupper nodded eagerly.

"To my knowledge, this is the largest green in the Statuary." They passed through an archway into a room with open lattices on every side. Chill winds gusted through the bright space, which was dominated by the statue of a man with four arms.

The green stone's milky transparency lent it a luminous quality. "Lovely stuff, songstone," Freydolf murmured, glancing at Tupper for his reaction.

The figure was markedly foreign, which was sure to delight the boy. Flowing robes topped full pants that had been gathered at the ankles so they puffed out, and the man's feet were clad in slippers whose pointed toes curled up.

"This is like your nightshirt!" Tupper commented, pointing to the full sleeves. "The one Carden borrowed."

"Aye. They must be the fashion on First Continent."

Bangles decorated the statue's ankles and wrists, and several necklaces were looped around his neck. One of the things Freydolf admired most about this particular piece was its sense of movement. Long, straight hair looked wind-tossed, and the overlapping layers of his attire seemed to be fluttering in an invisible breeze.

Running his finger along one of the many curlicues that decorated the statue's pedestal, Tupper asked, "What's this for?"

"It's meant to be a cloud."

Understanding dawned on the boy's face. "He's flying!"

"Aye. He's a creature from folklore among the people who live around the green mountain. According to some myths, they ride dragons, and in other tales, they're said to be able to fly themselves."

Tupper's eyes were wide, and he pointed at the green statue. "He can *fly*?"

"Nay, lambkin." He hid his smile. "No matter how wondrous a guardian stone may be, statues are still made from solid rock. They can neither fly nor swim."

The boy nodded his understanding, then asked, "Can we wake him?"

Freydolf rubbed the back of his neck with his free hand. "I'm not very musical, but songstone never criticizes." Pursing his lips, he managed a bit of whistling.

The statue turned his head toward the piercing notes. Smiling serenely, the statue stretched his arms skyward, extended them fluidly to either side, and with a graceful pivot, stepped from his pedestal.

Wasting no time, the young Flox said, "Hello. I'm Tupper."

The cloud-rider dipped his head before paying his respects to Freydolf, dropping to one knee and touching his hand to his forehead.

"It's good to see you again," the Keeper greeted, beckoning for the statue to rise.

Tupper poked curiously at the man's sleeves, which flowed like silk when he moved, then asked, "Does he have a job?"

"Not that I know of," Freydolf admitted. "But ignorance isn't much of an answer. We could check the archives to see if his maker left a record."

"He has a key."

A large key hung amidst the many baubles on the statue's necklaces. "So he does. It's probably just for decoration."

Tupper chose to address the statue directly. "May I see your key?"

To Freydolf's astonishment, the statue unhooked the item from its cord and passed it to the boy, who inspected it closely.

The Keeper muttered, "I didn't know he could do that!"

"It's a very nice key," Tupper complimented, earning another genteel smile. "Where does it go?"

The statue only shook his head, begging ignorance.

Tupper gave it back with a grave, "Thank you."

Recalling their original purpose, Freydolf asked, "Shall we proceed to the loggia?"

"Yes, please." Tupper waved goodbye to the green statue, who wandered off in the opposite direction.

When they reached their destination on the columned porch, the sculptor squinted at the sky, then sat upon bare stone. This spot saw plenty of sun, so most of the snow had receded. Placing the goblets at his side, Freydolf beckoned for Tupper to join him. "Have you chosen a name for her?"

"No."

"Think on it while I add my mark."

The lad nodded.

Taking his time, the sculptor inscribed neat symbols on a smooth patch he'd left on the underside of the statue's chin. Since Tupper didn't look as if his mind was made up, Freydolf quietly added a simple embellishment to his usual seal—a wreath of meadowsweet in token of his new name. He admired the effect as he rubbed his thumb over it, certain the addition could only be an improvement.

"Ready."

"You look very pleased with yourself," Frey teased.

Tipping his head to one side, the boy replied, "So do you."

"Aye. Well?"

Leaning close, the boy whispered his decision, and Freydolf laughed long and loud. "Clever boy! You remembered!"

"Is it good?" Tupper asked worriedly.

"Your choice is *excellent!*" the sculptor exclaimed, still grinning broadly. "I can't wait for you to spring her on Aurelius!"

The boy beamed, and Freydolf got down to business, placing the statue between them. "Some of your cider first, since she's yours," he impulsively directed. "Who knows, it may give her a sweeter temperament!"

With a look of supreme concentration, Tupper let amber liquid dribble from his cup onto the small creature's head. With a grunt of approval, Freydolf followed suit with a splash of wine. Swiping up the mingled liquids with one clawed fingertip, he tickled the lynx kitten under her chin and murmured, "Wake up, Rimbles."

26

Burning Bright

Tupper lifted his lantern higher, studying the complex patterns carved into the curving walls of a large alcove. He searched the profusion of stone flora and fauna, certain they held a secret.

"Found you," he finally murmured, poking his finger into a cleverly-hidden keyhole. Glancing down at Rimbles, the boy announced, "This is the sixth one!"

His little companion was batting at a cluster of stone flower buds with one of her over-large paws; however, at the sound of his voice, her tufted ears twitched, and she peered up at him. Freydolf had made the lynx kitten so cute, with her wide eyes, puffed out fur, and stubby tail. Tupper crouched down to tickle her chin, and she butted his hand affectionately.

"Let's find number seven."

Normally, he brought Brand along when he went exploring, but for Rimbles's first foray into the Statuary's passages, Tupper hadn't wanted to divide his attention between two companions. For today, he carried his own lantern, and he'd chosen the sunstone gallery in honor of his new guardian statue.

It intrigued him that the kitten didn't mind the darkness. Although she needed the touch of sunlight to wake, once golden stone stirred, it remained active until the sunset.

"This way," he said, letting Rimbles know he was moving on with or without her.

She was a bundle of feline curiosity with an independent streak, and he didn't want to lose sight of her. Thankfully, she seemed just as eager to keep him close. When he walked on, scrutinizing the ornate tunnel walls, she scampered after him, trying to catch the edge of his cloak.

Tupper was playing his usual game, like hide-and-seek for one. Whenever he explored the stone galleries, he chose a different thing to watch for—frogs, butterflies, sea shells, and so on. This time, he was searching for keyholes. He'd found the first in the heart of a flower, and the second in the eye of a stag. They were in sneaky places and funny places, so it took a sharp eye to spot them.

Locks and keys had been on his mind lately. The Triads had keys, as did the songstone statue near the loggia, and keys had a job to do. Tupper figured there must be locks for every key, and keys for every lock. He wished he could match them up, but the Statuary had more doors than all the buildings in Hayward put together.

Of course, the boy wasn't foolish enough to try to open one of the locked doors. He remembered what Freydolf had said about the Misbegotten—bad statues who needed to stay asleep. Still, the keyholes were his new favorite thing to find. It was as if Morven were whispering to him, telling him little secrets about herself.

Just then, there was a sharp *click* in the darkness ahead, and he paused to listen.

Rimbles launched herself between Tupper's feet, nearly tripping him and skidding to a stop in front of her charge. The little cat's back arched, and her fur stood out in every direction as she bared her fangs into the thick darkness.

"What's the matter, Rimbles?" he whispered, lifting his lantern higher.

Other noises came nearer—a snap, a scrape, a swish that stirred the air.

In a voice that trembled, the boy called, "Wh-who's there?"

He listened to the ominous silence for the space of several heartbeats, but then Tupper snatched up Rimbles, turned heel, and ran.

Light from Tupper's crazily swinging lantern scattered the gallery's darkness, but it quickly renewed its hold, surging back thickly in his wake. Deep as night, black as ink—the shadows hid his pursuer.

Between ragged breaths, the boy muttered assurances to Rimbles. "Frey will help. The statues listen to him. He'll tell this one to be nice."

Tupper sorely wished his words were true, but the workshop was far away. Too far.

A plan would be good, but thinking on the fly had never been one of Tupper's strengths. Tiny fears took root and flourished, sending the young Flox blankly scrambling up stairs and down, sprinting along straightaways, and skidding around corners. Even though Tupper wasn't really sure what was following him, he knew two things for certain. It felt big, and it was scary.

Knees shaking, he ducked into an alcove and tried to catch his breath. With each shaky heave, his mind cleared a little, and he realized that his lantern was giving him away. Still, he couldn't see without it. Or could he?

"Oh!" he gasped, fumbling in his pocket for his candle. Tupper had to set Rimbles down in order to open his lantern and light the stub.

As soon as the wick caught, he whispered, "Hurry," to the lynx and continued along the passage, leaving his trusty lamp behind.

Just ahead, the tunnel took a turn, and he stumbled to a stop, reluctant to move farther from the lantern's steady glow.

The candle guttered, and he cupped his hand protectively around the vulnerable flame, anxious for its survival. Maybe this was a mistake. Maybe he should go back for the lantern. Caught by indecision, Tupper stared fixedly at the beacon he'd left as a decoy.

Then, to his horror, something dark eased into the warm circle of its glow. A large muzzle wrinkled in a silent snarl, baring white teeth. An animal? There was an animal here? Tupper held his breath as red eyes lifted, seeming to stare straight into his, and he panicked.

That couldn't be a statue! It was a real monster! And it was hunting him!

Run!

With a whimper of dismay, the boy fled.

His bid for escape took on a surreal quality as time blurred. Every so often, a sound reached Tupper—clicks and snaps— letting him know that the beast was still on his trail. He had nothing to fend it off but a flickering candle and a sunstone kitten. Maybe if he found a stick or some kind of weapon?

Then suddenly, he remembered that Brand carried a sword.

Surely the Grif would protect him! If only he could reach the redstone warrior in time.

Redoubling his efforts, Tupper ran until his lungs burned, afraid to stop lest he collapse. When he rounded another turning and spotted daylight through an archway ahead, he nearly sobbed with relief. The Cavern! He was almost there!

Singeing his fingers as he desperately protected the tremulous flame he'd need to wake his friend, Tupper zigzagged between the statues that flanked the expansive gallery, aiming for his favorite fire-bearer's pedestal.

"Brand!" he cried, spying the familiar hooked nose and feathered cape. "Brand!" Tupper repeated as he all but collided with the statue, clinging to the stone man's waist as he shakily held the candle under his taloned hand.

Hiding his face against the warrior's armored chest, the boy swallowed hard when he felt the candle plucked from his grasp and an arm come around his shoulders in a protective embrace. Looking up, Tupper met the warrior's concerned gaze and panted, "Something's here! I'm scared! I ... I want Frey!"

The Grif peered over the boy's head, and his expression hardened.

Tupper looked, too. A large shape slipped between shadows, stalking closer.

Suddenly remembering his tiny guardian, Tupper raised a voice thin with strain. "Rimbles! Where are you, Rimbles?"

There was a skitter as the kitten broke cover, her body low to the ground as she streaked toward him. Their pursuer sped up, bearing down on her.

Tupper cried, "No!"

Without a thought for himself, he slipped free of Brand's embrace and hurried to meet Rimbles halfway. The lynx kitten leapt into his arms, winding him as her weight hit his chest. The young Flox's eyes bugged out when a much larger creature sprang for him. Those terrible fangs flashed within a dark maw, ready to bite, to tear, to hurt.

Tupper's knees buckled, and he tripped over his own feet, falling backward, and hitting his head. Light exploded before his eyes, fuzzed to gray, then narrowed to a pinprick before winking to nothing.

Out cold.

Freydolf straightened and glanced around his workshop, trying to figure out what had interrupted his focus. He'd been immersed in getting just the right curve to the golden statue's claws when ... what? Then, it came again—a rap at the door.

"Who ...?" he mused aloud, crossing the room.

Brand stood on his doorstep, clutching one of the old torches from the many brackets that lined the galleries, which was strange. There were lanterns aplenty, so Freydolf rarely bothered with them. Fire-bearers were certainly capable of taking the initiative and securing fuel for their flames when necessary, but why?

The Grif extended his hand beseechingly, and Freydolf stiffened. "Tupper?"

Nodding, the warrior stepped back, beckoning for him to follow.

With a muttered oath, the Pred rushed past, heedless of the icy bite of snow on his bare feet. Brand stayed close on the Keeper's heels all the way to the entrance to the lower colonnade, but when Freydolf paused at the bottom of the staircase, Brand took the lead, lighting the way as he ran along the passage that led toward the Cavern.

"What happened?" Freydolf demanded. Brand glanced helplessly at him, and the sculptor grimaced. "I know you can't speak, but put my mind at ease! Is the lad hurt?"

A nod.

"Is Tupper in danger?"

Brand's hand fluttered in a gesture of uncertainty.

With a sick feeling in the pit of his stomach, the sculptor picked up his pace. Dozens of questions whirled through his mind, but the answers would have to wait until he found the boy.

They burst through the Cavern's tall doors, and Freydolf begged, "Which way?"

The Grif pointed in the direction of his pedestal.

Freydolf charged across the room, calling, "Tupper! Can you hear me?" No answer came, but as he neared Brand's niche, Rimbles intercepted him, her fuzzy coat standing out in every direction.

Fearing the worst, the Keeper urged, "Show me where."

She dove between the legs of the nearest colossus, and he followed, only to be drawn up short by the unexpected sight of a regal beast sprawled across the path. Redstone eyes looked as if they'd been lined with blue kohl, and a thick tail banded with sunstone, titian jade, dapple, and songstone lashed and curled along the floor. Platt's masterpiece blinked languidly at him, looking completely smug, for between the creature's front paws lay Tupper's crumpled form.

Gritting his teeth, Freydolf snarled, "Graven!"

Tupper woke with a wince and a soft whine. His head hurt terribly! Opening his eyes, he scrunched them shut again, for the sun shone clear and bright through the workshop's tall windows. That made him frown. Why was he in bed during the day? Was he late? Oh, no!

He struggled to get up, but a firm hand pressed him back into the mattress. "Where do you think you're going?" inquired Freydolf in a low voice.

"Not sure," he answered honestly, his voice raspy. An underlying uneasiness made him reach for the sound. He'd been wanting Frey, hadn't he?

"Open your eyes," the man directed.

He did his best to obey, squinting up at the man as he tried to sort out what was going on. Freydolf tilted his head and stared hard at him. He looked really worried.

It took several moments for Tupper to realize that the sculptor was sitting next to him in his bed. The Pred may have been too tall to lie down in the fancy niche, but he looked comfortable enough with his back propped against the stone wall.

Taking hold of the hem of his master's familiar red tunic, Tupper was still at a loss, but he felt safe.

"Do you remember what happened?"

Tupper frowned in concentration, thinking back. "Rimbles!" he gasped.

"She's under your pillow."

That made no sense, but Tupper checked and found the still lynx kitten right where Freydolf said she'd be. "She's still," he mumbled, feeling all mixed up.

"I didn't let her wake this morning," Freydolf explained, "I'm standing in as your guardian for now."

"You are?"

"Aye. You had me worried." Reaching down, Freydolf ruffled his hair. "How are you feeling?"

"Not very good," Tupper whispered, for he ached all over. Edging closer, he urgently shared, "Something chased me. Was it a Misbegotten?"

The sculptor scowled, and he sounded angry when he replied, "Nay, though Aurelius would argue the point. Graven took you for an intruder."

"Graven." Memories of a shadowy shape with red eyes and white fangs flashed through the boy's mind, and he curled up on his side. "I don't like Graven."

"I don't blame you. I'm unhappy with him, as well."

Freydolf seemed to be speaking toward the other side of the room, which could only mean one thing. Hunching his shoulders, Tupper mumbled, "He's here."

"See for yourself."

Propping up on one elbow, Tupper peeked past his master, who acted as a barricade between him and the room's other occupant. Graven wasn't as big as Itak and Ilam, but he still took up much of the workshop's free space. Frey must have had to open the larger of the two doors in order to allow him inside.

He stared long and hard at the creature, which was by far the strangest statue he'd ever seen. Up until now, every one of them had been made from a single type of stone. But Master Platt's masterpiece was just as Freydolf and Aurelius had described him—cobbled together from every kind of stone.

Tupper had assumed Graven would look messy, but he was actually kind of pretty. Scary ... but a pretty sort of scary, like poison mushrooms or a rainbow-banded viper. The way the end of Graven's tail was twitching certainly made the boy nervous. Would he turn and pounce again?

Graven was definitely the work of a master, possessed of noble bearing, sleek strength, and a harmonious blending of colors. The tiger's moonstone body was decorated by stripes that flowed through the whole stone spectrum—redstone, titian jade, sunstone, songstone, freshstone, dawnstone, dapple, and brownstone. Starstone claws looked deadly sharp, and dazzle had been worked into an ornate collar fitted with crystals in varied hues.

The tiger sat with his back to the bed, snubbing its occupants, which suited Tupper just fine. Being ignored was far better than being prey.

"Why did you let him in?" Tupper asked in a small voice.

"This is his home, lambkin. In his own way, he was trying to protect it."

"From me?"

"Aye," the Keeper replied, his expression troubled. Freydolf carefully probed the knot that had formed on the back of Tupper's head, his dark eyes filled with regrets. "Please, don't be frightened."

The mosaic tiger turned his head then, glancing disdainfully at the boy he'd caught. Red eyes narrowed, and the big cat's lip curled just enough to display wickedly sharp, white fangs.

Tupper shrank back behind Freydolf, pulling his blankets up to his chin. With a weak shake of his head, he repeated, "I don't like Graven."

This had never happened before. None of his servants had ever fallen ill. A bump on the head shouldn't have needed more than a day's rest, but a fever had taken hold, leaving the boy pink-cheeked and listless. Freydolf was beside himself, for Tupper was burning up, and he had no idea what to do. Fears plagued him, and there was no one to turn to but the suffering child.

Kneeling beside the bed, Frey brushed his knuckles across a flushed cheek. Tupper's skin was dangerously hot. Gently shaking the boy's shoulder, the man pleaded, "Wake up, lambkin. You should drink something."

Fair lashes fluttered, and Tupper stared at him with glassy eyes. "I didn't water the trees," he mumbled, trying to sit up.

"Nay, lad." Pushing him back into his pillow, the sculptor assured, "It's winter. The trees are sleeping."

"Snow," he murmured agitatedly. "There are footprints in the snow."

Freydolf wasn't sure what to make of that, but he stroked the boy's messy hair in what he hoped was a soothing manner. "Are you thirsty, Tupper? Here, drink."

The boy turned his face from the cup.

Groaning softly, the sculptor said, "This isn't the best time to learn disobedience. Do as you're told, and you may do whatever you please in all the days ahead."

Tupper's brow puckered, and he clutched at his blankets. "If I don't sweep, Frey will hurt his feet."

Throat tightening, Freydolf said, "I promise not to make any messes until you're better."

"Don't let breakfast burn."

"As if I could eat," he muttered harshly, bowing his head, barely holding himself together. He couldn't lose this boy. Not Tupper.

A hot hand patted his cheek, and the man looked up in surprise.

The lad's gray-green eyes were more lucid, and he asked, "What's wrong?"

"You have a fever," Freydolf miserably reported.

With a guilty expression, Tupper touched his fingers to his lips, then placed them against the man's in a gesture of apology. "Sorry," he whispered.

Freydolf had never felt so helpless in his whole life. Voice cracking, he confessed, "*I'm* the one who should be begging forgiveness. I don't know what to do."

"Warm blankets, cold cloths, and tea sips."

The Pred straightened. "What kind of tea?"

"Bitter-bark," he replied, making a face.

"I can do that!"

"Good," he mumbled, giving a heavy-lidded blink. "Don't burn the water."

Freydolf cracked a smile and took his servant's small hand in both of his. "Don't leave me, Tupper," he fiercely demanded. "Promise me you'll get better."

Maybe the boy was simply fever-muddled, or maybe he understood what was at the heart of the man's plea, but with a whisper of a smile, Tupper said, "I promised to stay."

27

Avoidance

Freydolf woke to the smell of biscuits and nearly fell out of bed in his haste to get to the kitchen. The sculptor had barely slept over the last three days, so he'd been teetering on the edge of exhaustion too long and had inadvertently crashed into a deep slumber. Staggering through the door, he dazedly exclaimed, "You're up!"

Tupper seemed pale, and his fair hair was a tangled mess, but his eyes were clear and the firmness was back in his voice. "I'm better."

"Are you sure?" Freydolf asked, needing more reassurance.

"Yes." The lad paused in his meal preparations and quietly asked, "Where's Graven?"

"Out," he replied, gesturing vaguely toward the front door. "He's always been restless, so he's probably prowling the galleries."

Tupper nodded hesitantly.

Easing into a chair at the table, Freydolf gruffly said, "The two of you had a bad start, but it would be best if you could put that behind you. I was hoping to introduce you more properly. Start fresh."

"Maybe."

Gently pressing for more, the Keeper said, "You could be friends."

Silence stretched awkwardly before Tupper repeated, "Maybe."

Freydolf could hardly blame the lad. Graven had badly frightened him. Still, he felt a large measure of responsibility and empathy for the over-zealous guardian. Frey had assisted Master Platt in waking Graven, so he and the old Drom had been the big cat's first sight. Even if the statue's true attachment was to his creator, the Pred still rated a dash of deference. Graven didn't always listen to him, but he always returned to him ... or at least to Morven.

Wanting his servant to at least understand, Freydolf tried again. "Tupper, look at me."

The boy's gaze swung to his.

Tapping his own chest, Freydolf inquired, "How do I look?"

"Bad."

Amused by the boy's forthrightness, he prompted, "Why?"

"You need food and sleep ... and a bath."

"Aye," Freydolf agreed. "Just a few days without rest, and I'm a mess."

The lad tipped his head to one side. "I still need to light the necessary fire."

"Baths aside," the man grumbled, "I'm *tired*!"

"Yes, I understand." Fidgeting under his master's gaze, he added a soft, "Sorry."

"Nay, lambkin! That's not my point. I'm trying to explain about Graven."

The lad's gaze darted nervously toward the door.

Tapping his chest again for emphasis, Frey said, "I can't imagine going on day after day without sleep, but Graven has no choice. Master Platt's design gave him endless awareness." With a grim shake of his head, Frey continued, "You may not like him, but spare him a little pity. Graven cannot rest, and he cannot find the one he was made to protect. And because he's a statue, that will never change ... not for centuries without end."

"Statues get sleepy?" Tupper asked skeptically.

"Nay," the Keeper admitted. How did you explain world-weariness to one so young? With a crooked little smile,

Freydolf said, "It's more like being very sad."

Tupper stared at him thoughtfully, and for a moment, the man thought he'd finally gotten through, but the lad had the strangest way of interpreting things. With a quizzical expression, he asked, "Are you sad?"

"Nay, lambkin," Freydolf replied. Not anymore. "But I'm sad for Graven. Do you think you could ... try?"

The boy's struggle was apparent, but he grudgingly answered, "Maybe."

Tupper was good at avoiding trouble. Staying clean, keeping quiet, and following directions didn't exactly garner him praise, but nobody criticized him either. Back home, he was mostly ignored, not necessarily a bad thing when it came to bossy older sisters. All he had to do was stay still, and everyone else rushed past, caught up in their own busyness.

Things were a little bit the same with Freydolf, who easily lost himself in his work. Tupper could stoke the fires, light the lamps, sweep the floors, fill the water pitcher, and a half-dozen other simple chores right under the Pred's nose without once earning a glance. However, the moment the boy fell quiet, Frey would pause in his work and peer around the workshop, seeking him out.

He didn't mean to be a distraction, but at the same time, Tupper couldn't bring himself to leave. Not while Graven was lurking about the Statuary.

Tupper was indeed good at avoiding trouble, but he was becoming even better at avoiding tigers.

"Lambkin?"

Startled from his thoughts, Tupper glanced guiltily at his master. He'd been weaving nesting baskets for the hen house, but his hands had fallen idle. Frey noticed.

The man eyed him with concern. "Shall we stretch our legs?"

"Yes." Setting aside his work, Tupper slid from the safety of his bed and crossed to the door where he shoved his feet into his boots. Although Freydolf didn't make a big deal out of it, the man had definitely noticed that Tupper no longer went to the necessary alone. Trips to the storerooms and well were also carefully planned to coincide with the Pred's visits to the lower colonnade.

Freydolf casually said, "We may be gone for a while, but Rimbles can keep her mother company."

Tupper's little guardian lounged on the window ledge, her eyes half-lidded as she basked in an angling sunbeam. It was their little joke to call her the larger lynx's kitten, since she'd been carved from a chip off the same block.

The lad nodded obediently, but asked, "Why?"

Frey's smile showed a touch of fang. "There's something I want to do, and I'd rather not have your little one underfoot. She likes to trip me up."

It was true. Rimbles often made a nuisance of herself in the hopes of being picked up.

Tugging his cloak from its hook, Tupper asked, "Where are we going?"

"To the Cavern."

The faded blue cloak slipped from Tupper's fingers, crumpling on the floor.

Freydolf knelt to pick it up. Giving it a shake, he swung it around the boy's slim shoulders, amiably asking, "How many of the galleries have you explored from there?"

"Five."

"Not even half," said Freydolf. "Don't you want to see more of Morven's secrets?"

Eyes downcast, Tupper nodded.

"It would be a shame if you never went back into the galleries."

The lad peeped at his master out of the corner of his eye, utterly tongue-tied.

"Is it because of Graven? Is that why you hide in here with me?"

Color drained from the young Flox's face, then flooded back.

The sculptor was very good at noticing things when it came to Tupper. "Yes," he admitted.

"Aye. Come along," the man urged, opening the door. "And bring an extra lantern."

He trailed after Freydolf, who led the way into the six-sided room at the head of the stairs. Hanging his cloak on one of the many cloak hooks, he held out his hand, patiently waiting for Tupper to divest himself of snow-spangled outerwear. Leaving the spare lantern in the middle of the entry, he crouched and ordered, "Up you get!"

Unable to hide his relief, Tupper clambered onto the man's broad shoulders and clung tightly. No matter what they discovered in the galleries today, he would be safe.

Holding his lantern high, the Keeper descended the stairs and strode along the wide passage leading to the Cavern. Once through the tall doors, Freydolf set a course straight for Brand.

"You and he are friends," Frey remarked as he let the boy down.

"Yes."

"Aye, he's a trustworthy fellow. Did I tell you how he rushed to find me when you were hurt?" he asked. "Now that we're here, you could thank him."

"Can I wake him?"

Freydolf passed him the lantern.

Moments later, the red stone warrior's taloned hand rested atop Tupper's curly hair, and the boy flung his arms around the Grif's waist, much like he had on the day he'd been chased. It was really embarrassing when a sniffle escaped. Tupper hated being so nubless, but he held on tightly nonetheless.

"Thanks," he choked out. "Thanks *lots*!"

"Aye," Freydolf agreed, his deep voice ringing with approval. "You're one I can rely on, Brand. So I'm proposing a change."

Tupper blinked up at each of them, and Brand glanced between master and servant, his brows lifting quizzically.

"It seems this lad needs backup," the Keeper went on, tapping his boot against the circular disk of red stone on which the red statue always came to rest. "I'll be moving your pedestal today. Do you mind if I bring you closer to our home?"

Startled by the proposal, Tupper stammered, "R-really?"

"There's plenty of space in the entryway atop the stairs. And it would be more convenient for both of you, don't you think?"

"Yes!" Tupper could hardly believe his good fortune. Now, Brand could protect him from Graven! Adding a nod for emphasis, he begged, "Please."

With a flourish of his feathered cape, Brand bowed to the Keeper, accepting his offer.

"That's settled," Freydolf said, sitting right down on the floor.

Edging closer to his master, Tupper shyly whispered, "Thank you."

The Pred hummed. "There's something I'd like you to do in return, lambkin."

"Yes?" he replied uncertainly.

Frey reached up to grip his shoulder. "Enough hiding. Let me properly introduce you to that irascible tiger."

Tupper drooped. "Yes, sir."

Frowning, the Keeper revealed, "I've often suspected that the only reason Graven chases Aurelius is because he runs. If you keep trying to hide from Graven, he's sure to seek you out."

The boy flinched.

"Face him. He won't stand a chance against someone like you."

That didn't make sense to Tupper. "Why?"

Frey chuckled and repeated, "Face him, lambkin, just as you faced me. Something tells me your courage will be rewarded."

Tupper rubbed one of his horns, searching for enough courage to answer. Taking a deep breath, he promised, "I'll do my best."

Freydolf dragged himself to his cot and collapsed, tools still in hand, arm across his eyes. There was a soft rustling from the direction of Tupper's bed, and a moment later, the boy hovered over him, making a soft tutting sound.

"It's almost morning," the lad scolded, taking away the sculptor's rasps and rifflers, then plucking at the ties of his apron. "Did you finish?"

"Aye, lambkin." Slanting his gaze toward the finished sunstone guardian, he added, "There's nothing more I can do until Aurelius comes for her. We'll wait for him before I mark her."

Tupper's brow puckered. "That's a long time from now."

With a soft grunt, Freydolf replied, "That's why he leaves me odd bits of stone."

"But you finished them all."

Freydolf's heavy brows drew together. "Are you sure?"

"Yes." With a small smile, he said, "You did a good job."

Maybe *too* good! Frey couldn't ever remember finishing his work so far ahead of schedule. What was he supposed to do with himself in the weeks or even months that remained before his agent returned with a fresh commission?

Tupper pulled the blankets up over the man's shoulder, tucking him in. "There's that piece of songstone from the stream," he offered.

It would only last a day, but it would be better than nothing. With a rueful smile, he patted the boy's head, saying, "Back to bed, lambkin. Maybe tomorrow, we should do some exploring instead."

"In the galleries?"

There was no missing the hopeful note in Tupper's question. He liked it whenever Frey took a break from work to play tour guide through some section of Morven's maze. They'd gone a handful of times already this winter, which was more exploring than the Pred had done in years. It was a wonder how he'd managed to finish work early, considering how many breaks he'd taken for Tupper's sake.

"Aye, lad," he replied. "A whole day in the galleries, and if we're lucky, we'll run into Platt's peevish pet."

Tupper's expression suggested that *his* idea of luck ran to the contrary. "How early do you want to start?"

"Late."

The boy shook his head, then moved to douse the lanterns.

Once he was ensconced in his own bed again, he warned, "If you sleep late, I'll eat all the biscuits."

"Breakfast in bed," Frey drawled into the darkness.

"Crumbs in your sheets!" Tupper retorted, sounding scandalized. "That would mean an extra bath."

Freydolf chuckled, for the boy was surprisingly fun to tease. In his own way, he teased back. "Then I'll have to be careful not to waste a single crumb!"

Even though he couldn't see Tupper, Frey could hear the smile in the lad's voice when he answered, "See that you don't."

"Aye," he replied in docile tones.

To Freydolf's infinite amusement, Tupper softly echoed, "Aye."

They didn't catch sight of Graven the next day ... or the next ... or the next. Freydolf was pretty sure the tiger was off sulking in some corner, and it frustrated him. Just when he'd convinced Tupper to try for peaceful coexistence, his stripy nemesis decided to make himself scarce. Graven was ornery like that, just like his creator.

Spring was still several weeks off when the region experienced an early thaw. Freydolf's steps slowed as he crossed the courtyard, taking deep breaths of balmy air. This might be a good day to head into the upper loggia or out to the end of the southernmost gallery for a good bask in the sun. If the melt lasted long enough, they might even manage a trip down to the stream; fish would taste good after so many meatless days.

Plans spinning in his head, Frey strolled through the workshop door, cheerfully calling, "Tupper! What do you say we ...."

He trailed off. To his complete amazement, Graven was the only one in the room.

"You!"

The tiger gazed haughtily down his nose at the Keeper.

"Where have you been hiding?"

All Graven did was calmly fold one paw over the other.

"Wait," the man muttered, hastily peering around the room. "He let you in? Where's Tupper?"

The big cat's varicolored tail flicked and curled, but answers were not forthcoming.

Grumbling under his breath, Freydolf glanced about, this time noting that the beds had been stripped of their blankets. That meant his servant was most likely in the outer courtyard. "You wait here," he ordered, carefully closing the statue inside before hurrying to find Tupper.

Sure enough, his bedding and the boy's were strewn across the dry patches on the outer courtyard's pavement, corners anchored by rocks; however, the lad wasn't in sight. The Pred put his tracking skills to work and soon pinned down Tupper's location.

Sitting on a bare rock at the top of the slope where twelve heaps of unneeded stones steamed in the sun, Frey called, "Here you are!"

"Yes."

"What are you doing?"

The lad answered, "Picking."

Freydolf prompted, "Why?"

"Because they'll be snow-stuck again soon." Gazing out over the bare forest and white hills below, he added, "False spring never lasts."

"But what do you want them for?"

"You need them, and they need you." Tupper's eyes drifted out of focus for a few moments, and then he tried again. "Each other?"

Unable to hide his pleased smile, Freydolf waved him closer. "Show me what you've found."

The carry-sack he lugged over was nearly bursting at the seams. Freydolf spent several minutes rummaging through the boy's picks. Every last one of them made his fingers twitch in anticipation.

"These are good!" he murmured excitedly. "You're a first rate picker, lambkin!"

Accepting the compliment with a nod, Tupper said, "Now, you can find their secrets."

What a way to put it! The sculptor teasingly inquired, "Are you tired of my rattling around the workshop with nothing to do?"

"Yes. When you're busy, you're happy."

Trying not to show how touched he was, Freydolf asked, "You want me to be happy?"

Tupper tipped his head to one side. "Is that bad?"

Far from it.

28

Turn Back Time

Tupper sat on a cushion near the balcony's railing so he could look down into the workshop while he wove nesting baskets. Graven was too large to navigate the stairs leading to this haven, so the boy felt safe here. At the moment, Freydolf was below, leaning into the curve of the big cat's body and chatting quietly as he fiddled with a piece of songstone.

Part of Tupper wished he could be sitting with them, watching Frey work wonders with the bit of green rock, but something told him that Graven needed the company more than he did. After just a few days of watching the tiger, Tupper could tell he was agitated.

The young Flox knew just what to do when Freydolf's empty hands began to twitch. Choosing a stone from the carry-sack, he'd place it in the middle of the kitchen table. That way, once the man's restlessness drove him to pacing from room to room, he'd find the rock, fall upon it, and fill the rest of his day or night shaping it into something amazing.

Graven's restiveness was probably because of his maker.

Tupper already knew that when a statue couldn't do what it was made for, it spent its waking hours waiting, wandering, and wanting to do a good job. The white lady had been calmer ever since he'd begun adding fresh water to the urn next to her dry well. Ember had taken to mischief because he didn't have any chickens to mind, but the little fox was a champion rabbit-chaser. Even Brand seemed more content now that he had a lantern of his own and could spend his mornings and evenings accompanying Tupper.

It was a little different for the tiger, though. The person Graven was supposed to be guarding had died, so as much as the boy wanted to fix things, there wasn't anything he could do.

"Did you hear me, lambkin?"

Tupper blinked, then focused on Freydolf, who was standing with hands on hips. "No."

The Pred repeated, "I'm going downstairs. Do you want to come along?"

"No."

"Should I bring Graven with me?"

Tupper slowly shook his head. "He can stay."

Accepting the answer with a nod, the man strode out, and as soon as the workshop door clicked shut, the tiger's gaze swung upward.

Tupper set aside his work and announced, "I'm coming down."

Graven turned up his nose.

With a soft sigh, the boy picked himself up and tried to be brave. It was very obvious to him that Graven didn't want to be friends, and Tupper still found the proud feline intimidating. Freydolf had been very stern with the tiger when introducing them, so the boy doubted he was in danger. Graven no longer lay in wait for him in dark tunnels, but he was plenty grumpy.

While Tupper didn't really mind the tiger's version of the silent treatment, the boy wanted to change things. Graven's situation made Freydolf sad, but Tupper wanted his master to be happy.

As soon as the boy walked into the workshop, Graven turned his back. Sitting down in the corner, the boy stared perplexedly at the cat, hoping for inspiration. Eventually, the tiger relaxed into a supremely feline sprawl, scooting his haunches around to take full advantage of a sunspot. Rimbles did the same thing, which made sense since she craved sunlight.

Suddenly, Tupper realized something important, and several facts clicked into place. Graven had angled his body so that as many golden stripes as possible were catching the sun's rays, but wouldn't that mean the neighboring freshstone stripes were uncomfortably dry?

Not giving himself the chance to change his mind, Tupper hastened to the corner, thrust his hand into the water pitcher, and hurried back to the tiger's side. Without much thought to the consequences, he trailed his fingers along a wide, blue stripe, wetting it.

Graven's flank twitched, and he turned to blink at the boy.

"Is that better?"

The statue blinked again.

Tupper offered, "More?"

By the time Freydolf returned, every bit of blue stone was glistening, and Tupper was carefully running his fingertip around Graven's eyes, which were rimmed with more of the thirsty rock.

"What are you doing, lambkin?" the startled man inquired.

"Making him feel better."

The sculptor crouched down beside the tiger and asked, "Does that feel good, big fella? I wouldn't doubt it!"

Tupper ventured, "Should we try snow?"

Frey's eyes widened, and he practically leapt for the door. "Good idea!" he exclaimed, snagging the handle of a bucket on his way out. "Be right back!"

Graven curled his lip at Tupper, but the boy shook his head. "Don't grump. You like it, and you know it."

It wasn't as if the tiger could argue, so his was the last word on the matter.

Freydolf slammed back though the door, hefting a bucket of snow. "This should do the trick!"

"Do you want to?" Tupper stepped back, deferring to his master.

"Nay, lambkin. You should be the one to do it. Show him what you can do!"

Tupper nodded and singled out the dazzle stripes. Graven

sagged to the floor, practically trembling in ecstasy as the boy packed them with snow.

Freydolf whispered a suggestion in his ear, and with another nod, Tupper took a deep breath and launched into the lullaby he'd always sung for Aggie. He wasn't a very good singer, but the notes seemed to be resonating with the songstone as he worked his way from tip to tail.

The Keeper's eyes were dancing as he held up one finger after another, listing, "Sunstone, freshstone, dazzle, and songstone. Would you like to try the starstone next?"

"White stone needs starlight," Tupper pointed out.

"Aye, but ... wait a bit," he urged, hurrying into the kitchen. A few moments later, he returned, stirring the contents of a small bowl with his finger. "No harm in trying some homemade brine!"

Tupper accepted the dish and swirled his finger in the cloudy water, then painted the grainy liquid across the closest set of claws. Graven flexed them, pushing his foot closer to the boy, begging for more.

"You *do* like it," he mumbled, smiling to himself.

The experiment continued well into the evening, with Freydolf bringing out several different elements in succession— wine and spice, flame and steam.

"This reminds me of how Master Platt and I woke him," he shared in a low voice, passing fresh handfuls of snow to Tupper.

"But he's already awake."

"Aye, but it feels like we're turning back time," Frey said with a wistful expression. "I've never seen him so happy, not since ... then."

"We're here," Tupper murmured to the lonesome statue, adding a bit of his cider to the streak of wine on a golden stripe. "Don't be sad, Graven."

The big cat's ears twitched, and Freydolf gripped the boy's shoulder. "Call his name again!"

"Graven?" he repeated uncertainly.

Once more, the tiger reacted, and the Keeper's eyes flashed. With more authority, he said, "*Again*, lambkin, and don't stop!"

Tupper could feel the weight of his master's words, so he stood on tiptoe and stroked the green stripes that cut across Graven's cheeks; taking up a sing-song chant, he made the tiger's name the lyric to his lullaby.

Meanwhile, Freydolf crossed to his workbench for tools. Returning, he located his former master's mark on Graven's collar. "If anyone finds out, I may be vilified for tampering with another Keeper's masterpiece, but I know Platt wouldn't want his treasure left so lonely," he muttered, making deft incisions into white stone.

Leaning to one side, Tupper could see what the sculptor was doing. Freydolf didn't touch the original insignia, but just like with any of the rooms and niches in the Statuary, he added a border to show new ownership. When he was done, Platt's mark was wreathed with a garland of meadowsweet.

Scratching Graven's ear, Freydolf asked, "Can you feel the change? This boy can be yours, and you can be his!"

The statue lowered his head in order to bump his broad nose against the young Flox's forehead. It was a friendly gesture, and Tupper felt his heart lift. "Graven," he whispered, petting and patting for all he was worth.

"Aye, that's the way," crooned Freydolf, whose dark eyes were suspiciously moist. He had no troubles whatsoever producing the tears needed to set the seal. Pressing his thumb over the mark, he smiled lopsidedly at Tupper, then addressed the statue. "You are Graven, the pinnacle of Master Platt's craftsmanship, the famed Mosaic Tiger of Morven. I am Freydolf Meadowsweet, current Keeper of the legendary Moonlit Mountain, and I bid you take a new master. Let this boy be your charge."

Tupper could feel the magic in the air, thicker and stronger than the times when Olexi and Rimbles were awakened. It made his pulse race and his hands tremble, and when Graven's red gaze found his, he gave up on breathing. Something very special trembled in the air between them, then locked into place. In that moment, Graven accepted Freydolf's gift; his heart belonged solely to Tupper.

When the tiger's silent roar reverberated through galleries of stone, all the master-marked statues stirred in their sleep. They understood better than anyone what the shift in magic meant for Graven. The mountain herself took notice. Of her Keeper's confidence. Of the boy who'd unlocked it.

Every magical mountain had a mind of their own, and the legendary Moonlit Mountain's was in a whirl. She was old beyond knowing and patient as stone, but her Keeper's audacity gave her an excuse to be impetuous. Freydolf wasn't the only one who could break with tradition. Morven had a plan.

THIS ENDS BOOK ONE

Thank you for purchasing *Meadowsweet*. I do hope the tale was to your liking. If so, I shall borrow from Flox tradition and say,

"THE TRADE IS GOOD. MAY OUR NEXT BE BETTER STILL."

C. J. MILBRANDT has always believed in miracles, especially small ones. A lifelong bookworm with a love for fairy tales, far-off lands, and fantasy worlds, CJ began spinning adventures of her own. Her family-friendly stories mingle humor and whimsy with a dash of danger and a touch of magic. Follow your curiosity to CJMilbrandt.com, where you'll find more stories and story art. CJ's books are also on GoodReads.

Meadowsweet began as a personal writing challenge. The entire Galleries of Stone trilogy was written on the fly, posted in three hundred and sixty-six daily installments during 2012. Completely crazy. Entirely satisfying.

GALLERIES OF STONE
Meadowsweet
Harrow
Rakefang

GALLERIES OF STONE
2
Harrow
C.J. MILBRANDT

9 781631 230684